She knew what it
within her. Desire. The wanting and needing to touch this man, to kiss him. To do more than that with him.

Desire was a new experience for Jett. And it pounced upon her with an aggression that startled her. She wasn't sure how to handle it. She'd not known desire for another person. Not in Daemonia. Though the desire for things, safety and control had always resided inside her. And certainly she was no virgin who hadn't a clue what to do with herself regarding a man and sex. She had done things to survive.

No regrets, her darkness whispered.

No, of course not.

But now? Now she was free. And she wanted to explore the exciting feeling that warmed her from ear tips to toes. And everywhere in between.

TEMPTING
THE DARK
&
CAPTIVATING
THE BEAR

USA TODAY BESTSELLING AUTHOR
MICHELE HAUF
AND
JANE GODMAN

HARLEQUIN® NOCTURNE™

Recycling programs
for this product may
not exist in your area.

ISBN-13: 978-1-335-14696-0

Tempting the Dark & Captivating the Bear

Copyright © 2019 by Harlequin Books S.A.

The publisher acknowledges the copyright holders
of the individual works as follows:

Tempting the Dark
Copyright © 2018 by Michele Hauf

Captivating the Bear
Copyright © 2018 by Amanda Anders

This edition published by arrangement with Harlequin Books S.A.

For questions and comments about the quality of this book,
please contact us at CustomerService@Harlequin.com.

® and TM are trademarks of the publisher. Trademarks indicated with ® are registered in the United States Patent and Trademark Office, the Canadian Intellectual Property Office and in other countries.

Printed in U.S.A.

CONTENTS

Michele Hauf is a *USA TODAY* bestselling author who has been writing romance, action-adventure and fantasy stories for more than twenty years. France, musketeers, vampires and faeries usually feature in her stories. And if Michele followed the adage "write what you know," all her stories would have snow in them. Fortunately, she steps beyond her comfort zone and writes about countries and creatures she has never seen. Find her on Facebook, Twitter and at michelehauf.com.

Books by Michele Hauf

Harlequin Nocturne

The Witch's Quest
The Witch and the Werewolf
An American Witch in Paris
The Billionaire Werewolf's Princess
Tempting the Dark

The Saint-Pierre Series

The Dark's Mistress
Ghost Wolf
Moonlight and Diamonds
The Vampire's Fall
Enchanted by the Wolf

In the Company of Vampires

Beautiful Danger
The Vampire Hunter
Beyond the Moon

Visit the Author Profile page
at Harlequin.com for more titles.

TEMPTING THE DARK

Michele Hauf

Chapter 1

Savin Thorne stood before the weird, wavery, silver-blue vibrations that undulated in the midnight sky twenty feet above the lavender field. He waited. Twenty minutes had passed since he arrived in the beat-up pickup truck he barely kept alive with oil changes and the occasional battery jump. He'd gotten a call from Edamite Thrash regarding a disturbance in this countryside location, north of Paris.

He knew this area. It was too familiar. His family once lived not half a kilometer away. Yet when driving past the old neighborhood, he'd noted his childhood home had been torn down. Construction on a golf course was under way. Just as well. The bad memory from his childhood still clung to his bones.

To his right, Edamite Thrash, a corax demon, stood

with his eyes closed, his senses focused to whatever the hell was going on.

Savin could feel the undulations in the air and earth prickle through his veins. A heebie-jeebies sensation. The demon within him stirred. Savin tended to think of the nameless, incorporeal demon inside him as "the Other," for no other reason than it had been a childhood decision. She was upset by whatever was irritating the air. And when she stirred, Savin grew anxious.

Ed had been getting instinctual warnings about this disturbance for days, and tonight those dire feelings had alerted him enough to call Savin.

Savin reckoned demons back to Daemonia. The bad ones who had no reason or right to tread the mortal realm. The evil ones who had harmed mortals in this realm. Sometimes even the good ones who pushed the boundaries of secrecy and might have been seen by humans or who were trying to tell the truth about their species.

Savin wasn't demon. He wasn't even paranormal. He was one hundred percent human. Except for the part about him hosting an incorporeal demon for the past twenty years. That tended to screw with a man's mental place in this world. But most days he felt he was winning the part about just trying to stay sane.

A sudden whining trill vibrated the air. Pushing up the sleeves of his thermal shirt to expose the protective sigils on the undersides of his forearms, Savin planted his combat boots and faced the sky that flickered in silver and red.

Ed hissed, "Savin, did you hear that?"

"I did. I'm ready."

Behind them, hefting a fifty-pound sack of sea salt

out from the back of a white hearse, Certainly Jones, a dark witch, prepped for his role in whatever might come charging at them.

"Hurry up, Jones!" Ed called. "It's happening!"

With that announcement, the sky cracked before them. A black seam opened from ground to clouds. From within, a brilliant amber flame burst and roiled. A whoosh of darkness exploded out from the seam.

Savin cursed. That could be nothing but demons. An invasion? He felt the dark and malevolent beings, incorporeal and corporeal, as they flooded into this realm. Cool, hissing brushes across his skin. Wicked alien vocals. The gnashing of fangs and rows of deadly teeth. Tails scything the air. Claws clattering for flesh. And the ones he could not see vibrated a distinctive hum in his veins.

The protection sigils he wore tattooed on his body kept those invisible incorporeal demons from entering his system. As did the bitch demon he'd been serving as shelter to for twenty years. But that didn't mean he was impervious to an external attack by a corporeal demon. He was strong but did not hold a weapon.

The only weapons he required were his stubbornness and his innate ability to see and deflect most demons with a few choice warding incantations.

In the inky darkness, there was no way to count their numbers as they spread across the field and whisked through the air above the men's heads. Standing center of the freshly laid salt circle, Certainly Jones began to recite a spell. Ed swung above his head a black bone lariat bespelled to choke and annihilate demons.

For his part, Savin could recite a general reckoning spell that would reach about a hundred-foot circumference about him and send those demons back to Daemonia. So he began the chant composed of a demonic language he hated knowing.

"There are hundreds," Ed said as a curse as he avoided the salt circle with a jump. "We'll never get them all. Savin?"

He couldn't speak now, for to do so would shatter the foundation of the spell. Raising his arms, palms facing inward—but not touching—and exposing the demonic sigils on the underside of his forearms, Savin expanded his chest and shouted the last few words. And as he did so, the power of those spoken words formed a staticky choker between his fingers. He spread his arms out wide, stretching the choker in a brilliant lash of gold sparks. Then, with a shove forward, he cast the net.

Demons shrieked, squealed and yowled as they were caught by the sticky, sparkling net. Like a fisherman hauling up his catch, only in reverse, it wrapped up dozens, perhaps a hundred or more demons, and wrangled them back through the rift in the sky.

"I expel you to Daemonia!" Savin recited, then immediately prepared to begin again.

"That took care of at least half!" Ed called. "But some are getting away. Jones! How's it going getting that damned door to Daemonia closed?"

"Soon!" shouted the witch.

Savin's net, filled with yet more demons, wrangled another gang and whipped them back through the rift.

The dark witch, a tall, slender man dressed in black, stretched out his tattooed arms. Using specific tattoos as spells, he shouted out a command that gripped the serrated rift in the sky and vised it suddenly closed.

The night grew intensely dark. Not even a nocturnal

creature might see anything for the few moments following the closure of the rift to the Place of All Demons.

Savin dropped his arms and shook out his entire body like a prizefighter loosening up his muscles. He felt the air stir as a few creatures dashed above his head. None dared come too close, or try a talon against his skin. They could sense his innate warning.

No demon dared approach a reckoner.

Ed tugged out his cell phone from an inner suit-coat pocket, and the small electronic light glowed about his face and tattooed neck. The thorns on his knuckles glinted like obsidian as he punched in a number. "I'm calling the troops in Paris. We'll head to town. Certainly, will that seal hold?"

"For a while," the witch said. "But I'm not sure how it was opened in the first place. Had to be from within Daemonia. Which is not cool. Something wicked powerful opened it up."

The witch cast his gaze about the field. Dark shadows flitted through the sky, black on black, as the demons that had avoided Savin's net dispersed. The cool, acrid taste of sulfur littered the air.

Savin thought he heard someone walking across the loose gravel back by his truck. He swung around, squinting his gaze. He didn't see motion. Could have been a demon. More likely a raccoon.

"The energy out here is quieting," he stated. For the hum in his veins had settled. "I think we're good for now. But Ed will have to post a guard out here."

The corax demon nodded to Savin and gave him a thumbs-up even as he spoke on the phone to organize scouts.

Savin slapped a hand across Certainly's back. "Good going, witch."

"I can say the same for you. You took care of more than half of them. I don't know anyone capable of such a skill."

"Wish I could be proud of that skill, but…" Savin let that one hang as he strode back to the parked cars with the witch.

His system suddenly shivered. Savin did not panic. He knew it was the Other expressing her thanks. Or maybe it was resentment for what he had done tonight. He'd never mastered the art of interpreting her messages. So long as she kept quiet ninety percent of the time, he couldn't complain. Some days he felt as if he owed her for what she had done to help him. Other days he felt that debt had long been paid.

"I'm off," Ed said as he headed to his car. "I'll post a guard out here day and night. Thanks, Savin. I'll get back to the both of you with whatever comes up in Paris. If my troops find any of the escapees, we'll gather them for a mass reckoning. Okay with you?"

"I love a good mass demon bash," Savin said. But his heart could not quite get behind his sarcasm. "Check in with me when you need my help again." He fist-bumped Ed and the dark witch, then climbed into his truck and fired up the engine.

Alone and with the windows rolled up, Savin exhaled and closed his eyes. His muscles ached from scalp to shoulders and back, down to his calves and even the tops of his feet. It took a lot of energy to reckon a single demon back to Daemonia. What he'd just done? Whew! He needed to get home, tilt back some whiskey, then crash. A renewal process that worked for him.

But first. His system would not stop shaking until he fed the demon within.

Reaching over in the dark quiet and opening the glove compartment, he drew out a small black tin. Inside on the red velvet lay a syringe and a vial of morphine that he kept stocked and always carried with him. He juiced up the syringe and, tightening his fist, injected the officious substance into his vein. A rush of heat dashed up his arm. A brilliance of colors flashed behind his eyelids. He released his fist and gritted his teeth.

And the shivers stopped.

"Happy?" he muttered to the demon inside him.

He always thought to hear a female chuckle after shooting up. He knew it wasn't real. She had no voice.

Thank the gods he no longer got high from this crap. The Other greedily sucked it all up before it could permeate his system. A strange thing to be thankful for, but he recognized a boon when he saw it.

Flicking on the radio, he nodded as Rob Zombie's "American Witch" blasted through the speakers. Thrash metal. Appropriate for his mood.

Savin was the last of the threesome to pull out of the field. He turned left instead of right, as the other two had. Left would take him over the Seine and toward the left-bank suburbs of Paris. He lived near the multilaned Périphérique in the fourteenth arrondissement. Driving slowly down the loose gravel, he nodded to the thumping bass beat, hands slapping out a drum solo on the steering wheel.

When the truck's headlights flashed on something that moved alongside the road, Savin swore and slammed on the brakes.

"What in all Beneath?"

Was it a demon walking the grassy shoulder of the road? He'd *felt* more incorporeal demons move over him during the escape from the rift than actually witnessed real corporeal creatures with bodies. But anything was possible. And yet…

Savin turned down the radio volume. Leaning forward, he peered through the dusty windshield. The figure wasn't clawed or winged or even deformed. "A woman?"

She glanced toward the truck. The headlights beamed over her bedraggled condition. Long, dark, tangled hair and palest skin. She clutched her dirtied hands against her chest as if to hold on to the thin black fabric that barely covered her limbs from breasts to above her knees. Her legs were dirty and her feet almost black.

She couldn't be a resident from the area. Out for a midnight walk looking like that? Or had she been attacked? Savin hadn't passed any cars in the area, which ruled out a date-gone-bad scenario. That left one other possibility. She had come from Daemonia. Maybe? Corporeal demons could wear a human sheen, making them virtually undetectable to the common man.

But not to Savin's demon radar.

Shifting into Park, Savin spoke a protective spell that would cover him from head to toe. He was no witch, but any human could invoke protection with the proper mind-set. The demon within him shivered but did not protest, thanks to the morphine. He shoved open the door and jumped out. His boots crushed the gravel as he stalked around to the other side of the hood.

"Where in hell did you come from?" he called. Daemonia wasn't hell, but it was damned close.

The woman's body trembled. Her dark eyes searched

his. They were not red. Tears spilled down her cheeks. She looked as though she'd been attacked or ravaged. But demons were tricky and knew how to put on a convincing act of humanity. And yet Savin didn't sense any demonic vibes from her. He could pick a demon out from a crowd milling in the Louvre at fifty paces. Even the ones who had cloaked themselves with a sheen.

He stepped forward. The woman cringed. Savin put up his hands in placation. With the sigils on his forearms exposed, he advertised what he was to her. Just in case she was demon. She didn't flee. Nor did she hiss or spew vile threats at him.

Now Savin wondered if she had been hurt. And perhaps it had nothing to do with what had just gone down in the lavender field. Had she been assaulted and fled, or had some asshole abandoned her far from the city?

"It's okay," he said firmly. "I'm not going to hurt you. My name's Savin Thorne. Do you need help?"

"S-Savin?" The woman's mouth quivered. She dropped her hands to her sides. "Is it… Is it really you?"

He narrowed his gaze on her. She…*knew* him?

"Savin?" She began to bawl and dropped to her knees. "Savin, it's me. Jett."

Savin swallowed roughly. His heart plunged to his gut. By all the dark and demonic gods, this was not possible.

Chapter 2

Twenty years earlier

Savin grabbed Jett's hand and together they raced across the field behind their parents' houses. The lavender grew high and wild, sweetening the air. Butterflies dotted the flower tops with spots of orange and blue.

Jett's laughter suddenly abbreviated. She stopped, gripping her gut as she bent over.

"Wait!" she called as Savin ran ahead. "I'm getting a bellyache. Mamma's cherry pie is sitting right here." She slapped a hand to her stomach. "I shouldn't have eaten that third piece!"

Savin laughed and walked backward toward the edge of the field where the forest began. The dark, creepy forest that they always teased each other to venture into alone. Neither had done it. Yet.

Today he'd challenged her to creep up to the edge and touch the foreboding black tree that grew bent like a crippled man and thrust out its branches as if they were wicked fingers. If she did, he'd give her his Asterix comic collection. Fortunately, he knew she wouldn't do it. Jett was a chicken. And he teased her now by chanting just that.

"I am not!" she announced as she approached him, still clutching her gut. Her long black hair hid what he guessed was a barely contained smile.

"You can't use that excuse to get out of it this time." Savin planted his walking stick in the ground near his sneaker. The stick was one he'd found in the spring and had been whittling at for a month. He'd tried to carve a dragon on the top of it, but it looked more like a snake. "Girls are always chicken!"

"Am not." Jett stepped out of the lavender field and stopped beside him to stare into the forest that loomed thirty paces away.

The trees were close and the trunks looked black from this distance. Savin nudged Jett's arm and she jumped away from him and stuck out her tongue.

"I don't need your comic books," she said. "Anyway, I'll get them all when we get married someday."

Jett was the one to always remind him that they'd get married. Someday. When they were grown-up and didn't care about things like comic books and creepy forests. Which was fine with Savin. Except he thought maybe he should kiss her before that happened. And actually love her. Jett was a girl with whom he raced home from school, ran through the fields and played video games. They spent every day with each other. But love? Right now that sounded as creepy as the forest.

"Whatever." He stubbed the toe of his sneaker against the walking stick.

"Why don't you go in there?" she cooed in that cotton-candy voice she always used when she wanted him to do something.

It made Savin's ears burn and his heart feel like bug wings were fluttering inside.

"Maybe I will." He took a step forward and planted the stick again.

Looking over the forest, he thought for a moment he saw the air waver before him. Did something flash silver? Of course, a haunted forest might be like that. He didn't dare say "maybe not." So he took another step, and then another.

And he heard Jett's gasp behind him. "Savin, wait—"

He turned to see Jett's brown eyes widen. She pointed over his shoulder. When he swung around to face the forest, Savin didn't have time to scream.

Sucked forward through the air, arms flailing and legs stretched out behind him, he dropped the walking stick. Cold, icy air entered his lungs, swallowing his scream. Yet beside him he heard Jett's scream like the worst nightmare. The world turned blacker than the cellar without the lights on. And the strange smell of rotting eggs made him gag.

Of a sudden his body dropped, seeming to fall endlessly. Until he landed on his back with a crunch of bones and a cry of pain.

He lay there, silenced by the strangeness of what had happened. Had a tornado swept him off his feet and into the depths of the dark forest? Had the sky opened like a crack in the wall and sucked him inside? What was he lying on? It felt…squishy and thick, and it smelled like the worst garbage.

"Savin?"

Jett was with him. He sat up, looking about. The landscape was brown and gray, and a deep streak of red painted what must be the black sky. His fingers curled into the mud he lay on, and he felt things inside it squirm.

"Jett?"

"Over here. Wh-what happened? What is that!"

An insectile whine preceded the approach of a creature that looked like something out of one of those nasty video games his parents had forbid him to play. Jett scrambled over to Savin. He clutched her hand and they both backed away from the thing that walked on three legs and looked like half a spider…with a human face.

"Run!" Savin yelled.

They ran for days, it seemed. They encountered… things. Monsters. Creatures. Demons. Evil. They were no longer anywhere near home. This was not the outer countryside surrounding Paris. There was no lush lavender field to run through. Or even grass. Savin wasn't sure where they were or how they'd gotten here, but it was not a place in which he wanted to stay.

Jett cried as often as she wandered in silence and with a drawn expression. She was hungry and had taken on many cuts and bruises from the rough, sharp landscape and the strange molten rocks. Every time something moved, she screamed. Which was often.

This had to be hell. But Savin honestly didn't know why they were here. Had they died? They hadn't encountered people. But they did see humanlike beings.

Strange creatures with faces and appendages that morphed and twisted, and some even had wings. None had spoken to them in a language they could understand.

"I want to go home," Jett said on a tearful plea.

Savin hugged her close, as much to comfort her as for his own reassurance. He wanted to go home, too. And he wanted to cry. But he was trying to be brave. He'd hand over all his Asterix comics right now if only they could be home in their own beds.

"We'll get out of here," he murmured, and then clutched Jett even tighter. "I promise."

They tried to drink from the stream that flowed with orange water, but it burned their throats. Jett's tears permanently streaked her dirtied face. Her eyes were red and swollen. Her hands were rough and darkened with the gray dust that covered the landscape, and her jeans were tattered.

Savin had torn up his shirt to wrap a bandage about her ankle after she'd cut it on what had looked like barbed wire. But after she'd screamed, that strange wire had unfurled and slunk away.

They sat on a vast plateau of flat gray stone that tended to crack without warning, much like thin ice on a lake. No other creatures seemed to want to walk on it, so they felt safe. For the moment.

Savin had fashioned a weapon out of a branch from a tree that had appeared to be made of wood, until he'd broken off the branch and inspected it. It was metal. That he could break. But the point was sharp. That was all that mattered. He'd already killed something with it. An insect the size of a dog, with snapping mandibles and so many legs he hadn't wanted to count them.

"Do you hear that?" Jett said in a weary whisper.

Savin followed the direction she looked. An inhale drew in the air. For some reason it smelled like summer. Fresh and…almost like water. Curious.

"I miss my mama and papa," Jett whispered. She shivered. She shook constantly. They hadn't eaten for days. And Savin's stomach growled relentlessly. "If I die, promise me you won't let one of those monsters eat me."

"You're not going to die," Savin quickly retorted.

But he wasn't so sure anymore.

Jett stood and wandered across the unsteady surface, wobbling at best. Savin thought to call out to her, but his lips were dry and cracked. He wanted something to drink. He wanted his feet to stop burning because he'd taken off his sneakers after the rubber soles had melted in the steel nettle field. He wanted safety. He'd do anything to escape this place he'd come to think of as the Place of All Demons.

"I see water!" Jett began to run.

Savin couldn't believe she had the energy to move so swiftly. But he managed to pick up his pace and follow. She was fifty yards ahead of him when she reached the edge of what looked like a waterfall. *Actual water?*

"Jett, be careful!"

But she didn't hear him. And when she turned to wave to him, all of a sudden her body was flung upward—as if lifted by a big invisible hand—and then her body dropped.

Savin reached the edge of the falls and plunged to his knees. He couldn't see Jett. Her screams echoed for a long time. And what initially looked like clear, cool water suddenly morphed into a thick, sludgy black flow of lava that bubbled down into an endless pit. He couldn't see the bottom.

"Jett!"

He lay at the edge of the pit for a long time. Days? There was no night and day in this awful place, so he couldn't know. After he'd decided that Jett had died in the lava, Savin had vacillated between jumping in and ending his life, and crawling away. No one could survive such a fall. Perhaps that was for the best. He hoped she hadn't suffered. He hoped she was in heaven right now, happy and safe.

But as much as he wanted to give up, he also didn't want to die.

Savin finally crawled away from the lava falls. He hadn't the energy to stand. He'd lost his walking stick in the lavender field. The next creature that threatened him? Bring it on. He didn't like the idea of being eaten alive, but maybe the thing would chomp on his heart and kill him fast.

He crawled endlessly. Nothing tried to eat him.

Calluses roughed his fingers, and his T-shirt was shredded. He couldn't feel his feet anymore. And his throat was so dry he couldn't make saliva. So when he heard the voice of a woman, he thought it must be a dream.

Savin lay sprawled on an icy sheet of blackness that smelled like blood and dirt. Again, he heard the voice. Was it saying...*help me*?

It wasn't Jett's voice. Was it? No. Impossible. Though

his heart broke anew over her loss, he couldn't produce tears.

"Over here…"

With great effort, he was able to lift his head and saw what looked like lush streams of blackest hair. *Was it Jett?*

He crawled forward. His fingers glanced over something soft and fine, like one of his mother's dresses. It was blue and smelled like flowers. A woman lay on the ground, blue and black hair flowing about her in masses that he thought made up her dress. He couldn't get a good look at her face because he was too weak to sit up or stand.

"Do you want to go home?" the woman whispered.

He sobbed without tears and nodded profusely.

"I can help you out of Daemonia."

That was the first time he'd heard the name of this terrible place.

"Please," he rasped. "I'll do anything."

"Of course you will, boy. I ask but one simple thing of you."

"Anything," he managed.

"Come closer, boy. If you kiss me, I will bring you home."

Kiss her? What strange request was that?

On the other hand…all he had to do was kiss the woman and he could return home to his soft, warm bed?

Savin pushed himself up onto his elbows and looked back the direction from which he'd crawled. He'd promised Jett he'd protect her. He'd failed. He should stay in this awful place as punishment. But he wasn't stupid. And he wanted to see his parents.

"A…kiss?"

"Just one. And then you can go home."

Savin crawled closer to the woman until he hovered inches from her face. She smelled like a field of flowers. Her skin was dark blue and her eyes were red, as were the eyes of all the creatures in this terrible place. He wavered as he supported himself with a hand and leaned closer.

And then he saw her lips.

Savin cried out. He tumbled to the side and rolled to his back. Her lips were covered with worms!

"Just one kiss, boy. Your parents are worried about you."

Now a teardrop did fall. Savin gasped and choked as he could only wish for the safety of his parents' embrace. And then…he forced himself to lean over the woman and kiss her awful mouth.

Chapter 3

He was called a reckoner now.

Savin Thorne sent demons who had come from Daemonia back where they belonged. He was hired to do so and rarely hunted them himself. He left the hunting for others. Once the demon was subdued or contained—usually in some style of hex circle—then he stepped in and worked his magic. A demonic magic afforded him, he believed, because of the demon within him. She had hitched a ride to the mortal realm when she sent him home following that foul kiss. He knew it was a female. And he could not get her out of him. He didn't know her name, so had come to refer to her as the Other. He'd love to expel her from his very soul, but he'd tried every possible spell, hex and banishment without success.

He'd accepted that life from here on would be spent

sharing his bones and flesh with the demon he'd once kissed out of a vile desperation.

Rain spattered Savin's face and streaked through the headlight beams. The woman kneeling on the ground before him waited for his reaction. She'd called him by name. And her name was…

Mon Dieu, he'd thought her dead.

"Jett?"

She nodded, blinking at the falling rain. "I… I finally got out."

"Finally…" Words felt impossible.

It was incredible to fathom. This frail, dirtied woman was Jett? All grown up? Had she been in Daemonia all this time? Twenty years? If he had known she'd survived the fall, he would have found a way to get to her, to rescue her from the unspeakable evils. Somehow.

Savin's heart thundered. His fingers flexed at his sides. He didn't know what to do. How to react. He should have been there for her when they were nine and ten and lost in the Place of All Demons. He'd promised her he would protect her. And he had failed.

Yet somehow Jett had survived. Had she escaped through the rift that had opened earlier? She must have.

She must be so… Twenty years! She had no home. No life. She had literally been dropped into this world.

"Jett." Savin dropped to the ground before her, his knees crunching the wet gravel. Without reluctance, he hugged her to him. She was frail and shaking and they were both soaked from the rain. "I thought you were dead. Oh, Jett, I'm so sorry. It's really you?"

He leaned back and studied her face. He remembered the sweet round face of the girl with the long black hair

and the giggles that never ceased. Her eyes had been—
Yes, they were brown. It could be her.

It had to be her.

"You've gotten so big," she said, and then managed a
weak laugh. "Yes, it's me. Jett Montfort. I'm out. I'm…
Oh, Savin." She searched his eyes. Rain lashed at her
pale skin and lips. "I want to be safe."

"Of course. Safe. You are now. With me. I'll…"

What would he do? He couldn't leave her alone on
the side of the road. She needed a place to stay. Clothes.
Warmth. Food? How in the world had she survived in
such a place for so long? It didn't matter right now. She
was frightened and alone.

"Will you come with me?" he asked.

"Where to?"

"My place. I live in Paris. I'll help you, Jett. Whatever you need, I'll help you to get." And before he could
regret another vow, he said, "Promise."

She nodded, her smile wobbling and tears spilling
freely. "Please."

And when he thought to stand and help her up, instead Savin scooped her into his arms and carried her
to the passenger side of the truck and set her inside. He
tucked in her thin dress, which was nothing more than
jagged-cut fabric clinging to her torso. She was covered
with dirt and scratches, but the rain must have washed
away any blood. She'd been hurt. Traumatized, surely.

She was a strange survivor.

And he owed her his life.

"You're safe now." He squeezed her hand, then closed
the door and ran around to hop behind the wheel.

Legs pulled up to her chest and arms wrapped about

her shins, she bowed her head to her knees and closed her eyes as Savin drove into the city.

What strange luck that her escape into the mortal realm should be met by the one person she knew and had thought of many times over the years. It couldn't be a coincidence. And yet Savin was a part of the demonic world in a way that disturbed Jett. She'd watched as he stood before the tear between the realms and reckoned demons back to Daemonia. He was powerful. And dangerous.

To her, he could prove most threatening.

Yet in her moment of need, Jett had accepted his offer of safety. Because she was exhausted, tattered and worn. And yet triumphant. She'd done it! She had escaped to the mortal realm. And whatever happened next would challenge her in ways she couldn't imagine. She had prepared mentally, but the physical challenges would be unknown. She owned a specific power. She could survive this new adventure.

As the truck entered the city, she watched headlights flash past in swift beams of red and white. It had been a long time since Jett had been in a cosmopolitan city with vehicles and buildings of human manufacture. She remembered Paris. The historical monuments and buildings, the gardens and sculptures. The elite shops and the River Seine. It hadn't seemed to change.

She had changed. Everything she knew about every single thing had changed.

And Savin remained the one pillar she needed more than she could fathom. He'd grown older, as had she. He'd gotten big and tall. The man was a behemoth wrapped in muscle and might. His dark brown hair was still shoulder length and tousled, as it had been when they were children. But now he wore a mustache and beard and a brute glint lived in his eyes. He had become a man. A very attractive man.

Jett couldn't prevent the frequent glances out the corner of her eye to the man driving the truck. She had not seen such a handsome being in…a long time. And he occupied every air molecule with his presence. He overwhelmed the space in the truck. Being near him made her heart flutter, in a good way. That was something it had not done since she was a kid.

But was this man now her enemy?

No. She wouldn't think like that. She needed help from Savin. And possibly protection. Even though he was the one person she'd best run from, he was all she had right now.

When finally he parked the truck and jumped out to run around the front of the hood and open her door, Jett stared out at the dark building front where he said he lived. This was the fourteenth arrondissement. Not far from where she recalled a massive cemetery sat in Gothic silence amidst the bustling city. While she and Savin had lived in the country when they were children, their parents had alternated taking them into the city on the weekends to visit the parks and museums. Memory of those times made her heart again flutter.

Could she have back that innocence? Did she want it back? What *was* innocence but a foul waste of power? The darkness within her would not allow her to ruminate on the past for long. Just as well. Time to move forward.

Now Jett had ventured into the city again. With Savin. And he didn't suspect a thing about her, nor had he asked how she had survived for so long in Daemonia. Which was how it must remain.

She slid her fingers against the wide hand he offered, and stepped down onto the sidewalk. Her bare feet were scraped and bruised from running across the vast smoke-ice planes where cracks in the landscape were edged like razors. Pain had become but a bother to her. Healing would come quickly. Perhaps. She must be cautious about utilizing the skills she had been taught.

"Your feet hurt?" Savin asked when she wincingly stepped forward.

Pain in this mortal realm felt different than when she'd been in the Place of All Demons. It was acute. And the cool air brushed her skin roughly. A shiver ensured that she had grasp of the sheen she wore. She must be cautious.

Without another word, Savin whisked her into his arms and carried her inside the building and up four flights of stairs without a catch to his breathing. Jett clung to the front of his shirt, noticing beneath her fingers the hard, sculpted muscles. And he smelled like nothing she had smelled before. Freshly exhilarating, yet rough. It appealed so strongly she nudged her nose against his shirt and inhaled. Was this what the princess felt like when rescued by the knight? How many times had they played such a game when they were children, always alternating who got to be the rescuer and who had to lie in dismay in wait of saving?

Now that game had become reality.

Why she had such a silly thought startled her. She had tried not to think about the simple human life she'd lost while in Daemonia. Too dangerous.

He set her down, yet supported her by the elbow, before a door. A door inscribed with demonic repulsion sigils. Jett knew them well. One did not live in Daemonia for so long without gaining such knowledge.

She tentatively reached to touch one of the symbols—and flinched.

"Keeps the nasties out," Savin commented. "Necessary. But, uh… Hmm… You've just come from there. Must have some residual gunk on you that will alert the wards. Let me take them down for you." He swept a hand over the sigils and muttered a word she recognized as a demonic language. He knew so much? "There. Now it shouldn't tug when you cross the threshold."

He pushed the door open. Cool shadows invited Jett to step inside the narrow loft as easily as if she were crossing the threshold of her childhood home after returning from a day at school. No tug from the sigils, either. Whew.

Behind her, Savin muttered a reversal to seal the wards and closed the door. That action did pull at her system, but she disguised the sudden assault with an inhale and a sigh.

When she saw him reach for the light switch, she said, "No. Uh… I can see well in the darkness. I, uh… think it will take a while to adjust to the bright."

He lowered his hand. "Yeah, okay. There's moonlight anyway." He gestured to a line of windows that ran across the ceiling, skylights catching the moonlight. Pale illumination sifted down over furniture and the cluttered walls of a living area. "This top-floor apartment is small, but it has its perks. You thirsty?"

She was. And suddenly so cold, even though it had been warm outside. Jett rubbed her hands up and down her arms and glanced at the front door. No sigils on this side. Yet she was literally trapped now.

What had he asked? Right. She nodded. "Yes, water. Please."

He retrieved a glass from a cupboard and Jett marveled at the clear, clean water running from the tap.

She'd forgotten how pure things could be. Unadulter-ated by the darkness she had learned to caress and rely on for comfort. When he handed it to her, she held the glass for a moment, taking it in. So normal. She remem-bered when her mother would hand her a glass of water. Drink it down. On to the next adventure, like chasing rabbits through the cabbage patch with Savin.

"I'm not going to ask if you are all right," Savin said. Deep and calm, his voice chased away her shivers. "You can't be. You just came out of Daemonia. Maybe I should let you settle in and feel your way around the place for tonight?"

She nodded. "Please."

"I bet a shower will feel great. Come this way."

She followed him through the living room stuffed with dark, wood-trimmed furniture and saw many gui-tars hung on the walls. Amongst them she noticed more demon sigils scrawled on the bare-brick walls. Some glinted at her, but none seemed to notice her presence.

"I've only got one bedroom," Savin said, "but it's a king-size bed. Comfy. You can sleep in that tonight and I'll take the couch."

She didn't want to put him out, but—at sight of the bed, lush with a thick gray coverlet and pillows—pil-lows! She'd not laid her head on a pillow for so long. Jett decided to quietly accept the generous offer.

Ahead, he flipped on the light in the bathroom and she blinked and stepped back. It was so bright.

"Oh." He noticed her discomfort. "It's on a dimmer." He turned a dial and the light softened. "You can shower and there are towels in the cabinet. I probably have a shirt you can wear to sleep in. Does that sound good?"

She nodded again and realized she clutched the water glass to her chest. So precious, the clean water.

Savin rubbed his bearded jaw. His deep blue eyes beckoned her to wonder if they were real. Never had she seen such blue irises. Lapis lazuli, she remembered, was one of the stones she'd collected as a child. Though to consider his eyes now, they looked sad. Concerned.

"Tell me what you need, Jett."

She didn't know what she needed, beyond the temporary safety she felt standing before Savin's powerful build. In his home. Behind the sigils that would keep out demons. Of utmost concern was keeping any and all of those sorts away from her.

"This is good. I will shower and sleep. I feel like I can sleep." She rarely slept. To imagine lying for hours without nightmares? It seemed an impossibility. "You are too kind."

"It's not a problem. I'll be out on the couch if you need anything. You're welcome to wander about, help yourself to whatever appeals in the fridge. Just…uh, do what you need to do. Make my place your own. We'll talk in the morning."

Another nod was all she could offer. She didn't want to talk about that place. Not right away. In order to move forward, she needed to put that experience behind her. To truly be free. But she was curious how Savin had escaped and how he'd come to be a man who reckoned demons out of this realm.

"Good night," he offered. When he brushed past her, the heat of his skin shivered over hers.

Jett lifted her head and sucked in a breath. As she followed his exit from the room, the flutters returned to her heart and her skin flushed warmly. Was this what desire felt like?

Chapter 4

Savin did not sleep much that night. He lay there in the cool darkness, bare feet jutting over the end of the couch, thinking about the woman who slept in his bed not thirty feet away in the other room.

After watching Jett being literally sucked over the wicked lava falls in Daemonia, had he given up on her too quickly? Should he have lain there at the edge longer, waiting for her to emerge? He'd thought he had sprawled there for days. But he'd learned it was impossible to gauge time in such a place. He'd never cried so much as he had after losing his best friend. The remembrance zinged in his muscles with stinging aches and he almost thought to feel his skin burn now as it had then.

That harrowing experience had been seared into his very bones. It had become a part of him. It was him. It was the reason why he reckoned demons. Such creatures did not belong in this realm. No human should have to experience what he had lived through.

And now Jett was back. Alive, and seemingly sane. But how damaged must she be after living in that place for twenty years? He couldn't imagine. The demons he reckoned to Daemonia were often vicious, wild, physically disgusting and, many times, homicidal. For a human to exist in such a place, and with those creatures, for any longer than he had survived there seemed incomprehensible.

Yet there existed demons of all sorts, natures and aptitudes, and some were even—surprisingly—benevolent. Edamite Thrash being one such example. Savin could only pray Jett had been guided and sheltered by one possessing a modicum of kindness.

He had so many questions to ask. Why had they gotten sucked into Daemonia? It was something he'd asked himself thousands of times over the years. Never had he gotten an answer. Might Jett have brought back that answer with her? He wanted to know, if she could tell him. But he must be careful with her, allow her time to heal and to adjust to the mortal realm.

Hell, he was thankful she was alive.

Hours later, the sun prodded Savin out of a snore. He rubbed a hand over his head and then his shaggy beard. He needed a shave. He tended to avoid the manscaping bullshit and suffice with a shower and comb. He wasn't trying to impress anyone.

Except now a pretty woman lay in the other room. He didn't want to scare her. Might be time to dig out the razor.

Rising, he tugged off the long-sleeved shirt he'd slept in and unbuttoned his jeans as he walked toward the back of the flat. There were no doors between the living room and bedroom, so he peeked inside before entering. Jett lay still and was covered by the sheet, so he quickly snuck through the room and into the bathroom, closing that door quietly behind him.

Turning to meet his reflection in the mirror above the freestanding porcelain sink, he sneered at the gruff man who rarely smiled back. How long had his eyes been so dark and sullen? Was that the appearance of a wild man or a scruffy hermit? He really had developed a lack of concern. Kept the demons back, he figured. They feared his appearance. Heh. Not really. That was what the sigils were for. Protection and repulsion.

He traced one of the finely tattooed sigils on the underside of his forearm. Composed of circles within circles and some directional arrows along with demonic repulsion sigils. Sayne, the ink witch who'd put the bespelled ink down, had promised him they would be effective against most demons. Of course, he could never be impervious to all because there were so many breeds of demons in existence.

There had been one occasion when Savin met a demon who had not been repulsed by any of his sigils. That demon had initially been locked in a cage in the bowels of the Acquisitions' headquarters. Later, Savin had ended up working with Gazariel, The Beautiful One, to help track down a vicious vampiress intent on invoking a spell that could end the world by smothering all mankind with the wings of fallen angels. That was a long story.

Savin found his way into some serious shit at times. Like it or not.

Hell, he liked it more than not. Kept life interesting. And, well, it was what he knew how to do.

Flipping on the shower, he stripped down and grabbed the razor from the medicine cabinet. Time to make himself more presentable for his guest.

* * *

Jett sat up on the big, wide bed. She'd slept? Grabbing a pillow, she hugged it to her chest, burying her face in the rugged scent of Savin Thorne. She hadn't smelled anything so good. Ever. The man entered her pores on a brute whisper of masculinity and crisp fall leaves, and stirred up thoughts that didn't so much surprise her with their eroticism as rise to embolden her.

Was she still asleep and in a dream?

While she was in Daemonia, dreams had been elusive. Actually, nightmares might have been the only reverie possible there. When attempting to recline and rest, she'd learned to shut down her thoughts. To sleep? Surely, she had. According to Savin, it had been twenty years that she had been absent. A person couldn't survive so long without sleeping.

"Twenty years," she whispered.

Twenty years according to the mortal realm's timekeeping.

It was impossible to track time in Daemonia. Night and day did not exist. The seasons of gray and white and rust did. Gray crept in on mist and eeriness. White had shocked with ice and the crackly lava flowers she'd grown to enjoy despite their charcoal scent. And rust? Fire and screams.

It was late summer here in Paris. Perhaps. She hadn't taken careful note of the field and surroundings last night before Savin pulled up on the road beside her. But it was warm. Such comforting warmth teased at her skin. In all her time in that place, she'd not known such a gentle and undemanding temperature.

Now she was determined to open her arms wide and embrace it all. Take it back in and flood her system with the muscle memory of a normal life. She must once again become a part of the human race.

Was it possible? She didn't have a clue. But she would not relent until she was proved either right or wrong.

A clatter from inside the bathroom clued her she was not, indeed, dreaming. Savin must have finished in the shower. And before she could decide if she should leave the bedroom to give him some privacy, the door opened. Steam wafted out on a sage-scented cloud. And a god wearing but a towel emerged.

"Oh, you're up." Savin hooked his hand on the towel where it was tucked at his hip.

Jett dragged her gaze from his face—he had trimmed what had been a wild beard to something a bit more ruly—down over his wide and solid chest. That was a lot of muscle, and all of it was tight and undulated in curves and hard planes and... She had seen demons who looked like they pumped iron in a gym. They'd had muscles of blackest flesh or coldest steel. Some breeds' physical makeup had been so terrible as to reveal bone and organs. But this man? Those muscles did not wrap about a rib cage that lacked within it a beating heart. Savin Thorne was a hot drink of the clearest, cleanest water she'd ever desired.

"Did you sleep?" he asked.

"Sleep?" Adjusting her gaze from the tantalizing ridges of muscle on his abdomen, Jett hugged the pillow tighter to her chest, sensing a weird increase in her breaths. Which, when checked, she realized was want. Need. Hunger for the man's muscles pressed up against her body. "Uh, yes. Surprisingly. I think that's the best sleep I've had in ages."

"That bed is comfortable. I, uh…"

He glanced to the cabinet on the other side of the bed that stood up against the wall.

"Oh, you need to get dressed. I should let you have some privacy." She dropped the pillow and walked to the edge of the bed on her knees, but Savin beat her to the cabinet, and if she climbed off the bed, she'd step right up against him.

"It's cool," he said. "I'll just grab some things and change out in the living room. I'm sure you want to use the bathroom. You can use whatever you like. I might even have an extra toothbrush in one of the drawers. Toothpaste is in the cabinet."

Toothpaste. That sounded so decadent.

"How about we take a walk down the street and find something to eat?" he offered as he claimed some clothes. "Then we can talk."

"Talk?" Not about Daemonia. She wasn't ready for that. And she wasn't sure she would ever be. "Sure. It'll be great to get out in the fresh air. It's not something I've had…" Uh… No. She wasn't going to detail what was now her past. "Thank you, Savin. It was weird luck that you were out there in the country to help me."

"It was. But also not a coincidence." He took her in with a shadowed glance. His eyes were deep blue and his thick brows were low above them, granting him a dangerous mien. A force to, literally, be reckoned with. "That place where the rift to Daemonia opened last night is exactly where *it* happened."

Jett nodded. It. Yes, it had been. That day long ago when her life had been irrevocably altered.

"Sorry." He winced. "You probably don't want to talk much about all that. We'll take it slow. I'm hungry. Soon as you're ready, we'll head out. Feel free to raid my clothes. You might make a dress out of one of my shirts, you're so tiny."

He strode around the corner and Jett slid off the bed to look through the clothes cabinet. She'd found a T-shirt to sleep in last night and it hung to her thighs. Her hand glided over a pair of gray sweatpants with a string tie at the waist. It should serve until she could buy clothes that fit her.

Might Savin lend her some money to get her life established? She would need it because she had no means to a job or even knowledge of how to acquire the basics such as food, clothing and shelter.

Had she done the right thing?

The innate part of her that had seen to her survival in the Place of All Demons rose within her, reminding her she was not the same girl who had been taken out of this realm so long ago. She was stronger, and more vital. And she would have whatever she wanted, using her wiles if necessary. Let no man, or demon, stop her.

"I will," Jett whispered decisively. "And he will help me."

In the bathroom, she found a new toothbrush and Savin's comb. Her hair was a tangle and hung to her waist. Also, it was no longer the color it had been while she was in Daemonia. She wasn't sure if she missed that or not. She'd often worn it braided and back, but she no longer had consorts to aid or help her dress. Such a loss.

A moment to focus inward and ensure that all would be well—and secure—served her temporary solace. Maybe? She was trapped within something she was not in this realm, just as she had been in the other realm. And she was already questioning her decision to escape. She'd left behind things. Privileges. A certain status.

Jett shook her head. She had to stay on focus. She had wanted this. Had striven for escape. And the best person to help her achieve normality had been right there, waiting for her. Surely, that was a positive sign. For now, she was safe around Savin. Yet she could not overlook that the wards protecting his home pulled at her when she got too near the front door. She needed to be outside, free from any repulsive magic.

Pulling up the sweatpants, she tugged the ties and bunched up the excess. It still didn't fit smartly, so she'd be forced to hold them up while she walked. But the invite to get outside could not be refused. She craved fresh air and would swallow it in gulps.

Out in the living room and sitting on the couch, Savin strummed an acoustic guitar. When Jett entered, he stopped and stood, setting the instrument aside. "You found clothes. That's good."

She clutched the front of the pants.

"Or not." He winced. "There's a women's shop two buildings down from here. You want to stop in before we eat?"

"I'd appreciate that, but I have no means to pay."

"Jett, don't worry about it. You have nothing. I've got your back."

She nodded, again finding it hard to speak when he had already been so generous. At the same time, a part of her, the part that had shone and assimilated while in Daemonia, smiled and straightened her spine. Of course he should serve her and make her comfortable. She deserved it.

"Let's go out, then," she said. "I'm eager to breathe in Paris."

Chapter 5

In the women's clothing shop, Jett found some black jeans with sequins dashing down the sides of each leg seam, and a blousy red top. Black boots with high heels had given her a giddy thrill. Savin had suggested she grab a few more things, and while she had been initially reluctant, she quickly warmed to the shopping gene that Savin knew all women possessed. He didn't mind bulking up his credit card bill. Seeing Jett's satisfied smile had been well worth it.

Of course, the smile had been too brief. It was almost as if she'd caught herself in a moment of joy, then quickly slammed the door shut on the freedom. It would require time for her to rise above her experience, surely.

Now she sat across a metal table from him on the sidewalk before his favorite sixth-arrondissement café. Four bags were corralled around her. She looked over the menu while he had ordered black coffee and three *pains au chocolat*. That was the first course for him. He would go in for the potatoes next.

"I'm not sure what I want," she said, setting down the menu. "I feel hungry. Or do I?"

"You can have one of my pastries and then order something later if you're still hungry." He noticed her scowl. "It's not a test, Jett. You can try as many things as you like."

She managed a roundabout shrug-nod. He assumed it was overwhelming for her to be someplace so simple as a sidewalk café after coming from— Well, he wasn't going to ask about it. He'd wait until she brought it up. It seemed the kindest thing to do.

"Paris smells like I remember. Old, yet hopeful," she said after the waitress dropped off Savin's order. She accepted a plate with one of his pastries on it and picked up a fork. "And the fountain down the street sounds so happy."

He'd forgotten about that fountain. A guy could hear it if he really listened. He'd lived here so long it had faded into the background. Just another city sound. What his senses were most focused to? Demons. They brandished a distinctive hum to their aura. If one walked close enough to him, it registered as a twinge in his veins. Some, he even smelled the sulfur. And while they could cast a sheen over that hum, the scent and their innate red pupils, if Savin caught sight of them at the right angle, the red glinted.

Jett paused with her fork poised over the pastry. "Can I ask you a few things?"

"Of course. Ask away."

"You were sending demons back into Daemonia last night, yes?"

"You bet. I'm a reckoner, Jett."

"That is what I guessed. How did you ever come to do such a thing? And, uh…just how long have you been…back?"

He set down the pastry and brushed the crumbs from his beard. She wouldn't like hearing this, but he wasn't going to lie to her. Savin had a thing about loyalty to friends. He didn't know any other way to exist.

"I've been back," he said, "since I was ten."

Her jaw dropped open and the fork hit the plate with a clink. "But you were ten then. When we…" She pressed her fingers to her mouth, and her eyes averted to study the sidewalk.

"I was in Daemonia for what felt like weeks," he offered. "Maybe a month?"

"Time doesn't exist there," she said softly. The fragile pain in her tone cut Savin to the core. Should he have been so forthright?

"Right. No way to measure time there," he said. "But I did find a way out."

"That's so good for you." Her smile was again brief. Not easy. "And…your parents were there for you?"

"As soon as my feet hit mortal ground outside the wicked forest, I ran back home through the lavender field and straight into my house. My parents were over the moon. I didn't think my mom would ever stop hugging me."

Jett's eyes still did not meet his, and he could imagine what she was thinking. How she had lost that opportunity for a cheery family reunion. Hell, he shouldn't have mentioned that part.

"I tried to explain what happened, but they thought me…" He twirled a forefinger near his temple. "And when your parents asked me where you were, I didn't know what to say. Would they believe a kid who said some strange force sucked us into a different realm? Kids always get accused of having wild imaginations. And I remember your mom, in particular, was Catholic."

Jett nodded. Smirked at the memory. "To the extreme. So much guilt."

"Right. Religion is…not for me. Anyway, after giving it some thought, I decided that being lured into the woods by a stranger and the two of us being separated was the only story they'd believe. That's when the police arrived. They questioned me for hours. I cried a lot."

"I imagine so."

Savin lifted his chin and swallowed. Ignoring the stir of the Other within, he reached across the table and touched her fingers. "Those tears were for you, Jett. I just wanted you back."

She nodded and yet pulled her fingers from under his touch. Wrapping her arms tightly across her chest, she leaned forward, protecting herself as best she could. "Were my parents upset?"

"Inconsolable." He waited until she finally gave him her gaze. That soft brown stare that had once teased, cajoled and challenged him. "They loved you, Jett. But I know it was difficult for them to accept that I returned and you did not. Nothing was the same after that."

"What do you mean?"

"Well." How to say it kindly? Surely, she might seek her parents now. And while he'd been but a kid, Savin had understood exactly what had occurred in the neighbors' house down the street in those months following his return. The truth needed to be told. "Your parents split up about a year after it happened. I was still young and only heard the whispers from my parents, but I understood that your father moved out of the country."

"He did? That's… Wow." She sat back on the metal chair and pulled up a knee to hug against her chest.

"And your mother…"

"My mother?"

"What was her name again?"

"Josette. Josette and Charles Montfort."

"Right." Savin raked his fingers through his hair. "I'm not sure what happened to Josette. After your dad left, my parents told me never to speak to Madame Montfort because I'd upset her. So I walked the long way around the neighborhood to get to school. Not that I stayed in school much longer than a few years."

"But you were ready to enter middle school?"

"I managed middle school. Barely. My mom called it ADD. I knew differently. I dropped out in the first year of high school. The whole world, and the way I saw it, was never the same after— Well, I'm sure you understand. Anyway, I moved to the city when I was seventeen and lost touch completely with the Montforts."

"I see." Jett toyed with the pastry flakes on the plate, then rubbed her hand along her thigh. "I guess I can understand the divorce. My parents must have been shattered about my disappearance. They…fought a lot."

"I remember you telling me about hearing their arguments. It happens. People change and seek new directions."

"But another country? You don't know where my father went?" she asked.

He shook his head. And one final terrible detail. "He got remarried, Jett. That's all I know."

She nodded, taking it in. Her fingers clasped tightly on her lap. Everything about her closed. "I wonder if my mother is still in the same house."

"Impossible. That area we were in last night is where the lavender field once was. The houses were torn down years ago, Jett. There's only a thin line of trees left from the original forest. They're putting up new buildings and a golf course. I'm not sure where your mother went."

"Would your parents know? I mean…" She exhaled heavily, and when she met his gaze, Savin expected to see tears, but instead a steely determination glinted in her dark irises. "I have no one now. I need to start anew. But I can't do that without support. And survival aside, I'd like to find my parents. Because…"

"Of course. I can ask my maman for you. My dad died ten years ago."

"Oh." She dropped her gaze from his. "Death is— You resemble him, from what I remember."

Savin winced at her tone. It had been so…dead. Like she had forced herself to say something kind. Like she didn't really feel for him. It was a weird thing to notice. But again, he reminded himself, she had been through a lot.

"So you got out fast," she stated. "And did you always want to be a reckoner after that?"

He snorted. "Hell no. I had no idea what a reckoner even was until seven or eight years ago when John Malcolm—he's an exorcist—found me and told me I needed to be trained to do what I could do naturally. It's the weirdest thing I've never asked for, but have accepted because it seems that's what I'm meant to do.

It's a strange and repulsive calling. I just want to keep humans safe from demons."

She nodded.

"You need to know something, Jett. When I came back to this realm, a demon hitched a ride in me. I call her the Other."

"The Other?" she said with a gasp.

Yes, she remembered. They'd played a board game when they were kids that had been a bit like Dungeons and Dragons, and the creature who had lived in a dark cave had been called the Other. That was the name for the villain they had always adopted when playacting any sort of fantasy quest, adventure, or even when taking a tromp through the basement without the lights on.

Savin shrugged. "I was a kid. At the time, it was a name that fit. She's the one who helped me get home. The bitch is still in me. She's incorporeal. Can't get her out. I'm not sure how to. I've tried, believe me. But we've developed a mutual respect for each other's boundaries and I put up with her occasional fits."

"Fits?"

"When angered, she can toss me across the room. Freaks the hell out of me. She's been a bit prickly today. Weird. I'm chalking it up to our experience last night. But there are…measures I take to keep her calm."

"Measures?"

He reached into his back pocket and laid on the table a tin box that he never left home without. He had a few more tucked in all the other places he might need a quick fix, such as at home and in his truck. "Morphine. It seems to keep the bitch chilled without affecting me too much."

"Oh. Yes, morphine. It is a commodity in Daemonia. Smuggled in illegally from the mortal realm."

He shrugged. "Yeah, I knew that. That's how I figured it might be something I could use to control her." He tucked away the tin box. "Since my return, I've been able to see and feel a demon's presence. In my very bones, you know?"

She swallowed and nodded again, strangely telling in her silence.

"And for some reason," Savin continued, "I can invoke demonic rituals and languages to send them back to where they came from. It's been an innate skill after my return. So after Malcolm trained me, I figured I hadn't much choice but to become a reckoner. Wasn't as if I had a vibrant social life or dreams and goals of becoming a corporate raider or even a chef or fireman. I'm just weird Savin Thorne who sees demons and feels them all around. I've learned to work with it."

"You don't seem so weird to me. Rather handsome, too." She lowered her gaze, but her voice took on a confident tone. "You've grown up since I last saw you."

"So have you." He felt something close to a blush heat his neck. Savin quickly rubbed at his beard to hide his sudden nerves. Not that he didn't enjoy flirting with a beautiful woman. He just…was surprised by his sudden and easy interest in Jett's sensual appeal.

"So you can see demons in the mortal realm? All of them?"

"Not all. Most. And it's not so much that I can see them—some I can—as that they give off a vibration that I can sense when they are close. But some are clever and wear a sheen expertly. You know about that stuff, yes?"

Another silent nod.

"Right. Probably hard not to get educated on the demonic realm when stuck in that place. Listen, Jett, I know you probably want to avoid questions about Daemonia, but can I ask one thing?"

"Of course you can."

"Were you treated well?"

She straightened her neck and slid her palms along each chair arm. It was almost as if she had realized she was safe now and could be the woman she was. A regal confidence bloomed in her eyes. "Well enough. I survived. And I am in one piece. And now I'm here. That is what matters, isn't it?"

"It is."

Yet her confident front did not hide the fact that she was frightened. Savin could feel the fear coming off her.

The waitress stopped by and set the roasted potatoes, sprinkled with rosemary, before him. Jett decided on tea and he didn't push her to order more.

His cell phone rang and, seeing it was Ed, he told Jett he needed to take the call. "Yeah, Ed, what's up?"

"We managed to wrangle a dozen demons after leaving the site last night. I've got them contained here at the office in the basement holding cell. Would you be able to swing by and reckon them?"

He glanced across the table. Jett was poking about in one of her shopping bags, the tissue paper crinkling. "Sure. Give me a couple hours and I'll head over."

"Great. I'll give you more details then."

"The cellular phone has advanced measurably in my absence," Jett commented as he tucked away his phone. "I remember them being large and—what were they— flip phones?"

"They get smaller and sleeker every year. And the

cameras on them are amazing. I've even got a demon tracking app."

"What's an app?"

"It's a…" Savin chuckled. "A program designed to do something specific and usually make life easier. Though I'm not much for selfies."

"What's a selfie?"

"Something I think you would be excellent at." He winked, and her lift of chin preceded a slight curve of her mouth. Yes, she would put all the selfie queens to shame with her natural beauty. "I'll give you the tech talk later," he said. "You won't need to learn much to get up to speed. Except that swiping right can get you in more trouble than you are prepared to confront."

And that was all he was willing to divulge regarding his failed Tinder experiment.

"I have no idea what you just said, but I think I'll be fine without a phone for now. Getting up to speed on existing in this realm is going to take some time. You have somewhere you need to be?"

"Yes, that was Edamite Thrash. He's a corax demon. Good guy. I'd never reckon him. He keeps an eye on the demons in Paris and isn't afraid to move in when one steps out of line. Sort of the demon police patrol over Paris."

"Edamite Thrash." She seemed to make note of the name.

"I have some business across the river with Ed."

"Reckoning?"

Savin nodded. "I won't invite you along. I suspect you'll want to keep yourself as far from anything having to do with demons as you can."

"Sounds like a dream. But is it possible in this city?"

He felt awful that her dream was so dismal. "It is. Demons are populous in Paris, but the smart ones tend to mind their manners. I'll walk you back to the flat and then make it a quick job."

"I can find my way back on my own."

"I do need to get my truck." He wolfed down some potatoes and finished his coffee. Seeing Jett's longing look at some passing tourists, he offered, "Unless you want to walk by yourself for a while? I don't want to be too forward."

She gave him that silent nod again. Somehow submissive, which bothered him.

He tugged out his wallet and laid a couple twenty-euro notes before her. "You take that and go off walking by yourself. Buy what you want. If your appetite comes back, you'll be covered. Yes?"

"Thank you."

"I'll leave the door to my place unlocked. Don't let the demon wards freak you out. Sometimes they tug when you enter."

"Didn't even notice them last night," she offered airily.

"They're not all-purpose, but they've served me well. I'll loosen them up for you anyway." Because she probably still had residue from Daemonia on her. "And feel free to tuck your new purchases into a drawer. Make yourself at home, Jett. My place is your place until you feel like you need to get the hell out. Deal?"

"Deal."

He signed the check, then stood, and thinking he should shake her hand or something, he decided that was stupid. And would she get the friendly double-cheek-kiss thing? It wasn't something he ever did—why was he fretting about this?

Abandoning his ridiculous thoughts, he tossed out a "See you later?"

"I look forward to it."

So did he. Because those beautiful, sad brown eyes made him hungry for things other than food. A man shouldn't have such thoughts for a woman he hardly knew. And yet he did know her. The nine-year-old Jett. The intrepid, laughing best friend he'd promised to someday marry. Seemed like a long shot now. She was different. Could she get back to the usual? Did she want to? What had she been through?

He wanted to help her. He really did. And he needed to protect her. Things that came out of Daemonia might be required to return, no matter their species. Might someone—or something—come looking for Jett?

Jett wandered the cobblestoned streets and sidewalks through Paris, inhaling the smells of gasoline, cooked food and ancient limestone. The sounds of rushing cars, chattering tourists, Notre Dame's bells and the laughter of children lightened her mood.

The sights were both historical and contemporary. The old buildings that had been around for centuries, and that she could recognize, gave her comfort. The city had not changed in her absence. And the people had only marginally changed, fashionwise. But there were so many cell phones now. Did everyone carry them always? Including the children? How bizarre to want to walk down the street having a conversation with a person on the phone while your family or friend walked next to you, doing the very same.

The city was as she'd remembered, and yet those memories were so old everything had become new again. She found herself smiling despite not having used those muscles around her mouth for a long time. A satisfied sigh followed.

She could make this her home once again.

As she was weaving through tourists who crowded the sidewalks, the scent of roasted meat lured her to draw in the savory aroma. But she didn't feel hungry. After one bite of Savin's pastry, she had realized it tasted like stale paper. It was not what she'd eaten in Daemonia. All senses had been engaged during meals, lush scents and flavors combining to satisfy in the most bizarre manner. The humans would not know what to call the demonic foods, and some dishes might even repulse them.

She could grow accustomed to roast chicken and potatoes again. She must.

Savin had taken her bags back to his place, so Jett swung her arms as she crossed a busy intersection. The river was close. The water smelled dark, yet much cleaner than anything she had known in a while.

A passerby rudely brushed her shoulder and kept on walking, his attention on the cell phone at his ear. But the sensations Jett got from that quick contact shocked up her arm. *Demon.* It was an innate knowledge. He didn't turn to regard her. He couldn't know acknowledgment was required. Rather, submission.

That was a good thing. Maybe?

Part of her decided it was. The darkest part of her crossed her arms and gave a huffy pout. Really. Where was the subservience? Should not all demons know and fear her? It was going to take time to adjust to being just another face in the crowd.

Shaking off the surprise of having been so close to a demon—and not feeling compelled to follow—Jett wandered to the river's edge and leaned over the wide concrete balustrade. If demons walked the streets without notice, that meant surely the city must be populated with all species of paranormals. Something of which she'd not been aware when she was an innocent child.

And now knowing so much served her both bane and boon. All grown up and in the know, she could be smart and protect herself from anything that wished to harm her. If that *anything* knew who she was. Something she intended to conceal as long as physically possible.

Holding a hand out over the water, Jett closed her eyes and drew in the power of nature. Flowing water had always strengthened her. She harkened it to that fateful plunge over the falls. Rather, that *push.* She'd initially thought Savin had caught up to her and shoved her screaming and flailing over the edge. But she'd corrected that after the long fall. He hadn't been close enough. He could never have known what had occurred during that fall.

Similar to the fall an angel makes from Above? It was a tale she'd made up, a secret belief that had helped her through hard times. Innocence falling to destruction and ruin, and all that fantastical stuff.

But that truth wasn't something she could share with Savin. Maybe? No, she wasn't nearly so ready to completely trust the man. It had been twenty years. So much had happened. Both had changed and been altered by their stays in that nightmare place. Jett would be wise to tread carefully around the man who could reckon demons out of this realm.

Hearing the loud chatter of a woman next to her, Jett turned, expecting to find her conversing with another, and only saw the one woman.

"Technology," she muttered Savin's explanation. "What else has changed?"

For one thing, the movie screens. Or were they television screens? Whatever they were, there was one set up in the parvis before Notre Dame just across the river; it played a film on the cathedral's history. The screen was so large, and the images remarkably clear, even from where she stood.

The cars that zoomed past on the bridge were the same as she remembered, save newer and probably faster. The people all looked the same. Fashion in this touristy district still left much to be desired. Jett could spot a true Parisian by her smart, elegant style. Or there, the woman riding the bicycle in a skirt, with her high heels tucked in a side bag. Definitely a city native.

The food all seemed familiar. The Notre Dame Cathedral was still an awesome monument. The whine of tired children tugging on their parents' legs was familiar, as well. So much remained familiar to her, and that was heartening.

Yet where were the bowing sycophants?

Jett's eyes sought someone, anyone who might recognize her importance. And she realized her sheen was beginning to wane, allowing her darkness to rise, so she tightened her hold on it and spread her focus over her skin once again. Mustn't drop her mask. No matter how good it felt, or how much she desired recognition.

After walking awhile, Jett shrugged her achy shoul-

ders and yawned. The crowd and the bright sunlight
taxed her energy. She was beginning to require more
focus than usual to stay in this form. So she headed back
toward Savin's place, wandering quickly past the Montparnasse Cemetery and then the Luxembourg Gardens,
taking in all things, but also looking forward to rest.
She'd breathed enough fresh air for today.

Most of all, she looked forward to seeing Savin
again.

The only friend she had ever known had reentered
her life. And that was remarkable.

But what he'd told her about her parents. They'd di-
vorced. And he had no clue where either was right now?
Besides the memory of her best friend, her parents had
been her only connection to this realm. For the longest
time she had whispered the Catholic prayers her mother
had taught her, until the words had begun to literally
burn on her tongue. And long after she'd learned not
to invoke the Christian God in that place, the simple
image of her mother or father had worked to keep up
her spirits.

She needed to find them to truly return to this realm
she wanted to once again call home.

Arriving at Savin's building, she took in the vibrations cloaking the immediate area. Like Savin, she
could read the air and sense demons when nearby. As
well, she could vibrationally map out the living beings
in the area. Sort of like sonar, she supposed. Savin was
above in his home, already returned from his task. She
knew it because his scent carried to her. That delicious
essence of man that she'd slept wrapped in all night.

There were wards outside the limestone-faced
building. Invisible, yet she could feel Savin's signa-

ture sealing them. Wards against demons and a few
other species, perhaps vampires and werewolves. They
tugged at her musculature, as they had last night, when
she mounted the inner stairs and climbed up four stories, but it wasn't anything that would rip her apart or
send her screaming.

Facing the wards drawn on Savin's front door, Jett
rechecked the sheen she wore, a masterful disguise.
She'd need to relax and let go soon. Just an hour or so.
A means to recharge.

Yet the last place she could do that was inside a fully
warded reckoner's home.

Or maybe, it might serve as the safest place possible.

She knocked on the front door, then tried the knob.
It was open, and as she popped her head inside the
flat, Savin called for her to enter. A fierce tug at her
skin pulled and prickled as she crossed the threshold,
but she made it inside and closed the door behind her,
thus squelching the ward's seeking force. It sought to
repeal a demon. She was still strong enough to thwart
the weakened repulsion.

Now she dropped her shoulders and exhaled wearily.
"You beat me back," she commented.

Savin sat on the couch, a glass of what smelled like
alcohol in hand, which he tilted to her. "It was a quick
call. Four more demons sent back to where they belong.
And you have been out the whole afternoon. You walk
around the city?"

She sat on the wooden-armed chair across from the
couch and pulled up her legs to hook her feet on the
leather cushion. It was cool and not so bright in his
place, and she appreciated that. "Paris is beautiful. I

never appreciated the architecture when we were kids. So many people, though. I'm tired out!"

"Yeah, it's August and the tourist crush is ridiculous. No wonder all the locals head out of town this time of year. I left your new things in the bedroom for you. You want a drink?"

"I recognize the smell of whiskey from when my father used to have a 'sip' after an evening meal. But I've never tried alcohol. At least, not anything made in this realm."

"Really? I suppose." He swiped a hand across his jaw.

She sensed he tried to be tactful and not ask about her experience, which she appreciated.

"Want to try some?"

"I'd never refuse a challenge from you."

And while that statement was something that she would have said as a kid to Savin's challenging glint in the eye, now it felt bold and powerful. Adult. And in response, Savin's gaze seemed to slip across her skin in a welcome manner. Jett wriggled on the chair, lifting her chin. She liked to be admired by him.

He stood and collected another glass in the kitchen, then returned to pour her a portion from the bottle.

"Do you play all those guitars?" she asked as he handed her the glass. She sniffed it. Very strong, and not too appealing.

"Most are collectibles," he said. "A few are prized possessions. That one is signed by Chuck Berry. Saw him at a concert a decade ago and met him when he was exiting out the backstage door. I like to play my own compositions. A little blues à la Chuck Berry, a little Southern rock. Some headbanging riffs mixed with a touch of classical. I'm also teaching myself musicomancy."

Jett sat up a little straighter. "Is that some kind of magic?"

"Using music. But it's slow going. Hell, I tend to sit and drink far too much whiskey, and then my playing gets looser and more random. I suspect that's a good reason why I have yet to accomplish musicomancy." He winked and tilted back the remainder of his drink, then poured some more. "I use the diddley bow for the magic stuff." He gestured over his shoulder, and Jett noted a strange guitar-like instrument with a turtle-shell-sized body and a long, thin neck and only one string. "Made that one myself. That's another hobby of mine. Fiddling around with making things. Made a bunch of navigational devices that I use for my work, as well. Guess I got the creative gene from my dad. You remember when I took apart your Nintendo controller?"

"I don't think I forgave you for that. And I wouldn't necessarily call destroying things being creative," she teased. "You tended to take apart anything you could get your hands on."

"Yeah." He chuckled. "Now I put things back together. I figured out how it all works. Now I'm all about restoration and creation. No destruction."

Destruction. The word felt comfortable to Jett's senses. It had been so easy to destroy that which annoyed her. But just as she noticed herself smiling about such memories, she chased away the thought. She would not slip around Savin. She must not.

She sniffed her glass, then took a sip. It burned down her throat, but it was actually tasty. As she drank more, the burn lessened. Another sip and the dark liquid smoothened on her tongue. "I like this."

"Much as I hate to be the one to corrupt you, I can't argue an appreciation for a good aged whiskey."

"I am beyond corruption, Savin. So don't worry about that."

"Everyone is corruptible."

"Yes, well, there's nothing about me that can get any more corrupted. So trust, you won't harm me. No matter what vices or sinful challenges with which you should tempt me." She held out her glass toward him. Her voice thickened into a husky tone. "More."

Glass clinked as he poured her another portion. Then he topped off his drink. The lingering look he gave her was in reaction to her sensual tease. Good boy. He understood her. She could work with that.

"Can I ask you one thing? It's personal."

"I don't have any boyfriends, if that's what you're wondering." Jett chuckled softly and pressed the cool glass against her lower lip. The man was so sexy. And she understood the meaning of that word now. How quickly she relaxed around him. And desired. She was feeling…sensual. Must be the whiskey. Yes, she did like this drink.

"No, that's—" Savin looked over the rim of his glass. "Could you have boyfriends…you know…there?"

He wanted to know about her love life in Daemonia? Ugh. "Is that the question you wanted to ask?"

"Do I only get the one?"

Jett sighed and allowed her shoulders to relax against the comfy cushions. She crossed her legs, and with a slip off of the heel, she dangled her shoe on her toes.

"Fine. Ask me anything. But I'm allowed to refuse any answer."

"I don't want to grill you, Jett. But I am curious. In turn, you can ask me anything."

"You've been open with me so far. I owe you that much."

He leaned forward, resting his elbows on his knees, the whiskey glass dangling from one hand before a leg. "How did you survive in that place? Was there shelter? Buildings? Towns? A place of safety?"

"There's never safety in Daemonia," she said curtly. The whiskey slid quickly down her throat and she slammed the glass on the chair arm. "But there are dwellings. And cities and citadels. Castles, hovels and all means of residence. I…had a place to live." She couldn't tell him everything. She'd never get out of this flat in one piece if she did that. "And I was generally free from the treacherous elements that I'm sure you remember."

"So someone took you in? That's good. I couldn't imagine you wandering that horrible place for so long and on your own."

"There is no alone there." Jett cast her glance upward the windows fitted in the ceiling. The sky was darkening. Thankfully. "Nor was there a sun. But you know, the many moons were pretty. Save for the fire moon. That one hurt if I forgot myself and walked out beneath it."

"Like a sunburn?"

He might never understand that in Daemonia everything was multiplied, magnified, extremely enlarged, enhanced and so, so dangerous. He'd had but a taste as a child.

"A bit," she offered quickly. Now she stood and grabbed the half-empty whiskey bottle and refilled her glass. Growing more confident, she sat on the couch, snuggling up about two feet from where Savin sat and facing him. The whiskey warmed her, and the exhaustion she'd been feeling earlier cooled to a comfortable relaxation. "Any more questions?"

"So many. But I won't inundate you. I genuinely thought you were dead after that fall, Jett. Were you angry with me? For not coming after you?"

He lifted his chin just as their eyes met. Alpha in his command, and unwilling to show any weakness. She'd dealt with men like him. And yet she could feel his heart beating rapidly. He was frightened at his own emotions.

And she, well, she had long ago abandoned the sillier emotions such as fear, shame and empathy.

"I was never angry with you," she said truthfully. "And I hoped for so long that you had made it back home. My wish came true. I'm glad for that."

"I should have leaped over that cliff and tried to save you."

"It would have been a suicide leap, Savin. You were wise to stay put. Trust me on that one."

How she had survived the lava falls was a question she'd never gotten an answer to. And really, she'd decided long ago she didn't want that answer. There had been a reason she was whisked into Daemonia. A wicked, selfish reason for which she could never forgive the perpetrator.

Savin considered her words. Surely his next question would be, how had she survived? So she would redirect his thoughts. "What about you? Do you have any girlfriends?"

His brow quirked; then his lips dallied with a smile before he shook his head. "I'm not so talented with the suave and smooth. All that dating stuff feels awkward."

"A man so handsome and kind as you has trouble with women? Surely, you've dated."

"I have. I do. Eh. It never lasts. I'm human, Jett, but this demon inside me makes it difficult to relate to human women. I'm different than most. I know things I shouldn't know about things that shouldn't exist. And I have to protect that side of me from discovery. You know? I did date a vampiress once. I don't like the idea of getting bitten, though, and that did seem to be a requirement to a happy relationship."

"Did she bite you?"

"I wouldn't let her. It was tempting. I understand the bite is orgasmic. Oh, uh, sorry. I shouldn't talk like that around you."

"Why not? We're both adults. I am a grown woman." And she was feeling more of herself with every moment she sat near Savin. He'd toyed with getting bitten by a vampire? Jett traced the bottom tip of her canine tooth. It was sharp, but not as pointed as usual without her sheen. "I know things," she said. "Trust me, I'm not an innocent."

"All right, then." He considered his glass, and Jett sensed his sudden discomfort.

"Vampires! So many creatures walking this realm," she tossed out to break the tension. "All the things we once thought were only make-believe. All of them predators and prey."

"I've never been prey and don't intend to start. Trust me on that one." He chuckled and shook his head. "Hand me the bottle. Let's finish it off."

She grabbed the bottle and went up on her knees to slide closer to Savin, setting the bottle on his thigh. When he gripped it, she placed her hand over his. He turned his head, and the scent of him invaded her pores on a tease. As a woman, she had needs. And those needs screamed for satisfaction right now. A new turn at satisfaction, actually. One that she might not regret, or that would leave her shivering in revulsion.

"My turn to ask the questions," she said. "Or rather, I've a request."

He studied her hand still resting over his, and she released him so he could pour the last inch into his glass. He tucked the bottle on the other side of his thigh, then said, "Shoot."

Boldness had been bred into her over the long and unending years of her exile. And she was feeling her mettle now that she'd begun to acclimate to this realm. Jett touched the ends of Savin's dark hair and swept them over his shoulder. With the back of her forefinger, she traced along his neck up to the bristly beard hairs. He was warm, much more so than she'd expected. Fiery, even. But never dangerous, at least, not to her darkness.

"Do you think I'm pretty, Savin?"

Now his gaze locked on to hers, and she felt the heat of him scurry over her skin. It danced about her arms and torso and tightened her nipples. Mmm…he was not a man to be ignored.

"I do."

"Do you remember when we were kids and I asked you to kiss me and you said you couldn't until we were older because we'd have to be married and you'd probably have to like girls to do so?"

He nodded and, with a tilt of his head, chuckled

softly. "You remember that? I've always respected women. My mother taught me that."

"Yes, you are a kind man. But. Are we old enough to kiss now?"

Her finger wandered over his chin and followed the line of hairs below the center of his bottom lip. She traced lightly over his mouth. All the while his gaze was intent on hers. Desire smoldered in his deep dark eyes. And she could smell it on him, even though it was a scent that had usually offended her. Not so from Savin. He was a real man. Not a demon.

"Kiss me," she whispered. She moved nearer until their noses were close enough to brush. He smelled like the brisk Paris air and fiery whiskey, with a rich earthy tang of man.

"Jett, I—"

"Yes?"

A hush of his breath played over her lips. "Are you sure?"

"I never ask for things I don't want. That's a waste of words."

She ran her fingers along his cheek and back through his hair.

She would not kiss him. He must come to her. Otherwise, she would not know if he was merely doing as she asked or if he genuinely wanted to. But the heat of his body so close to hers was incredible. Tempting. And she felt dizzied, yet also emboldened by the alcohol. If he refused her request, it would crush her.

When his mouth met hers, the connection felt tentative for but a moment. Savin's hand slipped along her neck, gentle but guiding, as he tilted her head to better receive the taste of his desire. He invaded her with his presence in a way she had never known. And she wanted to keep it. To know him as only adults could know each other.

His mustache brushed her upper lip, and their noses nudged. Eyes closed, she gripped at his wavy hair. Their intense connection rocketed up the delicious tingle that began at her mouth and coiled rapidly throughout her body. Jett slid a leg over his lap, her knee hitting the whiskey bottle, and straddled him. He slipped a hand along her back, not breaking the kiss, instead keeping her firmly in place upon him.

She wanted to taste him, to drink the whiskey from his tongue. That wish was granted as he dashed his tongue along the seam of her mouth. Such a spectacular sensation giddied up her spine. The man's throaty groan clued her he enjoyed kissing her as much as she did him.

His tongue was hot and slick as he tasted her teeth, tongue and her lips. She copied his movements, daring him into a deep dance that ignited the coil of want in her belly, and lower. It was not a sensation she had known—too easy, too comfortable—and it alerted her for a few moments, but she would not let him know her caution rose. The width of his hand spanned her back as he gentled that sudden anxiety with the realization that he might only protect her and—if she was lucky— give her pleasure.

He must. She deserved it.

Bracketing his face with both palms, Jett tilted her head, seeking to devour his whiskey sweetness. When she brushed her hard nipples against his chest, again the man moaned. Yes, she liked his reaction. He was under her command now. And that empowered her.

Yet when he slipped out his tongue and kissed her

mouth, then bowed his forehead to hers to end the kiss, she wanted to greedily pull him back for another. So she did. This time the clutch of his hand against her hip was more urgent. And his other hand slid over her derriere and squeezed.

She wanted to feel his body against hers, skin to skin, to know what his muscles felt like flexing with movement, melding against her body, and to own him.

But she was getting carried away.

Jett lashed her tongue along Savin's lower lip, then met his gaze.

"Whew!" he said.

Exactly. And kneeling over him, firmly in his embrace, she could sense...something similar within him. The demoness he claimed had hitched a ride to this realm with his escape? The Other. Her presence was faint, barely a shimmer that traced the man's veins. And yet she wanted Jett to know of her presence.

Oh, she was aware.

Jett thumbed Savin's mouth. "I've never been kissed like that."

His eyebrow quirked.

"Actually, I've never been kissed until now."

"You're— Really?"

She nodded. "Finally, that kiss you promised me when we were kids has been granted. And don't think you have to stop giving them to me."

"That was an intense kiss. A guy would never know you'd not done such before." He looked aside. Were his thoughts going to places she didn't want them to go?

Jett kissed him again. She would claim this man, body and soul. Because that was what she did to survive.

Chapter 6

There was only one way to be safe, and that would mean relinquishing the power Jett had gained since living in Daemonia. She felt sure she could accomplish the task. She would never return there. Not even if a sexy reckoner decided her time was up.

However, to let go of what she had gained would be a supreme sacrifice. She'd not yet dared to test those powers here in the mortal realm. Perhaps they were already diminished?

But first, she needed an answer to a question that had haunted her all through her absence. And the only way to do that was to locate her parents; one or both. Though she suspected her mother might be the best bet, according to what Savin had told her about her father moving on after her disappearance.

Her father. He could be the missing key. What did she really know about her father?

She'd asked Savin if he could ask his mother about her parents. Since they'd lived so close when they were children, and she remembered their mothers being friends, perhaps Madame Thorne could aid in her search. With luck, she would have an answer to her oft-wondered-about question soon.

Teasing her finger along the granite countertop in Savin's kitchen, Jett marveled over the simple stone. Nothing like this in Daemonia. There the minerals and earth had been volatile and ever changing. One could never take a step without being certain one's foot would land on a solid or moving surface. It was good to be home. Almost home. Would she ever call a place home again?

Savin wandered in from the bedroom. The man wore loose-fitted jeans and a long-sleeved shirt that struggled to contain his biceps. "I'm heading out for some groceries, and I just got a text from Ed, the corax demon I reckoned for yesterday. He was the one who sensed the gates to Daemonia were opening, and was there the night you came through. He isn't sure Certainly's spell to close the rift is holding."

"And who or what is Certainly?"

"Certainly Jones is a man. A dark witch."

Yet another person of whom she should remain wary. Witches never survived Daemonia. The dark ones did like to conjure from that source, and such invocations never seemed to go well. At least, not for the demon.

"I thought you were the reckoner," Jett said. "How are you involved with wrangling demons? Do you hunt, as well?"

"Nope. Don't like to hunt. Dead giveaway, too, because demons sense me as easily as I sense them. But

I'm in on this whole keeping-the-rift-closed adventure, so I'll help Ed and CJ any way I can. You going to be okay here by yourself for a while?"

"Of course. I'm a big girl."

"That you are." His eyes twinkled, and Jett remembered their kiss last night. She would take another from him soon, if she had her way. And she generally did. "Any requests for food?"

"No, but if you could call your mother, I'd be appreciative."

"Right. I haven't forgotten. I might stop by her place today. She lives in the sixteenth near the park now. Has a nice little apartment. She's going to flip to hear you're back."

"Is that a good flip or a bad flip?"

"My mother knows about me and the demon stuff. She says she believes me, but I also know she can't bring herself to label her son crazy, even though she suspects that could be a possibility." He shrugged. "Such is life. I'm going to pick you up a phone while I'm out, too. Not that you need to start texting and taking selfies, but it'll be a good way for us to keep in touch when I'm gone."

"You are too generous, Savin. I feel as if I owe you so much already."

"Don't think like that. I'm glad I can offer you a place to stay. It's nice having someone around to talk to."

"And kiss," she offered, following him to the front door.

"And kiss." He turned and looked down at her. He was too tall and wouldn't be able to get close enough for a kiss without bending his knees. But Jett waited anyway. For a few seconds they held gazes. He seemed... nervous. "Uh, I should go, then."

"Kiss me first. I want to make up for lost time."

He leaned down and his breath hushed against her ear as he spoke. "It's impossible to get back time."

"Time grows longer when you kiss me."

His eyebrow quirked, followed by a slow smile that punctuated his cheeks with subtle dimples. Now, that was impossible to resist.

Jett initiated the kiss that lured her to her tiptoes and into the burly man's embrace. His arms wrapped about her back, and her body tilted against his. Their connection grew lush and deep. She moaned against his mouth. Pleasurable vibrations sparkled in her chest and shimmered lower. Standing in Savin's arms stirred her wanton instincts. This was a new feeling. Yet it teased at her darkness. How she wanted to push him against the wall and tear off his shirt—

"You sure do like my kisses," Savin said as he pulled away. "Or else you've had a lot of practice."

"I told you last night you are the first man I've kissed. I'm glad for that. And you tempt me to want to kiss you all day. Hurry back. I want to start up where we're leaving off."

"I like the way you think." He winked, then opened the door. "See you in a bit."

The door closed behind him and Jett felt the wards zap at her. Stepping back with a skip, she hissed at the intrusive repulsion. It was more an annoyance than anything. But now as she glanced about the kitchen and living room, she realized she was once again imprisoned. Even if she didn't mind the prison so much this time around, she could not breach those wards without pain.

She had to find her own place. Her own identity. And

yet she wanted to do that *and* keep Savin in her life. He fit her. It was as if they had never been separated.

This time her smile came easily as she spun into the kitchen.

Jett opened the fridge door and inspected the contents. Lots of sandwich meats, cheese wedges and bottled energy drinks in wild colors. She was a little hungry but had yet to figure out her appetite. She grabbed a bottle that boasted a protein-packed chocolate elixir and tested it.

"Not terrible."

Drink in hand, she wandered about the place. It was cool and quiet. The skylights beamed in subtle sunlight. Nothing too bright. She suspected it would take a while to fully adjust to the daylight. But the part of her that took comfort from the darkness prodded at her. *Stay in the dark*, it nudged. *Dark is safe. Dark is home.*

Rubbing a palm over her upper arm, Jett winced. Yes, the darkness was a safe and tempting place. There was so much light here in the mortal realm. Had her decision to escape here been wise?

Standing in the center of the living area, she suddenly felt lost, abandoned. Like a nine-year-old child who had been thrust into the unknown. Her cries would never be heard or comforted. She needed safety. So she began to allow the sheen to dissolve—

"No!" Jett lifted her head and fisted a hand at her side. The fall of her sheen stopped. "I can do this. I will do this. I am human."

And her dark half, defeated for the moment, slunk away into the shadows. But she would continue to lurch up closer and closer until Jett could no longer keep her back. How could she? That darkness was her reality.

She smirked. Savin had an incorporeal demon inside him? In a way, they were two alike. Jett had no idea how to ask him for help with her problem. And best she not. No reckoner was going to calmly take her by the hand and treat her kindly should he learn her truth.

Tilting back half the bottle of protein drink, she set it on the wooden chair arm and forced herself to think of anything but her past. Because that was where it now belonged—forgotten in the past.

Her eyes moved about the vast brick wall behind the couch. So many guitars. And the odd one with a single string he'd made himself. Fascinating. Savin practiced musicomancy? She wasn't sure how that magic was utilized, but it didn't sound like something she wanted to experience. Especially when wielded by a reckoner.

On the other hand, she needed to be smart and remain aware. Never look away and always glance over her shoulder. It was a motto that had helped her to survive. Best she learn everything she could about the use of music to invoke magic.

Jett strummed her fingers over the six nylon strings on one guitar. It sounded soft and simple. She imagined Savin could make the instrument sing. As he'd made her insides sing when kissing her. She was not a woman who could be satisfied with mere kisses for long. The man was an inferno, and she wanted to plunge into him. Flames were her sanctuary. It was where she felt most powerful.

Wandering into the bedroom, she approached the freestanding cabinet that stretched as high as her head. Half a dozen metal objects sat on top of it. Crawling onto the high bed, she stood on the mattress and leaned over to catch her forearms against the cabinet top. There were six different metal cases and objects. Brass housings edged them all and intricate carvings decorated the brushed metal surfaces. Wooden pieces were fit in here and there, and some gears and even a combination dial were attached to one of them. They resembled intricate navigational devices from a time long ago. Some had symbols embossed on the metal or burned into the wooden surfaces.

"Sigils," she said with knowing.

A few she recognized as demonic. She knew the words for them but would not speak them, for she could not know what such a recitation would conjure in this realm. Obviously, Savin also had that knowledge.

"His means to track demons?" she wondered as she tapped the cover of one case. But no, he'd said he did not hunt them. Which could only mean... "A device to reckon them back to Daemonia."

It was shaped like a book with an elaborate multitier brass wheel on the front and a dial in the center that did not turn to numbers but rather alchemical symbols. More sigils circled the wheel on four levels. Jett turned the center dial and heard a click. She tested the cover to see if she could open it; it did not. She supposed there was a code or series of turns to open it, much like a combination lock. The vibrations that hummed from the device were weak, yet she sensed it was perhaps honed to work only for a specific user.

Jett did not like being kept out of a secret whether it be delicious or dangerous.

With a sneer, she set that one aside and traced a fingernail over a circular device that featured metal bars jutting out from the center, and at the end of each bar was a small black crystal. Savin had mentioned he made these things. The craftsmanship was stunning. He was talented. As she moved a fingertip over each crystal, the device shook. It *felt* her.

A creak from the other room alerted Jett. She turned to check over her shoulder. Had Savin returned so soon? She listened for a few breathless seconds, then decided she was spooking herself. The thought was ridiculous. Someone such as she, spooked?

Never.

She would not understand these devices, and that was frustrating. With a snap of her finger she should be able to summon an answer.

Jett studied her thumb pressed against her middle finger, ready to snap.

"No longer," she said.

She must learn to exist in a new manner now. With new rules, or, rather, the old rules of the mortal realm she'd once known.

Replacing the device where she'd found it, she perused the rest of the items. At the corner of the cabinet sat a metal tin much like the one Savin had shown her at the café. Morphine? She opened it to find inside a syringe, and rather an old-fashioned one at that. It wasn't disposable or plastic like the sort she'd once seen her father's brother use because he had diabetes. This device was metal and wasn't rusted, but the glass tube did reveal discoloration. And nestled in the red velvet beside the syringe was a white vial with the fading word *Morphia* on it. An elaborate brass cap screwed on the top.

"Like something out of the nineteenth century," she whispered. It couldn't be sanitary or even safe for Savin's health.

He'd said he needed it to keep the demon inside him

subdued. Addicts in Daemonia drank morphine like some kind of sweet beverage and then lapsed into an eyelid-twitching reverie. If they had eyelids, that was.

What demon had hitched a ride in Savin Thorne to come to this realm? And why? If she was incorporeal, she had to have known before leaving Daemonia that she could never leave her host. Or rather, she might switch bodies, but only at great risk. Hmm… On the other hand, sometimes corporeal demons could only maintain that form in Daemonia, and a trip to the mortal realm reduced them to seeking a human host as an incorporeal passenger.

Should Jett have known about that apparent escape from Daemonia? It sounded as though Savin might have been there only a short while, so at the time, Jett wouldn't have had reason or the capability to tap in to what had occurred with his exit.

Now she was curious to learn more about his demonic passenger he called the Other. But she had to be careful because her sheen could crack at any moment. The last thing she wanted was for Savin to see her true nature exposed.

"I will learn what drives you, Savin. And I will have more than kisses from you. I need intimacy," she decided. "To finally feel like a real, human woman."

Ed had been heading out to meet with one of his troop leaders, so he directed Savin to speak to Certainly Jones, who worked in the Archives. The Archives kept a vast storehouse of all documents, texts and artifacts related to every known paranormal species. As well as the most rare and volatile magical objects, devices and even creatures. It was rumored that to obtain some of those things, by trick or by sword, they utilized retrievers in the branch called Acquisitions to do so.

Savin knew their methods were peccable, and that was fine with him. He wasn't big on following the law to a tee. And here in this realm, there was no paranormal code of ethics beyond "Don't make yourself known to humans."

But he was human, and he did know. And he was glad he knew about all the things that should only be myth or legend. Then some days he wasn't so glad. The things he had seen in his short lifetime would turn a man's hair gray and force him to drink. His hair was still brown, but the drinking part...

Upon entering the Archives, he'd let CJ test the wards tattooed on his skin for efficacy and deflection. With Savin's approval, the dark witch had whispered a spell to place a sort of "plastic wrap protector" over those tattooed sigils that could interact negatively with the wards in the building. Still, they retained their power to protect him should some*thing* wish to invade or harm him while he was here.

Feeling the wrapper tingle over his skin, Savin shook out his muscles with a good doggy shake. He then nodded thanks to the witch. "Ed says you're nervous about the wards on the rift."

"I am. And I appreciate you remaining involved in this, Thorne. It's good to have a reckoner handy when all Beneath breaks lose."

Beneath was the paranormal version of the humans' hell.

"I think Daemonia ranks worse than Beneath."

"Fair enough. I've been to Daemonia for a visit myself. Been there, done that, wasn't about to get the T-shirt."

Savin knew that, because CJ was the one he'd gone to in an attempt to get rid of his passenger demon. After his return from Daemonia so many years ago, CJ had been successful in banishing all the unwanted demons from his soul. Yet they both remained baffled on how to oust Savin's guest.

"Right, you know about that adventure," CJ amended. "I wish I had known you when I was full of demons. Would have been much easier to reckon them than the hell I went through getting rid of those bastards."

"It doesn't work that way, I'm afraid." Savin turned a shoulder against the office wall and leaned against it. CJ offered him a clove cigarette, which he took. "I can't reckon a demon within a human host. Tried it on myself."

"That's right. I forgot about that. Sorry, man. You've still got that bitch inside you?" He handed Savin a lighter, then blew fragrant smoke to the side.

"Yes, but let's not call her a bitch today. She's quiet, and I like to keep it that way."

"Got it." CJ leaned against the limestone wall beside Savin and the twosome shared the quiet as they inhaled the sweet smoke.

Despite him being a practitioner of dark magic, Savin liked Certainly Jones. The man had been around for longer than a century and was the ultimate laid-back, bohemian witch. And his woman was gorgeous. Savin had met her one time. Viktoria St. Charles was a cleaner, which meant she and her sister (Libertie, also a witch) cleaned up dead paranormal bodies before they were discovered by humans. She also had a sticky soul, which attracted wayward and lost souls. Interesting.

With the Other inside him, Savin wasn't sure what nature his soul was. *Did* she inhabit his very soul? Or merely this chunk of meat he called a body and used while in this mortal realm? He didn't look forward to dying and bringing her along with him. At the very least, he prayed death would release her. Because he'd felt her pull him away when he wanted to kiss Jett longer and more deeply earlier. Bitch.

Yeah, she could hear his thoughts. Screw it.

"Can I ask you something?" he said to CJ.

"Shoot."

Savin held the cigarette before him and blew on the end, brightening the embers. "When you were there, in Daemonia, how was it for you?"

CJ's heavy sigh said so much. No one in their right mind ever wanted to visit that place. But, apparently, CJ had gone there on purpose, for some magical quest. He'd gone into Daemonia of his own accord, and...well, as is usually the case, he'd gotten trapped there. His twin brother, Thoroughly, had to rescue him and bring him home. And with that return, Certainly had been accompanied by at least a dozen nasty incorporeal demons.

"You must understand," CJ started, "that a child's perception—your memory of the place—is going to be vastly different from a grown man's. And I am a man who went there on purpose."

"I know. I was scared beyond shitless. It was all I could do to survive and not go insane. And believe me, part of me thinks you're one hell of an idiot for walking into Daemonia like you did."

"Most of me thinks that, as well. But you know,

sometimes a guy has to make the leap and go for the adventure."

"I'm all for adventure. And that part of me admires your ballsy trip to the Place of All Demons. But is the place…hospitable? How can a person survive there?"

"I'm not sure it's possible for a human to exist in Daemonia for more than a short time. Time is weird there, you know?"

"I know." What he'd thought was weeks in that place had been a little over thirty-two hours by the time he returned to his parents' loving and worried arms. "Do you think a human could survive there for decades?"

Certainly shook his head and flicked ash to the side. "Not without becoming one of them."

"What does that mean? Like a demon?"

"Anything that isn't demon, and which stays there overlong, will ultimately assume, at the very least, some demonic qualities."

Savin hadn't known that. Could Jett…? No. He would have sensed if she had any demon in her. "But they change back to human when they return to this mortal realm?"

"If they don't have passengers. You know as well as I how difficult it is to come out of that place clean."

Savin blew out a breath and lifted his foot to stub out the cigarette on the bottom of his boot. He looked around for a garbage bin and, spying one by a desk, flicked it into the steel container.

"Why do you ask? You ever accidentally reckon a human?"

"No. Never." He hooked his thumbs at his belt loops. Should he tell Certainly about Jett? It didn't feel right. The witch had no need to learn about his houseguest who might have returned to this realm not as human as she seemed. Savin hadn't considered that she could have developed some demonic qualities. Hmm… She was sensitive to sunlight, and still the wards bothered her.

"Need more morphine yet?" Certainly asked.

CJ was also his supplier. The witch provided him with a clean yet powerful drug that appeased the Other. "Soon. Might have about a month's worth remaining."

"That old mixture is hard to come by. Requires wormwood and dragon's bane. Nasty stuff."

"It's the only thing that works."

CJ nodded. "I'll mix up a larger batch in a week or two. Should keep you in supply for a while."

"Thanks, man. So." Savin rubbed his hands together expectantly. "What's the plan?"

"Ed has two sentries posted out at the site. I visited this morning. I can feel the wards shaking. I think we've got a few days, at the most, before it opens up again."

"How to close it securely?"

CJ leaned against his desk, crossing his legs at the ankle. The guy was barefoot. Savin had never actually seen him wearing shoes. Witches were strange.

"The wards should have held securely," CJ said. "However, there is a reason this suddenly feels loosey-goosey to me."

Savin lifted a brow. "Yeah?"

"I feel as though something got out that wasn't sup-posed to," CJ offered.

"Like every single demon that made its way into this realm?"

"Not exactly. Some demons come here without mak-ing an indelible mark on the realm. They blend in and learn our mortal-realm ways. You know that."

Much as he wished otherwise, Savin knew he'd always have to coexist alongside demons.

"What I'm thinking is that something immense— not necessarily in size, but importance—needs to be returned to Daemonia in order to seal the rift and hex a good lock on it. If something that shouldn't have been allowed comes to this realm?" The witch shuddered. "Realm rules are big on stuff like that. Keeping the balance and all."

"Realm rules?" Savin whistled lowly. "Don't even tell me. I've got enough in this brain that I'd rather not know about, as it is. Something important? Isn't Ed finding most of the demons who got out? I reckoned a handful yesterday."

"He is, but you know demons can cloak themselves. They call it a sheen. Some are so talented they can walk right by you, rub against your skin, and you'd never think they were anything but human."

"I'm better than your average bear at sensing demons. I do have my demon radar sitting inside me."

"Maybe. But you don't sense them all, I'm sure."

"Probably not," Savin conceded. But how to know about the ones he couldn't sense? And did he really want to know? Besides, if it was important or immense, as CJ had described it, surely he would be aware of that disturbance to this realm.

"It's a hunch," CJ offered. "I'm going to spend the afternoon in the demon room, reading up in the Bibliodaemon."

"The Book of All Demons. Doesn't sound like light reading. How can I help?"

"Just stay alert to beyond the usual. Which I'm sure is pretty fucked for you."

"You got that one right."

"I'm going to defer to you as the expert on demons in this case. Did you encounter anything odd following the spell to close the rift?"

Savin shrugged. Jett was human and finally free. She couldn't possibly have an impact on the continuing issues. And if he did let CJ know about her, the witch might have questions. He didn't want to subject Jett to that. Not yet. Not until she was comfortable being back in this realm.

If he could help locate her mother, that might be a start to returning some normality to her routine.

"Savin?"

"Huh? Oh. No. All's the same. As usual. I'm going to head out. You've got my number if you need me. Do I turn left or right at the end of the hallway?"

"Right," CJ said. "Left always tends to lead one into the sinister, don't you know?"

Savin smirked at the joke. But not really a joke, since he did know his witchery and demon lore. "Talk to you later, man."

He strode down the hall, which was entirely of limestone, carved directly from the earth beneath Paris. So the dark witch didn't believe a human could survive Daemonia without becoming part demon? The notion disturbed Savin. If that was the case, would Jett know if she wasn't completely human?

And if so, would she tell him?

Chapter 7

Savin's mother, Gloriana, was wire-wrapping the new growth on her boxwood bonsai when he arrived at her cozy sixteenth-arrondissement apartment. He kissed her on the head—she was five foot two on a good day; he'd gotten his height from his dad—and she rubbed her hands together as she led him toward the kitchen, where it smelled divine.

"Just took some chocolate madeleines out of the oven," she cooed. "I knew I'd see you soon."

She had a weird sense for things like that. She always knew who was on the phone before picking it up (she still had a landline; cell phones weren't her thing), knew who was at the front door before answering and generally knew within a day or two when Savin would call or stop by. And yet the one time he'd mentioned such precognition to her, she dismissed it as woo-woo stuff. Good ol' Maman. She strived to walk a wide circle around her son's reality.

"I love the chocolate ones," he said as she set the plate before him.

Savin downed three cakes, which were still warm, then got up and checked the fridge for milk. "Your madeleines are the best, Maman. I still think you should go into business and start a food truck."

"I'm considering it."

"You are?" He took the milk carton to the table with a glass and poured. "That's awesome. You and Roxane?" Her best friend, who tended to convince his mother to check out the latest clubs and to wear the highest heels to prove that women in their fifties were only as old as they acted.

"Yes. She's got the marketing skills. I've got the recipes. It could happen."

"I'm impressed. Be sure you cruise around the fourteenth, will you?"

"Oh, *mon cher*, I will deliver yours special every day. I'm working on a cheesecake version. Would you like that?"

"I like them all, Maman, you know that." He downed two more moist and dense cakes in but four bites.

"Now, what's up?" Gloriana asked. "I just spoke to you last week and you generally go a few weeks without getting in touch. New girlfriend?"

Savin set down the half-eaten cake. "What makes you think that?"

She wiggled on the chair and smiled a toothy grin. "You've shaved that unruly beard, and your hair is combed."

"Am I really such a slob otherwise?"

"You do tend to avoid the mirror. So tell me what she's like."

"She's…" Savin pushed the plate of madeleines aside and stretched out his legs, preparing for this strange announcement. He and his mother had always shot straight with each other, even when it came to the weird stuff. "She's not my girlfriend, but she is an old friend."

"Oh? Like from school?"

"Jett Montfort is back, Maman."

"What? Did you say *Jett*? But she…" His mother's lower lip wobbled.

A few years after the event had happened, Savin had told her the entire story about being kidnapped to the demonic realm. After the media's interest had died down and his father had died. He'd had to. The truth had burned like a fire in him every time he tried to act as if it had been a kidnapping. He knew his mother had suspected he wasn't being completely truthful with her.

But as well, he knew the truth wasn't going to land on her believability radar. But she could get close. He trusted telling her things now. Weird things. She could believe him or not. Either way? She still loved him.

"Jett." She pressed her fingers to her mouth. "I can't— But how? Where has she been?"

"If I tell you, you'd never believe me. Well, you know, I told you the truth of it all. It was a wild tale, but every bit of it was true, Maman. I swear it to you."

She nodded. Tears glistened at the corners of her eyes.

"Jett was there, in that place, all this time."

Gloriana gaped.

"Suffice, she's safe now and looks well. I'm letting her stay with me until— I haven't thought beyond offering her a place to stay. I'm sure she'll want to find her own place. But she'll need a job first. Hell, she needs to assimilate and become a part of the human race again."

"The human—" Gloriana swallowed. "I can't believe it. It's been twenty years, Savin. And she just walked into your life?"

"Kind of like that."

"Oh." Again, Gloriana pressed her fingers to her mouth. "So she was there…with the…demons?" she whispered the last word.

Savin nodded. He'd described to his mother all he had experienced. And then she'd wrapped him in her arms. It might have been the first time he'd let out a breath and truly relaxed after that harrowing experience. It had been a long time coming.

"I'm keeping her safe," he said.

His mother nodded and grabbed a madeleine to nibble at the end.

"The reason I stopped by is Jett needs to find her mom and dad. She's alone in the world now and wants to reconnect. I figured if anyone had the smallest thread leading to either of the Montforts, it would be you. You were good friends with her mother."

"Josette and I were best friends. But, *mon cher*, you know she left not soon after the divorce. Just up and left her whole life behind. She didn't say a thing to me, and I haven't heard from her since. I can understand…" She looked aside. "You know she was angry with me?"

His mother had never told him that. But he could guess why. "Because I came back?"

She nodded, swallowed. "I understand, of course. Her daughter never came back."

"She has now."

"That's incredible. And you say she looks well?"

"She does. Do you think you can help Jett find her parents?"

"Well." She made the sighing thoughtful noise as her eyes traced about the kitchen. Then her deep blue irises brightened. "I'm not sure what good it will do…" She glanced down the hallway.

"What, Maman?"

"Sit tight. I have some things." She scurried from the kitchen and into the bedroom, where Savin heard her riffling through a large cabinet of craft supplies she ever fussed over. If she wasn't baking, she knitted and donated the sweaters to charity.

Savin downed two more cookies and another half glass of ice-cold milk. A man forgets about the comforts of home after living on his own for so long. If his mother were to invest in a food truck business, he would track her down daily for the treats.

"Here it is." Gloriana returned holding a rumpled brown paper envelope. She sat across from him and set the envelope on the table. "The Montfort house stood empty for a few months after Josette's departure. No realty sign, nor did I get a call from Josette. Finally, I decided to call the city and see what must be done. I was informed they would clean it out and take in hand all possessions, so I decided it would be best to sneak in and see if there was anything important left behind. Just in case Josette ever returned, you know?"

"Smart, Maman. You've always had a sneaky streak."

"And damned proud of it. Anyway, I found some family documents and important papers. Nothing much." She pushed the envelope toward him. "I haven't opened it since that day I took the papers out of their house. You give them to Jett. If they can help her, then I'll know my sneakery was worth it. I do believe there was mortgage info in there. Although the house has since been torn down. And there was bank account information. If those accounts still exist, Jett might be able to claim something for herself. Does she need money?"

"She doesn't have a job, but I'll help her out. You know I can." He didn't make the big bucks reckoning demons, but he did have a great financial investment adviser.

"You're so good, Savin. The two of you were like brother and sister. So close. I remember the day Jett told me she was going to marry you. I figured it would be the best thing that could happen to you. She calmed you. Kept you on course."

"You never told me that. Was I such a wild child?"

"Yes." She laughed. "Oh, yes, *mon cher*, you could never concentrate on a task for more than a few moments. What did they call it? ADD? I think it was that you got bored easily. You needed to feel the world against your skin, and sitting before a school desk all day drove you mad."

That was truth. There were days he'd cut out of school early just to rush home through the field. And yet another reason he'd dropped out in high school. "Music calms me now."

"It is good you have something to help you find peace. But never be afraid of your wild, *mon cher*."

Savin nodded, smiling. He'd given ninety percent of the details when telling his mother of that harrowing trip to Daemonia. But he could never tell her that he harbored a demon within him. That was definitely his wild. And he wasn't afraid of the Other. Just wisely cautious.

He grabbed the envelope. "I'm sure Jett will appreciate this. No idea where her mother is living now?"

Gloriana shook her head. "Sorry."

"You got any more madeleines?"

"I've put a batch in the fridge, but I can see that was unnecessary. Need more milk?"

"Yes, please."

When the sound of the front door opening alerted Jett, she quickly pulled on her sheen. Oh, but that pinched!

With Savin gone, she'd given in to her desire to revive her energy. Wearing a sheen was so confining. But necessary. Once it was dropped, she had inhaled deeply. Standing in her natural state had allowed her to breathe and relax. She had needed that.

With a dash into the bathroom, she checked her appearance in the mirror. She had put on some lipstick and blush and was feeling more human with every second that passed.

"Looking it, too," she said with a wink at her reflection as she turned off the light and headed out to greet Savin.

When she walked right up to him, gripped him by the shirtfront and pulled him down to kiss, he didn't protest. Which she took as a good sign. But it was a quick kiss. Long enough to give her a taste of what she desired, but short enough to keep her wanting. When he pulled away, a confused sort of acceptance wriggled on his face.

"I like kissing you," she offered quickly. "Maybe it's that I like kissing in general. It is a good thing."

"Have to agree with that one. You can kiss me anytime."

"Really?" She planted another quickie on his cheek, right over that delicious dimple.

"Really. But before you get carried away, I stopped by my mom's place. The bad news is she doesn't know where your parents are right now. But the good news is she did have this."

Jett took the large manila envelope he handed her. It was thick and wrinkled with age. "What is this?"

"Apparently, my maman snuck into your parents' house the night before the city came through to clear out things before they placed it under lien. Maman took out whatever looked important to her. She thought your mother might return someday, and had intended to give her these things."

"That was thoughtful of her. So what's inside?"

"I don't know. I figured that was for you to open." He held up a brown paper bag. The bottom corner was glossed with grease. "I picked up some chicken gyros on the way home. There's a little place down the street that makes the saltiest *pommes frites*. I love them crammed into my sandwich."

"Sure." She sat at the kitchen counter, rubbing her palms over the envelope. "But no salt, please."

"No salt— Oh. Right. Sorry. The gyros aren't salted. It's just the fries. You've got to try something. Jett, you haven't eaten much since you've been here."

"I know. Don't worry about it. I haven't developed an appetite for human food yet."

She could hear his swallow. Wondering what demon

food entailed, likely. He did not want to know. It had certainly taken her time to develop a taste for it. And by no means did demons go near salt. And she was not hungry, so she wasn't concerned.

"If I get hungry," she said, "I'll tell you immediately and make you run out for something. Deal?"

He nodded. "Does that mean I get to eat your fries?"

"You do."

He sat next to her and unpacked the food, which did smell delicious. But if those fries were indeed extra salty, she was not interested. And when she saw him pour white sauce over the sandwich, she decided there was no way she could work up a hunger now.

The envelope waited.

Inside was a stack of assorted papers. Some were neat and crisp, others folded, and a few were crumpled, having been compressed for years, and held a permanent fold crease.

"I don't recognize these company names," she said, glancing over the papers. The last time she'd been in this realm she had been nine. Adult responsibilities such as banks and bills had not been on her radar.

"That is the name of a bank, and that one…" He tilted his head as he read the paper. His hair brushed her cheek and Jett noticed a smudge of sauce on his mustache. "Looks like mortgage stuff. Must be for your parents' house. That, along with all the other houses in the area, was torn down last year to clear the land for the current construction."

"So, mortgage information is useless." She had to force herself to look back at the papers. How she wanted to lick his lips just now. To taste the flavor of the white sauce. And him. "The bank information might be handy," she said. "And this is…perhaps a list of phone numbers? No names on it. This might be important. Health insurance cards and my father's passport. Hmm, it's expired."

She tapped the small laminated photo inside the passport. It had been so long since she had seen her father, Charles Montfort. She'd never forgotten what he looked like. Yet now it felt as though she were looking at a picture of a stranger in a magazine. No attachment to the small portrait before her. Not even a skip of her heart in recognition.

But she couldn't let Savin know how alien the man appeared to her. "I got my black hair from him, yes?"

"I liked your dad," Savin offered. "He played catch with me more often than my dad ever did."

"If I recall correctly, your dad had a fabulous job jet-setting across countries."

"He was a pilot. And…a drinker. But he's dead now."

She hadn't remembered the drinking part. Strange, considering her own father had liked to tip back the whiskey. Had Savin's father turned to drinking after their kidnapping? And the way he'd dismissed the topic by stating he was dead. Jett wouldn't ask how he had died. She didn't want to stir up bad memories. Or try at empathy. She'd only just refreshed herself by dropping the sheen. Taking on human emotions could drag her down again.

"Those look like birth certificates." Savin tapped a yellowed paper. "What's that one?"

Jett turned it to read and sucked in a breath. "I don't understand this."

Savin leaned over to read the title on the page. "Certificate of adoption?"

"And the child's name on it is mine."

She met Savin's wide-eyed gaze. "You're adopted?" he asked.

"No. I mean, I don't think so. I'm not. I was… My parents never said anything of the sort."

She read through the document, her heart dropping with every word of evidence that claimed she had been born to a woman whose name was not her mother's and…there was no father's name listed, nor was it on the birth certificate.

And yet, even as her heart fell, the darkness within her nodded. Knowing. *You have always wondered…*

Besides the birth certificate, the certificate of adoption listed her parents' names, Josette and Charles Montfort, and a date of adoption. It was all very clear. And the documents were certainly official, to judge by the raised seal signed by a notary.

"I'm adopted," she said in disbelief. "I can't believe they never told me."

"Maybe they were waiting until you got older?"

She nodded, not comprehending, but also taking it all in, so deeply. There had been one thing she had wondered many times while in Daemonia. And to think on it now…

"I really was taken," she said with a gasp.

Because it had been said to her once—*you were taken*—but she hadn't wanted to believe it. No explanation had been given. Only that it hadn't been an accident that day she was sucked into Daemonia. She had been specifically targeted.

"Jett? What did you say? You were taken? Yes, I suppose you could call it that. We were both taken."

She collected the stack of papers before her and

placed her palms over them. Now the salty scent of
Savin's meal annoyed her. And she felt the immediate
need for fresh air.

"I need to walk," she announced, and slipped off the
stool and around Savin. Most important, she wanted to
get away from the tug of the wards that now seemed to
reach out toward her.

Savin caught her hand and met her gaze. Right now
she didn't want his closeness, or the perceived compassion she suspected. This was big. Too big to take
in while in the presence of one whom she must remain
cautious of.

"You want me to walk with you?" he asked. "We
don't need to talk."

It was a kind offer. The man cared about her. But…
She shook her head. "I need to breathe for a bit. Alone."

"Got it. I had an extra key made today while I was
out." He fished it out of his pocket and handed it to her.
"If I'm ever not home, you'll need it. I'll try to remember to soften the wards when I'm out."

"Thank you." She clasped the key and left quickly.

Inside she was screaming and clawing at the darkness that had constantly surrounded her in Daemonia.
A darkness she had welcomed and become. Because
she'd had no choice.

She was beginning to get answers. And she didn't
like them.

Chapter 8

Savin waited a few hours, but he couldn't sit around any longer and wonder if Jett would return to his place. She'd been upset by the realization she was adopted. He had to talk to her. And whether or not she wanted to talk to him, he could at least be there for her.

He grabbed his skull cap, pulled it on and left the flat. Wandering down the street beneath a fall of maple leaves, he decided that Jett could be anywhere.

When they'd been kids, their parents would take them into the city and they'd wander, mostly in the fifth and on the Île de la Cité, but they had visited and explored all the city parks and even the cemeteries. The best games were played in the creepiest of places. Would she remember? A graveyard held post down the way, so he veered toward it.

The Montparnasse Cemetery attracted Savin on those

occasions when he wanted to avoid the rush of tourists and traffic and get lost in his thoughts. Sure, there were plenty of camera-wielding tourists wandering about the cemetery grounds, but he knew the spots that were less frequented. Baudelaire's and Maupassant's graves attracted a lot of tourists. He avoided those sections and sought a back corner. The celebrities in Savin's ideal corner of the tombstone garden were long forgotten.

When he spied Jett sitting on an aboveground stone coffin, leaning against the headstone, her legs pulled up to her chest and arms wrapped around them, Savin smiled. She returned the smile as he approached, and patted the stone beside her as an invite to sit. He climbed onto the cool perch and stretched out his legs, then took off his hat and set it on his lap.

"Is it okay that I found you?" he asked.

"It is. How *did* you find me?"

"This is one of my favorite places to visit when I want to think."

"It's nice here. And it doesn't feel threatening. The dead tend to keep their secrets. If there even are any lost souls here. Feels…empty."

Indeed, Savin had never encountered a paranormal while here, not even a ghost. Surprising, considering the location.

He sat quietly beside Jett, figuring he'd let her bring up whatever she wanted to talk about. He wasn't about the third degree. Actually, it felt comfortable to sit beside her without speaking. In a manner, they were two alike. Together they'd been through some terrible things. They were bonded beyond childhood games and adventures. He liked that. Another person in the world he could relate to. The list was short.

After a few minutes, Jett leaned forward and said softly, "It was a weird thing to find out." Long dark hair fell over the side of her face and dusted her knees. "Adopted? I can't believe my parents never said anything. It's not like it's such a taboo thing nowadays. Is it?"

"Being adopted is nothing to be ashamed of. I haven't a clue why your parents didn't tell you. Although…your mother was a staunch churchgoer."

"Yes, Sundays were sacred to her." She smirked. "False gods and a controlling patriarchy. That's all religion is. There are demons far kinder than some religious zealots I've known."

Savin had to agree, but then, he was sure most of the major religions would pass on admitting him as a member. And yet he'd been trained by an exorcist, and their numbers were welcomed by the Catholic Church. And which institution was always claiming the most demon encounters? The Catholics.

He had to chuckle that most of those claims were unsubstantiated, yet they did get good press. The demons Savin knew were much smarter than to get caught in a human host. Most of them, anyway. And while exorcism was effective, a few rare demons were actually strengthened by the intrusion of the Christian rites. And such demonic strength from within utterly destroyed the human host. Tragic.

"This news doesn't change anything," he offered. "Josette and Charles loved you. They raised you. They are your parents."

"I know that. But do you know… It's silly to even wonder. I'm not an emotional person."

She tilted a glance up at him, and the Other inside Savin shivered. He pressed a hand to his chest but didn't think much of it. Or rather, didn't want to. The Other was cautious about Jett. To be expected from one who had just come from Daemonia.

Finally, Jett asked, "Were they sad after I was gone?"

"Of course they were. I only saw your mother the one time and she was in tears. My mom wouldn't let me near her after that. I upset her." He clasped Jett's hand. The simple movement worked like a squeeze about his heart. And yet the Other now cringed. Savin could feel it as a tightening in his insides that made him grit his jaw. What was up with her today?

"If I could change things," he said, "and make it so you had come back and I remained, I would."

"It is what it is, Savin. No sense in wishing to change the past. It's behind me now. Or I want to put it behind me. I need to move forward in this mortal realm. As a normal human woman."

"You are normal and human, but… I suppose it's going to take some time to adjust to this realm. Do you want to talk about it at all?"

Dare he ask her the burning question?

"If I did, it would only keep that horrible experience in my present. Can I put it out of mind, please?"

"Of course."

She dipped her head and Savin smoothed aside the hair from her face. It was soft and smelled sweeter than the shampoo he used. Chicks always smelled good without even trying. He figured it was an innate thing. When she turned to look at him, he thought he saw a glint of red in her pupils and pulled his hand away abruptly.

Jett's sudden smirk and soft chuckle softened his weird fear. "What?"

"Nothing." Had that been another alert from the

Other? He glanced aside. Ah. There. Outside the wrought-iron cemetery fencing a nearby streetlight flashed red. Whew! That was what had produced the strange illusion in her eyes. "You have beautiful brown eyes."

"Now you think them beautiful? You used to tell me they were the color of mud."

He shrugged. "I was an idiot when I was a kid. Now that I'm a man I've developed an appreciation for a woman's eyes."

"Just her eyes?"

"Eyes. Mouth. Hair. Everything else. It's all good." He cast her a long look but ended it with a smile. It was impossible not to feel happy around her. She was back in his life. And they were both grown adults. And the things he was feeling toward Jett right now could be a man's folly. Or an enticing dive into bliss.

"Your voice is so deep," she said. "It's sexy. You have grown to be quite the man, Savin." She turned over his hand and spread her fingers across his palm. "Your hand is wide and strong. Powerful. I bet you'd be a force in a fistfight."

"I try to avoid physical violence. Against humans, that is. I've had to punch a demon or two in my lifetime."

"Feels good, doesn't it?"

He lifted his chin at that comment. She'd said it with such conviction. The woman had punched a demon or two, as well. And she wasn't sorry for it, that was for sure.

Savin frowned. She should never have had to defend herself in such a manner. But thank the gods she'd had the moxie.

"You've seen horrors, Jett. I know that," he said quickly, needing to get out the words so she knew how he felt. "But they do not have to define you. You can make your future anything you want it to be." He clasped her hand against his mouth and held it there. "I'll do everything in my power to help you rise."

She turned to press her other hand over the clasp he held at his mouth and leaned in to bow her forehead to his. "I need that. Thank you for understanding."

The hush of her breath over his skin scurried desire through Savin's system. She smelled like cool limestone with a splash of flowers.

"I'm still thankful it was you who found me that night I made my escape. It was meant to be. The two of us belong together."

"I believe that. Things will get better for you. I promise."

She nodded and kissed the back of his hand before breaking their clasp. And in that moment, Savin wanted to kiss her to show her how much he was attracted to her, to bleed her warmth into his skin and know her scent viscerally—but something stopped him. A tightening of his muscles that stretched up the back of his neck.

The Other was not into romance this day.

To break the spell of discontent that had fallen on his shoulders, he asked, "You hungry?" If he didn't turn this conversation away from the Other, he'd need to shoot up now, and he didn't want to do that in front of Jett. "You haven't eaten much since you've arrived."

"I haven't. And I think I am hungry. You know what I could go for? Roasted chestnuts glazed with sugar. Do they still sell those?"

"Hell yes. There's a vendor not far from here that sells those and other sweets." He slid off the sarcophagus and offered her his hand. "Let's go get high on sugar."

The man was remarkable.

Jett couldn't stop from browsing over Savin whenever she had the chance. He led her to a trio of food stands selling various items and they each claimed a treat. Now they walked toward a bench beneath a yellow-leaved tree. Savin was taller than her by two heads and broad as a bodybuilder. So many muscles flexed and pulsed with his movement. Any shirt he wore seemed to struggle to contain all that man. And his deep voice. It crept inside her being and did things to her senses. Things she'd never imagined feeling. She felt a certain way when around Savin.

She knew what it was that coiled within her. Desire. The wanting and *needing* to touch the man, to kiss him. To do more than that with him.

Desire was a new experience for Jett. And it pounced upon her with an aggression that startled her. She wasn't sure how to handle it. She'd not known desire for another person. Not in Daemonia. Though the desire for things, safety and control had always resided inside her. And certainly she was no virgin who hadn't a clue what to do with herself regarding a man and sex. She had done things to survive.

No regrets, her darkness whispered.

No, of course not.

But now? Now she was free. And she wanted to explore the exciting feeling that warmed her from ear tips to toes. And everywhere in between. When gazing upon

Savin and taking in his masculine build, she felt her breasts become heavy and full. Her stomach swirled. And her pussy—well, she recognized the wanting ache for sex. For the first time in her life. Yet she also knew it sprang from the confidence she'd gained while inhabiting the darkness.

If she abandoned her dark side, would she also lose such feelings? She wanted the man. Dare she risk answering her sudden desperate desires when she knew the part of her that reacted in such a manner was not the part she wanted to encourage?

"My lady." Savin gestured to a bench under a tree just on the other side from a yard where children played. "You're almost finished!"

Guilty as charged. Her desire had manifested as a real hunger, apparently. Jett sat on the bench and licked the sticky sugar crystals from her fingers. She'd enjoyed this treat many a time when she was a kid. It was even better now.

"I think I finally got my appetite back," she said with a smile from behind another bite. More than one appetite, that was for sure.

"I guess so. Let me catch up."

He dug into the crepe he'd gotten at the stand next to the chestnut seller, while Jett was distracted by the shouts and laughter of the children behind them. So carefree and innocent. Unknowing of the dangers the world could present. Best they not wander too close to any demonic portals or—whoosh! Life would never again be innocent.

Adopted. Adopted?

Jett sighed, her shoulders dropping. She had never considered adoption, even though she had often wondered about who her father really was. As a frightened child, she'd dismissed the allusion to her real paternity as a mistake, a cruel trick to get her to submit and accept as the darkness had started to develop within her. Questioning her paternity had initially felt ludicrous, but she'd been so young. And had only wanted to be treated well. So eventually she had accepted that question as a real possibility.

"What are you thinking about?" Savin asked.

She glanced at him, unwilling to spill her secret pain. So she arrowed in on his upper lip, where his mustache was so thick and she knew the tickle of it during a kiss was the most exciting thing.

She touched his mustache. "You've got chocolate there. It's a lot." And then, without thought, she leaned in to kiss him. Tasting his mouth, the chocolate, and then dragging her tongue to lick the sweet treat. "Got it," she said, and sat back, crumpling up the paper her chestnuts had come in.

"That you did." He stared at her, his lips parted. She'd startled him? Good. She liked to maintain a certain amount of power, of control over men. Even if this was no longer her domain.

"If you don't finish that," she said, "I *will* go in for a bite. Just a warning."

He smirked, then offered the half-eaten crepe to her. She leaned forward and took a bite, and then another, her lips brushing his finger. The earthy taste of him combined with the sweet treat was the perfect tease to her appetite. She wasn't so much hungry for food anymore as she was for Savin.

A strange bell tolled, and as Savin pulled his cell phone from his pocket, Jett realized she'd like to have one of those. A telephone that had virtually all the information in the world on it with just a few taps of her finger? Hadn't he said he was going to pick one up for her?

While he spoke to the caller, she finished off the crepe and offered him a wink as she wrapped her fingers about his to get to the very last bits of it.

"I can come by soon," he said, then paused. When Jett looked up, the man was biting the corner of his lower lip, staring at her as she ate from his hand. "Uh… Yes, right. Sorry, I was distracted. See you in a bit, Malcolm." He tucked the phone away, then crumpled the paper and tossed it in the nearby trash bin. "You full?"

"Not even," she said. But it wasn't food that was going to satisfy her now. "What was the call about?"

"That was a friend. An exorcist. He's got a demon in a hex circle that needs to be reckoned. It won't take me long. But I should run."

"You are a very busy reckoner."

"Paris is a big city, and I'm the only one in town. I'll walk you back to my place?"

"Can I come along to the reckoning?"

"I, uh…work best without distraction." He waggled the finger she had licked, then winked at her.

"I like distracting you."

"I've noticed. I'll bring home something more substantial to eat when I'm finished, and wine. How does that sound?"

"Sounds romantic."

"You cool with a little romance?"

"I am. Are you?"

"I, uh…" He gave it some thought. "Yes, I am. I'm going to make this a fast reckoning. Come on." He stood and offered her his hand.

Once back at his place, Savin grabbed one of the intricate brass instruments from his bedroom cabinet that Jett had puzzled over earlier. He called out that he'd hurry back.

Jett rushed to walk him out the door, then skipped around in front of him. Standing on tiptoe, she kissed him. The taste of chocolate lingered and the sudden, wanting clutch of his hand against her hip sent a thrill directly to her core. The man knew how to take a woman in hand.

"Just so you don't forget about the romance," she said.

"Oh, I won't."

"And you'd mentioned getting me a phone?"

"Ah, right. Sorry. I was so eager to get the envelope Maman gave me into your hands, I forgot about that. Stores might be closed when I'm finished reckoning."

"We can go out tomorrow and shop for one."

"We can. See you soon." He kissed her quickly, then walked out, closing the door behind him. The wards repelled Jett back a few feet, and so swiftly she caught her palms against the wall behind her.

The man was off to reckon a demon back to the Place of All Demons. And Jett's thoughts immediately tracked to the adoption papers. If she was adopted—and apparently she had been—then who was her father? Could those cruel taunts as she'd matured in Daemonia have been true? Which would mean...

If her father was a demon, that would make her half demon. Or whole? With things as they were right now...

Jett closed her eyes and shook her head. Things had to change. She wanted something good. She wanted Savin. But he'd never have her if he knew her truth.

Chapter 9

The exorcist John Malcolm lived in a tiny ground-floor apartment across the street from Notre Dame. The main floor would suit a tall hobbit with an interest in religious clutter. The man was a former Catholic priest. Former being key.

After shaking Savin's hand and offering him wine, which Savin accepted, John led him down into the cellar, which was a remnant from the eighteenth century when an artist once used the subterranean rooms for mixing volatile paints and practicing brush techniques. The walls gleamed here and there with gold leaf and streaks of fading cinnabar and egg-yolk tempera. Savin entered and inhaled the limestone and oily scent. And sulfur.

"Been over a year since I've seen you," John commented as he pulled aside a metal-legged chair that had been positioned before the salt circle on the floor and set it up against the wall. "You're looking rather clean-shaven, Thorne. Who's the woman?"

Savin could but shake his head. Had he seriously been looking so dreadful that a mere shave made people wonder about his sex life?

John picked up the wooden cross from the floor before the circle and kissed it. The demon standing inside the circle suddenly spun about to face them and hissed, revealing two pinpoint fangs dead center of its upper mandible. Its skeletal black structure stood hunched because its head was twice the size of a human's head, and the horns curled around its ears twice in glinting red.

"Beelzig demon," Savin said, recognizing the skanky thing with ease. They were insectile in true form, though this one looked half in and out of the sheen. Their principal reason for existence was to get inside humans and slowly drive them mad with a burning need to eat dirt. The demon fed on the worms and bacteria in the soil. A human, if not exorcised, would eventually die from eating more than his body weight of dirt in one sitting. "How'd it happen onto you?"

"I took it out of a teenager this morning. The boy is in Hôtel-Dieu right now with possible brain damage. He'd been eating mud contaminated with toxins from a nearby field that had been sprayed with pesticides."

John set the cross on the chair and joined Savin's side, where they stood facing the despicable demon contained in the warded circle. "So does that mean there isn't a woman or you're just not talking?"

"I thought I came here to do a job."

The demon inclined its head as if listening carefully. "You did," Malcolm offered. "But you know my vows of chastity can be a burden. I need salacious details to brighten my day after seeing what this bastard did to that boy."

The man did not have to honor such vows, no longer being a priest, but for some reason Malcolm did. No judgment on Savin's part. But he couldn't imagine agreeing to not have sex. Ever.

"She's beautiful," Savin offered. "Long dark hair and sensual eyes."

John nodded. "Tits big?"

Savin's smile was easy. "Just the right size."

The demon hissed and jutted out its tongue at the two. "I will lick them for you, reckoner."

"Silence." John made the sign of the cross before him and the demon cringed.

But the beelzig didn't take its wicked regard from Savin. And he allowed it. Let the thing sniff him out, feel his presence. And know it had not long for this realm.

Savin shrugged off his coat and tossed it behind him, then rolled up his sleeves. This visit was business as usual.

"I can taste her on you," the demon said on a slithery tone. "In the air. On your skin. The earth she has trodden with bared skin is..." Of a sudden the demon stiffened and its eyes went wide as red beacons. "You must bow down before her!"

"Enough." Savin didn't need sex advice from a hideous demon.

Stepping forward, he began the reckoner's chant. It was something he'd devised himself, along with Malcolm's guidance. It had come from a deep and innate knowing. He hated it. But such was his life following his trip to Daemonia. It didn't pay to bemoan a situation he could never change.

He lifted his forearms and connected the sigils tattooed there, while keeping his palms facing outward from his face. And as the demon writhed and struggled and insisted he show his woman obedience, Savin focused on getting the ugly bastard out of this realm.

The chant to call out to Daemonia to receive one of its own was repetitious and a mix of Latin and Daemonic. Savin bounced on his heels, finding a visceral rhythm intensifying his focus. He needed to feel this weird magic in his very bones. The sigils on his arms glowed—and sometimes they sparked to flame. He was never harmed, beyond the mental toll of having to constantly deal with these bastards.

Could he find normal along with Jett? Was such a quest worth his consideration?

Halting his wandering focus, Savin shouted out the next few words to cement his vocal tones into the air and bring back his center to the task at hand. At his feet, the salt circle began to jitter and dance around the squirming demon. And while the beelzig yowled, the salt took to flame, as did the sigils on Savin's arms. He winced. This pain was worth it.

Ten seconds later, the beelzig let out a wicked yip and its form was literally sucked out of the circle, leaving behind but a scatter of ashy residue. Savin swept out his arms to each side, which extinguished the flames. He tilted back his head, closing his eyes, and whispered a blessing.

John Malcolm sprinkled the salt and the floor with holy water, echoed Savin's blessing and nodded to the reckoner for a task well done.

Savin rolled down his sleeves and grabbed the remainder of the wine and tilted it down. It was too sweet for his taste, but the ex-priest wasn't big on the good stuff.

"What do you think the creature meant by his statement that you should bow down to her?" John asked in his careful but exacting manner.

"Stupid demon tricks. They're always trying to distract my focus."

"Sure. But it sensed something on you. *In* you."

"The Other," Savin said flatly.

John nodded. But it wasn't a convincing movement. "You want to talk about anything, Savin?"

Like reveal he was harboring a long-lost friend who'd spent the last twenty years in the Place of All Demons? He didn't have time for all the questions Malcolm would have about that situation.

"Gotta get home to those perfects tits," he muttered, and handed John the empty glass. "This one was on the house. Pray the kid survives with as little damage as possible."

"You know that I do. If I'm not exorcising, I'm praying. I owe you one, Thorne!"

"Never!" Savin called as he took the stairs upward. "Always willing to help you out." He paused at the top of the stairs. "Keep an eye out for more assholes like that one. Certainly Jones doesn't believe the rift is going to stay closed."

"Yes, I sense that. Won't be a picnic, that's for sure."

Savin sighed. "Nope. Not a picnic."

After stepping out of the shower, Jett pulled on one of Savin's soft gray T-shirts. It hung to her thighs and it smelled like him. Earthy and wild. He wouldn't mind. She had only a few items to wear and hadn't bought any night wear. She'd love to wander about the flat naked, but she wasn't ready for that boldness.

Yet. The darkness within her could easily get into a nudie walk. And a flirtatious wink or a crook of her finger. But she was keeping that part of her subdued as best she could.

It was growing harder, though. Her true self wanted to rise. To be known. To have. And to claim.

Jett hadn't been able to stop thinking about Savin since he'd left earlier to go meet the exorcist. He'd almost kissed her in the cemetery, but something had tugged him away. The demon inside him? She'd not been able to get a good read on her. The Other. Who and whatever she was, that demon had become deeply embedded inside Savin. If Jett were to touch him long enough, she'd touch the demon and know her.

It wasn't as though the Other provided Jett any competition in catching Savin's romantic interest. But still. The incorporeal demon felt like a rival, so Jett was going to call her that.

In the living room, she sat on the couch and picked up the envelope that contained the adoption papers and a few other items. A deed to the house. With the land cleared and construction under way, that was useless. Apparently, the lot had been claimed by the city years ago after her mother left.

There was a bank account number in her name, which Jett found curious. She'd not had a savings account when she was a kid. Had her parents set up an account for her in hopes she might someday return? Had it been a college fund?

Had they hoped for her return? It hurt her heart to consider what they must have gone through, especially after Savin had returned. They must have hated him because he'd returned to his parents alive. Poor guy. She hoped they hadn't said anything terrible to him.

These human emotions were so…difficult. She felt as if she should perhaps cry, and then her darkness quickly wrangled that silly reaction.

Her disappearance had obviously been tough on her parents. Had the divorce been because of her absence? Possible. There had been many a night when she would lie in her bed upstairs and listen to the back-and-forth arguments in her parents' bedroom below. Despite that, she and her mother, as well as her father, had been close. They'd been a good Catholic family who attended church on Sundays, gardened, watched shows together in the evenings and spent a lot of time doing things in Paris. She'd been happy as a child. Could never have dreamed of the horrors that waited on the other side of the lavender field.

That stupid spooky forest. If she and Savin had never dared each other to approach it that day, might they have been spared?

Setting the envelope aside, Jett pulled her legs up to her chest and the T-shirt down over them, bowing her head to her knees. She did want to cry, and she'd spent her last tear a long time ago. Tears had not proved constructive in Daemonia. And they only gave one a headache. Nobody cared if you cried or that you might be hurting, whether physically or emotionally. And those who had cared?

"Dangerous," she whispered now as her memories threatened to make her scream.

Lifting her head and putting down her legs, Jett shook her head. And she summoned the power of denial that she had learned to own. "I won't remember. It's behind me now."

But ever in you, her darkness whispered. That gave her a shiver.

The front door opened and Savin wandered in. Seeing her on the couch, he nodded and said, "Hey. I picked up some food, as promised. Sorry it's so late. It took longer than I thought with the exorcist."

"I don't expect you to cater to me all the time. You have a life. I'm just lucky you're kind enough to let me into it. So, was the exorcist unable to cast out a demon? Is that why he called you?"

"Sometimes an exorcism merely brings the demon out from the human host in corporeal form. And then it stays. The exorcist needs me to send it out of this realm. It was a beelzig. Stupid bastard."

Jett knew that breed. They were ugly and lived in the vile, rusted earth of Daemonia. She shook her head. *Not going to think about that stuff, remember?* "That smells great."

"Roast chicken and potatoes. The place down the street knows me and what I like. When I asked for a double portion, they didn't blink an eye. I don't know if I should be offended by that."

"Big, strong man like you? Not at all. I'll have a little. I'm still quite satisfied from the treats earlier."

"I'm going to wash up first. You, uh, okay?"

Jett stood and tugged at the shirt, which hung to the top of her thighs. "Yes. Why do you ask?"

"No reason. Just wanted to make sure you're adjusting well enough." He gestured down the hallway, then wandered toward the bathroom.

And Jett couldn't help thinking that had been a suspicious question. What did he think about her? Should she be worried?

She opened the food bag and pulled out the boxes. The man shouldn't spend too much time wondering if she was okay. Instead, the only thoughts he should have about her should mirror her own about him. He needed to see her as a woman, and not the child he had once known. She wanted him to want her.

Perhaps seduction would be on the menu tonight.

Chapter 10

It was late after they'd eaten, but Jett wasn't tired. Nor, it seemed, was Savin interested in sleep. He poured them both whiskey and sat on the couch, so she sat next to him and clasped his hand. After studying their hands together a few seconds, he gave her a look that said so many things. A little surprised, maybe pleased, unsure and perhaps excited. She could hope. But he seemed to struggle with their attraction, so she'd play him slowly.

"Tell me about all these guitars." She tilted her head back and settled against the comfortable leather cushions, catching her bare feet on the edge. "Do you play them all?"

"Most." He tilted his head back, too, resting the whiskey glass on his thigh. The man's intense heat warmed Jett and she alternated taking in the sharp tang of the whiskey and the alluring temptation of his scent. "That one there. The one that looks like someone went after it with a chain saw and then rubbed tar into the cuts?"

"It does look tattered."

"Used to belong to Steve Vai. One of the rock-and-roll guitar gods. I've never played it. The pickups are damaged. It survived a mosh pit and rain and mud. I salvaged it. The one next to it is Jessica."

"The guitar has a name?" Jett eyed the violet electric guitar that had a sparkly gloss to it.

"Most do. Jess is my sweetie. Her tones are so pure and the harmonics—whew! She treats me right."

"How does a guitar treat a person right?" Jett turned on the couch and rested her head on his shoulder. His hair tickled her cheek.

"She seems to have a lot of patience, that violet vixen. I don't have the longest or most delicate fingers, so some riffs are difficult to master."

"Interesting. And what's that one with just the single string? Does she have a name, too?"

"No name, and I don't think that one is a she. That's a diddley bow. Made it myself. It's an American instrument that came out of the blues scene. I spent some time in the southern United States a few years ago and fell in love with the sound and the use of the glass slide. It's what I use to practice musicomancy."

A shiver traced Jett's arms at mention of that magic. She knew nothing about it, but instinctually something warned her away from it.

"Musicomancy is all about using the slide to sing the single string," Savin said. "A way of drawing out a demonic song and then controlling the demon so I can ultimately perform a reckoning. It's a challenge for my big, rough hands."

He opened his hand against hers. It was so wide Jett felt delicate next to him. Not something she'd felt. Ever. She curled her fingers about his and stroked the side of his hand. "Your fingers are calloused. Is that from playing so much?"

"That, and from the metal and woodworking I do. But that's a good thing. A guitarist needs to build up that protection when strumming steel strings."

Drawing her finger along the side of his hand, she traced over the half moth tattoo that, should he hold his hands together prayer-style before him, would form a complete moth. The black lines were so fine; she marveled over the intricate artistry. "What is the significance of the moth? Is this a hex?"

"I don't wear hexes. Those are witch things. Me, I'm all about protections and wards. But the moth is special. The ink witch that pricked it into my skin attached it to my soul. It's sort of a get-out-of-death-free card. If I'm lucky. And if it should come to something like that. One use only. And I think it would change me."

"How so?"

He shrugged. "The ink witch wasn't specific, but anytime someone cheats death? Well."

Yes, she'd seen the results of that in Daemonia. Far too often. But she'd never seen it happen with a human. It couldn't be pretty.

"Do you often encounter situations that make you fear for your life?"

"Honestly? No. Demons don't scare me. Nor can they threaten me overmuch with all the protection wards I wear. But I'm not impervious. I am merely human."

That word was not something that should ever be

employed against Savin Thorne. "I don't think you're
merely anything, Savin."

She let her hand drift from his and onto his chest,
where she slid it across the hard plane beneath his T-
shirt. The man was solid and hot, and she couldn't resist
digging her fingernails in. Just a bit. He felt so good.

Savin hissed behind a sip of whiskey. "Jett…"

"Yes?" She lifted her head, but inches from his face,
and studied his intent gaze. While she saw the darkness
that inhabited his life every time she looked into those
blue irises, now she also saw want.

Oh, yes, sweet, sexy man. The darkness inside her
wanted, as well.

Jett moved up, clutching his muscled pectorals as she
slid higher. Inhaling him. She smiled wickedly. Time
to get what she desired.

She kissed his mouth, tasting the bite of whiskey that
lingered on his tongue. He wrapped a hand across her
back and lured her onto his lap to straddle him. Both
his hands cupped her derriere and she settled against
the firm hold. He squeezed at her with a wanton groan.

Bracketing his face with her palms, she dove deep
into his kiss, wanting to fall as she had done that fateful day when she was a child. But this fall would not
be dangerous; it could only grant her a delicious thrill.
She wasn't afraid to seek Savin's darkness, because
she could match it with her own. Together they could
play in the dark.

Pulling her against him, he clung to her with greedy
clutches. His kiss sought and teased and tasted her. He
was at once playful yet also demanding. Jett willingly
gave up her control to him. She had never allowed anyone or anything in Daemonia to kiss her. Not on the

mouth. It was the most intimate and personal touch. Denying that contact had been her protection. And now she surrendered that carefully constructed wall of defense with pleasure.

"I want you," she gasped against his mouth, kissing him again and lashing her tongue against his teeth. "I need you, Savin."

She wouldn't dare to say it was because she wanted to know a real man. He would have too many questions. And really, the want was basic and feral. She simply needed right now.

He lifted her shirt and she raised her arms to allow him to slip it off. She wore no bra. That wasn't an article of clothing she'd ever worn or learned about. Her breasts were heavy and full and she pressed them against his chest. Savin groaned and cupped them both. When his thumbs brushed her nipples, she hissed a sharp, pleasurable gasp. Oh, yes, that was how a man must touch a woman.

Jett arched her back, which buoyed her breasts, and Savin's hot tongue seared about her nipple in the sweetest way. This was too much. And she wanted more, more and more!

She dug her fingers into his hair. Biting the corner of her lower lip, she closed her eyes and fell into the wicked, delicious sensations of him suckling at her breast. Her skin heated. Her system shivered. Her pussy grew wet. She pressed her hips to his torso, grinding, seeking the sweet spot that demanded attention, touch and oblivious surrender. Another place on her she had only discovered on her own; never had she allowed another to touch her there.

"Jett," he whispered as he switched to her other breast. "Oh, Jett."

Tugging at his shirt, she lifted it and he paused only a few moments to help her get it off. The man returned kisses and attention to her breasts as she dragged her fingernails down his hard, defined pectoral. For all her softness, he was her opposite in steely hardness.

With a nudge of her knee between his legs, she felt his erection. So hard, as if a shaft of steel confined within his jeans. Savin moaned as she pressed her knee harder against him. She wanted to unzip him, reach inside and wrap her fingers about his molten heat. Never had she so desired having a man naked beneath her. She needed to see him, to admire him.

To feel powerful here in this mortal realm.

Savin suddenly squeezed her upper arm. She looked up. Blew the hair from her face. He winced. Then he quickly kissed her on the mouth. But again, the squeeze about her biceps warned her against moving too fast. He pushed away from her.

Jett leaned in to kiss his jaw, along the line of his beard and up to lash her tongue at his ear. "Don't stop, Savin. Touch me. Everywhere."

"Want to." He groaned as he shifted his hips and she hugged her bared breasts against his chest. "Woman, that feels so good."

The hand he hooked at her hip held her firmly, and yet it almost seemed as if he were holding her back. Jett tested the hold by pushing forward and he increased pressure to stay her.

She tugged the flap of his jeans and released the button, but as she touched the zipper, the man slapped a hand over her wrist. "Wait."

"What? No. I want to see you, Savin. To hold you in my hand."

"I... Yes... Damn it!"

He pushed her roughly to the side and she slid off his lap. Standing, he gripped a thick clutch of his hair as he paced before her. His pecs pulsed and that six-pack rolled as if angry.

"What is it? It's her, isn't it?" Jett lunged for him, pressing her palms flat against his chest and closing her eyes. If she could make a soul connection with the man...

"The Other is screaming inside me," he said. "I can feel it more than hear it. Shit, I'm sorry. She's never done this before when I've been with a woman. It's like she wants out. Oh—damn! That hurts! I don't understand. Jett, I—"

She pulled her hands away from him and stepped away, setting back her shoulders and lifting her chin. "She won't defeat me. She has no right. I am her—"

She stopped from saying too much. But now darkness filled her. Suffused her being with her entitled power. She was in her element. What she had become. What she might always be.

What she wanted to run away from.

Or did she?

Savin exhaled heavily and gestured to the couch. "Put your shirt on. Please? I just... I can't do this with you. Not right now."

Jett picked up her shirt but didn't put it on. Instead, she stomped past him toward the bedroom.

"Sorry!" Savin called.

She muttered the word mockingly. But she wasn't angry with Savin. Instead, it was that incorporeal demon. Bitch.

* * *

Savin punched the thick wooden supporting beam in the center of the living room. His knuckles were calloused from previous punches. It was a reflex now. He no longer bled for his own anger.

He'd been cruel to Jett, shoving her away like that. He hadn't wanted to. Hell, he'd wanted to push down his pants and hers and get into it. The woman was incredible and her breasts in his hands had made his cock grow steel hard.

But that bitch. The Other. Why did she object to Jett? He'd had relationships and sex with other women and the demon inside him hadn't lifted a protesting finger. In fact, he sometimes got a creepy sense that she enjoyed the sexual experience as much as he did. Was it because Jett had so recently come from Daemonia? Had she remnants of that place on her that the Other couldn't stand to be near?

"You'd better get used to it," he muttered. Because he could not keep his hands off Jett any longer. He wanted her. He needed her.

Grabbing the diddley bow from the wall, he sat down and plucked out a few notes. She didn't deserve morphine tonight. That was a treat. If anything would suppress the Other, it was musicomancy.

She was not tired, and if she could not make out with Savin, Jett needed to get out of this place for a while. To breathe. To let off some sexual steam.

She pulled on a black dress that fit her curves tightly. The neckline exposed her breasts nearly to the nipples. They were both still so hard, and aching for Savin's mouth. Pressing her hands over her breasts, she closed her eyes—and heard a noise.

What was that awful screeching sound? It sounded like the worst death beetle dying over and over. It crawled over her skin and pricked into her pores. Body wavering, Jett clutched the cabinet for support. The brass devices on top of the cabinet wobbled. Her head filled with the racket.

Then she realized where it came from.

Staggering out to the living room, she saw Savin on the couch with the instrument he'd said he used to work musicomancy.

"What awful noise!" she growled. "Stop it!"

Savin's jaw dropped. He ceased—and then he did not. He plucked the single string as he wavered a glass slide over the neck. The sound cut down Jett's spine with an invisible blade.

She screamed and raced for the door.

Behind her, Savin stood and called, "Jett! What... what are you?"

Chapter 11

Savin let Jett leave. This time he wouldn't go looking for her. She needed some space and privacy.

And him? What did he need?

"Answers," he muttered.

The short riff he'd played on the diddley bow had affected her in a way he'd not expected. Only demons should have reacted so violently to the discordant tune. Jett had clearly been disturbed by it. So much so that she'd had to put herself away from it. And he had shouted after her...

"*Is* she demon?" he wondered with a sinking heart.

He slapped a hand over his bare chest, remembering the feel of Jett's fingernails sliding over his skin. Notching up his desire to new heights, fueling his need. Making her intentions perfectly clear with every kiss, every whisper, every sigh. His heart still pounded from their interaction.

Or was it because he might have been making out with a demon?

Any paranormal species that went to Daemonia—vampires, witches, harpies, sirens, whatever—could get in and out with few side effects. If the trip was quick. But it was known that anyone—paranormal or human—who stayed longer began to take on demonic traits. Some even changed to demon. It was like when demons came to the mortal realm. The longer they stayed, the more they risked developing human traits, and their demonic nature lessened, growing weaker until they were but shells that needed to return home or perish.

It would make sense that Jett, having been in Daemonia for so long, would have taken on some demonic traits. But.

"She can't be."

Why hadn't he had such suspicions immediately? A smart reckoner would have. He would have noticed that she wasn't right. Picked up the hum of her aura. Savin was ultra-tuned to their kind. Rarely did he miss one. And those he didn't pin as demon were masters of cloaking themselves with a sheen.

Had Jett worn an impenetrable sheen since arriving in the mortal realm? It seemed impossible to maintain for any amount of time. A demon had to be very strong to do so. Yet others did all the time. How many demons had Savin not noticed? And had innocent humans suffered because he had not?

He scruffed his fingers through his hair, tugging in frustration. Why hadn't she told him? There was no reason not to. Did she fear him?

"Of course," he muttered. "I am a reckoner."

He punched the air with a fist and a growl.

If Jett truly was part demon, he could well be her worst nightmare.

Arms swinging, Jett strode through the Paris streets. It was after midnight, but pockets of tourists still dotted the sidewalks. She passed over the river, drawing upon its natural power, infusing the strength of the flowing water into her system. Mmm... That was invigorating, most especially since the water was much cleaner than anything she'd ever drawn on in Daemonia. Now she marched onward with determination.

She'd unexpectedly revealed herself to Savin. And in that moment, he had known. He'd called after her as she'd fled his home, asking what she was. It might have been the wrong move to leave without an explanation, but her body had literally moved her over the threshold, despite the tugging wards, to get away from that place.

That terrible music! It had scraped inside her ears like the vilest insect chittering against her brain. Had she not been wearing a sheen, she suspected the sound might have brought her to her knees. The reckoner's musicomancy was indeed powerful.

And too revealing.

As it was, the escape through the wards vibrating with the dangerous sound had affected her. Jett didn't feel as though she could hold on to the sheen for much longer. Not without a breather.

How could she go back to Savin now? The man had been her only hope for finding her family and getting back to normal. Could he accept her if she revealed her truth?

Did she want his acceptance? Was she fooling herself that she could go back to how things once were? She'd been a child then. Even if she could fully integrate herself back into humanity, nothing would ever be the same. Those hadn't even been her parents! Everything she'd once held as truth, as a means to survival, had been shattered.

Feeling her eyes begin to tear, Jett shook her head and chased away the ridiculous emotion. An inhale drew up a shiver of darkness from within, instilling in her the confidence she'd almost lost grasp of. She would not shed a tear over silly pining for a normal family life. Nor even the hope for a romantic entanglement. Even if Savin meant more to her than a few kisses and touches. He had offered to protect her and had allowed her to stay until she could find her place in this realm.

Right now she felt her only place was so far away and in another realm. But the option of returning wasn't on the table.

Crossing a busy street that flashed with bright headlights and red and violet neon streaks, she veered away from a crowd that danced outside a noisy nightclub to the music drifting beyond the closed doors. Instead, she eyed a black metal door just ahead. She recognized the beefy bouncer standing solemnly with hands clasped before him. *Demon.* He needn't glance her way for her to pick up on his breed, but when he did, that confirmed what she knew. His red irises flashed with a glint from a nearby neon sign.

There was no name on the building before which the bouncer stood, but she could feel the vibrations of many demons, likely within and behind the door. Jett curled her fingers into fists. The pain of her fingernails digging into skin was acute. But it was a good feeling. That meant she was alive. A place of comfort was what she required right now. A dark, loud nightclub where she could release her sheen and scream like a banshee. And no one would know who she was.

Stepping up to the bouncer, she tilted back her head and met his gaze. Without a word, she delved through his skin and skull bone, needling into his feeble brain to work her influence on him. It was a handy skill she'd mastered while coming of age in Daemonia.

The bouncer's bottom lip quivered and his shoulders dropped in subservient acknowledgment. "My liege." He bowed, then pushed open the club door for her. "Enter, if you will."

Jett strolled into the pitch-black hallway. The utter darkness felt like a hug. The floors pounded with a frantic beat, pulsing up through her shoes and liquefying in her veins. The raucous beat led her onward. The darkness offered safety. And knowing this was a demon club decided her next move.

With but a thought, Jett shook off her sheen. The initial shiver of release was always orgasmic, and she sighed, which led to a satisfied growl. Her hair follicles tingled as the strands grew longer and spilled in long aquamarine waves down to her waist. All over, her skin prickled and took on a darker, dusky gray shade. Her fingernails grew to razor points and brightened to ruby. The demonic sigils that decorated her skin in violet and red lines, so fine no tattoo artist could achieve such, crisped to the surface with an exquisite sting that made her gasp. And her horns grew out from her temples in an obsidian curl that gently glided over her ears and tilted up to wicked points behind her head.

Smiling revealed canines that could tear, and even kill. Jett smiled with the utter pleasure of being back in the form she was most comfortable with. She entered the flashing red club lighting. One hand to her hip, she assessed the atmosphere with a regal lift to her chin. Ninety percent demon occupants. A sniff surmised the remaining breeds, which she determined were vampire or witch. Perhaps a few werewolves. No faeries. She didn't sense the weird energy of the sidhe species.

The club's décor was black and steel, burnished by red strobe lighting. A live band wielding guitars and a violin screamed to the masses from the stage. The crowd on the dance floor bounced as one, fists beating the air above their heads. Some of the heads were horned. A few tails whipped to the beat, their spaded tips slashing at skin and leaving in their wake fine cuts to spill black demonic blood.

The growls and rock-and-roll snarls coalesced into a wicked, thrilling welcome to Jett's innate darkness. She was demon. Or so she had become during her lengthy stay in Daemonia.

Survival? Sure, that had been foremost. But ultimately, she had grown into the form and had accepted it over any lingering human traits. And she would not be put back or disregarded in any way. The power she possessed gleamed in her sinews and tightened her muscles. Let no demon try to challenge her.

Striding toward the dance floor, she let the beat take her and bounced into the crowd. Head back and both arms outstretched, she reveled in the release of the confining sheen she'd had to wear to fit into this realm. To fool Savin. To win some time while she struggled to find her place.

Adopted? What the fuck was her father, then? She would find out. And whether she embraced him or punched him, who cared? Now was not the time for maudlin memory trips.

Shouting with the chants that surrounded her, Jett became the darkness she'd tried to ignore since arriving in the mortal realm. This was exquisite. And another lush, lung-deep growl felt appropriate.

When the dancers around her slowly stopped moving and the macabre merriness settled to a few drunken giggles, Jett spun to a halt and looked about. Glowing red gazes observed her with awestruck expressions and open mouths. Even the band ceased playing with a discordant scrape of the bow across the violin strings.

A particular male with small white horns sprouting above his ears and a switchblade smile stepped forward and bent to one knee. His hoarse voice held reverence. "My liege."

His actions were repeated by the circle surrounding her, and that waved back through the crowd until the entire club fell onto bended knee and bowed their heads, showing her their respect.

About time, her darkness whispered. *Screw hiding in fear. Let the party begin.*

Jett let out a wicked, throaty laugh and clapped her hands over her head. "We dance!"

And the nightclub burst into a frenetic collision of dancing bodies.

Chapter 12

Savin slept fitfully in the bed. He'd sat up drinking whiskey while waiting for Jett to return. After 2:00 a.m. he'd wandered toward the bathroom but had veered onto the bed and buried his face in his pillow that smelled of her. Sweet, dark and not at all like sulfur.

She was not a demon. She could not be.

He rolled over, and while his eyes were closed in the dark, he listened acutely. Nothing in the loft stirred. The distant noises of Paris's early-morning industry enlivened the air. Garbage vehicles rolled down the streets, collecting trash.

Had he been too trusting? No.

Maybe the musicomancy had malfunctioned? Very possible. He was so new at it and was far from a mastery of the magic. But he knew an incorrect spell should not have sent Jett fleeing with a painful scream.

Jett.

Jett.

He couldn't get her out of his brain. He'd invited her into his life, and the place she filled had been swept free of the cobwebs and welcomed her easily. She belonged with him. It was an instinctual feeling. And that wasn't because they'd been childhood friends. It was something more. Something he couldn't put a label to.

"Jett," he murmured in his half-sleep reverie. "Come back to me."

Jett stretched her legs out across the cool, sooted stone capping the aboveground sarcophagus in the cemetery she had wandered to last night after leaving the club. It had become a weird beacon for her. A respite tucked within the big city.

The sun had risen, but a nearby tree canopy provided shade. A pair of sunglasses was in order for her next shopping trip.

While standing in the center of the dance floor last night, surrounded by sycophants, she had felt her power rise. The inner strength and innate entitlement she'd grown into while living in Daemonia had suffused her system. She had been taken from this realm for a purpose, and she had fulfilled that purpose. She'd gained subjects and minions, and with the snap of a finger had decided the fate of so many.

And she had reveled in that power.

She still could. She did not have to forsake her demonic nature. She could keep it, hoarding it and using it as she wished here in the mortal realm. It came naturally to her. It would be a pity to abandon it completely. It had served her well.

And yet she shuddered now, so far away from the comfort of that dark club, and having successfully tamped down her darkness. Such power was a place she could not return to, did not want to return to. It had changed her. And that purpose? It hadn't been completely fulfilled. They'd wanted her for something more devious. It had been the last straw. She'd had to flee.

Jett tilted her head against the inscription that declared some long-dead woman a "considerate wife." Ugh. *Considerate.* She certainly hoped her epitaph would proclaim her wild, free and unabashed.

Or did she?

The shudder returned to remind her she wasn't the same Jett who had lived in Daemonia. A part of her had never left Paris and had only survived because she had clung to those roots of normality.

While she'd stepped into the exquisite feeling of control last night, today it saddened her that she had succumbed, if briefly, to that feeling.

She did not want to rule others. She did not require them to fall to their knees and worship her. And most important, she did not want to begin the next generation that would follow in her stead.

The only reason they had recognized her as a superior last night in the club was that she had released her sheen and allowed her demoness to rise. But now she again wore the sheen. It was the only way she could walk through Paris without turning heads. Wearing such a mask of humanity was tiring, but it also allowed her to stand aside and look over what she had been and what she could be.

She could be a woman, a human woman with goals and dreams and loves and hopes.

And Savin?

Would he still want to help her if she told him all? Dare she reveal the vile secret that had sent her fleeing to the mortal realm?

"Why?" she whispered, feeling the demoness speak up. "When I can have so much more by remaining as I am? What are these stupid thoughts?"

The stupid thoughts were what had brought her to this realm in the first place, had pushed her to escape. The need for more, for normality, for love and safety. But now that she was here, *could* she pull off human again? It seemed so…lackluster. Boring.

"No," she hissed at her dark side.

Whatever, the demoness inside her whispered dismissively. *You are a fool if you abandon me. Your kingdom asked so little of you!*

Bowing her head to her knees, Jett pushed her fingers through her hair and clasped them at the top of her scalp. No longer blue, nor thick and lush, it was simply black and wavy now. She preferred it blue—

"No," she groaned, and shook her head. "I am Jett Montfort. And I will not allow you to reign," she said to the darkness.

A pair of tourists wandered by, commenting in a language she did not know, and then shuffled past her quiet retreat.

When the next person, a lone walker, paused before the sarcophagus and did not move for a while, Jett looked up into Savin's deep blue gaze. No smile there, yet no accusation, either.

"Thought I'd find you here," he finally said. "May I?" He gestured to sit beside her and she nodded and slid over. "I didn't mean to scare you last night, Jett."

"You didn't scare me," the demoness insisted boldly. Then Jett bowed her head, reining in the dark. "I scared myself. Or rather, I reacted to your strange magic."

"I don't have any magic."

"You were invoking musicomancy."

"It's still a work in progress. But I told you it's only supposed to work on demons." He propped an elbow on his knee and turned to her. The brute stoicism she'd initially seen that first night he'd taken her to his home lived in his gaze. He was no man to mess with, to lie to or to attempt to trick or fool. And he knew about demons.

She knew what he wanted to hear from her. And even as she fought to maintain her secret, the dark inside her decided it was fitting and absolutely to her advantage to reveal her nature.

"A person can't survive in Daemonia for so long without taking on demonic attributes," Jett blurted out. How much dare she tell him? She'd feel him out and see where he stood regarding such a revelation. "I've been wearing a sheen since I escaped through the rift. I couldn't risk being seen in this realm. And when I learned you were a reckoner…"

"I only reckon those demons who have committed a crime against humans or have been determined to be a menace here in the mortal realm."

Which wasn't exactly a promise never to reckon her. And if he was attempting to send back all those demons who had entered this realm that night, wouldn't that include someone like her?

"I, uh…" Savin rubbed his hands together, then leaned back against the considerate wife's tombstone. "Okay. You're part demon. Nothing wrong with that.

You were there so long. It was inevitable. And I mean, demons come in all forms, types and demeanors. Just like us humans. They can be benevolent. Even more human than some of the humans I've known. But—" he pressed his palms before him and against his lips, letting out an exhale "—you've still got human in you, right, Jett?"

She nodded. Maybe she did; maybe she didn't. She couldn't know one hundred percent. Without the sheen, she sported horns and dark gray skin. Entirely demon. Yet surely, her innate humanness would return to her now that she'd left that horrible place. With hope?

No, you mustn't abandon me!

She winced at the cry from her darkness, which was entirely her, not a separate entity like the demon who lived within Savin.

"I do have humanity," she said, trying to convince herself as much as Savin. "I think. I don't know, Savin. This is hard for me to talk to you about."

He clasped her hand, and that startled her. That he could still want to hold her hand after what she'd confessed. After witnessing her flee last night.

"I'm safe for you, Jett. You can trust me with your secrets. I promise. I'll do what I can to help make things right. No matter what happened to you in Daemonia? You didn't ask for it."

"I didn't. You're right about that. And everything I did while there was with the goal of survival. I always looked ahead to a moment when I might make my escape." And there was nothing her dark side could say against that. "But there's something you should know. Something I learned while there. I was tended by a cortege that catered to my every whim, took care of me, treated me well. One grew to be my confidante. And… she confirmed that I was taken because of my father."

"Your father? Your adopted father or…"

"I didn't know then that I was adopted. Well, there were clues. But I didn't know how to process some of the things I was told when I was so young. Anyway, I could only think of the man I've always known as my father, Charles Montfort. But who was he? He had no ties to demons or the Place of All Demons. It made very little sense. So sometimes I tossed around the idea that my mother might have had an affair with another man. Perhaps a demon."

Savin tilted his gaze at her. "Josette Montfort never seemed the sort to go in for dark and dangerous."

"I wanted to believe she didn't know. It was the only option besides believing my real dad, er, Charles, was demon."

"He wasn't," Savin said. "I just know that."

"Right. So the affair scenario. Demons can do that. Wear a sheen or a human costume. Humans never know who they are interacting with unless the demons want them to know. And, well, I know how demons are. They seduce humans. It is in their nature to do so. They constantly seek the human experience."

She was revealing too much, and yet why the hell not? The jig was up. The reckoner had discovered her. But just let him try to reckon her. He wouldn't know who he was standing against.

Foolish, Jett thought. She didn't want to be a threat to the man. She wanted him to admire her, not label her an antagonist.

"It doesn't matter now what I suspected when I was there," she said, "because I now know I was adopted. I got the answer I most desired. So perhaps one or both of my parents was demon."

"Whew." Savin rubbed a finger along his bearded jaw. "That's a lot to take in. But it is possible. Like you said, demons make it a game at seducing humans. And if your mother had been human but knew the father was demon? A good reason to give the child up for adoption. And I hate to say it, but it would make your kidnapping into Daemonia less random. Though why *I* was taken along with you..."

"You were not the target," she said quietly.

He turned to meet her gaze.

"I was told that," she said. "You were so close, though, and were sucked in along with me. I'm sorry. If I could have changed it so you would never have had to suffer..." She shivered and clasped her hands about her legs. This human emotion stuff was draining. But she refused to allow her dark to rise. Not now. Not when he sat so close and she could feel his comforting warmth. He needed answers as much as she did.

"Jett, don't blame yourself. Ever. I survived. And for a while there we were together. We took care of each other."

"For that I was thankful. I don't know what I would have done had I landed in that place all alone. You gave me strength, Savin."

"You're a hell of a lot stronger than I will ever be. So, about being kidnapped. What were you told? Do you think your father—if indeed he was demon—wanted you to live in Daemonia? Did you ever meet him?"

She shook her head. "What I've told you is conjecture. I was only told I was taken because of my father. No explanation beyond that."

Mostly. She did know the exact reason—it was what made her flee—but she wasn't ready to reveal that yet.

But why not spill all? Savin seemed open to listening, and perhaps even to accepting her. And she had no intention of committing a crime or becoming a menace to society, which would then require him to reckon her.

They could do this. She wanted that.

You want him, between your legs and in your arms.

"So you know things," Savin said. "Can I ask a few questions?"

In for the dive, Jett leaned back beside Savin and gave him the go-ahead with a squeeze of his hand.

"I know it's tough for you now, and you don't want to talk about your experience there, but the dark witch who put up a binding hex on the rift between Daemonia and this realm expects that to shatter soon. We can't let that happen. And while I'm no demon hunter, I don't relish having to reckon hundreds or thousands of demons after they've been caught, if it's preventable."

"Nor do I relish another single demon coming to this realm. They need to stay where they are." And far from her.

Last night she hadn't encountered any determined to send her back to Daemonia. But that only meant none there had come from the Place of All Demons, or if they had, they were being as stealthy as she should have been. What was it called? Flying under the radar.

"So, part demon," Savin muttered. "I'm usually spot-on with detection."

"I'm wearing a sheen," she said. "I have been since I arrived. Not to deceive you. It is a necessary mask to walk amongst those unknowing in this realm."

"I can't believe I didn't sense the demon within you.

That must mean it is very weak. You're still mostly human, Jett."

She offered him a weak smile. It was difficult not to grip him by the throat and show him exactly how not-weak she was. But she had control over that side of her. For now.

"Is it difficult?" he asked.

"Very tiring. But I'm afraid of releasing it. And who knows, maybe it will become easier as the demon in me slips away? It's got to happen. I just want to be human again, Savin. To belong here in my home."

"What—" he dipped his head, and his hair concealed the side of his face "—are you like with the sheen down?"

Jett sighed. His curiosity annoyed her. And even if she did understand, she felt the prejudice in that question.

"You don't have to show me if you don't want to," he said. "I don't need to know. But, Jett, I mean it when I say I'm on your side."

He wouldn't be if he knew the complete truth.

Oh, she wanted him to trust her, and to help her. But her dishonesty would not make that happen. She had to tell him. To spill her truth. And if that scared him away, then so be it.

And if it made him come after her to reckon, then she would stand and fight to the death.

Because I am strong. The reckoner will bow to me as all others do.

Jett lifted her chin, feeling the dark energies infuse her system. She preferred him to know exactly what and who he was dealing with. "Savin…"

"Are you hungry? I'm hungry."

She slid off the sarcophagus and stood before him. "Sure, but I have to tell you everything. I need your trust. I need…" *Keep it innocent. He doesn't need to know how strong you really are.* "I need your help. I need…you."

"You have me, Jett. All of me."

"I'm afraid I'll lose you with my truth." Her darkness slipped. She quickly pulled it back up and used the power she owned to speak the next confession. She exhaled and spread her hands before her. "I was taken for a specific reason. To sit the throne," she said.

He cocked his head to the side.

"I'm the Daemonian queen."

Chapter 13

Savin stood abruptly.

A flock of crows pecking at a discarded bit of nearby food suddenly took to wing with an eerie chorus of caws. And Jett stood there before him, seemingly human and beautiful and so lost.

Or was she?

She held her head regally. Like a…

She'd confessed the most incredible and startling secret.

"You're…" He couldn't find the right words to express his mixture of dismay, shock, curiosity and downright revulsion.

"I had to tell you," she said. "I want you to know my truth, Savin. Then you can decide whether you want to help me or send me back to that terrible place."

He would never send her to a place she knew well yet did not belong in.

Or did she?

Who was Jett Montfort?

"Sit down," she said with a gesture to the sarcophagus. "I'll explain how it went down."

Savin crossed his arms high on his chest and did not sit. Then he realized he'd just closed himself off from her, so he dropped his arms and nodded, signaling his willingness to listen. It was the least he could do for her. Hell, what had just happened between them?

"I was brought into Daemonia by a queen," Jett said. Her voice was confident, modulated and precise. Chin lifted and hands hanging freely at her sides, she held herself with a regal air. "And then she fled."

Savin narrowed his brows. A queen had kidnapped Jett? And him, as well. Though, apparently, taking him had been a mistake. He'd been in the wrong place at the right time. Or had it been the other way around? Would his life have been different had he not been sucked into the Place of All Demons? Bizarre to even consider it now.

"It took me a while to piece together that she had wanted out of Daemonia," Jett continued, "but she had to find a replacement to take the throne in order to make that happen. In that legion of Daemonia they protect the queen greedily. Well, I imagine it is so in all legions. It is like here in the mortal realm with some of the countries. Royalty is not uncommon, and even revered."

The demonic legions were sections in the realm ruled by separate governance, a bit like countries or the states.

Savin nodded. "I know about the legions and royalty. I just never…"

He wasn't going to finish that sentence.

"As soon as the queen went missing," Jett continued, "there were cries of 'The queen is dead!' And then immediately after that, all gazes turned to me—shivering little nine-year-old me. And the shouts rose, 'Long live the queen!' I didn't know what to think of it.

"Well, you know what the conditions were like in that place. We were both near death and maddened by the experience. But I was sheltered and treated kindly amidst these strange creatures in a strange land, so at the time I thought it best to do as I was told. I was clothed and fed. My wounds healed and I began to think straight. I never stopped thinking of you, though." Her breath caught on those last words.

Savin swallowed. Alone and with no one to hold her hand, not a single friend… He couldn't fathom it. And yet. "Where did that queen go?"

"I don't know. I met her only the one time in the beginning when I was brought to her private chambers. It was right after I'd been scooped from the falls. I stood before her, tattered and shaking. She was vile and yet beautiful. Her skin was the color of a night sky splashed with indigo. She had a cackle laugh that I will never forget. Her red eyes seemed to burn my skin. She was the one who told me she knew my father and that was why I was there. I was so startled I didn't have the words to ask intelligent questions. You understand?"

Savin nodded. He would have been out of his mind had he been taken to such a place and told strange information.

"I was groomed and trained and coddled and dressed and taught how to be a queen. And as I matured, I learned that following rules was wise, but also that my newly gained title granted me power untold. I learned to wield it wisely, yet also always to protect myself. I never gave up hope of escaping. Someday."

A lift of her chin caught a glint in the corner of her eye. Was that a teardrop too proud to fall?

"So." Jett splayed her hands before her and said, "Throw me to the demons, I will rise their queen."

The tone of her voice held a wicked, dark edge and Savin felt he'd just heard the true queen. A woman who had grown into her power and embraced it. But for survival, or because she had learned to expect it?

"Call it my sad yet triumphant tale," she said. "I survived to escape. And yet here I stand before you, the one thing you have taken to task to destroy."

"Never destroy," Savin muttered. He did not do that. Reckoning did not harm demons; it only sent them whence they had come.

"Are you going to reckon me?" Jett asked in that same confident, and slightly challenging, tone.

Drawing in a breath through his nose, Savin straightened and met her defiant gaze. For the first time he saw a sheen of red in her irises. Barely there, but telling. He'd thought he saw it once before—in this same place—but had dismissed it as a reflection from a streetlight. What a fool. Yet he still couldn't sense her demonic nature as he could when around other demons. She wore the sheen well, and with an ease that amazed him.

"Reckon you? I don't know," he stated truthfully.

It hurt his heart to speak those three words. He wanted to know. He wanted to be positive that he would never harm her. He wanted only to protect her. But the situation had changed.

His alliances had been split.

"Thank you for your honesty," she said. "I've learned

to recognize those who would lie to get close to me, only to ultimately betray me. Very few speak exactly as they feel and act. But you do. You are a good man, Savin."

He didn't feel so good. But he had spoken the truth. For right now. Ten minutes from now? A day or more? Everything could change. Like it or not.

Jett asked, "Do you want me to leave your place? If I could get a small loan—"

"You can stay, Jett. Nothing has changed between us. And…" A sigh was unstoppable. "Everything has changed. You've laid a lot on me. I have to think about this. We'll figure this out. I promise I won't play the diddley bow when you're around. And… I'll see what I can do about adjusting the wards on my place."

She lifted her head, her eyes smiling before she did. "That's very generous."

"I won't completely take them down. I'm not stupid. I've got to protect myself from all the other demons in Paris."

"I understand that. Do you feel you need protection from me?"

He shook his head. "My job is to send demons back to Daemonia," he said. "The dangerous ones. Are you dangerous?"

"No."

"I believe you."

Jett smiled. "You really want to help me? After all you now know about me?"

He did. Because…

Savin grabbed Jett by the shoulders and pulled her to him and kissed her. She went up on her tiptoes to meet his mouth in an intense, hard crush of desire and want.

She was his girl. They had been friends since childhood. They knew each other. And he wanted her back in his life. Demon or not. Queen or commoner. No matter what it took, he wanted to see if this could work.

He broke the kiss and Jett's sigh dusted his mouth. "I think that was a *yes*," she said.

"That was a *hell yes*. I'm going to contact CJ, the dark witch."

"What for?"

"He's keeper of the Archives. That place has an entire room on demons. And the book of all demons, the Bibliodaemon, is constantly updated. Maybe he can find us some answers, like where that queen is who kidnapped you, and even who your father is. Come on. Let's go home."

With Savin's adjustments to the house wards before he'd left on an errand to pay monthly rent, Jett felt more relaxed sitting in the cool evening shadows of the living room beneath the skylights. He'd been gone for hours, but she'd taken that time to close her eyes and go within. It was something she had done when alone in her rooms. She'd cross her legs and place her hands on her knees, palms up. And seek that deep and hidden part of her, the innocence that still lingered.

She had never been alone. Always the presence of a watcher was felt but never seen. After a while she'd stopped caring and had simply proceeded with her life, breathing, sighing, living, dressing, sleeping, without a care for that presence.

Focusing and moving inward was initially a struggle, getting past the darkness, but there, she touched it. That giggle. The long-lost smile directed toward the sunshine. The memory of Savin telling her she had a cotton-candy voice. But now the memory was strangely overlapped by the rugged, masculine tone of Savin's adult voice. One that had the power to glide over her skin and creep under her clothing on a tempting touch.

Jett sighed as she imagined him holding her with his wide, strong hands. His mouth sought hers and then explored her skin, gliding, skimming, licking and tasting. Her nipples hardened and she pressed her legs together to capture the giddy shimmy at her mons. It was a delicious fantasy. And before she realized it, the darkness in her moaned with pleasure.

She did not relent the fantasy. It was too rich and something she'd never had. A man willing to please her and not ask anything in return. Someone she had chosen and not the other way around. A man—not a demon—whose gaze could melt her and make her heartbeat race. A man.

She so desperately wanted that man.

Shaking her head out of the dream, she emerged from the reverie and looked about. This sort of fantasizing was well and fine, but she'd best target her energies toward Savin when he was here. She must do everything possible to make him forget where she had come from and what she was. It could prove a monumental task.

She was always up for a challenge.

In the meantime, she was bored sitting in this small place. She needed to start her new life. And the best way to do that?

Her gaze fell on the brown envelope with the family papers inside. Jett pulled out a few, and when she touched the bank statement, she nodded. If she could find this bank, then they might tell her if she had an account and, if so, some money. It was what she required to become independent.

Chapter 14

Savin noticed as Jett paused before crossing the threshold into his home. He'd reactivated the demon wards upon returning home from his landlord's office but had forgotten to lessen them. It must take incredible energy for her to pass through without being torn apart or, at the very least, writhing in pain. Truly, she must be powerful.

A queen. Just how much of Jett was demon and how little of her humanity remained? It disturbed him, and yet it did not. And that realization worked to even further disturb him. Had he become so jaded to demonic existence?

"I can take the wards down," he offered as she closed the door behind her and stood in the cool afternoon quiet of the kitchen.

"That would be lovely for me, but not for you. You need protection from those who wish to harm you."

"Most demons know to keep a good distance between the reckoner and them. And I don't fear you."

"You should not," she said, meeting his gaze. Her smile was easy and so comfortable.

It was difficult to compare what she'd told him about being queen of Daemonia with the sweet, beautiful woman who stood before him now. Dressed in a soft red blouse and gray leggings, she exuded a feminine sexuality. He knew Jett was more human than demon. *She had to be.* He'd grown up knowing her. They had been best friends. And even now he couldn't push aside the need to protect her. To want to pull her close and know her. He desired her, no matter what species box she checked on a form.

Was that insane? She was *demon*. At the very least, part demon.

But if she spent enough time in the mortal realm, she would become completely human again. With hope.

"What are you thinking?" she asked. "Do you want me to leave? After all I've revealed I wouldn't be surprised if you wished to put up new wards specifically against me."

"I would never do that, Jett. Where were you?"

"Oh! I walked to the bank and asked about my account. It does exist and there's money in it."

"How much?"

"That's the problem. They could tell me I had an account but wouldn't give me access to it without identification. Driver's license or something with my current photo on it, like a passport."

"Both will take some time to get. I could—" Savin

rubbed his jaw "—find a guy who would make a passport for you."

Her smile twisted. "That sounds sketchy."

Savin shrugged. "I'm a sketchy guy. What can I say?"

Her sudden laughter reminded him of better times. He'd once thought of her teasing voice as cotton candy, and the laughter that bubbled up was surely a treat. Savin couldn't resist crossing the room to pull her into his arms. He threaded his fingers through Jett's hair and kissed her hard and deep. He didn't want to hear any more of her truths. The reasons why he shouldn't have her in his home. He wanted only to feel her heat against his mouth and his body. He wanted her in him and all over him. He wanted to get lost in her hair and skin and sighs.

Jett's palms slid under his shirt, gliding slowly up his chest and then around his back. Her nails dug in, which sweetened the intense moment. With a lusty groan, he slipped a hand down her thigh and around to cup her ass. That sweet, rounded softness in his hand encouraged him to press his growing erection against her groin. He was rushing toward his wants. The moment demanded he show her how he felt about her.

And this was what he wanted.

"Savin, yes," she whispered at his mouth. "But are you sure?"

"I'm never sure of anything," he said. "Just following my heart right now."

"I can do that, too."

"You want this?" He moved his kisses over her cheek and to her ear. "Tell me this touch is okay. My kisses. And…more?"

"Yes, a thousand times, yes. I need you, Savin. Let's have sex."

With that permission, he lifted her and she wrapped her legs about his hips. He strolled through the living room but paused by the supporting beam and nudged her against it, holding her there as the kiss demanded all his attention.

The woman's legs tightened about his hips, urging him closer. The exquisite rub against his hard-on drew up a pleasurable hiss from him. He kissed her deeply, with an urgency that showed her his need. Hell yes, he craved. Jett knew who and what he was. As he did her. They were going into this with eyes wide-open. And he was good with that.

He pushed up her silky shirt and she clawed at his shoulders. The sweet pain gave the Other a shudder, but he ignored the bitch. She would not interfere this time. He would not allow it. To do that, he focused on the smell, taste and sounds of Jett. She was summer and flowers tinged with an edge of wicked. Her moans spurred him on. He rocked his hips against her.

"Take off those jeans," she said with a gasp and a demanding tone. "I want to feel you against me." She wriggled from his clutch to stand and shoved down her leggings. "I want you inside me, Savin."

It wasn't a polite request. Savin preferred his women bold and to know exactly what they wanted. And this one did.

Shuffling down his jeans, he hugged his stiff cock against her soft nest of curls and groaned at the exquisite contact. "Jett, you're so hot. Are you sure…?"

"Quit asking me that. I am very sure. Inside me. Now!"

Resisting the intense inward tug that cajoled him to step away from Jett, Savin leaned into her, putting everything he had into moving toward her and never away. Screw the Other. This was happening.

With a grip of his cock, he glided inside the lushest, most delicious heat he'd ever known. The world changed. He groaned low and long against Jett's neck as he nuzzled his face into her hair. Closing his eyes focused all senses to smell and touch. Sweet, hot, wet energy. Lost inside her, he pumped slowly, then faster as her tight hug pushed him over some edge he didn't mind falling off.

This was his plunge into the lava falls. It had finally come to him. And he leaped freely and with arms spread wide to accept whatever dangers might come.

Gripping a hand at the back of his neck, Jett squeezed his hair tightly. "Yes, deeper. All of you, Savin. Don't stop. That is so… Ah!"

She shuddered against him. And he realized she had reached orgasm. How wondrous that she had. He normally had to work much harder to get a woman off. And that allowed him to release. With one firm, deep thrust, he came with a gasp—and then he had a sudden and intense need to pull out.

Savin pushed away from Jett, who clung to the wooden beam behind her. Had it been the Other? Or merely his better senses rising to the surface?

"Sorry," he gasped. "No condom. Forgot. Shit."

Jett nodded, huffing as she rode the lingering wave of her pleasure. Her breasts heaved within the dress. Her hair spilled messily across her rosy cheeks. "Right. That is something humans— Er, you have a condom?"

He nodded. "Bathroom."

"Then we're just getting started," she said in the most wicked and confident voice Savin had ever heard.

Savin had rushed to the bathroom and returned with a couple crinkly condom packages. It hadn't been a concern for Jett while in Daemonia. Demons had their own methods of birth control. Now, without missing a beat, they quickly returned to their frenzied lovemaking, this time on the bed. Gasps and moans were accompanied by the incredible freedom of skin upon skin, mouths tasting each other, heartbeats racing heartbeats.

When at the peak of orgasm, Jett felt the other demon inside Savin. When she sat upon Savin's hips, his cock fully hilted within her, and her body tremored with the most lush and unexpected bliss, a niggle of darkness shivered and tried to claw at her.

He called her the Other. She lived within Savin's body, inhabiting it, but not his soul. It was difficult for a demon to overtake a human's soul. Nearly impossible. However, if his soul had been occupied, then Savin would not even be Savin anymore. He would be whoever it was that was inside him.

Yet Jett wasn't able to delve deep enough to make that determination. And, honestly, she was too lost in the pleasurable moment to stop and attempt to dig deeply into Savin's being to learn that answer. She could do it. And she would. She wanted to know who and what lived within him. That was one determined—yet complacent—demon to have stuck around inside him for so long.

Lying down beside her lover, she kissed his shoulder and hugged him across the chest as the last delicious bits of orgasm pulsed in her belly. He smelled salty and fierce, his muscles tensing and relaxing in turns as his own orgasm played out. What an exquisite beast of a man lying beside her.

"That…was good," he murmured. The man panted, but his breathing grew more relaxed. How quickly he began drifting to a blissful sleep.

Would Savin let her step into his being and have a look around? Probably not. All manner of things could occur if Jett did such. She could learn things about him he'd rather no one discover. She could touch his soul, even. No human who knew what was up with such powerful magic would allow that. And Savin was a smart man.

And what would knowing prove? The demon was incorporeal. It could feasibly inhabit Savin forever. And, apparently, he'd developed a means to accept that, to even get along with the parasite. But the morphine he used so often could not be good for him. Even if most was sucked up by the Other, it was injected into his system. She hated that he had to use drugs to quiet the demon. He would be infinitely better if it were gone.

Jett would figure out who it was and, from there, could determine how to get her out. Because no other woman was going to dig her claws into her man. Savin was hers now. The sex had rocked her world and had connected them on a new level. They had moved beyond mere friends. She'd orgasmed…so many times. Never had she been brought to such a pinnacle. Treated as if a goddess. As if she was the one her lover had wanted to please, never mind his own pleasures.

And that was a good thing.

Savin's tight biceps pulsed against her arm as he

moved a little. His deep, throaty exhale sent a delicious shiver over her breasts and ruched her nipples.

Eyes closed, he slid a hand over her stomach and his thumb smoothed the underside of her breast. The man's growl hummed in Jett's throat and lungs. It felt like a universal signal. One that she answered with an arch of her back and a nudge of her shoulder against his.

"You feel like everything I've ever dreamed about," he said softly. "This is good, Jett. The two of us."

Indeed.

He nudged his head against her shoulder and kissed her arm. Then he quieted, perhaps drifting into reverie once again. Lying beside him was the only thing she desired. Ever.

Chapter 15

Savin whistled while he dried off after a shower. Jett had gone out to collect something to eat for them. He had told her to take the credit card from his wallet. And he felt on top of the world. He wasn't going to make excuses for feeling this way, either. He hadn't felt this good in a while. He'd made love with a woman he cared about—who happened to be half demon. Life went on. If anyone wanted to argue against that, he dared them to stand up and show him their teeth.

Tossing the towel aside, he strolled naked into the bedroom and sorted around in the drawer for some jeans. His uncombed wet hair dripped down his back, so he pulled up his jeans, then sat on the bed and lay back, wriggling to wipe his back dry. He was a guy. So sue him.

The front door opened and he peeked around to see

Jett. He'd left the wards down purposely, knowing she'd be gone only a short while. She blew him a kiss and he caught it.

And then he lay back again and closed his eyes as he listened to her sort through a bag and set things out on the counter. He'd just caught an imaginary kiss from a demon.

Half demon, his conscience corrected. And someone who had no intention of remaining that way.

She had been a queen, though.

What the hell are you doing, man? Do you know *what you're doing? Or are you love struck, following your cock instead of your brain?*

He honestly hadn't done that in a while. Hell, had he ever felt this way? Jett felt familiar to him, comfortable. Not like other women he'd met and had dated or with whom he'd had short-term relationships. She accepted him for everything that he was, including the Other within him. He could be open and honest with her. As she had been with him.

He sat up, wondering what the implications of a queen leaving Daemonia could mean. Did they know she was gone? If she had escaped, that would imply probably not. At least, not right away. Surely, they'd noticed her missing by now. Would they come looking for her? With the rift at a tenuous hold, what would a panic over a missing queen bring to this realm—and to Jett?

He rushed out to the kitchen and asked, "Are they after you?"

Jett set down a carton of apple juice beside a plate of fresh *pain au chocolat*. "They?"

"Your subjects. The inhabitants in the legion you ruled over. Did you…rule over them?"

She set a pastry on a separate plate for herself, then walked around him to sit at a stool before the counter. With measured confidence, she poured a glass of juice and took a sip before speaking. "I ruled. In a manner. I was more a figurehead. Someone who represented our legion and whom the subjects could bow to. But I did have authority. And I was meant to…"

"Yes?"

She set down the juice and sighed. "I had to get out of there now because plans were being made. I'd been put on the throne for more than the purpose of a figurehead. I was to breed."

"Oh, fuck. Jett. I'm…"

She shrugged. "I didn't want to tell you that, but I trust you. And after last night…"

He kissed her temple and bowed his head to her, so thankful that she had escaped. "You're safe now. I promise."

"I hope so. Do you really think…they will come after me?"

"I'm not sure. It was a thought that suddenly occurred to me. Doesn't Daemonia *need* a queen? And if they wanted you to breed? You said the former queen took you as a replacement. Maybe that was her only means to escape. Ensuring that another queen was in her place. Who will take your place?"

"I don't know. And I don't care."

"I can understand that, but…maybe you should care, Jett. Was there a scion, someone who would take your place?"

"No."

"Well, I gotta think that the queen who took you did

it for a reason. Maybe the same thing? She didn't want to be made into a breeding machine?"

"I know otherwise. She'd tried but was barren. She was not treated well after that fact was discovered. Which, I imagine, was her motive for making an escape." She took a few bites of pastry, giving it some thought. "You think I should fear capture?"

"You shouldn't. I will protect you."

"I am quite powerful. I can protect myself. But I won't disregard your offer of protection. Such a handsome man standing beside me as my champion?" She stroked her fingers down his bare chest and tucked two in at his waistband. "Will you be my champion, Savin Thorne?"

"Yes," he said without consideration. "I'm here for you, Jett. I..." He looked aside. The realization suddenly rose and it hit him hard.

"You?"

He clasped her hand. "I wasn't able to save you when we were young. I will not stop to save you now. I promise you that. I'm capable. And I'm strong. I know how to protect you. I am your champion, Jett."

She stood and kissed him, then pressed her hand over his heart. "I accept the offer, bold one. Now eat. And then? This queen desires more from you."

"More?"

She glided her palm over his quickly hardening erection. "Yes, more."

After a quickie on the couch that had led to a longer lovemaking session in bed, and then another against the bathroom vanity, Savin was feeling the champion. In a manner, anyway. Jett had asked if they could spend the day together, doing something—anything—that would not remind them of who they were, what darknesses lived within them. For they both harbored a darkness they'd rather not contain. And Savin had heartily agreed.

Now he and Jett stood at the top of the world, or reasonably close, as they looked down over Paris from within the Plexiglas-shrouded topmost level of the Eiffel Tower.

"I can see Sacré-Coeur," Jett pointed out with glee. "I love that domed cathedral. I want to go there. It's been so long. Can we do that next?"

"Of course. But, uh…it is a Catholic church."

"Yes. So? Oh." She wrinkled her brow. "Can I enter a place of worship now?"

"Generally? No. But to judge from your ability to wear a sheen with such ease, I believe you might be able to step on holy ground."

"Good. Then we'll go there."

Savin leaned against the window, the sights not as interesting to him as the woman who curiously gazed across the landscape and pointed out the landmarks she recognized.

He had dated many women in his lifetime. For a day or two, a few weeks, sometimes a few months. He'd never had a long-term relationship. Too difficult, considering his line of work. Yet he'd once yearned for simple domesticity with a former lover who had been a shoe model for a famous Parisian designer. She had left him for a stock-market trader.

Savin wanted a relationship. It wasn't a dirty word to him. When with a woman, he felt good. It wasn't that she filled him or completed him, but that she gave him a new outlook. And he needed more than his singular glance at life. He was a man who felt better when he could share his life and experiences with another.

But was Jett a person with whom he could hope to become involved? They had a history, and that mattered. But their history involved some pretty wicked stuff. And that mattered, too. They each knew what the other had been through. They understood each other.

Although he wasn't exactly sure what Jett's being a Daemonian queen meant. He felt sure she hadn't told him all. She'd been there twenty years. That was a lot of living. And surviving. He could be thankful she had risen as queen if only for the fact that they might have treated her far better than if she'd been forced to survive on her own and without any status. But to have been on the verge of being forced to breed? The thought of it made him shiver. He was so glad she'd gotten out of there.

She did have power. She wore a sheen right now, without seeming difficulty. So she must be strong. He'd felt her strength this morning while making love. He'd fallen into it and had luxuriated in it. And he wanted to do it again.

"What are you thinking about?"

He focused on her gaze and realized she must have been studying him for a while. Her smile was curious. He'd once wondered if her parents had named her Jett because her hair was so black. Not at all, she'd replied. Her father had suggested it, or so they'd told her, because he'd always wanted to fly in a jet.

A father who, apparently, hadn't been her birth father. Had Jett been sired by a demon? The implications were immense. Not least was the one that made him wonder who her demonic father could be. And was that unknown parent behind her being taken to Daemonia to replace the queen? What motives had been behind that move? Had he merely wanted his progeny to sit the throne?

"Savin?" she prompted. "Are you lost?"

"A little." He chuckled. "You want to know what I'm thinking about? Us," he confessed easily.

She blushed as she lowered her gaze and touched his chest.

He placed a hand over hers. "Will you be my queen?" he asked. "I don't want to worship you or put you on a pedestal. But I'd love to have you in my life. With me. At my side. In my bed. Here, holding hands, doing things we enjoy. Together."

She nodded.

"I realize you're only just getting your feet in this realm. Probably there's lots of guys out there waiting to meet you. And you'll want to explore and meet them, too—"

She pressed a finger to his lips to shush him. "I'm happy with where I am right now. With you. But are you sure you're prepared for whatever baggage I come with?"

He shrugged. "We've all got baggage."

"I'm going to wager mine's a bit heftier than yours."

"Probably. But I'm the strong one. I can lift a lot."

She smirked and gave his biceps a testing squeeze. "We'll see. I've been thinking about what you said about them coming for me." She glanced about, taking in the tourists around them, then lowered her voice. "I have to maintain my sheen. It'll keep them off my scent."

"Does it…wear you out? It must be difficult expending the energy."

"It takes a lot of work. But I'd never want you to see me…like that."

He stroked the hair over her ear and kissed her forehead. "Have more faith in me, Jett. There's not a lot that I haven't seen. I promise I won't disappoint you. Deal?" He held out his hand, which she clasped and shook.

"Deal."

"On to Sacré-Coeur?"

"Sure, but can we stop at the Louvre along the way? Do they still have that éclair shop in the gallery?"

"I'm glad you're getting your appetite back. I'm not sure, but we will find out."

They did still have the éclair shop tucked beside the top of the escalator. Savin treated Jett to a green apple and caramel concoction that had her swooning. She had gotten back her appetite and her penchant for sweets. Everything tasted so good. Was it because she'd had a taste of Savin and that had opened her to all the other delectable treats life had to offer? Most likely.

After the snack, they strolled through the Denon wing, which was crowded with tourists struggling to get a good view of the demure Mona Lisa.

"Remember when we got lost here?" Savin asked as they strolled out from that gallery into the hallway. Jett leaned against the wall to take in the crowd. "It was in one of the galleries with the eighteenth-century furniture."

"Yes, I remember that daring escapade into the past. We were firmly admonished by museum staff for hiding behind the King Louis XIV armchair. I thought for sure my mother was ready to faint."

"We didn't get treats that day," Savin noted.

"No, but we did get to see the security office. That was an adventure."

"Right, I remember that now. We played heist for weeks following, plotting methods to steal the *Mona Lisa* by hiding out in the guard's room until the perfect moment when we could make our escape."

His laughter rumbled and Jett clasped his hand, but of a sudden her attention was drawn down the long hallway to a crowd of teenagers dressed in black and chains. Someone brushed her shoulder, muttering "*désolé*" as he charged into the gallery. A definite feeling of recognition shivered up Jett's spine. Here, in this place that should hold only good memories, she could not escape the reminder that she was not the human she wanted to be. Would she ever be?

"I need to get out of here." She quickly strode off, knowing Savin would follow, and not wanting to converse when yet another accidental connection with a stranger could tease at her darkness.

The exit was just ahead. Even as Savin called after her, Jett picked up her pace. She fled upward, taking the twisting stairs to the glass pyramid aboveground, then exited out into the cloudy afternoon. Inhaling deeply the brisk air, she closed her eyes and caught a palm against her chest.

You are weakening, her darkness whispered. *You can stay strong if only you'll keep me at the fore.*

Jett shook her head. She didn't want to do that. She would not.

Why are you making this so difficult?

Savin touched her shoulder and bent to meet her gaze. "What happened in there?"

"Sorry, I had to get out as quick as possible. There were so many of them. I could feel them brushing my skin. It prickled intensely."

"Demons," Savin confirmed. "I sensed them. But then, they are always near. I've become oblivious. I obviously don't feel their presence like you."

"It's like walking through a cloud of mosquitoes," she said, knowing it wasn't the best way to explain it. "I'd love to slap them away, but then my identity might be revealed to them."

"Why didn't they react to you as you did them?"

"I'm wearing a sheen, Savin."

"Right. I need to do a better job at keeping alert for them. I can steer you away when I know. I'm sorry."

"You have nothing to apologize for."

"I want to keep you safe, Jett."

"I love you for that."

He smirked behind her fingers, then kissed the tips of them. "Should we head to a cell-phone store and get hooked up?"

"Yes, it's time I started acting like the rest of the humans."

He clasped her hand and kissed it. "You are human. Don't forget that."

They strolled out from the Louvre courtyard, footsteps crunching the crushed limestone, but Savin's phone rang when they broached a tourist-crowded sidewalk. He answered and stepped a few feet away from Jett, slamming a hand to his hip as he spoke in low tones to the caller.

She tilted her head to listen, but it was too crowded

to hear, and cars drove by, honking their horns at some emergency she couldn't guess at. From Savin's stiff posture and tightening jaw, she sensed whatever he was being told was not good.

Finally, he shoved the phone into a pocket and reached out for her. She took his hand and he pulled her close. "They've broken through again," he said.

And Jett's heart dropped to her gut. She didn't have to ask what that meant. The rift had been reopened. They were coming for her. She knew without doubt.

Daemonia would not rest until its queen had returned.

Chapter 16

Savin wanted to go directly to talk to Ed. And when Jett volunteered to walk home alone again, he didn't argue. He needed the distance, actually.

She was, or had been, a queen. What were the implications of that? Would Daemonia send troops after her through the newly reopened rift? It was something he had to keep in mind.

The two of them…had something. It was a beginning. A new chapter to their lives. And yet a strange plot twist had been introduced. His best friend, survivor of the most heinous horrors, was a demon queen.

Those demons who escaped Daemonia and caused trouble in the mortal realm then became his problem. Not that Savin expected Jett to cause trouble. Ah hell, so he'd already taken the leap to believing she was dangerous?

He should probably tell Ed about Jett. But then, would the man want to send her back? Even if she had taken on demonic attributes, she didn't belong in the Place of All Demons. Jett was an innocent. She belonged in the mortal realm. With him.

Up on the sixth floor, Savin strode into Ed's office. The clean interior boasted black marble walls and the entire outer wall was lined with windows. A massive conference table stretched half the length of the room. Ed's desk sat before the windows. On shelves along one wall were interesting objects that Savin knew were magical artifacts Ed had either collected or been given. Edamite Thrash's girlfriend was a witch and apparently he was smitten.

Ed stood waiting for Savin, leaning against his desk, arms crossed high over his chest. His slicked-back black hair revealed tattoos that crawled up his neck. On his hands he wore the ever-present half gloves, which exposed his fingers, but covered the poisonous thorns on his knuckles inherent to all corax demons.

"I just finished interrogating a bi-morph," Ed said.

Savin nodded. Those sorts were mighty ugly. But they had a strange penchant for lemons. He suspected, now that he got a whiff of the air, that Ed had employed that tangy treat as a means to twist the screws.

"The captive seems to know that there is only one means to securely close the rift to Daemonia."

"Which is?" Savin asked.

Sighing, Ed stood upright and splayed out his hands. "Apparently, one of the legion queens has gone missing. And until she's back where she belongs, upon her throne in Daemonia, the rift will never seal."

"A queen of Daemonia." Savin rubbed his jaw. What

the hell? And Jett just revealing to him that she was once a queen? How to play this one? He wasn't going to lay out all the cards until he knew if he could trust Ed. But he hated lying to his friends. "Are you familiar with such royalty?"

"I know every realm has its various royalties. There are dozens of legions in Daemonia. Like countries here in the mortal realm. The Casipheans—whom I'm most familiar with—descended from angels. But they are a dying breed. And the bi-morph didn't think this specific queen was Casiphean."

"So there's many?"

Ed shrugged. "Dozens of queens, yes. But only one is missing with whom we need concern ourselves. I've put in a call to Certainly Jones. He knows everything. And if he doesn't, he can find the answers in that crazy library of demonic lore in the Archives."

Savin had been thinking the same: to ask CJ what he knew.

"For now," Ed continued, "I'm going to call it and put out a hunt for a demon queen. There certainly can't be many running about Paris. In fact, I'm sure there can be but one."

And right under their noses. Shit. This was not how Savin wanted things to go down. But… "You need my help?"

"Thought you didn't hunt demons."

"I don't, but I can do whatever you need."

"For starters, there's a bi-morph in the basement waiting for reckoning."

"Will do." Savin rubbed his jaw, considering the information about Jett.

"Female problems?" Ed asked.

"Huh?"

"You've got that look. You got a woman that's making you smile and frown at the same time."

"Isn't that what they're supposed to do? Drive us men crazy?"

"In theory. But the good ones will do it with relish and make you love them even more for all the ups and downs."

"You and your witch have ups and downs?"

"Once in a while. She wants to travel and I'm happy right here in Paris. I've got a city to look after. Not that I'm doing a very good job of it lately."

"The demon queen will be found," Savin said. "And until she is, we'll have to batten down the hatches and keep a close eye on the rift. Can CJ put another hex on it?"

"Yes, but it's like slapping a flimsy plaster over a fatal wound."

"Right. Maybe I can do some asking around."

"About what?"

Savin shrugged. "You never know. I'll talk to people I know. See what information they might have on the local demon scene and if there's a queen wandering about we're unaware of. If she's powerful, she could put a sheen over herself that would—" Hell. Was he really going to lie to Ed?

"That would what?"

"Huh? Oh. Well, I just think she could walk right by us and we'd never know."

Ed's cell phone rang and he turned to answer it. He spoke to someone with half his gaze toward Savin. "Really? All bowed down?… Thanks. Did you get a description?… Yes, do that. Bye."

"What's up?"

"News on the queen already. Apparently, she showed up at l'Enfer last night."

L'Enfer was the nightclub owned by the Devil Himself. It was frequented by demons, mostly, and a few brave vamps and werewolves. Jett had gone there?

"My source said she walked onto the dance floor and everyone bowed before her. Started calling her 'my liege.' Most had never seen her before, but they all instinctually knew."

"Did they get a description?"

"No."

Whew! Of course, any description would be of Jett sans sheen. He wondered now what that looked like. She didn't want him to see her in her demonic form? He needed to see her truth.

"I'll head out to l'Enfer tonight," Ed said. "We've got an escapee queen wandering this mortal realm, and it sounds like no one will be safe until she's sent back where she belongs."

Savin nodded, swallowed. "Stay in touch, man. You said the bi-morph is downstairs?"

"In the holding cell. You are billing me for all these reckonings?"

"Hell yes." Savin nodded and left the man's office. As he stepped into the elevator, he blew out a breath. He did not like concealing the truth from Ed. He was a friend, and his loyalty to him ran deep.

His alliances were now sharply divided.

After reckoning the bi-morph back to Daemonia, Savin returned home with his mind at once racing and wanting to shut down. To help Ed and his efforts to keep Paris safe from hundreds, possibly thousands of demons coming into this realm? Or to stand beside Jett, a woman he cared about, yet who might prove his greatest enemy yet?

Jett wasn't the enemy. She hadn't asked to be queen. In fact, taking on the role might have been the very thing that had kept her alive all those years. In an odd way, assuming the throne had been a blessing for her.

But how to work for both sides? He couldn't stand back and *not* reckon those demons he was called to send back. But he would never reckon Jett. It was unthinkable.

There had to be another solution. And until he discovered what that was, he couldn't tell Ed he harbored the queen in his home.

He tossed his keys onto the kitchen counter but didn't call out for Jett. Due to their intimate connection, he sensed that she was not here. She was inside him in a way the Other never could be. And he wanted her there, racing through his veins, tickling over his skin and sighing against his heartbeat.

A glance revealed a torn piece of paper on the counter next to a pen. She'd left a note?

He read the words that were scrawled in that rounded style he recalled she'd used when they were kids. But no heart dotted the *i* this time. *Ran out for something to eat. Back soon!*

Savin's cell phone rang. It was his mom. She sounded excited.

"You'll never believe who just touched base with me."

He couldn't imagine—but then he tried a guess. "Josette Montfort?"

"Yes!"

He smiled at his mother's enthusiasm.

"I had put out a call to a long-lost friend I missed dearly on my Facebook page, and she messaged me. Said she was doing well and missed me."

"You spoke to her?"

"No, just the online back-and-forth. I didn't know how to tell her that her daughter had returned. I didn't want to do it online. You know? I asked her if we could meet for lunch and she's in the Bahamas. What should I do, Savin? She needs to know about her daughter."

"She does." But how to explain everything Jett had been through to Josette? "Maybe that's something that Jett should get to decide about. Yes?"

"Yes, certainly. You'll tell her I corresponded with her mother? Perhaps I can be a liaison to hook the two of them up on Facebook."

"Thanks, Maman. I'll tell her and see what she wants to do about it. How are those madeleines?"

"At this very moment Roxane and I are filling out forms to apply for a loan for the food truck!"

"That is awesome. Remember, your first stop has to be the fourteenth."

"Of course, Savin. But we've got a long way to go before we start baking. If the loan happens, perhaps next summer will see our maiden voyage. Oh, I'm excited about the possibilities! I'll talk to you soon. Let me know what Jett decides."

"I will. Love you."

He set the phone on the counter and exhaled. Was this good, bad or ugly news? How could Jett tell her mother what she had been through, and what she had become?

And yet would her mother have information about her real parents? And if so, would that lead them to a father who could very well be demon? Did it matter? Savin wasn't sure what knowing the father's identity would provide in Jett's quest to assimilate to the mortal realm.

On the other hand, if the demon was someone so important his natural daughter had been taken from the mortal realm to rule in Daemonia, then Savin would like to have a chat with him. He couldn't possibly know the hell he'd put Jett through. Or worse? The bastard knew exactly what he'd done to an innocent human girl.

Chapter 17

Getting a haircut and manicure was a strange luxury. Jett had been attended by many while ruling as queen. But she'd never simply relaxed into a chair and trusted the outcome. She allowed that to happen today. She'd needed this after telling Savin what she really was. Something to distract from reality.

Her long black locks that had previously hung to her waist were now trimmed to her elbows. Her hair felt so glossy she bounced as she walked down the street. A flash of silver in a retailer's window caught her eye and she went inside. Five minutes later, she wore black ankle-high boots studded with silver spikes on the toes. They went well with the black leather mini and red silk shirt, over which she wore a black lace vest that spilled long fringes about her waist. A pair of sunglasses kept everyone from noticing a red glint in her eyes.

Because she needed to drop her sheen. And soon. She was tired, and it was becoming harder to concentrate. The sheen was growing thinner. She could see that when Savin looked at her. He saw the red in her irises now. He hadn't before.

She considered finding an abandoned building and releasing her human shroud, but there weren't a lot of places in midcity Paris that would offer such privacy. And doing it at Savin's place? She'd done it after first arriving, but only after he'd left the place for a while. And now that he knew everything about her, it should be all right. But to reveal herself to him would not be wise. The man might believe he was okay with her being part demon, but she could imagine his reaction should he see her with horns, blue hair and gray skin.

That was not a party she wanted to attend. At least not with a man with whom she was growing intensely infatuated.

On the other hand, he hosted a demon within him. He was not so different from her. That was something that bonded them.

A short man wearing thick black-rimmed glasses walking toward her swept her with a look from legs to face and down to her breasts. As she passed, Jett heard him say, "Sexy."

Being called sexy made her feel good. Better than good. Never had she turned a man's head. At least, not a human man's head. Demons didn't count. Not here they didn't. Such attention could go straight to her heart.

With a wink over her shoulder to the man, who returned the wink, she strode on toward the river. Savin's place was a long walk off, but these boots were comfortable. And she intended to shine in the sun today and meet every wanton gaze with a flirty smile of her own.

Savin plucked out a chord on the diddley bow. It was the same chord that had sent Jett fleeing the other night. He'd just gotten off the phone with Certainly Jones. The witch was heading out to the rift to assess the damage. Savin had said he'd meet him there, with diddley bow in hand. Maybe combined with the witch's dark magic, the two could do something to slow or even stop the influx of demons.

He placed the instrument in its soft zip-up case. The body was convex and shaped like a turtle shell. It had a Bluetooth pickup so he could play the thing and amplify it over his phone. It was freaky crazy, but he wouldn't have an electrical outlet for an amp out in the field, so he was glad for the app. Jett had yet to return, but it was only early evening. She must be shopping. She deserved the freedom, so he decided not to worry about her.

Besides, when he saw her, he'd have to tell her about what had gone down in Ed's office this afternoon, and he did not relish having that conversation with her.

He opened the front door to a woman with her hand lifted to knock. Jett's smile beamed and she lunged up to kiss him. Shopping bags crunched against his back as her kiss opened his mouth and she tasted him as if she were starving. She tugged him toward her, so he stepped across the threshold and into the hall.

He wrapped an arm about her back and pressed her against the wall, not wanting to leave the kiss. The woman was delicious. And dark and mysterious. And so eager to meld to his touch and mouth. Yet she was demanding and took what she desired from him. A confident woman who would not be put back for any request.

A queen.

Shit.

Savin broke the kiss. "You're in a good mood."

"And I must have caught you on the way out?" She looked over his shoulder where he'd slung the case. "Have a concert to perform?"

"Kind of." He winced. No time to have the big discussion right now. That was an excuse, but he was happy for it. "I'm meeting the dark witch out by the rift."

"Right. Opened once again. That explains the annoying feelings of demonic presence I've felt all day." Her shoulders dropped, as did the shopping bags, landing on the floor. "You're going to use musicomancy?"

He nodded. "I'm still not so sure I can invoke it properly, but I mean to give it a try."

"It has been proved effective on me."

"Sorry about that."

"You should not be. You didn't know then what you now know. I'll let you get off to that adventure."

He sensed her unease. "I'd invite you along, but you're better off as far from that place as possible."

"I am a big girl. I do very well on my own. And I've got to learn self-sufficiency sooner rather than later. I might even attempt to cook a meal."

Savin's eyebrow quirked. "You ever cook before?"

"No." She chuckled, then waggled a teasing brow. "Don't worry, I won't burn the place down. I do recall helping my mother with her pies and cookies."

He'd forgotten about his mother's call with the information about Josette Montfort, but CJ was waiting.

"I look forward to whatever you create." He kissed

her on the forehead. "Remind me we've much to talk about when I return."

"Sure," she said as he started toward the stairs. "Uh, will you let down the wards for me?"

"Right. Sorry." Savin backtracked and spoke the Latin words that would release the protection wards. To his side, Jett noticeably shivered, as if shaking off a chill. "I'll leave them down while I'm gone."

"Thank you." She kissed him on the cheek. "I'm going to try on my new things!" She skipped into his loft and he closed the door behind her.

And Savin exhaled heavily. Could he trust CJ with the information about Jett's demonic nature?

Chapter 18

Watching the dark witch conjure a spell was mesmerizing. CJ stood in the center of a black salt circle poured on the tire-trampled grasses that edged the lavender field. He'd been speaking Latin for a while, and every so often punctuated those words with a good pull at the whiskey bottle he held in his left hand. In his right, he brandished a crystal wand, and when he drew sigils in the air before him, the magical symbols glowed green and lingered for minutes.

Savin stood before the truck hood with the diddley bow strapped across a shoulder. He put up a foot on the tire so he could prop the instrument on his knee. He needed to lay it flat to play it properly. The Bluetooth was activated. The phone app that would broadcast the musicomancy was set to play with the volume tuned to High.

Even though the rift was open, there was no discernible wavering in the sky to demarcate the tear as they'd seen that first night. It was apparent it was open to another realm. Savin felt the evil, cool vibrations pricking at his bones. He'd picked up the first tingles when he was about a mile away from the site. They hadn't seen any demons come through since arriving, but that didn't mean the incorporeal ones were not slipping into this realm. They could be ghostly figments that traveled about in search of a human host to fully achieve corporeality.

It was the corporeal demons Savin most wanted to catch. More often than not, they were assholes. They looked like monsters, acted like monsters, and not only did they scare the shit out of humans, but they tended to not care if they were seen. Very few bothered with a sheen.

CJ turned to him and nodded. As the dark witch spread his hands wide above his head, stretching out a magical green static of energy, Savin played the first lick in a series that he'd learned could incapacitate a demon.

Pressing the glass slide across the single string, Savin made his instrument sing a sorrowful cry that he at once loved to create and despised for the wickedness it was required to control. And then he took great satisfaction in knowing he could annihilate that wickedness and slam it back to the realm from whence it had come. A waver of the slide across the string teased up Savin's own brand of innate magic. It birthed in his soul and swelled in his bones. The sigils tattooed on his forearms glowed. That brief time he'd spent in the Place of All Demons had infused this skill within him.

And he would wield it relentlessly.

Sustaining a long and moaning note, Savin searched the sky. A flicker of red sparked above CJ's head and embers scattered over the ground.

"That was one!" CJ called.

Their combined magic had worked like a bug zapper to an incoming demon. Nice.

Savin slid another note into a commanding cry. Now, this was a weapon he could wield all day.

The cell phone Savin had picked up remained in the box. Jett ran her fingers over the smooth matte-finish box, marveling at the utter beauty of it. Just the box! It would be too complicated to figure out how to operate the phone, she suspected. And it didn't feel right to open it without Savin to help her with it. And really, she had no compulsion to walk the streets of Paris gabbing as all others did. Besides, she had no one to gab to.

She set the box aside, and with a preening gaze over the mess of Savin's amps and sheet music stacked beside the couch, she noticed a small radio.

"I do know how to operate a radio." She picked it up and played with the dials until a slow sensual tune sung by a woman with an incredible, longing voice captivated her. Shivers traveled over Jett's arms at the intense visceral connection she felt to the tones. Setting the radio on the wooden chair arm, she swayed and closed her eyes, turning about in the living room beneath the skylights.

Lifting her arms over her head, she whispered the release that dropped her sheen. Her hair thickened and grew blue. Her skin prickled as it darkened. And the horns at her temples stretched out and over her ears.

"Ah…"

Respite.

* * *

Savin bumped fists with Certainly. The witch hadn't managed to close the rift, but they had cleaned up dozens of incoming demons. And that had seemed to put up a warning beacon. They hadn't witnessed any new arrivals in the past half hour they'd stood by, waiting, sharing the dregs in the dark witch's whiskey bottle.

"You know they'll start coming through as soon as we leave," Savin commented.

"I'm going to mark a blood hex on the ground that will, at the very least, give them pause. It's not much, but it's all I can do until we find that queen. Ed tell you about that?"

Savin nodded. "Yep." He picked up the diddley bow from the truck hood and opened the passenger door to place it inside on the seat. "I should head out. I'm drained. Gotta go home and recharge."

CJ waggled the empty whiskey bottle. "This didn't do it?"

"That makes me tired after a reckoning. I can barely keep my eyes open as it is. I'll check in with you tomorrow."

"Thanks. I have to hit the road, too. Vika complains when I'm out too late. The twins are a handful."

CJ and his partner, Vika, had twin boys. Savin figured they were toddlers, but hell, who knew, they could be rowdy teenagers. He nodded and climbed in behind the steering wheel. The witch cast ash and salt across the ground and began to stomp out a ceremonial chant as he pulled an athame across his palm. What kind of father was that to have?

Savin drove out of the field and onto the gravel road. He led such a weird fucking life. The whole idea of having children, of being married and *domestic* teased at him. And yet it felt wrong to fit *ordinary* into his lifestyle. But the dark witch did it. CJ worked at the Archives, cast out demons and dealt with magical shit all day; then he headed home to the family—for all Savin knew—to have cupcakes and tell bedtime stories. So weird.

Yet maybe not. Maybe the weirdos were the humans who had no clue what paranormal crap was going on right under their noses.

"Hell." Savin turned toward the city. He was the weirdo, no *ifs*, *ands* or *buts* about it.

Despite being weird, he didn't aspire to normal.

Now he wondered if two weirds—he and Jett—could make a right. Or even a family. He wouldn't mind having a child or two to deal with and love. Someone to read a bedtime story to? He could imagine doing such a thing. And he would never make his child feel unworthy or insignificant, as his father had done. Blame it on the alcohol, but Jacques Thorne had taken a drastic one eighty after Savin's return from Daemonia. Not a day had gone by that he hadn't fallen asleep on the couch with a whiskey bottle in hand. Rarely had he time for Savin, and when he did, it had been to berate him or tell him he could have done whatever it was Savin had been doing so much better.

Savin didn't miss his dad much, and that was a shame. A man should have a strong father figure to look up to, to mold his life after.

Jett was lucky to have been adopted. He couldn't imagine what would have come of her had her real mother and demon father raised Jett. Would she have grown up in Daemonia? That was too fucked to consider.

Half an hour later, he parked and jogged up the stairs to his place. He was exhausted from all that reckoning, but knowing a gorgeous woman waited for him lifted his spirits and gave him renewed energy. He strode inside the apartment, strengthening the wards behind him as he closed the door. It was dark, but he heard the music immediately. So she'd found the radio?

"Don't look at me!" Jett called out. She dashed out of the living room.

And Savin immediately knew he'd caught her unawares. Must have taken advantage of his absence to release her sheen. He flicked off the radio and tightened his fist. He'd just spent the evening vanquishing so many demons.

Demons were assholes. He hated them. He hated the Place of All Demons. And he hated...

He didn't want to hate her. He did not. Did he?

Why couldn't he sense her demonic nature? Closing his eyes now, he concentrated, focusing, searching for that hum in his bones. Nothing. A man should consider that lacking sense a good thing, but he wasn't sure what to make of it.

Jett spun around the corner from his bedroom, casting him a shy glance. She looked human. Was human. *For the most part.* She had pulled on the sheen. "Everything go well?"

He set the instrument case on the kitchen counter and nodded, sure if he spoke right now that his voice would quaver with the anxiety of walking in to find a demon dancing in his own home. Had he been mistaken to not tell CJ and Ed about Jett?

"Uh, were you…?" he started.

"I'm sorry," she offered, rubbing a palm up her bare arm. "I shouldn't have done that here. It tires me to keep up the sheen."

He put up a hand. "I understand." He did. But he didn't want to.

"I attempted to make a meal, but…" She glanced toward the kitchen and for the first time Savin picked up the scent of something burnt. "Can we order out?"

"Sure. I can run out and get something. Give you more time to yourself?"

"No, I'm good. I don't want to be alone now. Can you just make a phone call?"

Whatever demon had been dancing in his living room had retreated. Jett was now that sweet, innocent, frail woman he'd found by the side of the road. And all he wanted to do was wrap her in his arms and make everything safe for her.

Savin tugged out his phone and pressed the speed dial for his favorite local restaurant. The girl who took his call knew his usual, and he doubled it. It would arrive within the hour.

Jett sat on the couch, stretching her legs before her as she sat sideways. Her arms on her knees and chin resting on one forearm, her hair spilled…not so far as usual.

"You cut your hair?"

"Needed a change. You like it?"

"I do. But it doesn't matter what I think about your appearance. That's all for you."

"Is it? You don't care if I'm a mess or a glamour doll? What if I didn't comb my hair for a week?"

"I'd still find you attractive."

Her lip wobbled. "You find me attractive? Even knowing...?"

"Even knowing." Though truthfully, a part of him still couldn't wrap his mind around the fact that his girlfriend was part demon. "I'm sorry you feel that you have to hide your true self from me, Jett. I wouldn't be upset if you wanted to drop your sheen more often."

"But it's what you work against. Things like me."

He sat on the sofa and lifted her head by her chin. Her brown eyes were glossy. "You are not a thing. You did what you had to do to survive. I know that."

"Oh, Savin, I need your trust so much right now."

"You have it."

She moved onto her knees and glided to him, pressed her hands to his cheeks and kissed him. He didn't protest, because he didn't want to. He wasn't going to allow his brain to process the fact that he was making out with a woman who was also part demon.

Sliding a hand up Jett's hip, he slipped it under her shirt and groaned as her incredible warmth seemed to heat him to the boiling point. Her body hugged his and made everything on him instantly hard. She'd never been kissed before he had kissed her? Hard to believe. Or maybe he was that good a teacher. Heh.

Jett made quick work of removing his shirt, though it got hung up on his biceps. "How do you get such hard, big muscles from reckoning demons?" she asked.

"Reckoning requires a strong body, so I lift weights. Whew! But I am tired out from this evening's work. CJ and I managed to extinguish a few dozen incoming demons."

"Extinguish? I thought when you reckoned them you merely sent them back to Daemonia. Do you kill them?"

"I said that wrong. Well, yes and no. CJ and I combined our forces and—yes, it kind of worked like a bug zapper to the incoming. But no, I don't generally kill them. Reckoning sends them back, all in one piece."

He winced. Why did he feel as if he were reassuring her of something that could happen to her in the future?

"I see. You said you're tired?" She kissed his forehead. "Then let me do all the work. You sit back..." Her fingers danced down his abs and unbuttoned his fly. "And let me take care of you, lover."

Not a single protest came to mind. Savin lifted his hips as she unzipped him and pulled down his jeans. Felt great to let his shaft out of its confinement and... Yes... The woman curled her fingers into a nice, firm grip.

Jett dragged her fingertips over her tongue and winked at him, then placed her wet, hot fingers around him and began to work him up and down. Slow, and then faster. And then so slow he wanted to grip her hand and make her go faster. But... No, that was good. The tension she used was just right. Then she torqued her grip to the left and then...

Savin tilted his head back against the couch and groaned deep from his chest. Not a thing wrong with this situation. And when he felt her lips on the swollen crown of his cock, he nearly lost it. It was only when she tongued him that he had to grip at her hair and the couch and began to shudder as orgasm dashed up on him much quicker than expected.

The door buzzer rang and Savin shouted as he came, then swore because he was in no condition to answer the door. Damn, the woman had hit him hard and fast.

Jett stood. "Food is here. You want me to answer?"

Lost in some kind of wild and delicious high, he was capable of reaching into his back pocket to pull out his wallet. "Credit card is in there."

She took it and approached the door. "Wards?"

Breathing out a few exhales, Savin stood and pulled up his jeans. "I got this." She handed him his wallet, then cupped his cock through the jeans. "Mercy, Jett."

"I did okay, then?"

"Okay?" He grabbed the doorknob. "I don't think there's a rating high enough for that performance."

She mocked a bow and then climbed onto a stool before the counter.

He winked at her but opened the door and took the delivery from the man, promising him the usual tip. Closing the door, he joined Jett at the counter.

"Ribs?" she guessed.

"There's a place that makes them like I remember my dad used to cook on the grill. Whew!" He shook out his hands and then found his place. Segueing from the high of orgasm to answering the door was weird as shit. "Okay, I'm cool."

"You're not, really. And I'm happy for that. Your cock is so big. I like it." She winked.

And he would be hard again in no time.

Jett took a tin container and peeled off the foil cover. "I remember eating at your house. Often. Your parents were so good to me."

"We had good times when we were kids." He set plates and forks out and joined Jett on the next stool.

"We can have good times as adults."

"I thought we already were."

She kissed him and handed him a sauce-laden rib. "That we are."

Chapter 19

Jett licked her fingers and then stuffed the empty food containers in the garbage bin. Savin had wandered into the bathroom for a thorough wash. He'd eaten all but one of the ribs. For some reason the meat hadn't appealed to her. But she'd eaten the Gouda potatoes after testing them to be sure they hadn't been salted.

Demons and salt. Gave her a shudder. Though she was half demon, so she couldn't know how some things would affect her here in the mortal realm. Like knowing that her eyes could give off a red glow, even when sheened. Or that if she wasn't careful with her sheen, her skin might darken and look ashy. Gray ashy, not a normal skin tone. And oh, if she let even a portion of her horns out. On the other hand, it could be considered by some as body modification. Humans did a lot of weird stuff to alter their appearances nowadays.

It was late, nearing midnight, but the day had been good. Because even after almost catching her without a sheen, Savin still had wanted to have sex with her. The man desired her. And he did care about her. She felt that.

"There's a few things I need to tell you," he said as he wandered back into the living room.

The man was a walking advertisement for sex. Those jeans hanging low on his hips revealed all the many tight, hard muscles on his abdomen and chest. His arms were solid and big. And that tousled hair gave him a wild, virile look that made Jett weak in the knees. She wanted more of him. Inside her, filling her, tasting her and owning her.

Never had she had such a thought about a lover while in Daemonia. She had not considered them lovers, actually. Merely things to entertain her. Things she had not allowed to kiss her. She was glad for that caution now.

Refilling her whiskey glass, and one for Savin, Jett walked over to the couch, handing him the glass as they both sat. He downed the two fingers of whiskey, got up and retrieved the full bottle.

"Might need this," he said.

"Is what you have to tell me that terrible?"

"I, uh… I'm not sure. I'll start with the maybe-good thing first."

"Okay. But first." Jett held up a finger to pause him while she downed the swallow of whiskey. With an exhale, she held up her glass for him to refill it. "Okay, go."

"My mom is on Facebook," he started.

"A book of faces?"

"Huh? Oh. Right. The internet has really exploded and become this sort of social hangout since you've been gone. There's a thing called Facebook and everyone is on it. You can post about your life and see what other people are doing."

"Like a means to spy on them?"

"No. Well. Maybe." He gave it some consideration. "Normal people use it to stay in touch with friends and relatives. I'm sure there are creeps who use it for nefarious means. Anyway, my mom, after I'd talked to her about your parents, decided to try to contact your mother on Facebook. And…she did."

Jett clutched the glass to her chest. "Where is she? How is she? Did she ask about me?"

"My mom didn't know what to say about you, so she didn't mention your return. We both feel it's up to you how, or if, you want to make contact with Josette. Apparently, she's living in the Bahamas."

A much-admired vacation spot. Jett recalled her mother cutting pictures of the island from magazines and pasting them in her dream scrapbook. The memory loosened a tear at the corner of her eye, so she quickly swiped it away.

"How is that possible?" she asked. "How could your mother have learned these things about my mom without actually talking to her?"

"Through the internet. It's like email, but Facebook messaging is instant. What matters is that Josette wrote back to my mother that she was in a good place and didn't foresee coming back to Paris. That was all the contact my mom had with her. But she has Josette's Facebook information if you want to contact her."

"I do. I mean…" Jett sucked in the corner of her lip.

What *did* she want to do? Her mother was alive, and apparently well. Living in her dream getaway. That was good to know. She must want to know about her daughter. Yet Jett had been gone for twenty years. Had her mother believed she was dead all that time? How would it impact her to know she was still alive?

And no longer completely human.

"Right." Jett tilted back the rest of the whiskey. "I have to think about that one."

"She's as close as a computer message," Savin said. "But I'm sure you'll want to weigh the pros and cons about contacting her."

Jett took the bottle from him and poured herself more. "Do you think I should contact her?"

She handed him the bottle, and this time Savin drank directly from it. "I can't tell you what to do. Your mother will most likely be elated. But it would be weird for her, too. Might take her some time to figure everything out, as it has taken for you. She thinks—well, you know—she thinks you're dead."

Jett toggled the glass on her stomach.

Savin leaned over and kissed her on the shoulder. "You just need some more time to adjust to being here."

"And to forget about the past."

"And…" He sighed heavily. "CJ and I managed to destroy and/or send back dozens of demons this afternoon. But there's something you need to know."

She turned to look up into his deep blue eyes. She trusted those eyes. They would not hurt her. "Tell me."

"Edamite Thrash interrogated one of the demons he captured and the thing told him how, exactly, to close the rift and seal it."

"Which is?"

"They want their queen back." As he met her gaze, Jett saw the stoicism return to his demeanor. "We send her home to Daemonia, and the rift can be sealed."

A stunning revelation, issued with a cruel calm that shouldn't surprise her. The man did do that for a living. And he was trying to protect innocents. She had no qualms about that. Save that she was also an innocent. In her core, she was. Despite the darkness that clung to her.

"I'll never reckon you, Jett. Promise."

"But I'm their queen. You have to send me back."

Jett stood up from the couch. She paced toward the kitchen, keeping her back to Savin. He got up and pulled her into a hug from behind. She initially struggled, but when he wrapped his wide arms about her and hugged his head aside hers, she could no longer resist the need for the safety he offered.

"I promise you," he reiterated. "My word is good. I will not reckon you to Daemonia."

"But so many could suffer if you do not send me back. The people of Paris…"

"We're keeping things under control. For now. CJ's fix on the rift should slow the influx, but… I'm going to the Archives early tomorrow to see what CJ has found in the demon room."

"The demon room?"

"They have a room for every paranormal being that exists. Filled with source materials, documents, histories, artifacts. There's got to be something in that room that can help you."

"Make me completely human again?" She turned in his embrace and her wide eyes pleaded with him.

He hadn't considered that option for her survival. Daemonia would not want back a queen who was merely human. That could be a way to save Jett. And…

He nodded. "And maybe we can find the other queen.

The one who took us in the first place. If she's still out there, we can send her back."

A twinge at his insides gripped him like a vise about the spine. He let go of Jett and stepped back from her. She stood before him, seemingly weak and defeated, an innocent woman. Looking so frail. He wanted to hug her again, to hold her tight to make her know what he said was the truth.

But something kept him from doing so. And then he realized what it was. Or rather who—the Other.

Bitch.

What did she have against Jett? And why had she allowed him to make love to her without interference, yet at moments like this it was as if she cringed in horror at their closeness? It had been a few days since he'd given her morphine, and he wasn't about to shoot up again so soon. The bitch could go through withdrawal for all he cared.

"What did the dark witch say when you told him I was the queen?" Jett asked quietly.

"I didn't tell him. Wasn't sure how. Also, didn't feel he had a right to know. Yet."

She nodded. "Yet." He reached for her, but she turned a shoulder to him. "I'm tired."

Right. This was too much for both of them right now. Savin grabbed the whiskey bottle and nodded toward the bedroom. "You should get some rest. In the morning I'll head to the Archives. I don't think I'll sleep much, but I'm going to try."

"You need to be strong." She bowed her head. "Thank you, Savin. For telling me the truth. You could have kept it to yourself."

"Secrets only grow. I want you to trust me, Jett."

"I do. I'm going to think about my mom. I'm not sure it would be a good idea to contact her right now."

"Give it some thought." He started to lean forward and kiss her on the forehead, but the Other turned him toward the couch.

Just as well.

"Good night," Jett said softly. She padded into the bedroom.

He listened to the sheets rumple as she climbed in, and her sigh as her head hit the pillow.

Savin tilted back another swallow of whiskey. He'd once told a friend this stuff had been brewed by trolls. He'd like to punch a troll right now. A big, blocky bit of stupid that could take a punch like a sand-filled punching bag.

He wanted to beat out his anger and frustration on something, that was for sure. But how to attack that which lived within him?

He eyed the tin of morphine of the shelf beside the couch. "Bitch," he muttered.

Jett woke from what felt like a refreshing slumber. She stretched out on the bed, then immediately noticed that Savin had chosen to sleep on the couch last night. The information about her mother and the subsequent heart-wrenching decision that had to be made—to seek her out or not—had not lended to a sensual snuggling session following. Nor had the fact that the queen was needed to close the rift.

Just as well. She was thankful that he'd been truthful with her.

Now to figure what should happen next.

She did not want to go back to that literal hell. No one could make her take a single step toward that realm.

But no matter if she planted her feet firmly, Savin did have the power to send her back. He was a reckoner. He could send any demon back to Daemonia.

He'd said he wouldn't reckon her. And she did believe him. But it pained her to know she would be forcing him to go against his loyalties to the job he performed. Reckoning was all he knew. What would the consequences be if he refused to do that job?

Surely, the man hadn't reckoned all the demons who had come to this realm from Daemonia. Some were smart, and perhaps others blended easily into society, becoming a part of the human race. They might not present harm or a danger to humans. No need to send them back from whence they'd come.

She hadn't harmed anyone. And didn't want to, either. Yet she had worn the crown and still felt that power within her. A power that was stifled too much lately.

Sliding out of bed, Jett wandered into the bathroom and twisted on the shower. Checking her reflection, she sneered. Her skin had gotten pale and her hair wasn't as glossy since she'd escaped that place. If she were in her demonic form, she would glow. Literally. And she would feel her strength so much more.

Keeping up the sheen was growing more difficult. And yet she sensed it was also getting easier. Was that because some of her demonic nature was changing, going away? Could she ever become completely human again?

Savin had said he'd look into that today. Something about a book on demons. And now, when she took a moment to slip through the bedroom and glance out into the living room, she didn't see him on the couch. It was late, around eleven in the morning.

"He must have left for the Archives."

She hoped he could find what they both desperately needed.

Chapter 20

Savin wandered into the demon room behind Certainly Jones.

"Must be freaky working here with all these strange artifacts and—" Savin bent to peer into a glass cylinder container that was about two feet high and filled with clear liquid. Inside floated what looked like a jellyfish, but it was thorned and its eyes were red. "Hell fish."

"Got it on the first guess. This is not one of my favorite rooms." CJ led him toward the Bibliodaemon, the Book of All Demons. "The witch room is comforting to me. And, not surprisingly, the unicorn room is fascinating."

"Unicorns exist?"

"Everything fucking exists. Don't you know that by now?" The dark witch wandered ahead.

Savin could but shrug. He knew all the myths and

legends did exist, but he hadn't seen them all. He'd love to see a dragon soaring through the clouds. And hell, he wouldn't mind throwing those much-desired punches at a troll. But for some reason the unicorn still challenged his sense of reality and fantasy. Couldn't there be one legend that really was made-up? A fantasy that people could entertain and not have ruined by reality.

"If you tell me unicorns are assholes, you're going to shatter a childhood fantasy," Savin said as he joined CJ before a large book on a dais.

"Never met one. They are fierce, is what I know. There are always assholes in every species, most especially humans, yes?"

"True enough. So what have we got here?"

CJ stepped onto the steel dais and, using two hands to grip the thick leather cover, opened the book randomly. The tome was massive, stretching about three feet long and two feet wide, and it was a good two feet thick.

"The Bibliodaemon." CJ rubbed his hands together with more eagerness than his dislike of the room should have warranted. "This is the book that records all demonic happenings, spells, hexes, possessions and exorcisms, heritage, and breeds. Most species have such a book."

"What about us reckoners?"

"You're not exactly a species, more a rare tradesman. And humans have enough books recording their antics, do they not?"

"Most history books are often proved inaccurate."

"Perspective," CJ said. "It changes as we grow and learn, and uncover and disprove the falsehoods that were generated by the past." The witch threaded his fingers from both hands together before him and flexed them outward. "Now, what are we looking for?"

"Information about the queen of Daemonia."

"There are many."

"Yes, but the one from the particular legion where the rift opened up. Is that possible to locate? An identification can only help to catch and send her back."

But would a search show Jett's face? What Savin wanted to find was the former queen who had taken him and Jett, who had also ruled over the same legion. This was going to be a tricky search, no matter the outcome.

"I'll take a look." CJ closed his eyes and held his hands, fingers spread, over the book as he murmured in Latin. The thin pages began to slowly turn, whispering across one another, then picked up speed. CJ said over the flicking pages, "It's like an internet search. Only, you know…"

"The old-fashioned way." Savin leaned against the dais, the sweep of the pages brushing his face with a cool breeze. "What part of Daemonia did you, uh, visit?" he asked, just for conversation. But also, if the dark witch had been there when Jett was queen…

"Probably this same area we're searching now. I didn't mark down the territory. It was…eh, a spur-of-the-moment decision to do some reckless magic. I paid for it. In spades."

CJ had told him that he'd been possessed by a dozen demons upon his return to the mortal realm. One had been a pain demon and, upon his return, had forced CJ to harm himself. That hadn't been nearly so terrible as the grief demon, though. Savin couldn't imagine. Well, he could. He didn't know what kind of demon lived inside him, but for the most part she was quiet. Unless, of course, he kissed another demon.

Was that it? Could the Other be jealous? It didn't make sense. It wasn't as though he and the Other could be intimate in any way. More intimate than him wearing her inside him, that was. Whew!

He really wanted to unload her, but there didn't seem to be a way to do it. Not without a supreme sacrifice. That was something he had never wanted to face, and would not.

"Here's something." CJ leaned over the book and read while Savin peered over the edge of the page. The dark witch's long black hair fell over the paper, and his fingers, heavily tattooed with all sorts of spells, drew a line down the page as he silently took in the information. Finally, he stood and tapped his lower lip. "It seems one queen disappeared a while back and was replaced with a half-breed. That's the one who is currently missing, the half-breed by the name of Jettendra."

Savin muttered the name, thinking it could easily be an elongated form of Jett. She'd not told him that. Not that she would. "And the former queen's name?"

"Fuum."

"Fuum? Sounds like a bad rash."

CJ chuckled. "Apparently, Fuum went missing and the half-breed was left in her place, already designated to take the throne."

Savin knew that much from what Jett had told him. "So where is the former queen?"

"Why? Shouldn't we be focused on Jettendra? It says she escaped recently to the mortal realm, but there are no dates. It always takes these books a while to update the details, but when they do, they are incredibly accurate. I wonder if it was the night the rift first opened."

It had been. And hell. "But why veer focus from the former queen? I mean, it's always good to have options. More choices will ultimately make it easier for us, yes?"

CJ studied Savin with such a delving gaze, Savin felt sure the witch was tapping into his soul. Something witches could do without a guy even knowing it had happened. He crossed his arms over his chest and met CJ's gaze with as sure a stare as he could manage, though he wasn't feeling at all confident with the stuff he was not telling CJ.

"You know something," CJ finally said. "And I need to hear it."

A knock at the door lifted Jett up from her inspection of the diddley bow Savin used for musicomancy. She didn't dare to touch it but wondered how easy it might be to cut the string.

Another knock sounded. Had Savin forgotten his keys? He would have told her if he'd expected company, and surely he wouldn't have left her to greet that company on her own.

From outside the front door a woman called Savin's name.

Company? Jett hustled out to the kitchen. She'd donned black leggings and a silky red sleeveless shirt that hung below her hips and sported a few rhinestones decorating the low-cut scoop neckline. She looked presentable. And the wards were loose enough that she could leave and return on her own, so she was good.

Gripping the doorknob, she tried to get a sense for

who—or what—could be on the other side of the door, but her senses didn't twitch.

Opening the door, she was surprised to find an older, glamorous blonde woman holding a plate of something that was wrapped with cling plastic.

"Oh?" The woman peered beyond Jett, searching the kitchen. "Savin isn't home?"

"I'm afraid not. You've missed him."

"Oh, but you must be Jett."

"I…" Jett narrowed her gaze, wondering who the woman was.

"I'm Gloriana Thorne, darling. Savin's mother. And you have been away a very long time."

Chapter 21

Savin stepped back from the steel dais and turned about, taking a moment to weigh his options. He could walk out the door, but he never ran away from a threat. And CJ was no threat. The witch simply wanted the truth. Which Savin had and should share with him. But…could he trust the dark witch wouldn't go to Ed with the information? Why keep the info from Ed? Perhaps if he told him everything, the corax demon would agree that Jett should be protected and not sent back to the Place of All Demons.

Like that was going to happen.

"Thorne?" CJ prompted. He jumped down from the dais, his bare feet landing on the cool limestone floor. The witch stood as tall as Savin and was formidable, but Savin knew, were it a battle of might and muscle—without magic—he could take the witch. With ease.

"I guessed right, didn't I?" CJ said. "There's something you haven't told me. Has it to do with the rift and the demons?"

"It does," Savin finally said. "I didn't think telling you and Ed what I knew was necessary. Initially. And I've been protecting her..."

"Her? Protecting who?"

Savin toed the base of the dais. He had to be honest with Certainly. His loyalties to his friends were paramount to him. "You know all about me being kidnapped to Daemonia when I was a kid."

"Yes."

"Remember I told you about the girl who was with me?"

"You said she died. Fell over a cliff into some sort of lava falls?"

"That's what I thought. Until I found her wandering the roadside that night we first closed the rift. She'd been living in Daemonia all this time, CJ. Has done everything she possibly could to survive until she had the opportunity to escape. Her name is Jett Montfort. She was my friend then, and she is now. She hasn't lived in the mortal realm for twenty years. She has nowhere to go, no one to care for her. I've taken her in."

CJ blew out a breath and hooked his thumbs at his pants pockets. "Wow. For a human to survive so long in Daemonia..." Then he met Savin's gaze. "She must have become demon. At least part."

Savin nodded. "She has. I'm not sure how much. I know she's still human. But demon, too. Except she can pull on a sheen even I can't detect."

"That's a powerful demon." CJ's gaze grew more discerning. "I've been there. I can't imagine surviving so long. And I'm a dark witch. How did she, a mere human, manage such a feat? A ten-year-old girl? All alone?"

"She was nine. And…she still hasn't given me all the details. I haven't pressed her for information. She's been through a lot. She did what she had to do to survive."

CJ nodded. "Smart girl. But what you're telling me raises a lot of questions."

"I know. But I don't think it's fair to treat her like a criminal or even a target that needs to be sent back to Daemonia. She doesn't belong there, CJ."

"She *didn't* belong there. When you were kids."

That comment bit. Hard. Where did Jett belong now? Was she more demon than human? *Could* she exist as a mere human now?

"So now she's back in the mortal realm," CJ said. "And she's living with a demon reckoner."

"I probably wouldn't have been her first choice for a roommate, but it's how things played out. I was there at the right time. I have to believe we were meant to find each other."

"There are no coincidences. The universe knows exactly what it is doing." CJ nodded. "Yes, you were meant to help her. Or, at the very least, to have her in your sight so she was accounted for."

Savin winced at that explanation. He didn't like CJ's manner of seeing things in more than one way. And not always the best way, either.

"So…you didn't tell Ed and me because you thought she wasn't a problem. She's not a threat to humans."

"She's not. Jett wants to live a normal life. But there's something else you need to know. She just told me. It changes things. I don't want it to change things. And maybe it doesn't have to if everyone involved has all the information and we look at all the options rationally and with Jett's best interests in mind."

The dark witch lifted his chin. "And that is the 'something else' I need to know?"

Savin pressed his lips together and squeezed his eyelids shut. This was not a betrayal against Jett. It couldn't be. He only wanted to help her.

He opened his eyes and said, "Jett is the missing queen."

Gloriana Thorne strolled into the kitchen and set the plate she was carrying on the counter. She turned and, with an assessing summation, took in Jett from head to toe. Jett remembered Savin's mother as always smiling and friendly to a fault. She'd eaten over at their house often and had even stayed some nights when she and Savin would watch a movie, popcorn in hand, and fall asleep on the couch.

"You've grown up," Gloriana finally said. "You're beautiful, Jett."

"Thank you." She lifted her chin. The darkness within loved to be complimented. "You haven't changed at all. Very glamorous. Savin always called you his movie-star mama. Did he…" She worried her lower lip, but again, her darkness would not allow her to cower or feel less-than. She was who she was, and damned proud of it. "Did Savin tell you everything?"

"He did."

"Even about…"

"The demon place?" Gloriana sat on a stool and patted the stool next to her, which Jett slid onto. "I always took everything Savin said about demons and such with a huge grain of salt. But I've watched him over the years. He was not a boy, nor is he now a man, who lies with any sort of ease. I can't imagine he made it all up. Even knowing how he loved to play those silly make-believe games about dragons when you two were young."

"He didn't make anything up. I swear it to you."

Gloriana shook her head. "I believe you. Because for you to suddenly appear after twenty years? There's something to all those tales Savin told me. I've known it since he first told me when he was a child. Here." She shoved the plate toward Jett and peeled back the plastic wrap to reveal delicate fan-shaped madeleine cakes. "We have a lot to talk about."

"Your Jett—the little girl you were once friends with—is the queen of Daemonia?" CJ leaned back against the dais, taking in that information. The witch looked flummoxed, and Savin could understand that feeling.

He was still out of sorts about the whole thing, and yet not. He knew where his alliances stood, and they were with Jett. She needed him. End of story.

Or was it a continuation of their story?

"Then all we need do is send her back to Daemonia," CJ said. "Close the rift, seal it and all is well. But I'm suspecting that is not your first choice in this problem-solving endeavor."

"I won't reckon Jett. She escaped that place, CJ. She was taken there against her will and forced to survive. Now that she's free I will do everything in my power to ensure that freedom."

The witch nodded, yet Savin did not release his clenched fists. He wasn't angry; he was feeling his power. Let no man stand against him.

"Then Paris will be overrun with demons," CJ stated simply.

"We can find another way. There's another queen," Savin said. "Jett told me that she—we—were taken by the queen and then that queen disappeared, leaving Jett behind to assume the throne. What was her name you read in the book?"

"Fuum. You think that queen escaped to the mortal realm, as well?"

"Possible. We have to search for her."

"How? Where? If Jett has been there twenty years, that means Fuum may have been here twenty years. She may no longer be in Paris. She might be dead. Who knows?"

"It's a long shot, but I owe Jett that much. I have to search for the other queen. You've got spells to track demons. I've seen you do it before."

"Yes, but to locate a specific one? Do we even know who she is?"

"What does the book say about her?"

"Right." CJ returned to the Bibliodaemon and read aloud, "Fuum. It says she did escape to the mortal realm by transforming herself into an incorporeal demon. I would assume she's taken on a human body since. But there's nothing more on her after that." CJ tapped the page. "Ed needs to know about this. He's assembling troops as we speak, Savin. I don't think it'll be long before the humans notice demons, perhaps even get hurt by them. The influx is increasing."

"Then I've got my work cut out for me. As do you. I need a tracking spell for the former queen. Can you fashion something using the info in that book?"

"I…might be able to." CJ jumped down again to

stand before Savin, and this time his gaze wasn't so much delving as compassionate. "Are you sure this woman is worth it?"

"She's my best friend, CJ."

"Is she really? She's lived in the Place of All Demons for twenty years. Hell, a lot longer according to how time works there. Are you sure she's the same person you once knew? You were kids then. And she is, at the very least, half demon now. If I were her, I'd use every trick in the book to maintain a rapport with the reckoner who rescued me. To keep him from reckoning me. And to stay under the radar until…"

"Until? CJ, she's one tiny human woman with an unfortunate past and a huge desire to step as far away from that past as possible. I promise you, she's not a threat to anyone. I will personally take the blame if she does become a nuisance. And I can say that because I know and trust her."

CJ put up both hands in surrender. "Very well."

Gloriana had suggested they go outside for a walk in the subdued fall sunshine while they talked. So, with a madeleine in each hand and sunglasses in place, they walked beneath the shade of chestnut trees creeping over the chain-link that surrounded a public garden.

"You're quite remarkable," Gloriana offered. "To have survived what I can only imagine are incredible horrors. I never wanted to think too much about the place Savin described to me, but I confess it was difficult not to imagine…things. How are you, Jett? Here." She tapped her temple.

"I feel fine. I mean, I know I'm not fine. I know it's called having baggage. And I have a lot. But all I want is to get back to normal. To be a regular woman and to forget all about that time away." She finished off the last madeleine. "I've been thinking about contacting my mom, but I'm not so sure it's the right thing to do. If she believes me dead, maybe that's better."

Gloriana heaved out a sigh. "She was devastated by your loss. And then with the divorce... Well, she's been through a lot. But it has been twenty years. She might be able to face this new trial. And it's not a trial, is it? She'd be getting her daughter back."

"Gloriana, did my mother ever tell you I was adopted?"

"No. I'd forgotten about that. Oh, dear, I must confess something to you. Your mother had never mentioned anything of the sort to me, but when I was looking for things to rescue from your abandoned house, I did happen upon the adoption papers. It was a surprise to me at the time. And I haven't looked in the envelope I stuffed all that information into for...well, over a decade. You just reminded me of that now. Is that the first you learned, when reading those papers?"

"Yes. It was a surprise."

"I'm sorry. But you must know your parents loved you so much."

"I do know that. And I can accept it. But I'm still not sure it would be wise to contact my mother. And if I did? How to tell her the truth? She would never believe I've spent the past twenty years living amongst demons," Jett said plainly.

"Most certainly not. I think it best you maintain the story Savin initially told the police about being abducted."

"Perhaps. I'd have to invent some details. I'll think

about it. I want you to know, Gloriana, that Savin can trust me. I promise you. I'm not…evil." At least, she hoped she was not.

"Yes, well, I hadn't considered that until you brought it up." She angled across the street toward their departing point. "Do you know Savin once told me something when he was nine? He said he was going to marry you when he grew up. And he might even consider kissing you, too."

"He did?" Jett felt a blush ride the back of her neck. Well, she'd felt the same way then. Yet it hadn't been an adult longing, a sensual kind of attraction between them then. Kid stuff.

Things had changed. He'd kissed her. And so much more.

"Yes, and I would pat his head and tell him he should go right ahead and do that. But to wait until he got a bit older." Gloriana sighed heavily as they neared the front door of Savin's building. "But now?"

Jett brushed her palms together to disperse a few cake crumbs. "Now?"

"I have to be honest, Jett, I certainly hope you don't attempt to sway my son's head toward his ridiculous childhood fantasy of marriage. I could not condone it."

Jett's jaw dropped open.

"If what Savin has told me is true, you're a…why, you're a creature."

"I, uh—no," Jett said on a gasp. Tears pooled at the corners of her eyes.

"Oh, *cherie*, I know you didn't ask to be taken away and kept amongst those nasty creatures, but it's the truth. And my son has only ever fought to keep the streets of Paris safe from your sort."

The way she said *your sort* hurt Jett's heart.

Gloriana ignored Jett's obvious dismay. "You have to look at things from his perspective. He rids the city of demons. You are one of those…awful things."

Over Gloriana's shoulder Jett noticed a figment of black mist forming. Her senses immediately picked up demon, and the sulfurous scent spilled into the air and her nostrils. Along with that she could only think, *Danger.*

She grabbed Gloriana by the shoulder. "You need to get inside now!"

"Unhand me!" The woman shook off Jett's grip and clutched her purse to her chest. "You see? You're wild. A thing!"

"It's coming at you!" Jett lunged to push Gloriana against the brick wall.

As she did so, she heard Savin shout from down the sidewalk, "No!"

Chapter 22

At sight of Jett attacking his mother, Savin charged forward. He managed to shove her away and wrapped an arm around his mother, moving in front of her to block her from Jett.

"What the hell?" he blasted at Jett.

"Didn't you see it? The mist demon?" Jett protested.

He had not seen anything but Jett attacking his mother. And if a demon had been that close to Gloriana, he would have seen it, no matter its speed. Savin turned his back to Jett and slid his hand down the side of his mother's head as he inspected her face. "Are you okay?"

She was startled but smiled up at him. "Yes, I'm fine. I'm glad you arrived when you did." She glanced over his shoulder to Jett. "What's wrong with her?"

"It wasn't me," Jett insisted from behind him. "There was a demon."

"I didn't sense anything," Savin said. "A mist demon? Those are obvious, Jett."

Jett dropped her mouth open, at a loss for words.

"I'm going to take my mother home. All right, Maman?"

"Yes, please, Savin. I'm feeling shaken. I was only being nice to her."

"It's okay. Where's your car?"

"I didn't drive here. I took the metro."

"My truck is in the lot. Come on."

With an arm around his mother's shoulders, he walked away from Jett without looking back. He couldn't bear to look at her after watching her bodily fling herself at his mother. And a sniff at the air did not scent sulfur. Mist demons were smelly. And even after they'd gone, their scent lingered. And if not for a noticeable scent, he should have felt the thing's hum before even getting close.

"She came at me so angrily," Gloriana said. "Why would she do that?"

"What did she say to you?" he asked as he and his mother turned the corner.

"She didn't say anything. She just lunged. I think I might guess why. I had told her I didn't want her involved with you. She reacted. She's a wild thing, Savin. Jett Montfort is not the same girl you were friends with twenty years ago."

After witnessing the attack, he had to agree.

Even if his mother had said something so inconsiderate to her, Jett had no right to attack. In broad daylight on the sidewalk with so many walking by.

Had he missed something? *Had* there been a demon? He stopped before the passenger door of his truck and helped his mother up and inside. She clasped his hand, still shaking. No matter what had gone down, he would find out.

Jett watched Savin walk away with his mother. He'd yelled at her. Had believed she had been trying to attack his mother.

Her chest ached and her throat grew dry. She wanted to cry out for him to please listen to her, and that she would never harm his mother. Not anyone. But if he hadn't seen the mist demon, then she had no proof of her innocence. It certainly must have looked as though she were attacking Gloriana.

Without a glance back at her, Savin turned the corner.

And Jett kicked the door to the building. "Damn it!" Had she just lost Savin's trust?

She had reacted. Thinking to grab Gloriana and pull her away from the demon, which was gone now. Why had it dared to materialize like that in public?

The darkness inside Jett straightened. She knew. It had wanted her to see it. To challenge her to act out in public. Did it know she was the queen? Had they already sent minions to find and retrieve her?

"Let them try," she said, curling her fingers into fists. "They will have a fight."

And then she dropped her tight pose and bowed her head. She didn't want this. Not here in the mortal realm. Would she ever be free from what Daemonia had made her?

Savin returned to his place after nightfall. His mother had still been shaken when he walked her up to the front door, so he'd sat with her awhile. When she'd begun to sweep the spotless kitchen, he knew she was getting back to herself. In that time, his anger had settled. And he'd given the incident some thought. Jett would never have purposely tried to harm his mother.

He wanted to believe that.

Finding a half-full bottle of whiskey on top of the fridge, he then sat on the couch and picked up the diddley bow. A slip of the glass slide across the string would send out wicked vibrations to any nearby demons. Jett was not here, so he didn't worry about how it would affect her.

Did he care?

A mist demon. He'd seen them before. They were exactly as they sounded: a swirl of insignificant black mist. Red eyes seemed to bobble within the figment about head level. Sometimes they possessed a sharp tail that could snap around and slash across flesh, searing through blood and bone as it cut deeply.

He'd not seen it. But had it already fled by the time he'd noticed Jett lunging for his mother? Had the shadows created by the overhang from the building disguised the ghostlike creature? They could be fast, misting out of sight as quickly as they had a tendency to appear.

He wanted to give Jett the benefit of the doubt. And he should talk to her, listen to her side of the story. But she wasn't here. He'd not expected her to be here. If she didn't return tonight, he figured it was because she truly was guilty and couldn't bear to face him.

He grabbed the whiskey bottle and took a long swallow. He fitted the glass slide on his middle finger. Time to dally with some demons.

* * *

Jett returned to Savin's home well after dark. Despite knowing she was probably not welcome here now, she had nowhere else to go. She hadn't money to stay at a hotel. And while the cemetery might have provided a private place to snuggle up against a tombstone for the night, it had begun to rain. She was finding it difficult to keep her sheen on with the fresh water falling from the sky.

She hated feeling so dependent on another. *It is beneath you.*

She nodded in agreement as she took the stairs upward. How easy it would be to simply let go and be and look the way she really was. But worry over Savin's opinion of her appearance aside, she still had to think about the reactions from other humans. Not a wise move.

At the front door, she paused with her palm facing the demonic wards. She felt them more acutely than she ever had. She was growing weaker. She had to either drop the sheen to get past the wards, or else suffer a wicked pull to cross the threshold.

She glanced along the floor and to the corner of the hallway not five feet away. The idea of settling in for the night curled up in a ball did not appeal. And besides, she was not one to give up and hang her head in defeat.

With a heavy sigh, and an inhalation of bravery, she gripped the doorknob and turned it. It wasn't locked. But as she crossed the threshold, her body felt the electric prickles and vibrations that fought to keep her out. She was still too strong for expulsion, but oh, that hurt. Right in her heart. It thudded loudly and her nerves twinged, curdling a moan in her throat.

Stepping inside and closing the door shut off the wards. Jett pressed her forehead against the wall, breathing in deeply to work through the lingering pain. Savin had not loosened the wards as much as usual. And she could guess why.

It was time she figured out how to survive, how to get money and to support herself. She had a way to get in touch with her mother. Would she help her?

Creeping in through the kitchen, Jett paused in the living room. Savin lay on the couch, a whiskey bottle not far from the hand that was splayed out over the floor. His legs stretched across the hardwood.

"Savin?" she whispered. "Is it okay that I stay here tonight?"

With a grunt, he rustled, obviously sleeping, or had been very close. "Jett? Was worried about you."

"You were?"

He made a come-here gesture with his fingers. Jett approached, smelling the whiskey and sensing he'd probably used the alcohol to drown his apprehensions about her. Warranted.

"I'm sorry," she said softly. "I wasn't trying to hurt her. But if you didn't see the mist demon, then I understand how it was difficult to believe me."

"It's over," he muttered, still teasing sleep, for his eyes were closed. "Sit here."

She sat on the edge of the couch, and his torso hugged up against her derriere. He was so warm, and beyond the whiskey he smelled dark and delicious.

"I should let you sleep," she said.

"Yes. Long day. Tired," he muttered. "Kiss me? Good...night?"

That was either the whiskey talking or— Jett wasn't

going to overanalyze the request. Any chance to kiss the man would be met. Always.

She bent and kissed Savin. The arm he'd had out-stretched wrapped across her back, but not possessively. He was sleeping and dreaming or maybe in a half-wakeful reverie. So she would make it the best dream he'd ever had. Straddling him on the couch, she deepened the kiss, diving into his whiskey sweetness and tasting his throaty growl. The man's body was solid and hard beneath her legs and chest, and she pressed her breasts against him. Her nipples hardened, stirring her need for pleasure.

He didn't seem awake enough to want to have sex, but when his hand slid up under her shirt, she pulled it up higher to give him access to her bare breasts. Mmm, that soft, not-so-focused touch giddied her. And then she felt him resist with a slight shove against her rib cage. The demon within him?

"Shh…" Jett kissed him again, lulling him toward sleep. "Let's just hold each other."

She didn't need to make love to him. And right now she had a more important goal. She wanted to dig in and see if she could read the demon lurking inside her lover. And she might be able to if Savin agreed, or…if he were not fully in his senses. Taking his slight nod as a signal he approved of her suggestion as permission, she glided her fingernails down his chest. A kiss to his firm mouth. A brush of her lips over his beard. She nuzzled her cheek against his. He was like a big cuddly cat whose purrs were more like wanting growls.

His hand at her breast dropped the clutch as he drifted into reverie.

Fine with her. And much better if he wasn't fully aware.

Jett bowed her head and focused within on her darkness, summoning her demon. She would not shift, but she would use the skills she had learned while sitting the throne. Reading others was a necessity for survival and everyday rituals such as assessing work tasks and punishments. Incorporeal demons were tricky and liked to hide out in human bodies or even another demon. The only way to tap into them was to send her detection senses through skin and bone, moving like an invisible finger to touch the demon's essence.

Digging in her nails, but not so firmly that they drew blood, Jett pressed her fingertips about Savin's left pectoral, right above where his heartbeat had slowed to a relaxed pace. Whispering a word to command obeisance, Jett connected.

The Other within him jerked and lifted her head. She knew Jett was coming in but was not so subservient to allow it with ease.

Jett had to move quickly. She forced out her influence through her fingers and swirled it in through Savin's skin and muscle and felt the tug as she entered him and saw the Other. With her eyes closed, a figment of the one who inhabited Savin formed in Jett's mind. Tall, lithe, long hair and...so ancient. She had served... something. It wasn't clear to her yet. Yes, a female...

...that she recognized.

The Other growled and Savin's body jerked. The incorporeal demon inside him fought back at Jett's intrusion with a remarkable power of her own. Jett's fingers left Savin's chest as she was bodily flung away and off the couch to land on the floor in a sprawl. She lifted her head and eyed the sleeping reckoner. Thank goodness, he hadn't woken.

And yet she knew exactly who she had seen. That bitch!

Understanding emerged. What a foul and wicked plan the Other had taken. Her name was not Other, though. It was Fuum.

"Very tricky," she muttered. "Now the game has changed."

Chapter 23

Savin shut off the shower and heard his cell phone ring. Hand dripping, he reached out and grabbed the phone. "Ed, what do you got?"

"A news report about the sudden, strange increase in demonic possessions. It's on France 24."

"What? Humans don't believe in that crap. Well, you know. The smart ones don't."

"In a perfect world they would all believe it myth. Apparently, exorcists are getting a workout. And the possessions are focused specifically here in Paris."

Savin blew out a breath. He hadn't heard from John Malcolm. Was it because he was too busy?

"CJ was able to work out a tracking spell for the queen," Ed said. "We're going to activate it as quickly as possible. I'd like you to be there."

"I can…"

Could he walk in and watch as the guys attempted a spell that would ultimately, if it worked, lead them to Jett? Savin stepped out of the tub and slapped the dry towel over a shoulder. Had CJ told Ed about Jett and the fact that there was another queen out there somewhere?

"How about in a few hours?" Ed said. "At my office."

"Sure. I'll see you soon."

He set the phone on the vanity, then pulled the towel off his shoulder and used it on his hair. He'd woken on the couch this morning and had snuck past Jett, lying in the bed, and into the bathroom. She was probably still snoozing. It was only around 7:00 a.m.

He remembered her coming in late last night and he'd asked her for a kiss. He might have been swimming in whiskey and half-asleep, but he'd felt the intensity of their touch and could not deny he'd needed it. And then something strange had happened that he wasn't too clear on. Had Jett been disgusted by their kiss? She'd pulled away from him so quickly. And…he had dozed pretty fast after that. He didn't have a clear memory of what had gone on.

Whew! He never overdid it on the whiskey like that. What the hell was wrong with him? He had to get it together. Had his whole life suddenly turned upside down because of a woman? While most men would find that fact strangely welcome, he wasn't sure how to take it. Because was the woman in his scenario even human?

Wrapping the towel about his hips, he opened the bathroom door to find Jett sitting up on the end of the bed, waiting for him. She was naked. Looking every inch a human. It didn't take long for his erection to rise and salute beneath the towel.

"Morning," he mumbled.

"We need to talk." She patted the bed beside her.

"Sure, but, uh, it's going to be mighty hard for me to concentrate with you doing your Venus thing."

"My Venus thing? Oh. Sorry." She grabbed a T-shirt from the pillow and pulled it on. "But what about you, looking all Greek god and glistening with water— Ah, shit, Savin, I have to tell you this. I can't get distracted by all that...candy."

"Candy?" He smirked. Never heard his abs called candy before.

All right, so he was on board with the woman fucking up his life a bit. But she was right. They did need to talk. And both were aware of how far that talk would progress if they were not fully clothed.

He pulled up the blanket from the bed and wrapped it about his shoulders. "Better?"

"Sure. But not really. Just sit." Impatient, she got off the bed and paced before him as he sat on the end. "I know we're still not okay with the thing that happened to your mother. You may never believe me—"

"My mother wasn't hurt, just more scared by your sudden need to grab her. For now, let's pretend it never happened. I think that can work for both of us. Okay?"

"If you say so. But your mother hates me now."

"We'll leave that for her to worry about. So what do you want to talk about? Is it about last night? Sorry, I was in my cups, as they say. If I said or did something wrong..."

"No. It wasn't you, it was me. I was bold. I shouldn't have— But I had to know—"

He grabbed her hand, stopping her pacing. "I don't know what you're trying to tell me, but you need to know what's going on out there. Ed reports the influx of demons is growing. Incorporeal demons are taking up residence in humans. The exorcists are busy."

"I suspected as much. My skin crawls with recognition of so many demon entities," she said, meeting him with a direct and defiant look. "You need to send back the queen."

Savin nodded. "That seems to be the fix. Ed wants me to meet him this afternoon. The dark witch has developed a tracking spell for the queen. I'm hoping it can locate the old one, but we don't even know if she is in Paris."

"She's right here," Jett said.

"I know that, but I still haven't figured a way to avoid the spell zooming in on you."

"I'm not talking about myself. When I said she's right here..." Jett pulled her hand from his clutch and placed it over his heart. "I mean, she's right here. Inside you."

"What?"

"Savin, last night when we were making out on the couch... I sort of took advantage of you. You were... I needed to get answers, so I looked inside you. I was able to briefly connect with and see the demon within you. And I recognized her."

Stunned that she'd done such a thing, without his permission, Savin wanted to charge out of the room. But something kept him on the bed. A shiver inside him. The demoness knew that Jett had seen her. What did the Other fear?

"You *know* her?" he asked.

Jett nodded. "She's the one who had us brought to Daemonia. Savin, the demon who hitched a ride in you is Fuum, the former queen. The one who kidnapped me and put me in her place so she could escape. I know it. I felt her and she felt me."

"Fuum." The same name CJ had read in the Bibliodaemon. The former queen who had disappeared from Daemonia.

The shivering inside Savin turned to a jitter. His arms and hands began to shake. A piercing burn stretched from throat to gut. This was not a nervous reaction to hearing the uncomfortable truth about his latest romantic entanglement. Savin had experienced this before. And it never ended well.

"Leave," he said curtly.

"What?"

"Just get out of the apartment. She's going to blow."

"She's—" Jett nodded. "You can't control her?"

"Not when she gets angry." He stood and stretched out his arms, the blanket dropping behind him. "Oh, man, it burns inside me."

"Unhand him!" Jett cursed. "Or I will make you regret it!"

Savin gritted his teeth. His body moved toward Jett, and his feet felt as if the Other controlled them as he tried to stop the movement. The Other was pushing him, commanding him.

"Get the morphine," he managed through a tight jaw.

Jett searched the cabinet top. "Where is it?"

"In the living room."

She ran out and he heard her collect something. Savin punched the wall and shouted because his knuckles opened and blood ran out. "You're the queen?" he said to his disgruntled passenger. "I will send you back!"

Bodily, he threw himself against the wall. His shoulder crunched upon impact and he dropped. His entire body shook as the darkness within him went on a rampage.

Jett plunged to the floor beside him, and the stab of the needle entered his neck.

Savin swore at the pain. He grabbed Jett by the shirt and whipped her across the room. It hadn't been him! She landed hard against the cabinet, toppling the demonic devices. With a shake of her head, Jett said something in the Daemonic language and then…she shifted.

Chapter 24

She had never wanted to drop her sheen before Savin. But now was no time for vanity. Or to be ashamed of her true nature. The demon inside Savin was powerful, and the Other was determined to hurt him, and Jett, at all costs.

Even as her horns grew out and over her ears, Jett lunged forward and gripped Savin by the shoulders. The connection, her hands to his skin, shocked her influence into him and jolted the demoness. Savin yowled, but it wasn't his voice that sounded, but rather the former queen's.

"You can't make me harm him, you nasty bitch," Jett said firmly. "But I will make you regret ever hitching a ride in my best friend."

Focusing her will, she seared a vicious hex through Savin's body and felt the demoness within shudder and jerk. Jett was more powerful than the one who had stolen her so many years ago, and she would make her know that now.

Savin's head rocked backward, hitting the wall. Jett held his shoulders firmly, exercising her strength over her enemy. Her lover slapped a hand through the air, landing it on Jett's waist. He gripped but did not clutch her for long. His arm dropped weakly. He couldn't take much more of her influence coursing into his system. Two powerful hosts of darkness battled within him—and only one could win, rendering him incapacitated.

No. This wasn't the way. She did not want to hurt Savin.

Jett released him and stepped aside. Spreading back her arms, she drew in her vita from the prone man on the floor, retracting what darkness she had put out in an attempt to defeat Fuum. It came to her in sparks of crimson that electrified her system upon reentry.

The Other's vibrations shivered to nothing. Savin let out a gasping exhale as his demonic passenger relented. Fuum had been subdued thanks to Jett's intervention. And likely the morphine had kicked in. Savin's eyelids fluttered, but he managed to catch his palms against the wall so he did not drop to the floor. He glanced to her, mouth gaping.

Satisfied, Jett nodded and then was sweeping her hands over her head in preparation to pull up the sheen—when Savin grabbed her by the wrists.

"No. Don't put on a sheen," he said. "It's getting harder for you, isn't it?"

Suddenly humiliated to be standing before one she wanted to see her in only the best light, Jett bowed her head and nodded.

His eyes took her in, gliding along her dark gray skin and up over her face, which she knew altered slightly, narrowing, the flesh clinging to the bone. And then the horns that she'd learned to take pride in captured his attention.

"You're beautiful, Jett. It doesn't offend me to look at you like this."

"You might want to believe that. And speaking it sounds good to both you and me. But now that you've seen my true appearance, you'll never forget it." She sighed. "I am this thing, Savin."

"You are Jett." He reached to touch her horn, but she flinched away and he retracted his hand to his chest.

"I'm sorry," she said. "I didn't mean to hurt you."

"You didn't. Just zapped the strength out of me for a bit there. I know you were fighting her."

"She knows who I am," Jett said. "And she knows that I know who she is. I've subdued her, but she takes her strength from you. You are a strong and mighty man. She'll rise soon enough."

"I know. But I think the morphine kicked in. I know when it does. I feel her make a sort of giddy shiver. It's…weird."

"I'm so sorry you need to do that. You shouldn't have to."

"The drug used to affect me, but I've become immune to it over the years. Either that or she sucks it all up before it can even influence my system. I don't miss getting high, that's for sure."

"Have you tried to expel her?"

He nodded. "Yes, it won't work."

"But exorcists—"

"John Malcolm has tried to exorcise her. No go. And

I can't reckon her out of my own body. It's just not possible. And…well, some sacrifices aren't worth it. Like I've said, I've learned to live with her."

"But now you don't have to. If we can get her out of you and you can reckon her back to Daemonia, then I won't have a thing to worry about."

"That sounds great. In theory."

Jett lifted her head but remembered her horns. No matter what he said, she knew he could only ever see her as *not human* from now on. She swept her hands over her head and pulled on the sheen. Her body segued from tight and muscled to firm and pale skinned and the horns receded with an inward tug.

And Savin pulled her to him and kissed her, drawing her body against his and pressing into her as if they could become one. His mouth tasted her slowly, deeply. The feel of his body, so commanding and strong against hers, weakened her need for shame, to believe that he could not adore her. Dare she hope they could have a future together?

"That's how much you offend me," he said as he withdrew from the kiss. "I know that's what you were thinking. But don't waste your well-being on such thoughts. We're good."

His words brought tears to her eyes. "How can we be?"

"I know a lot about demons, and where you've come from. And I know you, as well. Oh, sweetie, don't cry."

She sniffed and wiped at a teardrop. "You only know the nine-year-old me. I've changed, Savin."

"Have you?"

"Of course, I—I've matured. I've changed! And I'm not an innocent."

"Never thought you were."

"I really do want to be human again. And oh, when you kiss me. Savin." She stepped out of his embrace and crossed her arms over her chest, immediately regretting the distance from him, but feeling she had to tell him her thoughts or risk losing him forever. "I've been with…others. It was a means to learn and experience— Well, I am a woman. I couldn't ignore my changing body or my growing desires."

His expression softened, but he didn't say anything.

"I thought that sex was what pleasure was. You know? It's what I received and I knew nothing else. But now. Here. With you. When you touch me and kiss me. Oh. I know now that what I had then was never true pleasure. Only you have shown me that. And when you look at me, I see in your eyes such honesty and…is it admiration?"

"It is, Jett. And I'm glad I've been able to make you feel good. But I wish when you looked in my eyes you could see that I trust you, too."

"Be honest, Savin. We stand on opposite sides. How can we each ever truly trust the other will work for our best interest?"

"You can trust me because I give you my word. I… wasn't able to protect you when we were kids. That kills me. And I've atoned for that ever since. But now? I will protect you, Jett. You have my word. And we'll find some way to send the Other back to Daemonia. I promise you."

She nodded, still not willing to completely trust him. He believed he could do such a thing, but was it possible? That be-damned conniving queen! She was to blame for all this. And all this time Fuum had hidden away inside Savin, him not being the wiser that he harbored the very demon who had irreversibly changed both their lives.

"I need to go meet with Ed," he said. "He and CJ have a tracking spell for the queen. Maybe it's time you come along and I introduce you?"

"So you can offer me as a sacrifice?"

"Never. I just want Ed to understand that you are no threat to any in this realm, and that our focus needs to be directed on the other queen."

"I am not a threat." Jett shivered and wrapped her arms across her chest. Was she? Every day she felt the darkness within her recede. And that was a good thing. Now to fight for her right to remain here, as a human. "If you think it will help, I'll come along. And if it's a trap, then so be it."

He kissed her. Hard. Then bowed his forehead to hers. "How do I make you trust me?"

"You earn it."

He nodded. "Then I will."

Chapter 25

When Jett and Savin walked through the door, Edamite Thrash turned abruptly from his position standing before the windows at the end of his vast, ultrasleek office. He pulled his hands from his trouser pockets, and his fingers flexed into claws.

Jett felt his gaze go right to her and she sensed his discomfort and recognition. She also recognized him as a fellow demon, but his vibrations were cool and quite different from what she was accustomed to. He was kind; she knew that. But also leery of her. He wore an aura of restrained power and she guessed he would not hesitate to wield it against any who betrayed him, or who had done wrong.

A corax demon, she knew, could shift to an unkindness of ravens and fly off, then shift back to human shape, clothing intact. The demonic sigils visible on his neck above the white dress shirt resembled a black raven's feather. As well, sigils decorated his hands, but most were covered by the half gloves that must conceal the thorns she knew grew on all corax demons' knuckles.

"Ed, I want you to meet Jett Montfort," Savin said as they stopped in the middle of the marble-floored office. He still held her hand, which provided her the added courage she required because she hadn't known what to expect from this visit. But now that she had read Edamite, she knew she could control him. If need be.

Ed crossed the room and shook Savin's hand, and then the demon with the slicked-back dark hair looked to Jett. He didn't extend his hand to shake, and his brows quirked. "Demon."

Savin nodded. "She's my friend. I've known her since we were kids."

Further consternation crimped Ed's brow.

"I need to catch you up on things," Savin said, "and I ask you to listen without judgment. I told CJ about her yesterday. I want you to have the same information."

Ed crossed his arms high on his chest. His eyes did not waver from Jett. And she held her gaze firm, yet softened it, not intending to throw out any defensive vibes. But she held her sheen on tight. For now.

Savin laid it all out. How Jett had escaped to the mortal realm that night when the rift to Daemonia opened. How she'd been staying with him since then, and how he'd just learned she had been their queen. A title she had assumed for survival, he made clear.

"She is not a threat to anyone in the mortal realm," Savin finished. "Nor to you or me."

Ed, who had taken to leaning against his desktop,

stood now and wandered to the marble-topped bar along the wall. He poured a shot of whiskey and drank it. Then he offered Savin a drink, but he refused. The corax demon let his gaze fall slowly over Jett. He didn't offer her a drink, but she wouldn't expect it, either. He didn't trust her.

If this man had taken it upon himself to protect Paris and police the local demon population, then he was doing a good thing for the humans. And it ultimately protected him and those demons who simply wanted to exist and not ruffle feathers. Without knowing her personally, Jett could only be a threat to him.

Unless she could prove otherwise. And she hadn't a clue how to do that.

Ed let out a hefty exhale and approached them. Now his demonic vibrations felt a bit stronger. Jett lifted her chin, forcing out her influence as a warning. The demon stopped and nodded, sensing her challenge.

"This fucks things up," he finally said.

Indeed.

"It doesn't have to," Savin said. "What if we can exorcise the demon from inside me and send her back in Jett's place?"

Savin had also told Ed that she recognized the Other as the former queen, Fuum.

Ed nodded, finger to his lips in thought. "Possibly. But I thought—"

"Yeah. Exorcism is out. How easily I forget that." Savin now walked over to the bar and poured himself that shot of whiskey. After tilting it back, he turned to Jett and silently inquired if she wanted any. She shook her head. "So that's what we've got to work with right now."

"A mess?" Ed posited.

Savin shrugged and poured another two fingers, quickly making work of the amber liquid.

Should she sacrifice and go back to Daemonia? It was the sure way to close the rift. And as Ed had mentioned, humans were beginning to notice the outflow from that realm. Possessions were occurring frequently. The news media were reporting exorcisms on the rise. And in Paris specifically. They could not let the rift remain unclosed for much longer.

But she didn't suggest she be the sacrificial lamb. She desperately did not want that to happen.

"How can we get Fuum out of you?" Jett finally asked Savin. "There must be a way, beyond exorcism. The dark witch might know a way."

"I've talked with him about it." Savin poured another shot. "There is a way. And you know it." He and Ed exchanged glances that Jett could not read. They knew something they were not telling her.

"What is it?" she asked. "If you need my help…"

"There is one way to scrub the demon out of Savin," Ed offered. "And that requires his death."

Jett tugged Savin's hand, forcing him to turn and look at her. "Is that true?"

Savin shrugged noncommittally.

Ed said again, "Yes, it is true. He's gone over this with Certainly Jones. Years ago, the witch found an expulsion spell for Savin's situation, but it'll kill Savin to remove the demon within. And now I figure it is because she was once a queen. Very powerful. I assume she's been able to root into him."

"It's nothing," Savin said to Jett, and he looked away.

But Jett wasn't about to let him dismiss it so casually. "It's not nothing. It is your life."

"Sending the Other back to Daemonia will close up the rift and save you," he said.

Jett dropped his hand and crossed her arms. "There will be no sacrificing of one's life today."

"Then we'll do it tomorrow," Savin said coolly.

"I'm not going to let you do that," Ed said. "There's got to be another way to get that bitch out of you, Thorne. And I'm siding with your girlfriend. No sacrifices."

"Yet you would sacrifice me," Jett said defiantly to the corax demon.

His smirk was more evil than he might have wanted to display. "I don't know you enough to trust you. And you *are* their current queen."

"What if I can find a replacement? Such as the one inside Savin did with me? As long as there is a queen to sit the throne, then that legion in Daemonia should be appeased."

Ed shrugged. "There is a time element here. Your kind are flooding the mortal realm."

"My kind? They are your kind, too, Edamite Thrash. More so, because I assume you are full demon. I am not. Do you forget that?" She beat her fist against her chest. "Half of me is human. And I can feel my demon side growing weaker every day."

Ed approached her, hand out and palm facing her. Jett backed up, and when her shoulder nudged Savin, he put an arm around her waist and held her protectively.

"We're not going to sacrifice Jett, either," he said to Ed. "What are you doing?"

"I'm just trying to get a read on her." The demon did not relent.

And so Jett would give him what he wanted. She

pulled out of Savin's grip and pressed both her palms to Ed's temples, forming a connection that would open them both to each other. She saw his life, his triumphs and failures. His love—he loved a beautiful witch. And she touched his raven core that squawked and beat its wings frantically at her unwelcome invasion.

At the same time, she gave him her truth. Her fall into the lava, which had burned and iced at the same time. Her hurried and bewildered ascension to the throne, and her desperate need to do as she was told for survival. She showed her ability to put a vile demon to heel, her ease at reading all others and her unrelenting power.

When finally Ed was able to push away from her, he stumbled backward, catching himself against the desktop.

"What did you do to him?" Savin asked.

"I gave him my truth. And I showed him who his queen really is."

"You are never my queen," Ed said with a sneer. "I am not from Daemonia. They are all…filth." Jett lunged, but Savin caught her about the waist. "But…you are right," Ed continued. "Your human half is growing more prominent. Should we send you back to Daemonia now, you may not—"

"It's not happening," Savin interrupted. "Jett stays in this realm. Done deal. So let's come up with another plan."

Ed eyed Jett and she saw in his eyes defeat and a reluctant submission. He nodded. "Yes, another plan. CJ should be here by now. He mentioned tracking the queen. But if we know where both are…?"

Savin rubbed his chest. "Right. Hmm…"

"What if there is another?" Jett suggested.

"How many queens are there?" Savin asked.

She shrugged. "I don't know. How many queens does the world have? Many, yes? Fuum and I cannot be the only ones."

"I believe the specific queen for your Daemonian legion is the fix," Ed said. "There's CJ."

The glass office doors opened and Certainly Jones strode in. He took one look at Jett and slashed his hand before him. The sigils on his left hand glowed a bold emerald.

The repulsion spell pushed Jett off her feet and she landed in Savin's arms.

"CJ, this is Jett!" Savin said as he helped her to her feet. He charged toward the witch, who held his ground with palm extended and wards glowing. "Stand down!"

The dark witch thrust a glinting green hex toward Jett. She managed to dodge it and put up her palm in retaliation.

Ed called, "No! You cannot practice your demonic magic inside my wards!"

A second round of hex from the witch was this time caught by Savin, right on the chest, as he jumped to stand before Jett. Savin yelped and clutched his stinging chest.

The witch swore and reversed the spell, drawing back the magic into his hand, where he crumpled the hex and dropped it over a shoulder.

"What the hell? She's not going to harm anyone," Savin insisted. "Man, that hex hurt! Jett, stay by me." She clutched his hand, but he could feel her rage in the tight grip. "Settle," he cautioned her quietly.

"He was going to hex me!" she protested.

"Sorry. I may have rushed to a conclusion—" CJ started.

"This is ridiculous." Jett tore her hand from his grip and marched past the witch toward the door. "I am out of here!"

Savin took a step after her but then stopped. She needed to get out of here, away from the wicked energy of the lingering hex. One that still burned in his lungs. Whew! He glared at CJ.

The witch shrugged. "I didn't realize it was *your* Jett. It would have only shackled her, had you not taken the brunt."

"The brunt." Savin pressed his fingers to his chest and winced. All in all? That had been a mere tap. "You're slipping, witch. Didn't even knock me off my feet."

"It wasn't designed to—" CJ silenced himself with another glare from Savin.

"I told her she could trust the two of you," Savin said. "Good going. Now we've a Daemonian queen wandering the streets of Paris. And I'm going to wager she's pissed."

Jett charged across the street and raced blindly forward. Sure, Savin had tried to protect her. Feebly. The dark witch had actually blasted a stream of magic at her! What kind of hello, how are you, had that been?

She'd trusted Savin. Had he walked her into a trap?

Much as her darkness cajoled her to believe just that, Jett fought to remain on Savin's side. He'd been just as surprised as she when the witch walked in with hell blazing in his eyes.

She'd had to get away from them all. They needed to send a queen back to Daemonia to end the influx of demons into this realm, and she was an easy target.

Yet they had another option. The demoness who clung to Savin's soul. If he had so many friends like witches and other demons, surely between them they could figure a way to oust Fuum from Savin's body and send her back. It couldn't be that difficult to accomplish for men who were demon, or as a reckoner whose sole task required him to have an intimate knowledge of demons.

However, to do it without killing Savin was key. She didn't want that. Never.

Shoving roughly past a man talking on a cell phone, Jett sneered when he flipped her off. If he only knew how easily she could take away his voice.

Should she?

She paused at a red light and turned back to listen to the man who walked a circle on the sidewalk. Some kind of business chatter about stocks peaking. To buy or sell? He talked so loudly. Was he not aware that everyone could hear him? Did no one respect personal boundaries anymore?

Jett muttered a few words that began a spell, but the laughter of children interrupted her. Two kids, probably around ten years old, ran down the sidewalk with kites in hand. The moment curled into her chest and lessened her anger. The darkness receded and she turned to face the crossing. The light was green. She crossed without concern for the noisy businessman.

Turning down a narrow alleyway, she rubbed her palms over her arms, whisking away the tension. A walk in the fresh air was what she needed. A few raindrops splattered her cheeks and she actually smiled. Yes, she really did want to exist in this realm. And to do so, she had to get control over her darkness.

Or find a way to remove it from her completely. Could the dark witch help with that? No, she didn't trust him as far as she could spit.

A left turn and then another left lured her close to the scent of a river. She wasn't near the Seine, but she remembered a canal that jutted out from the river on the right bank where she walked. Had to be close.

The sudden sensation of another nearby—demon— slowed her pace. No. She didn't care. She must not. Let them be wary of her. If they were smart.

Venturing forward, she heard voices and slowed. Now the shiver of recognition shook her shoulders. A demon was just around the corner. He was powerful and…speaking to a human, if she guessed right. His sensual voice and promising words would appeal to any woman who wanted to be praised for her beauty.

Darkness rising, Jett tightened her fist. "There is only room for me in this realm." She rushed around the corner.

The human woman saw her and fled. And having lost his prey, the demon, who sported long dark dreadlocks and a furrowed brow, turned to growl at her. Fangs lowered and glinted. And when Jett sensed he would lunge for her, instead the demon cracked a smile and shook his head.

"It's about fucking time," he said. "You, my lovely bastard child, have been very naughty."

Chapter 26

Arms held slightly away from her body and fingers curled to ready as weapons, Jett walked a tight half curve about the demon who had just called her naughty. And…his child. Her entire body was tight and ready to defend. Yet as she took in the demon's arrogant grin and assessing gaze, she saw so many similarities between the two of them. Her breath left her in a hush.

"I heard you'd come to the mortal realm," he said, propping a hip against the brick wall and assuming a cocky pose before her.

He was lanky and his wrists were wrapped with leather straps and buckles. His arms, revealed by a sleeveless shirt, were blackened with so many tattoos Jett could not determine where one sigil began and another, possibly a skull design, ended. His hair was as dark as hers. And his nose long and…so much like hers. Eyes glowed red now that the human had fled. Jett could not determine if they had been brown, like hers. The one thing that drew her interest the longest was the glowing sigil between his brows that formed a symbol denoting his rank and heritage. Only demons of royal birth wore such, in various places on their bodies.

Jett absently touched her hip, where beneath the silk shirt a sigil to match the one on the man's forehead heated and glowed.

He noticed and nodded. "Yep, it's me. Daddy dearest! Sorry I didn't stick around for all that child-birthing stuff. Cramped my style. But look what I did for you. A queen! And then you flee the throne, you ungrateful bitch."

Jett lashed out and slapped his cheek, dragging her fingernails across the human skin he wore. Dark runnels of blackest blood oozed down his cheek, and she wiped the thick substance from her nails across her pants.

"Ah, that's sweet." He lashed out a very long tongue, licking away the blood even as the slashes healed. "So, you going to speak to me, or do I have to narrate this little tête-à-tête? One way or another, it's going to end with me kicking your ass back to Daemonia where you belong."

"I do not belong in the Place of All Demons," Jett hissed. Her body shivered, and she knew it was nerves, and fear. She mustn't cower before this vile man, father or not. She lifted her chin, assuming the regal mien she had grown to accept. "How dare you speak to me with such disrespect!"

The demon laughed in a low rumble and shook his

head. "Fair enough. My girl knows how to play the queen, that's for sure."

"I am not your girl."

"Beg to differ, Jettendra. You've got my blood in your veins."

"And who else's? Did you rape a frightened human woman? Is that how I was conceived?"

He swiped a dismissive hand between them. "Rape is boring. I prefer seduction. And…" He blew out a breath. "I don't remember them all."

"You are despicable."

She stood before her demon father. And she had never felt more repulsed. Not even in the twenty years she had lived in Daemonia. He was vile and idiotic and— Hell, *this* was her father?

The demon held out his hand to shake. "Drav," he offered. "Seventh underlord of the clan Tratch."

Tratch. Yes. That was the legion she had ruled.

Jett considered his hand, and when she did not shake, he grabbed her arm and pulled her to him, chest to chest. His gaze held her speechless, and…she had not felt so helpless since that day she was tossed into the falls and taken to the throne.

"That's right," he said. "You grew to become a powerful half-breed, but you'll never be full demon like Daddy. Cocky is good. But you watch yourself, youngling. I can eviscerate you with a sweep of my hand. But I won't." He shoved her away from him. "Because we are going to get you on your way back to Daemonia so whoever is in charge can seal that damned rift and keep all the deplorables out of my territory."

His territory? Jett guessed Edamite Thrash might have qualms about such a bold statement.

"No one is going anywhere until I have the answers to the questions that have haunted me for years," Jett said. "And you may wish to believe you are stronger than me…but I have a reckoner on my side."

Drav mocked a shudder, which shook his dreads. "Yeah, I noticed. Disgusting. Why the hell did you hook up with him?"

"I don't owe you any details regarding my love life."

"Ah. It's a love life, is it? So you've fucked him. That is some kind of ill shit. Cripes. But hey, just means you're as fucked-up as your daddy. Good going!"

"Who are you?" Jett insisted, because she wasn't certain she could endure standing in the demon's presence for much longer without flaying him to a heap of demonic sludge. "Royalty? Why are you not in Daemonia sitting the throne yourself? And why me? Why kidnap an innocent child and force her to such servitude?"

"Servitude?" His laughter sounded like stones clacking against wood. Jett clenched her fists. "You were treated like the queen they made you, sweetie. Don't deny it."

"I was stolen from a safe home in the mortal realm and forced to another land to learn ways unfamiliar to me. I was a frightened child! They insisted I breed for them! I barely escaped becoming a broodmare."

"Yeah. Well. Had to be done. Fuum was getting antsy."

Jett gripped her father by the throat and squeezed. She pushed some of her influence in through his skin, and she could feel his skeletal structure shudder. "Fuum?"

"You are good at exerting influence," he managed

through his compressed trachea. "Pain gets me off, sweetie."

Jett shoved him away from her, and his shoulders hit the wall so hard the brick cracked. The demon slipped on that malicious grin again and clapped slowly as he nodded in appreciation for her display of power.

"Enough with the dramatics," Jett said. "Tell me about you and Fuum."

Drav exhaled, his shoulders dropping. "Fine. We'll get the catching-up shit out of the way, and then down to the real nitty-gritty. Fuum. The worm bitch. I was having a fling with her at the time—"

"In Daemonia?"

"Sure. I used to go back and forth between realms all the time. The advantages of being born into legion governance. As a Tratch I was privileged and have always had the ability to move from one realm to the other at will. But you know that. You didn't need any special release to get here. You just had to wait for the right moment, eh?" He winked.

Jett sneered at him.

"Right. So we were getting it on, and Fuum wanted to come to this realm, and I was willing to help her. The best way to do that? Replace her seat at the throne with another queen."

"But I was not a queen," Jett protested.

Drav swiped a finger over a lingering trace of black blood on his cheek and showed it to her. "You had the royal blood, sweetie. And I had the influence. So I searched for my by-blow—uh, that would be you. You were an easy find."

"Your— How many half-blood children do you have?"

"Truth? Not a hell of a lot. Surprising, considering my frequent copulation habits—"

Jett put up an admonishing palm between them. "Just stick to the details."

"Right. I located my daughter who had been adopted because, well, your mom didn't survive the birth. That's kind of a side effect of having a demon's baby, if you're a human. Can't be avoided. Anyhoo. I found you and had you brought to Daemonia. Stupid little boy got taken along with you, though. That wasn't part of the plan. But then again, he did serve Fuum as a vessel to get to this realm. All in all, it worked out swell."

"I hate you."

"Yeah? That feels so good." He slid a palm over his chest, and Jett could not look at him any longer.

She turned away, crossing her arms and sighting the nearby canal. Moonlight glinted on the water. Silver and clean and not at all like anything in Daemonia. She had never expected to meet her father. And she would never have guessed it would go down like this. What an utter asshole.

"I heard that," he said. "I'm good at picking up thoughts from my blood kin. Asshole. Idiot. Whatever you want to call me, I'm still your daddy."

And here she had been troubled to learn she was adopted? Not anymore. Josette and Charles Montfort had been the best, and only, parents she'd ever had.

"Why didn't Fuum leave Savin's body after they arrived in this realm?" she asked.

"That was the annoying glitch to the whole plan. Bitch tricked me. She didn't really want to come here and set up house with me. She just wanted a ticket out of Daemonia, so she used me to get you to sit the throne. Grabbed the boy and headed off on her own sweet way."

"She dumped you?"

Drav shrugged. "No big loss. Hey, I got to claim a daughter as a queen out of it. Do you know the privileges that grants me now? Man! I can waltz into Daemonia with armloads of illegal morphine and toss it around like candy and no one is going to stop me, the queen's father." He lifted his chin and pressed a hand to his chest. The entitled mien did not look half as good on him as it did on her.

"How come you never visited me the entire time I was there?" Jett asked. "I should think you'd have a care to thank the one who gave you such privileges."

"I'm not into family reunions."

"You're lying."

"And you can read thoughts, too."

So she could. Must be the family blood. Ugh. Jett did not want to know what was going on in the man's mind.

"I never visited because I didn't want to get tangled up in the royal mumbo-jumbo stuff. If they had inducted me into your court, I would have been stuck there."

"Just like me?"

"Oh, come on, enough with the pity parade. I don't care what your reason for leaving the place was. You needed a vacation? Fine. You've had it. Beautiful Paris. Rendezvousing with your lover. A reckoner. Really?" He again dismissed the statement with a sweep of his hand. "Whatever. Women always have such strange taste in men. Now it's time to skip back to the throne and be a good little queen for our legion."

"So Daddy's privileges will not be revoked?"

"You got it, sweetie."

Jett thrust out her hand, forcing a vile hex at her father. It slammed him into the brick, this time fitting his body into the hard structure in a spume of dust and painful growls.

"I am not your sweetie." Jett turned and walked toward the canal.

As far as meeting the father for the first time went, she'd mark that one as Avoid All Future Contact. Now she was walking away from him. For good.

When an arm hooked about her neck from behind and her throat constricted, she instinctively bent forward in an attempt to toss off the attack. But Drav clung to her, and everywhere his fingers touched her skin, she felt his wicked influence seep inside and begin to take control.

Savin walked the streets for hours. This time he was not going home without Jett. The sun had set and the sky was dark, for the moon was new and no stars could ever breach the illumination of Paris. He'd held such intense focus during his walk, senses focused toward any demon he neared, that his temples now ached with a burgeoning headache.

He stopped by the steel guardrail that edged a stairway leading down to the canal. He picked up vibrations from a few demons in the distance, but none felt familiar to him. Not that he'd ever detected Jett. And why was that? Why could he not know—had he never known?—what she was?

Was it because it was better that way? Better for his heart and soul. No matter what makeup she now was, she would always be his girl. And if that meant he had to love a half demon, then he was in for the fall.

When he heard a sniffle below near a patio edging the canal, Savin looked over the balustrade. And saw the lush black hair that glittered without moonlight. Because she always shone to him.

"Jett!"

He rushed down to the patio and she turned and plunged into his arms. He kissed the crown of her head and felt an instant release of the head pain as her warmth melded against his. It never felt wrong to hold her.

"I'm glad I found you," he said. She nestled against his chest, silent save for tears. "I had no idea CJ was going to react that way. I'm sorry."

She didn't speak, only clung to him tighter.

"I love you, Jett."

She nodded against his chest. "I… I wasn't trying to hurt him. Maybe…maybe I was."

"Huh? Jett?"

Then Savin noticed the dark figure sprawled at the edge of the canal, his head tilted back and long dreadlocks swept by the water. His mouth was open and black blood drooled out into the water.

"What happened? Demon?" Savin asked.

Jett nodded against his chest. She tucked herself up even tighter against him and he wrapped his arms across her back. Much as he wanted to inspect the body, he wanted even more to hold Jett.

"He tried to hurt you?"

She nodded.

"I'm sorry I wasn't here for you. Damn it," he swore softly. "I can never seem to be in the right place when you need me most."

And that fact hurt him more deeply than anything ever had. Even the sour looks his father had given him or the vile interactions he'd had over the years with those demons he'd reckoned couldn't match the utter devastation at not being able to protect Jett.

"His name was Drav," she said, and lifted her head to meet his gaze in the darkness. "He was my demon father."

Savin didn't know what to say. How could she know that? Had he come looking for her? Had she sought him? What was going on?

"He told me everything. And then he insisted I return to Daemonia. He was going to take me there at any cost. And... I almost fell victim to his influence. But you know, men are men, no matter their form and physicality."

Savin wasn't sure what she meant.

"I kicked him in the crotch and that bought me the few seconds I needed to pull up everything I had within me. I ripped out his heart and tossed it in the canal."

A matter-of-fact recitation of a truly nasty encounter. Yet Savin was only glad she had triumphed. He kissed her forehead and tasted her sweetness.

"I don't want the darkness to win," she whispered. "Help me?"

"Always. Come on, I'm taking you home."

They stood and, upon considering Drav's body for a moment, Jett suggested Savin shove it into the canal. The demon would decay quickly and become but a thick sludge in less than a day. It was the way of those born completely demonic. Death in the mortal realm did that to their bodies.

They walked hand in hand in silence. No words were necessary. Savin understood she was helpless regarding the demon inside her. Her darkness? Now that her greatest threat had been extinguished—the father who wanted to send her back to Daemonia—he would do what he could to help her rise above the demon she still wore within her. He'd read all the books, master all the spells, even consult witches, wizards or warlocks, if that was what it took to save Jett from her darkness.

At his place, he took down the wards and then left them down after he'd closed the front door. He knew it drained her to have them activated. He'd risk it for tonight.

Jett wandered quietly into the bedroom and pulled off her clothes. Savin stood by the wall, watching as she undressed. With no moonlight sifting through the clouds, shades of gray filled the room, but he saw the shape of her against the bedclothes. So beautiful. A match to the darkness he held within his soul?

When she turned and held out her hand to him, that was the only invite he needed. Savin pulled off his shirt and unbuttoned his jeans. He crawled onto the bed and kissed her.

Chapter 27

The next afternoon, Jett walked into the living room, which resounded with acoustic guitar music. Savin did not play the diddley bow, thank whatever gods for that. Instead, it was a classical piece that featured rapid arpeggios and some high notes that sang to her inner desire for all things beautiful. She lingered by the wooden support beam, not wanting to interrupt and hoping he'd continue through to the end.

He was a dichotomy of dark and light. As was she? Perhaps. But did their opposing sides balance each other out when needed? Or when they were both at their darkest, would they be hell to deal with? Maybe that was what was required to see this current situation to a resolution? Both mining their darkest powers to fight it back?

It was an idea. But she wasn't sure Savin would get

behind it. She had exercised her greatest skills last night to defeat Drav. So easy to rip out a demon's heart. To hold it in her palm and feel the beats that had given her life. That had marked her as not completely human. An outcast in the mortal realm. She hated him for that, for his callous decision to use her as a means to get Fuum out of Daemonia. And for what? Fuum had ditched him immediately and remained in Savin. And Drav had walked away. Just another failed romance.

Jett closed her eyes. She had been a pawn. Who had risen to queen.

She did not want that. She wished to shuck any part of Drav from her body and bones. This morning she felt the exertion as an all-over muscle ache. Every day she grew…lesser. The sheen was getting easier to keep up because… Was she losing the demon inside her? There was less and less to hide now.

The music ended abruptly. "Didn't see you standing there."

"I didn't want you to stop," Jett said. "It's beautiful."

"Some Scarlatti. I like the classic stuff as much as the blues."

"I remember you started taking guitar lessons that summer before we…" She didn't need to finish that sentence. "You wanted to be a rock star."

Savin set the guitar aside and patted the couch beside him. Jett joined him and he wrapped an arm around her shoulders and brought her in to hug against his chest. "Doesn't every kid want to be a rock star?"

"I don't remember what I wanted to be."

"A nurse," Savin said easily. "Don't you recall all those times you'd bandage my wounds after our adventures? And that time I actually broke my arm?"

"Oh hell, I do remember that now. Your mother was so freaked that I'd splinted your arm with branches and your torn T-shirt."

"I think the emergency room doctor was impressed. I was."

She snuggled her head against his chest and listened to his calm heartbeat.

"How are you today, Jett? After…last night."

"I'm tired, but not upset. It was either him or me."

"I know that. You did what you had to do." He kissed the crown of her head. "I think I've always loved you, Jett."

She closed her eyes, letting the words flow in, but a little unsure how to process the confession.

"You're my friend, my confidante," he said. "My partner in adventure. You know me."

"I *knew* you," she clarified. "We used to be those things, Savin. And…much as I would like to continue the way we once were…can that be so?"

"We just have to get through this mess with the open rift and the queen," he said. "Then it can be. If you want it to be."

"I do. I mean, I think I do. I'm not sure I know what love is."

"You loved your parents. You loved that mangy cat that used to hiss at me every time I'd come over."

"Oh, Snoodles! I forgot about him." Memory of that ginger cat dashing up and down the carpeted stairs after a piece of string warmed her heart. "I really did love that stupid cat. He hated you."

"I put up with the scratches because I wanted to be near you. I didn't know it when I was a kid, but you were my world, Jett. And it feels like now you've stepped back into my world for a reason."

"What if that reason is to challenge you? To make you stand up to the darkness I am and send me away?"

He sighed and hugged her tighter. "I hope not. I really hope not. But if anything were to happen to me, just know that I love you. From my heart. In every way possible."

She pressed her lips to his hand and kissed it. She didn't know how to say she loved him. Wished she did. But for some reason the word didn't feel right. It could be her darkness. It could simply be that she had so much learning and growing yet to do.

"Do you remember when we would sing?" she asked.

Savin chuckled. "Oh yeah. All those Saturday-morning-cartoon songs? Ha! We knew every single one."

"And we'd sing them at the top of our lungs while perched in the massive oak tree in your backyard."

"Those were good times."

"Savin." Jett swallowed and lifted her chin to meet his gaze. "Those songs kept me alive. When I needed to not lose hope and remember that I was human and that I might someday escape the terrible place, I'd sing one of those songs. Only in my thoughts, mind you. But I'd hear your voice singing along with me. You were always there with me."

He bowed over her and hugged her tightly. And Jett thought she heard him sniff at a tear. Her heart warmed and she clung to her sexy lover. She never wanted to let him go. His heartbeats buoyed her. Maybe she did love him.

Jett sat before the laptop computer that Savin had placed on the kitchen counter and inspected the screen.

After his mother had refused to help with further liaising between Jett and her mother, she did forward Josette's email address to Savin. He'd sent Josette an email stating he had some information about Jett, and Josette Montfort had replied with a desperate plea to learn more.

So now Savin suggested she send her a letter online. This email program would enable her to write to her and send it. Her mother would have the letter as soon as she clicked Send. And then it was in her hands to reply or not.

Heartbeat thudding, Jett closed her eyes. She needed this to erase the lingering foulness of meeting her demon father from her very soul.

Savin leaned in and kissed her on the cheek. "I know. Give it some thought. You don't have to tell her all the details."

"I can't lie or make something up. You said you told them we were kidnapped by humans?"

"That's what I decided I needed to tell the police and our parents so they wouldn't think I was crazy. Later I told my mom the truth."

"But my mother only knows that original lie?"

"Yes."

So she must have concluded that her daughter was harmed, maybe even abused or tortured, and very likely dead by the hands of cruel humans. What a terrible mis-truth to have to live with. Yet it had been twenty years. Surely, her heart had healed and she had moved on. "I don't know how to do this."

"Maybe just start with a hello. I'm going to head out and scavenge up some food. Give you some time to yourself. When you're done typing what you want to say, just hit the send button and then I've shown you how to close the program."

She nodded. Her fingers shook over the keyboard, so she pressed her hands together and tucked them between her legs. "Thanks, Savin. Pick me up something sweet?"

"You always were a sugar freak."

That made her smile. Would they ever get back to the way they were twenty years ago? She didn't want that childhood friendship anymore. She wanted them as adults, in love and sharing their lives. And he'd said he loved her.

Did she—*could* she—love Savin Thorne?

The front door closed behind him. And she missed him already.

He'd lied to Jett. He would pick up something to eat. But first a detour was in order. There were things he needed to take care of. Much as every mile he drove farther from Jett killed him, Savin pressed onward until he arrived at the field where it had all begun.

Savin walked out into the field beneath the rift. A man couldn't see the tear between the two realms, but he felt it. The air was still. Quiet. He didn't sense any demons lurking or coming through. But it wouldn't remain so for long. The afternoon was growing into evening. He'd left Jett before the laptop, knowing she needed some time alone for such a momentous thing as contacting her mother. He didn't know how to help her with that. It had been difficult for him, as a ten-year-old, navigating his own return and concocting the story about being kidnapped.

Yet here he stood. He'd survived and thrived. And

he'd walked a path he hadn't chosen but had been led toward. Never would he have purposely sought to reckon demons. But really, what other choice had he? And he did the job well. But he didn't take pride in it. It was just the thing he did. To survive. To move along with life. To exist.

Just as Jett had done for so long.

Was there something else out there for him? Could he have a real life? What was that to him?

Family was the first word that popped into his brain. Yet the image of green grass, a picket fence, a puppy and a backyard swing set replete with one or two children made him shake his head. A foolish notion. Who was he to believe he could father a child and take care of it and teach it morals and values when the only example that child would have was a man who sensed, talked to and reckoned demons?

No life for a child. Nor for a wife who just wanted to be normal. Because a wife was necessary for a child. Savin had never looked at a woman in such a manner as future wife potential. He had promised Jett when they were kids they'd get married. Stupid kid stuff. But…not really. He'd meant it last night when he told Jett he loved her. Now, as she was. As the person—part demon—she had become. He could imagine spending his life with her. They got each other. And they each had secrets that only the other could understand. She fit him.

But there was only one way to keep her safe in this mortal realm. And that decision suddenly became less tough than it had been years ago when he first learned the only way to get the Other out of him. He knew what he had to do. And he would do it for the woman he loved. Because if he couldn't have the picket fence, she deserved a chance to live as a human and to have that opportunity at building a family.

Behind him, a white hearse pulled onto the grassy off road and parked. He'd asked Certainly Jones to meet him out here. Meeting at the Archives only raised red flags. And he knew the director of Acquisitions, Ethan Pierce, would question him if he got wind of his frequent visits. He didn't want to make trouble for anyone. As well, CJ had wanted to check out the rift.

The witch wandered over, his tall, lithe figure moving the air with a wicked vibe. Always dressed in black, and that long black hair and so many spell tattoos marked him as the dark witch he was. Savin did not fear him. Yet, much as he didn't trust witches, he respected CJ's power. Always good to have such an ally.

On the other hand, the witch was on his list after yesterday's fiasco in Thrash's office.

"Surprised you contacted me," CJ said as he approached.

"You're the only witch I trust. And that's a tough one to admit after what you did to Jett."

"I apologized. I reacted. I do shit like that sometimes."

"Yeah." Savin heaved out a sigh. Didn't they all?

CJ handed Savin a corked glass vial sealed with black wax. Savin sniffed the seal and jerked away from the vile smell.

"You don't smell it," CJ said. "You drink it. Preferably fast. Or it'll come back up on you." He dug out a folded paper from his coat pocket. "This is the incantation. But, Savin." He laid a hand over Savin's, enclosing the paper between the two of them. "Give me a few more days, will you? There's got to be a better way. I can find the answer in the Archives."

"I asked you about this years ago, CJ, and you looked then. What's changed?"

"Maybe my determination? There's a hell of a lot of information to go through in the demon room. My search last time wasn't focused, or as motivated as it is now. You know what enacting this spell means. I am only giving you this stuff because I also know what it can do on the other side. Sealing this rift is paramount."

As if on cue, a sudden flash in the sky spit out a black cloud. Both Savin and CJ ducked to avoid the onslaught. And while the dark witch called out a Latin incantation and cast a hex into the air, the demons escaping into the mortal realm seemed oblivious, quickly spiriting away from where the men stood.

The sight left Savin with a foul taste in his mouth. "I'll give you one more day. But I've seen the news reports. The demons are growing bolder. We'll have a disaster on our hands sooner rather than later."

"Ed and I are doing our best."

"I intend to, as well." Savin stuffed the vial and paper in his coat pocket. "Thanks, CJ. Can I ask you another favor?"

"Always."

The witch walked closer to the edge of the field and Savin followed, standing side by side with him. They looked out over the twilight, which cast purple and red across the tree-jagged horizon.

Savin swallowed but then summoned the courage required. "If all goes as it should in a couple days…promise me you'll keep an eye out for Jett. I've already called the bank and had her name placed on my accounts. She now owns everything I own. I wouldn't have it any other way. But she needs guidance. The demon she still wears is power-hungry and, well—"

"I got it," CJ said. "Will do. Promise." He held out a fist and Savin met it with a bump of his own fist. "But it's not going to come to that," CJ added. "I hope."

Savin wanted to have as much hope, but he could not stand by and idly wish for the best. He'd made plans and was ensuring Jett's security. Now to let the chips fall where they may.

Chapter 28

Savin sorted out the takeaway meal on the kitchen counter. Jett, looking gorgeous in a soft, floaty red dress that resembled something a woman would wear to a wedding, climbed onto a bar stool, knelt and watched him.

"You going dancing?" he asked.

"No. I love this color and I wanted to look nice for you when you got home."

"You always look nice. I can't imagine you looking un-nice."

"What about with horns and gray skin?"

"Still pretty."

"Liar." She picked up a fork and tested the peppered potatoes, sans salt, at his request to the chef.

"Nope. Not lying. Did you send an email to your mom?"

"I did. I told her I was in Paris. Didn't know how to tell her what I've been up to the past twenty years, though. I mentioned you'd taken me in and I've been relying on you for strength. I asked her if we could exchange emails to get to know each other again. She hasn't replied."

"It's only been a few hours."

Jett bowed her head and stabbed her food.

"It could take days for her to find the email," Savin encouraged. "Some people don't check their account that often. It'll be okay." He kissed her, then sat beside her. "So tonight is for seduction, eh?"

"Why do you say that? Because I'm in a red dress?"

"Yes. Red wilds me, Jett. Especially when it's on you."

"It does? Like a bull?"

"You'll have to find out for yourself."

They exchanged winks, and that made getting through supper all the harder for Savin. Because if his plans went well, then there would be very few teasing winks they would again share.

After dinner, Jett picked up the acoustic guitar from where he'd set it beside the couch and held it out to Savin. "Will you play for me? I want to dance."

"Yeah? I might have some dance music in me." He took the guitar and sat on the couch. Anything to keep his mind from impending doom, right? Strumming a few chords, using the *rasgueado* flamenco technique he'd once tried to master, Savin lit into a slow E minor run.

"I recognize that," Jett said as she twirled before him. "You and your mother used to listen to it when we were kids."

"This is like soul stuff."

"It's what the Spanish ladies dance to. Your mother used to do a dance for us, if I recall. Yes?" She stretched up an arm and performed a delicate wrist curl and then stomped her feet. "So the bull is rising already, eh?" She winked and turned, doing her best impression of a flamenco dancer.

Indeed the bull inside him, if there was one, pawed at the ground, wanting more. More Jett, always Jett, stop the world and make this moment last forever. Savin strummed a series of chords and slapped the guitar body in punctuation of the call to a free-spirited dance. He'd never been to Spain, but he'd love to visit.

That dream was now dead. As were all other dreams. The only one he had left danced before him, laughing as she bowed to him in a graceful denouement.

"Let's go to Spain," he said suddenly, setting the guitar aside.

Jett climbed onto his lap, straddling and kissing him. The floaty red material brushed his skin in a sensual tease. "You mean it?"

He did. But his heart had been speaking much faster than his brain could race to stop it. And suddenly Savin couldn't hold it all in any longer. He kissed Jett deeply, longingly, tempering his need to take her swiftly and wildly. He wanted to know her beyond the intimacy they'd shared. He needed to know her soul deep. Could he have that?

"I wish we could get married." He spilled out his heart. "I wish I could get you pregnant, over and over, and we'd raise a brood, living in a sweet little place out in the country. I wish for so much, Jett."

"Why can't we make those wishes come true? I'm in."

"You are? You know that's not possible. As long as the Other lives inside me..."

Jett met his protest with another kiss. This one burned against his mouth in the sweetest way. He wanted her to mark him so he would forever taste her on his lips and on his tongue and in his heart. She already lived there, deep inside him, and had carved out a niche much deeper than any wicked, demonic former queen ever could.

Jett he wanted to keep inside him. To never lose.

Was he giving up too easily? Perhaps he should give CJ those few extra days he requested? If it would see him and Jett fulfilling the wild wishes of his—

A knock at his front door startled Jett to stand upright, alert. Savin wasn't expecting anyone. It could be CJ or Ed. But neither made it a habit of visiting.

When he stood, Jett put up her hand to stay him.

"What is it?" he asked. Inside him, the demoness clenched at his spine and twisted. Savin winced, clutching his gut at the strange need to fold over on himself. "It's vile," he gasped. "A demon?"

"We'll not open that door," Jett said firmly. "Are all your wards up?"

He'd forgotten to put them back up after coming in with the food. And he'd been leaving them low since learning they weakened Jett. He shook his head.

"You've got to pull them up and strengthen them," she said.

"But they'll hurt you."

"I'll survive. But you won't if we don't keep whatever is out there out."

Jett stood by as Savin grabbed one of the demonic devices from the bedroom. He set to twisting the dials and brass knobs that would turn up the juice, so to speak, on his house wards. With every twist, she felt the repulsive vibrations tweak at her nervous system. It tightened her jaw. Her fingers curled into fists. But she breathed through it and summoned her queen to rise above it. She stood inside the protective wards, so they could do no more than keep her inside. Yet she wouldn't be able to help Savin in any way.

"Done," Savin finally announced. "Shit, Jett, you're in pain."

He bowed over her where she sat on the floor, back against the couch and hands splayed beside her. He caressed her head and studied her gaze. Such gentility in her protector. She loved him. Truly, she always had. And she wanted what he desired, to marry him and have children and live out on a quiet little country cottage.

But it seemed the only way to solve the problem was for one or the other of them to sacrifice. Only one would be left standing.

"I'll take care of this." He dashed for the door, and, reciting a demonic litany, he thrust forward the device as he opened the door.

Insectile skittering clawed the outer walls, and a screech resounded in Jett's ears. That had hurt whatever demon had vocalized, she knew that much. When she smelled flames and her darkness lifted at the scent, she followed the curiosity to stand and peer around the corner. Savin stood with his arms together, sigils facing outward—and they flamed.

He was marvelous. Truly, a hero in every sense that appealed to her.

When he dropped his arms, the flames hissed out and Savin kicked the door shut. He turned, startling when he saw her right behind him. "Jett, you should be more careful."

"I don't fear you." She wrapped her arms around him and hugged him. "You are my protector. You're not hurt? From the flames?"

"Never. The fire slips over my skin without burning me. Don't know why, but that's how it works."

She had always felt so comfortable near flames. And now she had returned to another comforting fire.

"Kiss me," she whispered. "Touch me, Savin. Make me yours. Please."

He lifted her into his arms, and as he passed by the kitchen, she did not sense the intruders outside the door. The wards had repelled them. For now. Savin carried her into the bedroom and laid her on the bed. When she looked into his eyes, she did not notice the inner pain from the wards. She had but to maintain a connection with him.

His kiss fell upon her like redeeming sunlight. Hot and lingering, and oh, so welcome. The tickle of his beard over her skin softened her anxiety and teased up a smile against his mouth. She pushed her fingers into his hair and clung to him, keeping him there at her mouth. Wanting to breathe all her pain into him and, in turn, take his away from him.

"You are my flame," she said. "My comforting flame."

"I don't want to burn you."

"Oh, yes, you must. Burn me with your heat, Savin. I need to feel you deep and hot within me."

Savin's wide hand strayed down her shoulder and to her breast. The less-than-gentle squeeze of her nipple shocked a vibrant pleasure thrill through her. Arching her back, Jett lured her lover down onto her and into her arms. He bowed his head and licked a trail down her chin, shoving down the strappy sleeve of her dress. Nudging aside the fabric, he claimed her nipple with his hot tongue.

He supped upon her and, in the process, teased her senses to ultra-alert. She felt beautiful, wanted. *Not a horned demon queen.* She felt as if she'd never revealed that side of herself to Savin. She felt…loved.

Dragging her dress down as he followed with his tongue, Savin skated over her skin, lower and lower, circled her belly button, then tugged to get the dress below her hips.

"Yes, kiss me there," she said. Her senses soared with every delicious trace of his tongue.

His fingers wrapped about her hip as he lowered his mouth to kiss her mons and nuzzle into her hairs. The anticipation of welcoming him into her most intimate place made her spread her legs. But he lingered there, at the top of her thigh, his breath hushing hotly, and his mouth kissing here, then there, then moving lower and aside until, finally, she felt him enter her with his tongue.

Jett gripped the sheets. Her head tilted back into the pillow. Her nipples, tight and hard, cooled in the evening air. He dashed tastes and touches and suckles everywhere about her pussy. His wicked touch felt so right. She had not to command or request his submission. She might be queen, but this man was the champion she had always desired would ride in on a white stallion to rescue her from the darkness of Daemonia.

A stallion would have perished in such a place. And her knight had instead waited for her to rescue herself. But now the real saving had begun. He could lift her soul to the surface, to plunge through the flames and touch the light with his gentle protection and willingness to love her.

Savin's hair spilled over her thigh. Jett reached to clutch at it as his ministrations focused on her swelling clit. It pulsed and ached and hummed. Her entire body answered with a tightening, pleading urge to jump. To fall once again over the edge.

And this time she fell into Savin's arms.

Chapter 29

In the morning, Savin felt the threat as deeply as Jett had. Her spine tingled with a pricking electricity. They both knew demons were in the area, perhaps even the building. They were looking for her. Daemonia had sent scouts to retrieve their missing queen.

Would they know she had destroyed Drav? Despite his claims to royalty, he'd seemed insignificant. Else why had the legion not insisted he remain at court? She had done away with him out of defense, but Jett suspected Drav would not be missed by any in Daemonia.

But had the scouts she now sensed come for her or Fuum? It was possible they sensed the demon within Savin. Either way, if they succeeded in breaching Savin's wards, the results would not be pretty. So when Savin had to run out, this time he increased the efficacy of the wards, locking Jett inside with a powerful shield.

She rubbed her arms and pulled up her legs on the couch where she sat, feeling as though she were hiding and not standing up to the threat, as any queen should. This was not her. She was stronger.

If she could fight off those lurking, would that success show others she was a force not to be threatened?

She glanced to the front door. She could walk outside. As simple as that. To keep Savin safe.

Savin hung up on CJ. The dark witch reported finding something interesting in the Archives. Not the thing necessary to keep both Savin and Jett safe, but he felt he was getting close.

Uh-huh. Close. Like that was going to help matters.

Savin strode down the sidewalk, following the eerie sensation that clued him a demon was near. Not a corporeal one. He couldn't see it, but it was close enough he could reach out and grab it, he felt sure. Grabbing wasn't possible with the incorporeal kind. They tended to seek humans to inhabit. And while Savin could reckon them, the reckoning wasn't something he could whip out like a magical spell and—*poof*—the demon was sent back to Daemonia.

He needed a few minutes, at the very least, to summon a connection to the Place of All Demons. Knowing he didn't want to let the thing run free, yet also knowing he couldn't call attention to himself on this busy, tourist-filled street, Savin quietly put his forearms together to connect the demonic magic he possessed and began to chant under his breath while keeping the demon's aura in range.

He walked swiftly, roughly shouldering someone out of the way. They angrily called after him, but he couldn't pause for politeness. The incorporeal demon turned a corner. Savin hurried and rounded the corner and…bumped into a pregnant woman holding her stomach. She moaned and winced.

"I'm sorry, mademoiselle."

"No worries," she said. "It was so sudden."

"Are you…in pain?" Was she going to give birth? She wasn't overly large, but by the manner in which she clutched her stomach, he could tell she was pregnant.

"I'm fine now. Must have been one of those Braxton Hicks. You barely brushed me, monsieur. No worries."

And yet, as Savin took his hand away from her arm, he felt it. The shiver of darkness that seemed to laugh at him. The incorporeal demon had found a host. Hell. Had it entered her baby?

She required an exorcism. It was the safest way to rid the human body of an incorporeal presence. But how to tell her that?

She started to walk away, and Savin searched his brain for a way to tell her what had just happened to her without having her flee from him thinking him insane. If he let her go, that poor child…

A car pulled up to the curb and she waved to the driver. A man leaned over and opened the passenger door.

"Wait!" Savin called, but the car rolled away. He fixed the license plate in his memory, then pulled out his phone and tapped the info in a note. He would need to find her if the rift was not closed.

He could stop the damned thing, which had likely come from Daemonia, by closing the rift. Because when he was closing it, all the escapees would be sucked back inside even if they did occupy a human host. The door would be slammed behind them, and all would be returned to normal.

As normal as this crazy realm could get.

He couldn't protect everyone. But how many more innocents would be taken over by demons? He'd never been taken to task for protecting the city from demons such as Ed did. But he could not stand idly by and allow this to continue.

"This has to stop."

Savin dialed up CJ. The connection crackled, and he only heard CJ say he was "still looking" before it cut out. The Archives was many stories below ground. Cell reception was always iffy there.

"Still looking," Savin muttered.

Not good enough to close the rift. But he did have a spell he'd tucked away in a drawer at home that would drag the bitch inside him out, kicking and screaming, and send her back from whence she had come.

One queen was as good as any other.

With a decisive nod, Savin dialed his mother.

"What's up, *mon cher*?"

"Hey, Maman, just wanted to call and tell you how much I love you."

Jett walked outside Savin's building and found a place on the sidewalk where passersby would not bump into her. Projecting a morsel of her influence outward, she ensured that they wouldn't notice her beyond yet another uninteresting tourist. And then she spread out her arms and closed her eyes. With all her senses, she sent out a message to any demons close enough to hear: *Beware. Do not challenge me.*

Suddenly she was gripped by the upper arm and

hurriedly moved toward the building door. "What are you doing outside?"

"I couldn't sit idly by," she said to Savin. "I had to let them know they could not come near me without a fight."

"You risk being seen by humans."

"I am half human," Jett protested. She tugged her arm from Savin's grip as they entered the building lobby. "Or did you forget that?"

"No. I'm just— I'm worried for you."

"I can take care of myself. As I did with Drav. Besides, I influenced those in the area to only see what they expected." She pressed her hands akimbo and met his blue gaze. He was only concerned, but if she allowed him to be her knight, he would lose himself. And she didn't want that sacrifice. Savin was supposed to live. "Where were you?"

"Out for a walk. I saw something disturbing. A pregnant woman hosting an incorporeal demon. It's probably in her baby. Hell, Jett, we need to end this."

"You said *we*. Does that mean you are willing to work with me?"

He winced. "I don't know how you can help."

"I can communicate with those who have recently come from Daemonia."

"What about the ones after you? Let's go inside and talk about this." He glanced around them. "I can't risk anyone walking by hearing us." He pointed up the stairs and she started upward. "Please trust me, Jett."

At his front door she took his hands and kissed him. "I will trust you if you will trust me."

"I do, I swear to you," he said, closing the door behind him. He took a moment to reinforce the wards and

Jett hissed at the intrusion to her system. "Too strong?" Savin asked.

"No, I'm good." But not really. She wanted this to end as much as he did. Dealing with having to worry about her sheen and Savin's wards was driving her mad. This was no way to normal. "So what do we do now?"

"I'm heading to the rift later with Ed and CJ. And CJ is still searching for a spell to draw out Fuum." He thumped his chest. "You hear that, bitch?"

Of a sudden Savin's body thrust backward and his shoulders slammed into the wall. He cracked a smile at Jett. "She heard me."

"Don't cajole her," Jett said. "I need you in one piece if we're to…" Could she say it? She'd confessed she loved him. But how to surrender to something so untouchable as that normal life they both wanted.

"We'll have it." Savin pulled her into his embrace and kissed her. "I know exactly what you're afraid to say. But I'm not. I'm going to fix things for you, Jett." His phone buzzed with a call. He silenced the ringer and kissed her again. "Let me hold you."

But he didn't say, out loud, *One last time.*

The phone on the bedside stand buzzed, indicating a message. Savin ignored it and nuzzled his face against Jett's neck. Her hair felt like silk, her body like home. Was he doing the right thing?

"I want you to be happy," he whispered.

"I am." She was drifting into reverie, perhaps even sleep. They'd exhausted themselves with each other, and life was not more perfect than it was in this moment.

Fitting.

Holding her until he felt sure her breaths were now

those of sleep, Savin carefully slipped off the bed and pulled up his jeans. The skylight beamed in moonlight that illuminated the room with an eerie quiet. He wandered out into the living room and, slipping his hand in between the couch cushions, pulled out the vial and instructions CJ had given him the other day.

Sitting cross-legged on the floor, Savin set the items beside him and took a moment to look across the shadowed display of guitars on the wall before him. The diddley bow he used for musicomancy leaned against the end of the sofa. He owned a Rickenbacker that had been signed by Tom Petty. The Flying V had Ace Frehley's signature scrawled in black Sharpie across its silver-speckled body.

Good times, that. He'd miss music. But then again, how would he know what to miss if he was not even alive to think that?

With a decisive inhale and exhale, Savin opened the paper and read the spell. It involved drawing a circle about him, so he chanted the words as he drew that circle with his finger and then arched it up over his head to enclose his seated figure in a sort of cone that now glimmered with the activated magic.

Savin's skin prickled. The Other sat up at attention. He hastened the ritual.

Reading the final words silently to fix them to memory, he uncapped the vial and tilted the sludgy ingredients down his throat. It tasted…not terrible. Then, bringing his palms together to unite the moth halves, he spoke the words…

…and the demon within him clawed for hold at his soul.

Chapter 30

Jett rolled over on the bed, awakened by the cell phone vibrating on the nightstand. Savin was not in the bed—he must have wandered into the bathroom. She grabbed the phone and read the text. The dark witch Certainly Jones reported: I've found an option. Coming over right now.

An option? For what?

Sitting up, she noted the bathroom door was open. He wasn't in there. Had he left? It was late, but not early-in-the-morning late. Must be around midnight. She'd dozed into such a blissful sleep after their lovemaking. There was no man she desired more than Savin, and when he kissed and touched her, he made her believe she could be whole again.

Human.

She shouldn't have challenged him so outside the

building. She didn't want to alienate him. They needed to work together. She needed him as much as she suspected he needed her.

A strange noise sounded from the living room. Scratching?

"Savin?"

Instinctually, she spread her senses through the air, mining for demonic presence. Nothing.

Sliding off the bed, Jett grabbed the T-shirt Savin had been wearing earlier and pulled it on. It smelled like him, rugged and wild. But as she wandered into the living room, her footsteps quickened to race to Savin's side. His pores emitted a thick red smoke that coalesced in the air above his prone figure.

Jett screamed and shook him. He murmured something. She saw the paper on the floor with spell sigils drawn on it and the empty vial that reeked of foul things. "What have you done?"

Of a sudden the red smoke sharpened and began to form. Jett's heart dropped because now her senses felt the demonic presence. And she knew who this was. The former queen, Fuum. The one demon who had destroyed her life, and Savin's as well, had been freed and was taking shape.

An insistent knock on the front door was followed by a man's call to let him in. Jett sprang up. It must be the dark witch. She started for the front door, but an arm lashed out and caught her across the neck. Jett's feet left the floor and she tumbled backward, landing painfully on hands and butt.

"CJ, she's out!" Jett called. "I can't get to the door."

"You have fouled everything," the now-solid form of Fuum growled at Jett. She stood tall and regal, her long midnight blue hair flowing out as if blown by the wind. Her black flesh hugged tight to her skeletal bone structure, and the bits of red mist surrounded her like fabric from her shoulders to her knees. "I will not go back!"

"Nor will I!" Finding her strength, Jett stood. An eye to Savin on the floor showed her he did not move, and she worried he might be dying. Edamite Thrash had said that the demon within him could not be removed without his death. "What have you done to him?"

"I've kept him alive and well all this time." The bitch grinned a shark's smile.

The front door slammed inward, and the dark witch stumbled inside.

With a flick of her finger, the demoness pinned CJ to the wall. "This does not concern you, witch."

"Shit, he performed the releasement spell," CJ said. "Savin?"

"He's there on the floor," Jett said. "Is he going to die?"

"Of course he is," the demoness said. "He no longer has me to keep him alive. Men. They never know how much they need us women until it's too late."

"With you out of this realm, he can live," CJ called. The witch recited some Latin, and that allowed him to peel himself away from the wall.

"I'm not going anywhere…" The demoness hovered in the center of the living room, then tilted her look directly at Jett. "Without taking Drav's progeny with me."

"Oh, he's dead," Jett challenged. "Not that you'd care."

Fuum lifted a brow. "I don't. The idiot served me one purpose. But I do care that you are not where you belong."

Knowing what was coming, Jett released her sheen. Horns curled out and back over her ears. Her skin tightened and the sigils glowed as her skin darkened. She drew up her protective wards just as she felt Fuum hit her hard.

"Keep her busy!" CJ called. He plunged to the floor beside Savin.

"Gladly," Jett said.

She pushed at Fuum and managed to shove her away from her. The demoness's back hit the wooden support beam and she yowled. Releasing all the magic she could summon, Jett directed it toward Fuum. The old queen matched her. And Jett realized she was not so powerful as she had been in Daemonia. Truly, she was losing her demon. Yet Fuum could only match her. She had not so much strength, either.

How easy it had been to destroy that which annoyed her while sitting on the throne. And to rip out a man's heart. But she did not want to kill Fuum. She had to keep her alive so Savin could send her back to Daemonia.

The witch knelt over Savin, reciting a spell. He dusted him with ash and salt. Dragging his gaze over the guitars on the wall, CJ asked, "Which is the one you use to perform musicomancy?" Savin did not respond. The witch slapped his face and joggled him, stirring Savin from the depths of death. "Which one!"

"Single...string..."

With a snap of CJ's fingers, the diddley bow flew across the room and landed in the witch's grip.

Jett felt the demoness's tendrils digging into her, seeking a space where her defenses might crumble. Her strength was growing; she must be feeding off Jett's magic. And Jett's energy was quickly depleting. She wouldn't be able to hold her off much longer.

She saw the witch hold the diddley bow over Savin, and her lover lifted a hand to strum the string. A sudden, nerve-biting tone filled the room. The demoness was whipped away from Jett while Jett was also flung away. Her shoulders hit the wall hard, and she dropped to the floor in a sprawl.

"Continue!" CJ commanded the weak reckoner on the floor. "Let me help you up."

CJ managed to pull Savin upright and prop his back against the couch while the demoness dove for the diddley bow. Her fingers burned into the wooden body.

With a spoken hex, CJ caused the demoness to recoil, but only momentarily. She lunged for the witch, gripping his hair and pulling him away from Savin.

The reckoner leaned against the couch, immobile, yet his eyes were open. And when they met Jett's gaze, she pleaded silently with him; she wanted him to know how much she loved him, that he meant the world to her. That she forgave him for not being able to save her when they were kids.

"I love you!" she shouted.

The reckoner dragged the diddley bow to his lap. Head tilted back against the couch, he plucked a few discordant notes, then a few more. The demoness dropped the dark witch, who rolled to his back and shuffled away against the wall to sit near Jett.

Savin's playing lured the demoness to him. Her form was at once solid and then wispy red smoke that hovered over him, her face fully formed, moving but inches from his.

Jett's body cringed at the sound, but the clasp of

CJ's hand about her wrist grounded her. "Don't listen," he said. "Listen only to me. I will speak quiet words of strength." He began to whisper and Jett turned her focus from Savin's music.

Meanwhile, Fuum floated toward Savin, lured by the music. She bent, placing her face close to his as if to draw in his scent or position herself to lash out a wicked tongue to taste.

And then Savin whispered to the demoness, "Kiss me..."

"My lover." Fuum pressed her mouth to Savin's.

The reckoner plucked out a trill of notes and, seeming to gain strength from the kiss, segued into a riff that took a life of its own and formed harmony at the same time. The instrument wailed at the demon and she coiled away from her contact with Savin and into a twist of yowling pain.

CJ clutched Jett's hand and began to chant louder. She felt his magic enter her. He was keeping her here, so she surrendered to his dark magic.

A shimmery rift opened before them. The red queen screamed. Arms flailing and curses flying, she was sucked in through the rift, which then flashed and closed up.

CJ dropped Jett's hand. "It's done. I've got to go."

She grabbed his wrist. "Where?"

"To the rift at the edge of town. I'll call Ed. We can seal it now that the queen has been sent back. But I have to hurry before she again escapes. You take care of Savin."

"Will he die?"

"No. He...shouldn't." The witch winced. "He needs

you now, Jett. Give him the strength that he once got from the incorporeal queen. Give it all to him."

With that, Certainly marched out of the place, closing the door behind him.

Jett crawled over to the couch, where Savin held the diddley bow clutched in his embrace. She stroked the hair from his face and gently pried the instrument from his hands.

Softly, she kissed his forehead and then his mouth.

"I'm not sure how to do this," she said, "but whatever I have is yours. Take it all from me, Savin."

Breaths came slowly. A monumental effort. Savin had mustered up the energy to strum the expulsion spell on the diddley bow. He was vaguely aware that the Other was now gone. The queen called Fuum. No longer inside him. And he felt…empty.

Savin tried to lift a hand to clutch at Jett's hair, but his extremities felt leaden. She straddled him. The weight of her lightness buoyed him. The sweetest kiss landed on his forehead. And then that softness touched his mouth. Like a redeeming elixir, she gave to him that which he'd never thought imaginable.

Freedom.

He was now free of the demon who had lived within him for twenty years. Because he had found Jett and had been forced to face the decision to give up his life to expel the demon inside him. Which he had done. And with every breath, he felt his life slipping away.

"Don't leave me, Savin," she whispered against his mouth. "We have our whole lives ahead of us. I need you here. In this mortal realm. By my side. Your hand in mine." She clasped his heavy hand and he wasn't able to curl his fingers. "Just try, Savin. For me? Please, don't die. CJ said… I must give you my strength. I'm not sure how. But I'm going to try this."

The press of her palms, one against his forehead, the other over his heart, felt like a zap from a life-saving emergency device. Savin's body jolted, but the movement rocked his rib cage and he moaned. Was this how it had felt when she ripped out her father's heart?

Again, he was jolted. She was doing something to him. He wasn't sure what it was. But she could take his heart. It belonged to her. When he opened his eyes, he didn't see the black-haired beauty whom he had likely loved since he was a child. He saw red eyes and blue hair and horns that glinted like specularite.

Jett. His Jett. In all her demonic glory. He loved her so much he wanted to tell her, but his tongue would not move.

This time when he felt the jolt, it was followed by the intrusion of sharp, pricking tendrils that seemed to poke in through his every pore. Heat gushed through his system. It glowed red behind his eyes and flickered like flames. The vibrations he felt when a demon was near were pronounced, only tenfold. Jett chanted a demonic phrase that sounded deep and earthen and older than the stars. Her throaty hums vibrated in his bones. They entwined, their souls.

"Your get-out-of-death-free card!" Jett declared.

She grabbed his wrists and pressed his palms together, and Savin smiled as he was thankful he'd told her about this. Would it work? Jett held his palms together tightly. His palms heated and flames formed. Jett swore but did not let go of his hands.

It felt as if the sides of his hands fused together, burning, yet without flames. The moth wings fluttered and peeled away from his skin to take flight.

Savin gasped in a choking breath as if he were rising from the depths of a molten lava pool. Had she done the same after falling over the cliff?

"Stay with me," Jett said in a voice that defied him to stay. To not make the leap. To be brave enough to stand at her side and face whatever the future would push at them.

The moth landed on his chest, right over his heart, and then it danced off and into the darkness.

"Yes," he murmured. The vibrations began to undulate and his muscles twitched. He could lift his hand and landed it at Jett's hip. And the flash behind his eyes brightened like the sun. He sat up abruptly. She slid down his legs, observing him with those eyes that were swiftly growing brown.

"Jett, I love you," he said.

She held up her hand and he slapped his other hand into hers. And her energy, her vita, flowed up his arm and into his heart. He watched her hair drip away the blue color and shine richly onyx. And just as he reached to touch the horn that curled over her ear, it dropped away from her skull and, glittering madly, diffused and scattered to dust as it spilled over his leg and the floor.

Jett hushed out a heavy exhale and bowed her head against his shoulder. Her body relaxed against his and she curled up her legs. He embraced her and kissed her forehead. He wasn't going to die this day.

Chapter 31

Days later

The life force Jett infused into Savin saved him from death. And in that moment, he in turn had taken from her all that was demonic, and she became as human as she had been that day long ago when fate lured them to the edge of the lavender field. Which wasn't entirely human, thanks to her paternity.

They confirmed these things with the help of Certainly Jones, who read their auras. But as well, now when Savin looked into Jett's eyes, all he saw was her. The woman he loved, sans red gloss to her brown irises.

Jett, on the other hand, wasn't ready to completely mark herself off as human. She had lived in Daemonia for a long time. The entitlement that had come to her by sitting the throne lingered. And while she would never wish for the return of horns, she sensed there were tendrils within her that would ever remind her of those dark days. She didn't say that to Savin. He didn't need to know a bit of the queen yet lingered. In her blood would always flow Drav's legacy. Like it or not.

With the rift sealed, the city of Paris returned to as normal as it could be with the paranormal species walking its streets and existing alongside humans. Demons would always be a part of the population. And the smart ones knew how to survive and blend in. Ed Thrash continued to police his kind. And Savin was ever on call for another reckoning.

He would not give up his job. Because the call to reckon demons had not changed. And yet now he didn't feel it was so much a curse as a privilege to be able to keep his fellow humans safe from the dangers they must never know lurked so close.

The day was bright and Jett laughed as sunshine hit her face. Savin clasped her hand and led her toward the cemetery, where they both felt comfortable. It was their place now. It didn't remind them of death and misery, but rather, it honored the parts of themselves they'd allowed to pass on.

Skipping down a narrow stone lane ahead of him, Jett glanced over her shoulder. Her smile was so bright. And that blue dress with the flowers all over it was like summer in the autumn. He couldn't imagine being happier.

Actually, he could. If all went well.

Jett stopped at the sarcophagus that they favored for afternoon picnics and sat on the edge, waiting for him to catch up to her. As he arrived before her, Savin knelt on one knee and took Jett's hand. Her look told him she had no idea what he was up to, and it pleased him that he could surprise her.

He wanted to fill her life with only the best surprises from now on. For good or for ill, he would be there for her.

"I love you, Jett," he said.

"I love you, too. Why are you kneeling?"

"It's what a guy is supposed to do."

"What do you mean— Oh." Her eyes glinted. "Really?"

"I've done a lot of growing up over the years, but I think I've done the most the past days you've been back in my life. And I've kissed you, so… I can finally ask you the important question."

Jett pressed her fingers to her lips, beaming.

"Will you marry me?"

She plunged forward to wrap her arms about him, and Savin stood, taking her with him as her legs hooked behind his hips. Their kiss was filled with wonder and joy. Heartbeats fluttered and raced. And finally, their future looked bright.

* * * * *

Jane Godman writes in a variety of romance genres, including paranormal, gothic and romantic suspense. Jane lives in England and loves to travel to European cities that are steeped in history and romance—Venice, Dubrovnik and Vienna are among her favorites. Jane is married to a lovely man and is mom to two grown-up children.

Books by Jane Godman

Harlequin Nocturne

Otherworld Protector
Otherworld Renegade
Otherworld Challenger
Immortal Billionaire
The Unforgettable Wolf
One Night with the Valkyrie
Awakening the Shifter
Enticing the Dragon
Captivating the Bear

Harlequin Romantic Suspense

The Coltons of Red Ridge

Colton and the Single Mom

Sons of Stillwater

Covert Kisses
The Soldier's Seduction
Secret Baby, Second Chance

Visit the Author Profile page
at Harlequin.com for more titles.

CAPTIVATING THE BEAR

Jane Godman

This book is dedicated to my grandchildren. They bring so much joy to my life just by being in it.

Chapter 1

Lidiya Rihanoff was doing her best to be objective about the situation, which wasn't easy when she was caught up in the center of a screaming, sobbing crowd.

She had spent the last hour slowly working her way through the hysterical throng until she found herself a place up against the crash barriers. It had proved surprisingly difficult. Lidi had trained with warriors. She knew how to deal with combat situations. This was different. Faced with an adoring group of rock fans who did not want to relinquish the opportunity to get up close to their idols, she was at a loss. Her usual street-fighting tactics wouldn't do. Eye gouging and throat punching would have brought her to the attention of the police officers who were standing at regular intervals along the route. In the end, she resorted to strategically using her elbows. When that didn't work, she dealt out a few surreptitious ankle kicks.

Now she was pressed right up against the barrier, with a clear view of the movie theater and its red-carpeted steps. From the mounting fervor, and the way the security guards were pacing back and forth along the street, she guessed the stars were about to arrive at any minute.

It was winter, but the temperatures in the South of France were like a summer day in her home country of Callistoya. Sweat beaded her forehead and trickled down her spine as she was jostled and pushed. Even so, she couldn't remove her sweatshirt. Beneath it, her long-sleeved T-shirt was torn, the shredded material revealing the injuries to her arm. She couldn't risk drawing attention to herself.

"Here they come!" The woman next to her spoke English, a language in which Lidi was fluent. Her screech was accompanied by a curious gesture. Putting her fingers on either side of her head, she made them into devil horns. A quick glance around revealed a number of other people doing the same thing. She laughed at Lidi's bemused expression. "Sign of the Beast."

Two stretch limousines drew up to one side of the theater. On the opposite side of the street, hundreds of photographers were already in position with their cameras poised.

A man bounded out of the first vehicle before it had stopped, and the flashbulbs went wild in time with the crescendo around Lidi.

"Who is he?" She had to mouth the words to the helpful stranger.

"Khan. Lead singer." She got up close and yelled her

response directly into Lidi's ear. "The woman with him is his wife, Sarange."

Lidi watched as the group of glamorous figures exited the cars and posed on the red carpet. Her new friend bellowed out an excited commentary. Next came Torque, the rhythm guitarist, with his blonde wife, Hollie. The dark-haired, muscle-bound man with the brooding expression was the drummer, Diablo. Then there was the lead guitarist, Dev, and the bass player, Finglas.

Lidi paid only scant attention. Her interest in the members of the internationally famous rock band Beast began and ended with their ability to lead her to the man she was seeking. Was he here? She scanned the group on the red carpet. He had to be here.

As if the intensity of her thoughts had somehow communicated themselves across the distance between the crash barriers and to the building on the other side of the road, a man strode down the steps. He was talking on his cell phone, clearly engrossed in his conversation.

Lidi's breath caught in her throat. Just from his height and the width of his shoulders she knew it was him.

She gestured to the woman next to her, not trusting her voice.

"Ged Taverner." A little shiver ran through Lidi as she heard the name. "He's Beast's manager."

Ged Taverner. That was what he called himself now, but Lidi knew his true identity. The tall, imposing figure she was looking at was Gerald Tavisha, the rightful king of Callistoya.

She had heard so much about this man that his nearness almost took her breath away. Until his exile he had embodied everything the warrior-heroes of the magical shifter state of Callistoya held dear. Chivalry, honor and a deep, abiding love of their country.

Lidi would never understand why he had stayed away instead of raising an army and fighting the man who had stolen his throne. But all that mattered now was that she had found him.

As she gazed across the distance between them, a new sensation swept over her. Stinging and cloying at the same time, like a hit of hot sugar surging through her bloodstream. It was the craziest feeling, a wild urgency that made her want to vault over the barrier and throw herself into Ged Taverner's arms.

She looked around her at the longing faces. Mass hysteria. That must be what she was experiencing. Despite her noble upbringing, she had put her dignity aside and been infected by the mood around her. But she wasn't here to be part of this. She was a Rihanoff of Aras. She could rise above it.

It didn't matter what she told herself. The feeling persisted, growing stronger, becoming a wild, yearning ache throughout her body, but centering very specifically in the throbbing pulse between her legs. Everything around her came sharply into focus, every sense heightening until she was quivering with tension.

What exactly is happening to me?

Her concentration became centered on Ged and it appeared she was not the only one suffering. Frowning, he looked up from his call, the cell phone held slightly away from his ear as he scanned the crowd. Excitement powered through Lidi as a new realization hit her.

It's him. He is the reason I'm feeling this way.

Across the yards that separated them, she knew he could feel the same longing that was driving her demented. An invisible cord between them was being tightened, drawing them closer together. Heat burned up the air between them. The urge to go to him and wrap her body around his was becoming a storm in her blood.

Because of the distance, she couldn't see the finer detail of his looks, but her impression was of strength and muscle, of ruggedly carved aristocratic features, a square, stubborn chin, wavy, butterscotch-brown hair, and eyes that faced the world with the same bravery and determination as her own. It was the look that had embodied Callistoya. Once. Before the unthinkable had happened.

Just as she thought she couldn't take any more, the group on the red carpet began to move. With a final wave to the fans, they made their way inside the theater. Ged remained on the steps for a moment or two after they'd gone, a look of confusion on his face.

Finally, with a reluctant shrug, he turned away and the spell was broken. Lidi shuddered as her body tried to deal with the return to normality. She almost laughed out loud. Normality? For her, there would never be such a thing again.

She had come here to find the only man who could save her father and her country. It had not been part of her schemes to also find her mate. But the decree of the fates was absolute. For every shifter there was a match. One true life partner. The rush of feeling she'd experienced when she gazed at Ged could mean only one thing. The fates had decided he was the one for her.

Stifling a groan, she tried to get her errant emotions under control. *Arousal? Attraction? Gazing longingly at the handsome bear-shifter king? Being struck dumb by my fated mate? I don't have time for this right now.*

Lidi had a plan and she was determined to stick to it. Resolutely, she turned to her helpful new acquaintance.

"Do you know where the band are staying?"

Ged Taverner tried to concentrate on what the man standing next to him was saying.

"Small venues are a nightmare." Rick, Beast's head of security, gazed moodily out at the crowd of fans. "Give me an arena or a sports stadium anytime."

Ged managed a suitable reply, saying something about the importance of this theater in Cannes as the most suitable place in which to screen the premiere of the band's documentary. The whole time, his mind was preoccupied.

What the hell had just happened?

One minute he had been walking down the steps, talking on his cell with a French national newspaper about an interview, the next...he shook his head. It had been like a bolt of lightning, hitting him full-on as he walked out into the sunlight. He had no idea where it had come from, or what had caused it. When he had raised his head, seeking the source of the enchantment that held him helpless, he had known with absolute certainty that it was coming from somewhere in the throng of fans across the street.

As his eyes scanned the crowd, he had been in the grip of the most powerful emotion he had ever experienced. No matter how hard he tried, he couldn't shake free of it.

Who are you?

Ged was a shifter. His bear senses had kicked in, taking over from his human perception. Although it wasn't his dominant sense, his sight was good. Even so, trying to pick out one person among the mass had been impossible. But scent…that was a different matter. He could pick up a smell twenty miles away. The delicious aroma from the other side of the street had made his nostrils flare. It reminded him of clean, warm fur. Of winter sunshine, fresh, clear water and deep, dark pine forests.

How could he have been so sure the origin of that new fire in his blood was female? The answer was simple. Not only was his reaction to her knee-weakening and breathtaking, it was also zipper straining. His tailored pants had started to feel snug and he had dug his hands into his pockets, cursing the fate that had decided to put him in this predicament while he was wearing a tuxedo. Scratch that. He had cursed the fate that had decided to put him in this situation. Period.

Because he knew what had happened. Of course. Shifters were creatures of tradition. Their lives were ruled by legend and magic. Ged, along with every other werebear, had been brought up to respect the ancient traditions that ruled his life.

There is one mate for each of us, and we will know our mate instantly.

He had heard other shifters talk about that moment of recognition. He'd even seen it happen recently for two of his friends. That moment of seeing their mate for the first time and knowing there was no going back. They described it as being like a drug, an injection of pure, undiluted passion direct into the bloodstream, delivering a perfect high. An instant, uncontrollable addiction.

Ged understood all of that. But there was no way it could happen for him. A king in exile? Even if he had any sort of order in his life, he was a *bear*. Other shifters could do the mates-for-life thing. Callistoya werebears were notorious for the control they had over their emotions. Even if he was prepared to accept the concept of instant, lifelong passion, it wasn't happening with someone he hadn't even looked in the eye.

That was what he tried to tell himself, but his body was giving him other messages. When the time came to go into the theater, it took all of his considerable strength to turn away. Every nerve ending was crying out to cross the street and find her. Every fiber of his being was alight with the need to grab her, claim her and never let her go.

Need her. Now.

The strength of that feeling hadn't faded once he was inside the building. The burn wasn't as fierce, but it was still there. He still hadn't seen her face, but she had started a fire in his blood and it was raging out of control.

He sat in the elegant theater, surrounded by celebrities, and watched the images on the screen. At least, he assumed that was what he did. He had no memory afterward of watching the documentary that had consumed so much of his life over the last twelve months.

At the after-party, he accepted the congratulations and praise, laughing off any suggestions about the awards that were likely to come flooding his way. He knew the movie, a snapshot of six months on the road with Beast, was good. The strength of the story was in the editing. The truth would never be told. The world would never be ready to learn that one of the most famous bands on the planet was really a group of shifters.

As he drank too much champagne and discovered that, as usual, there weren't enough dainty canapés to fill his large frame, part of Ged's mind was disengaged from the elegant occasion.

Who was she? It couldn't be coincidence that she was here in Cannes at the same time as him...

A strong grip on his shoulder shook him out of his musings. "I've got to hand it to you." Khan, the band's lead singer, gestured around the room, encompassing the group of designer-clad guests. "You sure know how to throw a dull party."

Ged laughed. "Tonight is about money and influence, not about getting wasted and behaving outrageously. Make sure Torque knows that *before* he sets fire to the drapes, will you?"

"I guess that means swinging from the chandeliers is forbidden?" Khan was a weretiger. Intuition wasn't his strong point, but the two men had been friends for a long time. His eyes scanned Ged's face for a moment. "Everything okay with you?"

How the hell was he supposed to answer that question? If he told Khan the truth, his exuberant friend was likely to insist they set off right now on a quest to find the mystery woman. Because he was blissfully happy in his own marriage, Khan would seek the same thing for Ged.

Ged didn't want to be forced to make excuses or lie. He knew his friends sometimes speculated about his true identity. He was the man who had rescued them all from danger or captivity, the person who had brought this unique group together. They owed him an allegiance that went beyond loyalty, but he had never disclosed the details of his background to them. How could he? Sharing the details of his past would be on the same level of madness as trying to find himself a mate.

"I'm fine." He tilted his empty champagne glass toward Khan. "Do you think there's any chance we might find some brandy in this place?"

* * *

To Lidi's surprise, the crowd began to disperse as soon as the band was inside the theater. She turned to her companion, whose name was Allie. "Shouldn't we wait for them to come out again?"

Allie gave her a pitying look. "Rookie mistake. They've played nice and given the paparazzi what they wanted. It's possible they'll come out this way and sign a few autographs, but it's more likely they'll leave by a rear door and go straight to the after-party."

Lidi experienced a moment of panic. She couldn't have come this far only to fail now. Clearly she needed to stick with Allie, who was suitably dressed for the weather with an embroidered scarf wrapped around her neck and long boots encasing her legs. The other woman seemed to know what she was doing and was willing to share her information.

"What do we do now?"

"The party is being held at the Palais Hôtel, where the band are staying—"

Lidi brightened up. This was more like it. "How do we get inside?"

"We don't." *Don't?* Clearly Allie didn't know who she was talking to. Telling Lidi what she couldn't do was an instant challenge. "Oh, don't get me wrong, some of these women will try it, but it's a waste of time. Security will have them out of there so fast their feet won't hit the ground. That's if the hotel management don't call the police and let them spend a night in the cells for trespassing."

Lidi allowed herself to be led along the street with the rest of the crowd. She took a moment to appreciate Allie's unusual looks. Lidi came from a land where most people had the classic brown hair and golden eyes of the Callistoyan werebear, a close relative of the Siberian brown bear. With her silver-blond hair, pale skin and light gray eyes, Allie was striking.

"So what are we doing exactly? Trying to get another glimpse of them?" Lidi hadn't risked life and limb and traveled all this way just to *look* at Gerald Tavisha.

Allie gave her a sidelong glance. "What else were you hoping for? Did you think one of the guys was going to look your way and fall instantly in love?"

There didn't seem to be an answer to that. Because although it wasn't what she had expected to happen, the insta-love that Allie was joking about was exactly what *had* happened. However, maybe now she had been removed from the center of the furnace, *love* was too strong. She couldn't seriously have fallen in love with a man she hadn't even spoken to. Desire was probably a more apt description for what she was feeling. Good, old-fashioned lust.

The initial wild exhilaration had subsided. Thank heaven. There was no way she could have endured that level of panting eagerness for long. Even so, her whole body was quivering. It was like the aftermath of her most strenuous workout, with an additional heat zinging through her bloodstream. Every impulse was urging her to return to that theater and find her mate.

Lidi knew what arousal felt like. She was an adult shifter with a full range of both human and bear emotions. Although human and shifter time worked differently, thirteen years ago, her country had been thrown into unimaginable turmoil and she had sworn to devote her life to fighting to restore its equilibrium. Unusually for a bear shifter, Lidi's human emotions were dominant.

It was an inconvenience she had sworn to overcome. She was a warrior with no time to waste on feelings.

That was what made her reaction to Ged so difficult to understand. He was the man she had come to find. She needed him. As she accompanied Allie along the seafront promenade, Lidi bit back a laugh. Oh, yes. She *needed* him; that had become glaringly obvious. She only had to think about the instant connection between them to experience a thigh-clenching response.

She had to overcome these troublesome cravings and focus on the true reason she was here. Lidi always battled to maintain command over her feelings as well as her muscles. All those years of directing her energy into maintaining a mind and body that were at peak fitness had to be put to good use now. For some reason, her reaction to the man at the theater had been extreme. Maybe it was the stories she had heard about his bravery. Possibly it was the fact that he was the true ruler of her beleaguered nation. A legendary hero and a man of mystery.

Lidi had spent years training her body. It was hard, strong and fast, and it served her well. As for her emotions…well, she was having to work a little harder than usual to get them under control. It was an obstacle she hadn't anticipated, but she had never backed down from a fight. She wasn't about to start now.

They reached the Palais Hôtel, a dazzling white structure that faced the glittering waters of the Mediterranean. The imposing building consisted of a central block with two attached wings forming a U shape. Pretty wrought iron balconies were decorated with blue-and-white-striped parasols and lipstick-red geraniums.

As they were ushered behind yet more barriers Lidi surveyed the hotel thoughtfully.

"Beautiful, isn't it?" Allie sighed. "One night in a top-floor suite costs more than I earn in a year."

"Is that where the band will stay?" Lidi shielded her eyes against the sun with one hand, viewing the rooms directly beneath the terracotta roof tiles.

"They always have the best rooms, and in this hotel, that means the fifth floor." Allie regarded her warily. "Don't even think about trying to get in there." There it was again. That word. *Don't.* "The place is wall-to-wall celebrities this weekend. You won't get a foot inside the gardens before you're noticed. And while Beast's security team are okay, you don't want to take your chances with some of the others. Vicious thugs all of them."

Allie's words might almost have been issued as a dare to Lidi, who was focused on the edifice across the promenade and in particular on those balconies.

Many people believed that bears couldn't climb. Some people had died while clinging to that hope. Lidi, growing up in the shadow of the Callistoya mountains, had spent her childhood scrambling up the steep slopes alongside the mountain goats. The hotel was busy, of course, and scaling a building always carried an element of risk. But those wrought iron railings were almost too good to be true. If they were replicated at the rear of the hotel, and if she waited until the early hours of the morning…

Allie was still outlining the reasons why attempting to get into the hotel would be a bad idea. Tearing her gaze away from the building, Lidi cut across Allie's explanations with a final, very important, question.

"Will the band's manager also have a room on the top floor?"

Chapter 2

Ged couldn't sleep. The gamble he'd taken on the documentary had paid off. If the initial reviews were anything to go by, it looked set to be a huge success. He'd made the most of the party, renewing old contacts and developing new acquaintances.

His hotel suite was comfortable, with every luxury at his fingertips, but it was 3:30 a.m. and slumber still eluded him. Even his online contacts had fallen silent. It was that strange, predawn time when it would be easy to believe he was the only person in the world left awake.

The familiar restlessness surged through him, the need to *do* something stronger than ever. He glared at his electronic tablet, searching through his contacts. When he drew a blank, he tossed it aside in annoyance. *Nothing?* He wanted action and his usual sources weren't helping.

Stretching full-length on the bed, he willed his body into something that resembled a relaxed pose. Even if there had been a task for him, he was in no frame of mind to undertake it. Coiled tight as a spring, he needed to get his head straight before he went charging off on a rescue mission.

Ever since he had been driven out of his homeland by his enemies, the urge to help others had been Ged's driving force. There were many ways he could have done that. Working with children, donating a percentage of his earnings, volunteering in a deprived country...the list went on.

He didn't have to risk his life rescuing other shifters who were in danger, but that was what he had chosen to do. He knew what an analyst would say about his motives. Danger, excitement, risk...all of those were factors. But there was more to it. Ged had grown up knowing from an early age he was the heir to the throne of Callistoya.

Monarchy and immortality were strange partners. The werebears of Callistoya had eternal life, but they were not invincible. Like other shifters, they could be killed by silver, fire beheading and some illnesses. Since their magical kingdom had always been peaceful, Ged had expected his father's reign to last forever. Then everything had changed. Ged had barely reached shifter maturity when his father had been murdered and he and his brother, Andrei, had been forced out of their homeland.

Driven into exile, his rightful place on the throne snatched from him, his reputation ruined, he had attempted to return and fight back. That was when he had discovered that his enemies had used magic, as well as villainy, against him. Though prepared to fight evil, he had been unable to combat the sorcery that barred him from entering Callistoya.

Although his old life had been snatched away, Ged had been raised to serve and protect. His duty to others came first. Even though he no longer had a country over which to reign, those feelings of service and honor hadn't gone away. They had simply found a new direction.

Raised voices distracted him from his thoughts. Standards must be slipping if the tiniest sound was allowed to penetrate the luxurious corridors of the fifth floor of the Palais Hôtel. When the commotion continued, he paid closer attention, his finely tuned hearing distinguishing individual sounds. A woman's cry of protest was followed by a scuffle and a grunt of pain.

Frowning, Ged got to his feet. Pulling sweatpants over his boxer briefs, he went through to the sitting room and opened the door to the corridor. The sight that met his eyes was unexpected.

One of Beast's security guards was lying on the elegant rug, clutching his groin and groaning. At his side, a uniformed member of the hotel's staff was slumped against the wall with both hands clasped over his nose. Blood was seeping through his fingers.

In the center of the corridor, Rick, Ged's friend and trusted security manager, was grappling with a tall, slender woman. From where Ged was standing, it looked a lot like the woman was winning.

As if to confirm that judgment, Rick's opponent chose that moment to break free of his grasp. Instead of escaping while she had the chance, she neatly spun around and delivered a back kick direct into Rick's chest. Across a distance of several feet, Ged heard the air leave his friend's lungs in a rush as he dropped to his knees.

Torn between admiration for the neatness of the move and concern for his friend, he stepped forward. "What the hell is going on here, Rick?"

Rick managed to gesture toward the woman and wheeze out a few words. "Climbed...the damn balconies."

Over the years, there had been some daring attempts to get close to the band. Fans had hidden inside delivery trucks, tried to stow away on board the tour bus, even disguised themselves as journalists or caterers. But risking life and limb to scale a building followed by an assault on security staff? It was a unique approach.

Ged's intention, as he stepped forward, was to take over where Rick had left off. Whoever this woman was, she was a formidable fighter. Even so, she wouldn't stand a chance against him. As she swung around, *it* hit him. It was the same rush of arousal he had felt earlier, concentrated now because she was so close. The overload of pure sensation made him feel slightly dizzy.

Twin realizations, both equally potent. She was a bear shifter. And she was his mate.

Dark brown eyes, flecked with gold, regarded him for a moment or two; then she smiled. The expression had the same effect on him as the kick to the chest had on Rick. It drove the breath from his lungs. Unlike Rick, Ged managed to remain on his feet.

"I needed to see you."

He gazed down at her, unable to speak. This couldn't be happening. The fates couldn't be *this* unfair. It was bad enough that his mate appeared to have come storming into his life in search of him—and he would have to *turn her down*—but why did she have to be so damn gorgeous?

He became aware that Rick, who was getting to his feet with difficulty, was talking.

"Shall I call the police?"

The woman took a step closer to Ged, placing one hand flat on his naked chest. "Please. I have to speak with you."

He half expected to look down and see her palm print burning its way into his flesh. That was how her touch felt against his skin. She branded him in that instant, and it was the most perfect thrill he had ever felt. Oddly, it brought his senses back into clarity.

Yes, she was the most beautiful woman he had ever seen…but she was in trouble. Although that was apparent from the plea in those incredible eyes, there were other, more tangible clues. She wore flat, leather ankle boots that had taken such a beating they were almost useless. Her jeans were faded and stained and the long-sleeved T-shirt she wore over them had a tear that left one sleeve hanging half-off. The exposed flesh of her arm was a mass of scratches and cuts, some of them deep enough to appear serious. Her long, dark hair was pulled back into a ponytail, but the sheen was long gone, as though it hadn't been properly washed for some time.

In their human form, both male and female bear shifters were generally above average size. This woman was tall, her head reaching almost to Ged's shoulder, and her build was similar to that of an Olympic swimmer, long and lean with endless legs, broad shoulders and slim hips. But she was too skinny for her frame. It was the false thinness that follows illness or extreme dieting. The pallor of her skin and dark shadows under her eyes seemed to confirm Ged's assumption that she hadn't been eating properly just lately.

Yet she kicked the hell out of three guys? All because she wanted to see me? Even a bear shifter had limits, and she looked like she had been pushed to the end of hers, yet she had found that inner strength. This had to be a story worth hearing.

"No police." There was a good chance he would regret that decision later, but she was a shifter and she was in trouble. Helping in these situations was what he did. Ignoring the look of reproach in Rick's eyes, he held the door of his suite open for the woman to step inside. "Do whatever it takes to cover this up..." They were familiar words to Beast's security manager. "I'll speak to you later."

When he entered his suite, his unexpected guest had discovered the hospitality tray. Having already devoured half a pack of cookies, she was gulping mineral water so fast it was running down her chin.

Ged closed the door, leaning against it as he watched her. "I think you'd better tell me what this is about."

She nodded, leaving a grimy mark as she wiped the back of her hand across her mouth. "I am Lady Lidiya Rihanoff. My father is the Count of Aras...and I have come to take you back to Callistoya."

Lidi sat on the floor as she ate. Ged had ordered several items from the room service menu and was slouched in a chair watching as she worked her way through them. Ordinarily, the sight of his naked upper body might have proved a distraction, but she was too hungry to care. Or perhaps she was growing accustomed to being in a near-permanent state of arousal.

"When did you last eat?"

She gave it some thought. "Two days ago. I think."

"You think?" Until now, she had been under the impression that all bear shifters had the same brown eyes. But Ged's were different. Darker and more intense, set under heavy lids, with a gleam that made her want to check how her hair looked. Since she already knew the answer, she didn't bother. Her hair, like the rest of her, looked awful.

She paused with a donut halfway to her mouth. "I didn't have time to think about food."

"Clearly." He nodded at the remains of her repast. "What happened to your arm?"

Lidi glanced at her torn T-shirt, wincing slightly as the memory of breaking a window and scrabbling through it came back to her. "This?" She managed a shrug. "It's nothing."

It wasn't true. It actually hurt like hell, but he didn't need to know that.

Ged leaned forward, his clasped hands between his knees. "Let's get one thing straight, shall we? You broke in here and beat up two of my employees and a hotel security guard. I could have handed you over to the police, but I didn't. Start lying, or keeping information from me, and I may change my mind." He kept his gaze on hers, letting the message sink in. "Let's start again. What happened to your arm?"

"I hurt it when I escaped from the dungeons beneath the grand palace." Lidi tried out a defiant head toss. It didn't quite have the flourish she intended. Up close, Ged was too imposing, too attractive…too *everything.*

She attempted to regain her composure, not an easy thing to do when she was sitting at his feet, tired, dirty, and aching all over. "You must remember that place. It used to be your home."

If there was a flicker in the depths of his eyes, it was momentary. "Why were you in the dungeons?"

"Can't we talk while we travel?" When Ged shook his head, she huffed out a sigh. "Your stepbrother, Vasily the Usurper, imprisoned me and my father when I refused to marry him."

A frown pulled his brows together. "It may be a long time since I've been in Callistoya, but last thing I heard, Vasily had claimed the throne. Shouldn't you be calling him King Vasily?"

Lidi tilted her chin stubbornly. "I will never swear allegiance to that man."

He studied her thoughtfully. "Since your words imply loyalty to my side of the family, perhaps you can give me news of my uncle?"

Could he really have cut himself off so completely from his homeland? Callistoya was a magical place situated in the heart of the vast expanse known to humans as Siberia. Visible and accessible only to shifters, it did not exist on any mortal map. Even so, Lidi had heard how close Ged had once been to the uncle who had remained in Callistoya as leader of the resistance.

"Eduard Tavisha is working hard to rally those loyal to you." She watched his face. "It's a difficult job in your absence."

He was silent for long moments, his expression closed. She got the feeling he was gazing back into the past before he roused himself. "What about Vasily? How is the new king's reign going?"

"Badly. Vasily is struggling to maintain power. There is opposition from factions loyal to you. Vasily thought he could reinforce his position if he married me. Aras is a territory in the northern part of the kingdom."

Ged nodded. "I know of it."

"My father has great influence over the northern nobles, most of whom are loyal to you. Vasily reasoned that a Petrov-Rihanoff marriage would strengthen his claim to the throne." Her lips twisted into a bitter smile. "And I am a wealthy woman in my own right."

"There seems to have been a lot going on since I left Callistoya. Maybe I should have done more to keep up with the news from home."

"Yes." When he started to laugh, she looked up at him in confusion. "I don't understand why that's funny."

"It isn't. It's tragic." He stared down at her, his gaze taking in her disheveled appearance. "How long have you been traveling?"

The swift change of subject threw her off balance and she had to think about it. "Two, maybe three, weeks."

There was a brief silence as he registered that information. "I've never heard of anyone escaping from the palace dungeons before."

"No, nor have I." She shuddered at the memory of it. "Once I passed through the Callistoya border, I walked for miles within the mortal realm. The first town I reached was in the human land known as Russia." She bit her lip, uncomfortable with the next part of her story. "When I was there, I stole food and I managed to hot-wire a car. A few times, I was able to fill the vehicle up with gas and drive off without paying. Once I reached Austria, security was much tighter and I had to abandon the car."

All Callistoya bear shifters were good at hiding their feelings—mainly because they learned from an early age that emotions were a disruption to their lifestyle—but Ged took *enigmatic* to a whole new level. It was impossible to tell what he was thinking. "What did you do then?"

She laughed. "I did a lot of walking. Sneaked onto trains without paying when I could. Hitched a few rides."

"What?" His exclamation startled her and she took a moment to process what had prompted it. The realization that he was being protective caused a flare of warmth to start deep inside and spread through her body.

"I'm a bear shifter, remember? I was never in any danger from humans."

The way he sank back in his seat was an acknowledgment of the truth of her statement.

"How did you know where to find me?" he asked. "I don't advertise that I'm the former king of Callistoya."

"I overheard Vasily talking about you. He has spies in this world who discovered your whereabouts." She had intended to deliver the bad news in stages, but, under Ged's direct gaze there didn't seem to be any hiding place from the truth. "He still sees you as a danger, and if he suspected you were going to return to Callistoya, he would have you assassinated."

Ged had a very expressive mouth, she noticed. It was particularly evident now, as his lips curled in contempt. "Would he now? Vasily must have grown himself a spine since the last time we met."

"All I know is he has my father locked up." She got to her feet. "Can we go now?"

"Lidiya—"

"It's Lidi. No one ever calls me Lidiya." Why was she worrying about what name he was using when her father was depending on her?

"Lidi." He ran a hand through his thick brown hair. "If you know why I left Callistoya, you must also know why I can't go back."

"No." The word was almost a sob. "We can work with the resistance, get the people we need. Together with your uncle and my father's friends, we can fight Vasily."

He got to his feet and she felt the impact of his nearness all over again. He was too potent. His height, his presence, his masculinity...they all had the effect of driving everything out of her mind except the need to be in his arms. Determinedly, she clung to the image of her father languishing in a prison cell.

"There is more to it—"

"I know that thirteen years ago, Vasily told everyone you left Alyona Ivanov to die at the hands of the same men who murdered your father." The words burst from her lips before she could stop them, and Ged flinched as she said the name of his murdered fiancée. "I don't believe the story that you abandoned her...or that you killed her, then murdered the others to cover it up."

"I can't go back." If Ged cared that his stepbrother had spread a rumor that he was a spineless coward, or worse, it didn't show. There was no inflection in the words, only finality.

Lidi had come prepared to beg, to plead, to offer her family's wealth, her own fortune and allegiance. Anything. Nowhere in her schemes had she allowed for this scenario. One in which she faced a man who differed so completely from her expectations. She had believed the romantic folk stories about Gerald Tavisha. There were rumors about an exiled king who devoted his life to the rescue of endangered shifters. When she looked into Ged's eyes and saw the blank look in their dark depths, she was forced to question the truth behind those legends.

Her whole body slumped in defeat. She had pinned every hope on finding Ged and persuading him to help. Now she faced a return to Callistoya and the prospect of discovering another way. Giving in to Vasily's plans wasn't an option, but her choices were limited to her own ingenuity.

Squaring her shoulders and stiffening her spine was hard, but she managed it. Turning away from Ged? That proved more difficult. How had she reached this point so fast? Dependence on another person wasn't on her agenda. It never would be.

To her annoyance, she felt tears sting the back of her eyelids and burn her throat. Back home, she was known for her stubborn chin tilts. This one didn't quite work.

"I'm sorry to have wasted your time."

Ged muttered a curse as he crossed the room. Lidi already had her fingertips on the door handle when he reached her. Placing his hands on the wooden panels either side of her shoulders, he leaned in close.

"Don't go." What was happening to him? He didn't do empathy or tenderness. He certainly didn't change his mind. Yet, the second he had turned Lidi down, he was regretting the harshness of his response.

She turned around, the action placing her in the circle of his arms. Not quite touching, but temptingly close.

"I have no reason to stay."

"We both know that's not true." Getting up close to her had been a mistake. The attraction between them couldn't be forgotten, no matter how much they might wish to fight it. Lifting a hand, he cupped her chin, rubbing his thumb along her jawline.

"Don't." Lidi turned her head away. "For the last three weeks, I've only been able to wash in rivers and streams. I can't imagine what I must smell like."

"You smell incredible." That was part of the problem. Lidi's scent was driving him crazy. She smelled of the forest. Of fresh air, new rainfall and pine needles with a hint of the wild honeysuckle that reminded him of home. He rested his forehead against hers briefly, fighting the temptation to do more. "God knows, I don't want to change anything about you, but why don't you take a bath? Then I'll deal with those injuries to your arm and you can get some sleep. Even if I can't come back to Callistoya with you, I can help in other ways." He smiled. "I can book you on a flight to Siberia faster than you can steal a car."

She regarded him thoughtfully and he could see she was weighing her options. After a moment or two, she relaxed and nodded. "A bath would be heaven."

Ged showed her to the bathroom. Once he could hear water running, he took out his cell phone and called Rick.

"Any problems?"

"Other than the fact that you've got a crazy woman in your room?" Even though they were friends, Rick rarely crossed the employer-employee boundary when he was working. Now Ged could sense the anger and frustration in his voice. "Yeah, everything is *très bien*, as they say around here."

"The two guys who were with you, are they okay?"

Rick snorted. "Well, Marty's gonna be talking like an overexcited schoolgirl for a day or two, but the hotel guy's nose isn't broken. I managed to persuade him it was all a misunderstanding. When I say *persuade*, I mean I gave him a barrel full of cash to forget it."

"Thanks." Rick always came through for him and for the rest of the band. Although Ged had never shared the truth with the other man, Rick must know there was something unusual about Beast. Even if he hadn't guessed they were all shifters, he had seen enough over the years to figure they were *different*. He had covered up werewolf attacks and dragon flights, as well as a few less dramatic supernatural events. "Can you get me a first aid kit?"

"Are you hurt?" He could hear the concern in Rick's voice.

"It's not for me. And bring some women's clothes to my room."

"What sort of women's clothes?"

"How the hell do I know? The sort women wear." Ged drew a breath, reminding himself it wasn't Rick's fault his whole world had been turned upside down a few hours ago. "Go to the boutique in the lobby. Make up some story about your niece losing her suitcase. Tell them she's tall and slim. They'll do the rest."

He ended the call and went to stand at the window, looking out at the view of the Mediterranean. When he'd arrived in Cannes, his head had been full of business deals and upcoming concerts. His usual distractions. Now he was barely seeing the beautiful promenade, the dark waters and the first light of dawn streaking the sky. Instead, his mind was focused on a grander view, one that encompassed dramatic mountains and sweeping forests.

From the moment he'd been forced to leave Callistoya, he'd made a conscious effort to put it from his mind. But he would never be able to erase it from his heart.

That old expression *bear with a sore paw*? That had described Ged for a long time. He had been angry about everything. Furious that the places he visited weren't the same as his home. Judgmental of the people he met because they were different to the Callistoya nationals, annoyed that he had to explain his wants and needs, when in the past everyone around him understood them. Gradually, he understood what his rage was about. He didn't hate new people and places. He just missed his old life.

Ged had no idea what had happened to him on that awful night when almost his entire family, as well as his fiancée, and most of his father's council were murdered. He believed he had been either drugged or subjected to a powerful magic spell. He vaguely recalled standing at the entrance to the palace with Alyona at his side as they greeted the guests for their engagement meal. His next memory was of waking at the bottom of a deep ravine here in the human realm.

That was just the start of the nightmare. A frantic dash to his homeland had ensued, but his attempt to cross the invisible border into the magical land known only to shifters had proved futile. Somehow, the man who was the rightful monarch had, from that day forward, been locked out of his own kingdom.

Tortured by frustration and guilt, he had finally been forced to accept defeat and refocus his energy on a new life.

He hadn't wanted this new start, but it had been forced upon him. Telling himself he had to come to terms with that, he had channeled his royal training into new experiences. He could either make the best of what had happened, or spend the rest of his long, immortal life ricocheting around the human world in a fugue of self-pity.

That was when the idea for his alter ego had been born. As a child, Ged's favorite literary character had been Baroness Orczy's Scarlet Pimpernel. The story of the society fop who led a double life as a daring rescuer during the Reign of Terror that followed the French Revolution had gripped his imagination. The palace corridors would ring with sounds of mock sword fights as Ged and his younger brother, Andrei, acted out heroic combat scenes.

Rock band manager by day, shifter rescuer by night. Ged had become his own version of his childhood hero. But the ache in his heart had never gone away. And Lidi's presence had brought the homesickness and the memories back. Stronger, sharper and more painful than ever.

I'm a bear. We don't do feelings. He bit back a laugh. *Yeah, keep telling yourself that whenever the homesickness hits.*

He looked up as the bathroom door opened and Lidi emerged. Wrapped in a fluffy white bathrobe, she had dried her hair and it hung in soft waves almost to her waist. His heartbeat stuttered at the sight of her, a new realization hitting him.

It didn't matter what he told himself about old loyalties and past promises. He had become engaged to Alyona for the sake of his country, their union born out of politics. not love. He had convinced himself back then that he could have been content with a marriage of convenience. Right now, it was as if the fates were laughing in his face.

The moment Lidi had walked—or stormed—into his life, everything had changed. His feelings for her went way beyond anything physical. The fates had decided she was his mate. Whether he liked it or not, that meant he was responsible for her.

What he had to do now was find a way to make his past and present work together in a way that didn't bring the future crashing down around them.

Chapter 3

Lidi viewed the first aid kit with suspicion. "I can't take this robe off. I'm not wearing anything underneath it."

Ged groaned. "Comments like that aren't helping me concentrate on the practicalities."

She knew exactly what he meant. They were sitting inches apart on the bed and his nearness was so tempting it was sinful. Inexperience didn't count. Her imagination was going into overdrive, heat surging through her in waves that were pleasurable, tormenting and wildly inconvenient.

Since Ged seemed determined to deal with her injuries, she reluctantly slid the robe off her left shoulder and down to the elbow on that side, clutching it tightly in place across her breasts with her other hand.

She already knew the cuts on her arm were bad.

When she had broken the tiny bathroom window of her prison and forced her way through, she had been aware of the jagged shards tearing into her flesh. Because she had needed to slither down a steep wall and get away from the palace as fast as she could, it had been some time before she was able to take a look at her wounds. All she knew was, as she ran, she could feel hot, wet blood soaking her sleeve. When she finally stopped, everything had swum out of focus and she lay panting on her side until the world righted itself.

"How did you keep going with injuries like these?" Ged's hand on her elbow was gentle as he bent closer to examine the damage to her flesh.

"I had to." That was what she had told herself at the time, forcing herself on, one pain-filled step at a time. "Once I had managed to get out of that cell, it would have been crazy to let anything stop me." She managed a smile. "I was even wearing the clothes I'd been captured in. You don't think I'd have chosen to make that journey in ankle boots and without a warm coat, do you?"

His face was inches from hers as he raised his eyes to look at her, "This should have been stitched when you did it, and you're lucky these wounds didn't become infected."

"I bathed my arm in fresh water whenever I got the chance. And I'm a shifter. You know as well as I do that we heal fast."

"Are you always this stubborn?"

Lidi started to laugh. "Let me see...my father once asked my mother if an evil spirit tricked them and substituted a mule shifter for their bear baby. Does that answer your question?"

He smiled. "After three weeks, it's too late for stitches. All I can do is apply a balm and put a dressing on your arm."

Lidi watched as he scooped lotion out of a tub. When his fingertips touched her arm, she flinched and Ged raised questioning brows.

"Am I hurting you?"

"A little." It was true, but her reaction had been more about the impact of his touch. Or rather, the intention behind the contact. He wanted to heal and comfort her.

Their DNA was half-human and half-bear. While bears were solitary creatures, shifters mated for life. Until they met their mate, they were free to live by human rules. But Lidi was a Callistoya noble, constrained by centuries of formality and duty. Their land had not moved in step with the mortal realm.

Her mother, in particular, had been determined that her daughter should observe the traditions of the ancient name into which she had married. From the day Lidi was born, Olga, Countess of Aras, had sworn her only child would marry well. She would train her daughter to rise above her instincts and marry for convenience instead of love. Even if she found her fated mate, Lidi, as the daughter of an aristocrat, would not be allowed to spend her life with him. Her parents would choose her partner. With that in mind, Olga had raised her in the ways of the bear.

There had been one problem with that plan. From a very early age, it was obvious that Lidi was unlike other bear shifters. Words like *unusual* and *flighty* were always attached to her. Her father scratched his head over her while her mother described her as *overemotional*, possibly the worst character trait she could conceive of. No matter how hard they tried to confine her spirit and mold her to their expectations, Lidi didn't change. Among her werebear counterparts, she was quicksilver to their lead. Ruled by her powerful human emotions and intuition, she refused to conform, preferring a life of rebellion to one of compliance.

During her early years, Lidi's mother had played the part of a bear in the wild. Demonstrating affection, protection and devotion, she had remained close to her daughter only until Lidi reached an age when Olga judged she could survive on her own. After that, mirroring the actions of a bear mother in the wild, she had tenaciously cast her aside. It was a tactic that worked effectively for most werebears.

But Lidi wasn't like most werebears. She could still remember the shock and distress she had endured. The mother who had protected and cared for her one day was coldly turning her back the next. Her half-human heart had shattered, her two-year-old cries echoing through the stately corridors as her governess dragged her away. Even now, she awoke sometimes to find her pillow damp with tears and her hand outstretched as though reaching for her mother's skirts.

Ged's fingers smoothing the herbal-scented balm over her damaged flesh was the first positive touch she had encountered since her mother's last embrace. It was almost too much to endure.

He used gentle, circular strokes to apply the balm, the action stinging slightly while also warming and soothing. Everything faded away except Ged and the point where his fingers caressed her. With a sigh, she gave in to temptation and rested her forehead against the smooth, hard muscle of his shoulder. Just this once, she would let someone else take over. She would allow herself these few minutes of bliss, of surrendering to the feeling of every care and hurt being smoothed away. By the time he finished, she was almost asleep.

Ged carefully placed adhesive dressings over the cuts. "They should stay in place without bandages." He held out a couple of painkillers. "Now take these and get some sleep."

"I have to get home—"

His fingers on her lips silenced her. "When you travel on a plane and the crew give you the safety information, they tell you to fit your own oxygen mask before helping others."

She frowned. "I have no idea what you're talking about. I've never been on an airplane. This is the first time I've left the kingdom of Callistoya." Her voice was muffled by his hand.

Ged laughed. "I should have remembered we come from the land that time forgot. I was trying to find an analogy to explain how you should take care of yourself before trying to look out for your father. Sleep will refresh you."

The bed *was* tempting, and what Ged was saying did make sense. Exhaustion hit her all at once, leaving her feeling as though she'd run into a brick wall. "Okay. I suppose a few hours won't make much difference." If she was less tired she might actually be able to think of a way out of her predicament.

Within minutes, she was nestled between crisp sheets and plump pillows. Although her troubles tried to intrude, her body relaxed and she began to drift into slumber. She was conscious of the tiny sounds Ged made as he moved around the room, but the knowledge that he was close by added to her sense of well-being.

For now, she would let him take care of her. There would be enough time tomorrow to continue the fight.

"We have a problem."

Although it was tempting to tell his security manager to deal with whatever it was and leave him alone, Ged knew it must be important. Rick wouldn't bother him unless it was serious.

He glanced over at the bed where Lidi was still sleeping soundly. Ged had remained awake, checking his emails and fine-tuning arrangements for forthcoming appearances. He had also checked on flights to Siberia, planning the best way to get Lidi close enough to her own magical land without enduring another epic journey.

There was a major problem to be overcome before he could send her on her way. International travel required a passport. As far as the mortal world was concerned, Lidi didn't exist.

The whole time, his mind had been preoccupied with more than the logistics. How could he let her go back, knowing the danger she faced? No one knew better than he did what Vasily was capable of. Yet, having glimpsed that determined gleam in her eye, he had a feeling stopping her would not be an easy task. If only it was as simple as she believed. If he could just take her hand and walk at her side across that invisible border. Even without the spell that had been cast to stop him, the barriers were insurmountable.

"I need you to come and check something out." For

the first time ever, Ged could hear a note of fear as Rick spoke.

Although his intuition was telling him that tremor in his security manager's voice should have him heading for the door, his newfound responsibility to Lidi made him pause. "What is it?"

"A group of men have stormed the foyer. Hotel security have managed to lock down the lower floor, but they don't know how long they'll be able to hold them." Rick sounded slightly incredulous. "The manager thinks it could be a terrorist attack."

Ged muttered a curse. "Wake the others. Tell them to come to my room. See if you can get me real time pictures of what's happening downstairs."

"I'm on it." Now he had been given a focus, the hesitation was gone and Rick was all action.

Ged ended the call and glanced in Lidi's direction again. Although he didn't like the chances that this was a coincidence, there was a possibility the attack could have nothing to do with her presence here. The hotel was full of celebrities. The terrorists—if that's what they were—could be taking advantage of the shock factor of a strike against some of the world's most famous names.

Even as his mind went through that reasoned argument, his gut was telling him another story. His protective instincts were on high alert. Some additional sense had been triggered when he met Lidi. His mate was in danger. There was no need to wait for confirmation. He could *feel* it. And, for a man who didn't do feelings, that was a powerful motivator.

He headed through to the sitting room, closing the bedroom door behind him. Rick arrived a minute or two later. "The manager has sent some images to my cell phone." He handed it over to Ged.

The black-and-white footage showed four men entering the hotel lobby. Even though the pictures were grainy, Ged could tell these men were big. Tall and broad-shouldered, they moved with a steadfast confidence he would recognize anywhere. They were bear shifters. There was a good chance that when they shifted they would resemble Siberian brown bears. Just like him, Lidi and the entire population of Callistoya.

"What makes the hotel staff think it's a terrorist attack? I don't see any weapons."

On the screen, the men began to smash up the reception area, systematically tearing apart the elegant decor with their bare hands. When the hotel security staff approached them, they were flung aside like rag dolls.

"When the manager called me to warn me what was happening, a terrorist attack was his suggestion. That was because robbery didn't seem to be the motive," Rick explained. "The guy was a wreck. I don't think he knew *what* was happening. The hotel security system allows the manager to isolate each floor. Right now, these guys are contained on the first floor. The elevators have been shut down and they can't gain access to any of the other floors," Rick said. "The problem is that the guests are going to start waking up about now. Once that happens, word will filter through to the outside world."

"The guests are trapped on their own floors." Ged pointed out.

"For now. These guys are still on the rampage in the foyer. It looks like they are trying to gain access to the elevators or the stairs, so that makes it appear that the guests are the target. The manager is locked in his office with those security staff who managed to get away."

"Have the police been called?"

"They're outside the hotel and the manager is communicating with them. They're holding back from storming the building because some of the security staff who were injured when these guys stormed in are still trapped in the lobby with them. It's a hostage situation that has the potential to go badly wrong."

They were interrupted by the arrival of the rest of the band. The lead guitarist, Torque was accompanied by his wife, Hollie.

"Sarange volunteered to stay with the kids," Khan explained. He and his wife never traveled anywhere without their two children. The friendship group had recently expanded further to include Torque and Hollie's twin baby boys.

"What's up?" Torque asked.

Ged measured the situation. If he said too much in front of Rick, he risked giving away his own shifter identity and that of his friends. It came down to how much he trusted this man. He shrugged.

"There is a group of bear shifters smashing up the lobby." Just as he'd anticipated, Rick didn't blink.

"Friends of yours?" Khan asked.

Ged shook his head. "There is also a female bear-shifter aristocrat asleep in my bedroom—" he held up his hand to prevent any comments "—we don't have time for jokes. I suspect she's the reason they're here."

"Do they want to harm her, Ged?" Hollie's calm question got straight to the point.

"She's escaped from captivity. I'm guessing they want to return her."

Diablo flexed his muscles. "Then let's take them out."

"It's not that easy. There are a lot of people around and there are security cameras everywhere. The police are outside and I figure the press will be onto it soon, if they aren't already."

Ged was trying to formulate a plan as he spoke. The worst nightmare of any shifter living in the human world was the loss of anonymity. Mortals enjoyed books, movies, comics, and games about werewolves and other supernatural entities. Let them get the tiniest hint that such beings existed alongside them and all hell would break loose. The peace shifters had enjoyed for centuries would be shattered. Old enmities would resurface, hunting season on shifters would probably be declared, there was a possibility experimentation might be sanctioned… Shifter Zoo? It didn't bear thinking about.

"The police are here. Maybe we should let them take care of it?" Rick suggested.

Ged shook his head. "Those guys down there won't hesitate to shift if they're cornered. The place they come from is…unusual." How could he explain his homeland to his friends? Callistoya had always been ruled over by bear shifters. For that reason, the tiny kingdom remained hidden from human sight. "They belong in a land where shifting isn't hidden or private. They won't understand the need to steer clear of publicity. No, we have to corner them somewhere away from cameras and other people."

"I'll get a plan of the hotel," Rick said.

"Lidi climbed the balconies," Ged pointed out. "Is there any chance the intruders could try the same tactic?"

"I don't think so. They're locked into the foyer right now and can't break out. Plus, their focus seems to be on the interior of the hotel." Rick turned back as he reached the door. "When you come down to the lobby, don't take the main staircase. There's a smaller one that the staff use. You'll have the element of surprise if you come that way."

Ged nodded. "Get the manager to tell the guests to stay in their rooms. I don't care what message he gives them. Faulty electrical wiring, poisonous gas in the air, a problem with the early-morning croissants…leave it up to his imagination. Just make sure they stay where they are."

When Rick had gone, Ged became aware of his other friends regarding him with curiosity. In all the years they'd known each other, he'd never revealed anything about his past, or shown any interest in a woman. He guessed the questions would come later. Would he answer them? Now was not the time to make that decision.

"Our first job is to override the hotel's security system. I want to shut down every camera in this place. Then we need to back these intruders into a corner of our choosing while making sure they can't gain access to the upper floors. If we can do that and also make sure none of the guests know anything about it, I'll buy you all a meal in the best restaurant in Cannes."

"Will the bear-shifter aristocrat be your date?" Khan was the only person who had the audacity to ask such a question.

"Don't push your luck, tiger boy," Ged growled. There was a hierarchy in the shifter world, but in this group it didn't matter about tigers, dragons or wolves. Ged was in charge. Always.

Khan held up a hand in a peacemaking gesture and Torque stepped into the silence that followed. "Hollie and I will check out the security system." He took his wife's hand. "Nothing like a little dragon breath to fry the electronics."

Ged watched them go. "Dev and Finglas, I want you to check out the elevators. They aren't working right now because they are locked down, but once Torque and Hollie screw up the system they may start up again."

Dev, the snow leopard shifter who was the band's lead guitarist, nodded. "We'll disable them." He and Finglas, the werewolf bass guitarist, went out of the room.

Ged turned to Khan and Diablo. "A bear, a tiger and a panther. The three of us against four bears. How do we feel about those odds, guys?"

The sound of the bedroom door closing made him look up. Lidi was dressed in the clothes Rick had delivered earlier. Jeans and a gray sweater fitted her slender figure perfectly. Her long dark hair was tied back and, although she was still pale, she looked refreshed.

"The odds just improved." The determined look in her eyes was stronger than ever. "Because now we're four against four."

Ged took Lidi to one side, speaking quietly so only she could hear. "You're injured."

"I was injured when I climbed the outside of this building and fought three men." Did he seriously think he was going to shut her out of this, whatever *this* was? She had to remind herself that he didn't know her very well. If he did, he'd know all about her tenacity. "I heard what you were saying. Four bear shifters? They are here to either take me back to Callistoya or to assassinate you. Maybe both."

"You think Vasily sent them?"

She nodded, her lip curling at the thought of the man who had masterminded a massacre so he could usurp the throne of Callistoya. Vasily was everything Ged was not. Vain, ambitious and cowardly, he preyed on the worst characteristics of his followers. Every bear shifter Lidi knew took pride in his or her strength, courage, intelligence and loyalty. Vasily deliberately undermined those values. He targeted groups within the kingdom who were vulnerable and preyed on their insecurities.

Even so, Vasily had been surprised when he had seized power at the strength of feeling against him. Callistoya had been weakened by the death of its beloved king together with most of his council, but it was a land of tradition and Vasily had no direct claim to the crown. His mother had married King Ivan, Ged's father, after his first wife died. Since the king's first marriage had produced two sons—Ged and Andrei—they were the rightful heirs to the throne.

Callistoya had been a peaceful nation when Ged's father was alive, with only minor skirmishes in the outlying regions and uprisings when the crops failed or the taxes were raised. Ged's father had been a strong king who knew how to deal with those problems, but Vasily was good at stirring up trouble. He had incited the rebel forces in the east of the country. They claimed that an area of land belonged to them, not to the Crown, and demanded freedom from taxation. Vasiliy supported them, keeping the feud going until they refused to back down despite King Ivan's offer of a peacekeeping council. Then, having argued with his stepfather over money and titles, Vasily joined the rebels, his presence strengthening their cause and providing him with a ready-made army.

The night King Ivan died would be remembered in Callistoyan history as a night of betrayal and bloodshed. Lidi was unsure of all the details, but she knew it was the occasion of Ged's engagement to Duchess Alyona Ivanov. Negotiations between the king and Vasily had been ongoing, and Vasily had agreed to suspend hostilities and attend the celebration. As a sign of his commitment to peace, he had pledged to accompany his mother, the queen, to the party.

He and a group of his men had been welcomed into the palace and an evening of feasting and entertainment had ensued. During the night, the king and most of his entourage had been slaughtered in their beds.

At some point before the murders, Ged and his brother, Andrei, had disappeared. The following day, Vasily had announced to a stunned nation that he was taking over the throne. The murderers were never brought to justice, although suspicion naturally fell on Vasily.

When Vasily was crowned, many of Callistoya's subjects were outraged. They had been convinced that Ged, their true king, was still alive. Vasily had used the death of Alyona against him. On the night of the massacre, Alyona had been found dead in Ged's bed. She had been strangled before a silver knife was plunged into her heart. If Ged was such a hero, Vasily asked, why had he deserted his betrothed in her hour of need? Or was the truth more sinister? Was Ged the person responsible for her death? Had he killed the others to cover up for his guilt? If he was innocent, why hadn't he come back to Callistoya to clear his name? The whispering campaign had filtered throughout the kingdom until a seed of doubt had been planted against the man whose name, until then, had stood for honor and decency.

Ged's uncle, Eduard Tavisha, now the leader of the resistance, had done his best to end any speculation about Vasily's claim to the throne. The matter was simple. Ged was the king. Next in the line of succession was his younger brother, Andrei. After him, there was a cousin. No matter how much noise Vasily the Usurper made, he was no relation to the Tavisha family. He had no right to the crown.

Vasily had greeted Eduard's proclamation with rage. Ged had confirmed his unsuitability to be king by fleeing like a dog with his tail between his legs, he declared. Only Vasily's own strength of character had saved the day when he stepped in and took over. Since most people knew he had been behind the massacre, his protestations, far from fooling anyone, only made the situation worse. Seeking a way to strengthen his position, his gaze had turned to an alliance with the noble house of Rihanoff.

Looking back, Lidi supposed she could have dealt with Vasily's proposal more diplomatically. He was known for his vindictive nature and her point-blank refusal had provoked an angry response. Determined to get her to change her mind, Vasily had tried persuasion, moved on to threats, and ended by throwing Lidi and her father, the Count of Aras, into prison.

"I *know* he sent them," she said in reply to Ged's question. Vasily was cruel as well as vengeful. He would have her followed to the ends of the earth rather than allow her to escape him.

"If his men have been trailing you, why have they

waited until now to attempt to capture you? It would have been easier to do it when you were alone and on the road."

"Who knows? Maybe they wanted to find out where I was going. Once they knew I was with you, it would have changed everything." She squared her shoulders, feeling the pull as she moved her injured arm. "There is only one way to find out."

He was staring at her in that disconcerting way he had. As though he was looking *through* her, seeing something in her that captivated him. It was the look every woman should want from a man. *If* she wanted a man…

"Are your friends really big-cat shifters?" She attempted to deflect his attention by glancing at the two men who were still standing near the door.

"Ah, hell. I'd forgotten we weren't alone." He ran a hand through his hair. "How do you do that, Lidi? How do you make me lose sight of everything except you?"

"It's not deliberate." Without thinking, she reached up a hand and brushed back the lock of hair that had flopped onto his forehead. "And it's mutual."

Touching him only confirmed what she already knew. Heat pulsed through her at the brief connection, and she saw Ged's eyes widen. There was no escaping this attraction between them. Unwanted and inconvenient, it was burning them both up.

He caught hold of her hand, his strong fingers wrapping around hers. The delicious tingling sensations continued, but his touch grounded her. For the first time since her mother had walked away, she felt safe and protected with another person.

"We have to go." The regret in his eyes matched her

own. Taking a breath, he turned to his friends. "Khan, Diablo...this is Lidi. She's coming with us."

She could see the interest in their eyes as they looked at her, particularly when their eyes dropped to take in their clasped hands.

Khan smiled at her. "Nice to meet you, Lidi. Now can we please go and kick some bear butt?"

Diablo clapped a hand to his forehead with a groan. "One day, Khan will think before he speaks. Sadly, I don't think it's going to happen anytime soon."

Khan was protesting in an undertone as they headed toward the door. "What did I say?"

"First impressions count. You just sounded like you were excited about kicking naked asses."

Khan gave a snort of laughter. As Ged opened the door, his mood changed, becoming instantly serious. They made their way along the corridor in silence. Although her own body was on high alert, Lidi was also aware of the coiled strength of her companions. They were a team, communicating in gestures and eye movements. She had engaged in coaching sessions with the Aras guards, and her training had been rigorous and demanding. Even so, she sensed something in this group went beyond her experiences. She had always felt there was an element missing from her instruction, a higher level that remained stubbornly out of her reach. Now she was witnessing it, and it had nothing to do with experience or skill. It was about trust. These men knew they could count on each other, no matter what.

They avoided the main staircase, heading instead for a door marked *Réservé au personnel*. Ged took the lead as they went down the stairs. Lidi was behind him with Khan next and Diablo at the rear. When they reached the second floor, a man was waiting for them. Although Lidi tensed for action, she recognized him. He was the guy who had tried to stop her from getting to Ged when she climbed into the hotel. She recalled that just after she had broken free of his grasp and kicked him, Ged had called him Rick.

Rick's eyes flickered briefly to her face and he rubbed his chest reminiscently, but he gave no other sign that he knew her.

"Did you get a plan of the first floor?" Ged spoke in a low voice.

"Yeah. There is a storage room behind the kitchens. It has no windows, so no one can see in, and Torque has shut down the security cameras. If you can get these guys in there, you will be out of sight of the rest of the hotel. There is also an exit that leads to a delivery area, so I can bring a vehicle to the door and…uh, dispose of any evidence."

Ged placed a hand on his shoulder. "Good work. I need you to direct us to this room and then get the hell out of the way. This will be messy."

Lidi understood what he meant. His friend was a human and he didn't want him caught up in the middle of a shifter fight. She knew her world was unique. Callistoya was inhabited by bear shifters, and diversity had barely touched their magical realm. It was only since her escape that she had encountered humans. Of course, since she was half-human herself, their ways, although occasionally unusual, weren't completely strange to her. The biggest difference was when it came to combat. Then, of course, a human didn't stand a chance against a shifter.

Rick accompanied them down the remaining stairs.

As they drew closer to the lobby, they could hear noises. It sounded like the intruders were trying everything they could to gain access to the upper floors.

"They haven't figured out yet that the system has been overridden," Diablo murmured. "The locks have been disabled, and they could just walk through."

"What are they saying?" Khan asked. "It sounds like they're speaking Russian."

Lidi turned to look at Ged, the only other person who could understand what the men were saying. She saw his face tighten with anger as he listened to the furious comments of Vasily's men.

"Close," Ged said. "It's the language of Callistoya, their homeland. They're know Lidi is here and they're trying to find a way to get to her." He gestured to the door. "Let's go."

They stepped into the foyer together and Lidi took a moment to view the damage. It looked like a hurricane had blown through the building. Furniture had been overturned and ripped apart as though a child had thrown a tantrum and destroyed its dollhouse. Ruined light fixtures dangled from the vaulted ceiling, and the doors on one of the elevators were hanging half-off. As they moved stealthily toward them, two of the intruders were using a table as a battering ram, attempting to pound their way into a room that Lidi guessed must be the manager's office.

Close to the entrance, two figures lay on the floor, their uniforms soaked with blood. Lidi couldn't see any signs of life from either of them. Nearby, a woman was curled in a fetal position with her hands over her head.

Ged moved forward, drawing the attention of the intruders. All four of them turned their way. One man lunged toward Lidi, his hand reaching for her arm, but Ged stepped between them.

"Touch her and you die." There was no doubt about it. Ged meant what he said.

The other man's lips drew back in a snarl. "She is the reason we are here. She is an escaped criminal and our orders are to return her to justice."

"On whose authority?"

"I am Pyotr. I act on behalf of King Vasily of Callistoya."

Ged drew himself up to his full, impressive height. "You have been misinformed, my friend. There is only one king of Callistoya...and you're looking at him."

Chapter 4

There is only one king of Callistoya and you're looking at him.

As he spoke the words, Ged's well-laid schemes came crashing down around him. As he faced Pyotr and Vasily's other thugs, he knew the truth. He couldn't stay away. The crown of Callistoya belonged to him, and no matter what he had to do, he would return and find a way to wrest it from Vasily so he could wear it with pride.

He had a moment or two for that thought to register before Pyotr shifted. Lightning fast, Ged gave a signal to his companions. There were a lot of myths around shifting, many of them originating in the books and movies of human culture. It wasn't a long, protracted and painful process. Shifting was as natural as breathing. It was about reaching deep inside and finding the inner animal, then relaxing into those memories and muscles. For

Ged, it was a split second in which he closed his eyes as a human and opened them as a huge Callistoyan bear. Shrugging aside the remnants of the clothing he hadn't had time to remove, he rose onto his hind legs.

In the wild, bears avoided fighting. Armed with tremendous strength, large claws and teeth like knives, they were wise enough to know they could inflict severe injuries on each other.

To avoid physical conflict, bears used vocalization and posturing to demonstrate their dominance and intimidate an opponent. This allowed them to establish a hierarchy within which they could interact without violence. A bear's place in the social structure was based on its size, strength, age and disposition.

As the two groups faced each other, it was apparent Ged had the advantage. He was the alpha, towering over the others, his superiority obvious. They should have bowed before him. But this wasn't a forest and they weren't fighting over a mate, or a kill. They were shifters, not wild bears. They retained an element of their human senses even in their bear form, and Vasily's men were here on a mission—one that didn't allow them to back down.

Even Lidi, who should have been subordinate to each of the males present, had an agenda that suppressed her bear instincts. Instead of signaling her subservience, her stance was combative. Standing tall, with her head held high and her golden eyes alert, she was the most beautiful sight Ged had ever seen.

Although there was nothing he'd rather do more than spend time admiring Lidi, either in human or bear form, there were more urgent matters to take care of right now. If his opponents were surprised to be faced with a tiger and a panther as well as two bears, they didn't show it. As they charged forward, it was clear they were used to fighting as a unit.

Bring it on.

The lobby was filled with the sounds of claws scrabbling on marble, deep bear grunts and harsher cat cries as solid, muscular bodies connected. Ged squared up to Pyotr. His aim, as always in a bear fight, was to bring his adversary down. Once a bear was on the ground, it was easily defeated. Using his superior height to his advantage, he lunged, striking out with his huge claws. The blow caught Pyotr behind his ear, slicing through thick fur and connecting with flesh.

Pyotr staggered back but retaliated with a smack to the side of Ged's head that made his ears ring. It shouldn't have happened. Pyotr was an inferior opponent, but Ged's attention was divided between his own struggle and what was going on with Lidi. His protective instincts were overriding his self-preservation, placing him in unnecessary danger.

What had he been thinking of? Allowing her to get involved in this brawl was madness. Even though she clearly knew how to handle herself in a fight, she was much smaller and lighter than the other shifters. As he dug his claws into the flesh of Pyotr's shoulder, drawing him closer in preparation for a bite, Ged risked another glance in Lidi's direction.

He saw at once that there was nothing to worry about. Her speed and agility were astounding, making everyone around her—even Khan and Diablo—appear slow and lumbering in comparison. Relying on tactics that were unusual for a bear, she dodged the swipes of her much larger foe, ducking under his huge paw and emerging behind him to deliver her own hits. It was working. Ged could see blood staining the other bear's fur and heard his growls of frustration.

Conscious that at any minute the manager's door could open, the guests could defy the instruction to stay in their rooms or the police might decide to act, Ged knew they had to move the action away from the public space. He pulled Pyotr to him and sank his teeth into the other bear's shoulder. The temptation to rip into him and finish it there and then was overwhelming, but bear entrails in the lobby? Try explaining *that* to a forensics team.

Instead, he hauled Pyotr in the direction of the kitchens, trusting his companions to accompany him. From the noise level just behind him, he guessed they had followed his lead.

Once they were inside the storage room, Pyotr sensed what was happening and knew he only had one chance. Lowering his head, he charged at Ged's midsection with his teeth bared. It was a brave move, but Ged had seen it before. Pyotr was expecting him to drop to all fours to protect his belly, at which point the other bear would tip him over. Instead, Ged waited until the last moment, just before Pyotr's lethal teeth connected with his flesh. Then he gripped the other shifter and, using his monumental strength, flipped him onto his back.

Surprise registered in the depths of Pyotr's eyes as Ged placed both paws on his chest. The final move was swift and brutal. With his thorax crushed, Pyotr was dead within seconds, leaving Ged free to help his friends. Although, as he drew himself up to his full height once more, it looked like his companions were doing just fine on their own.

Khan, the deadliest weretiger of them all, had one of

the bear shifters cornered. Ged recognized his friend's stance. From the way Khan's huge fangs were bared and he was poised to crouch, he was going in for the kill. In another corner of the room, Diablo was shaking another of the intruders around like a rag doll.

That left Lidi. She was still facing up to her massive challenger with a dexterity and bravery that astounded him. With jaws snapping and claws slashing, they were engaged in a classic bear fight, but, as Ged watched, the large male raised a paw and slammed Lidi against the wall. With a snort of rage, Ged made a move to intervene.

Before he could get there, Lidi was springing back from the tiled surface. As the male swung at her, she ducked low and came up at his side, dealing him a blow in the kidneys that made him howl. When he reached for her, she slipped behind him. In a move that made Ged's lips twitch into an appreciative smile, she hurled herself onto the other bear's back, clinging on as she clamped her jaws onto the tender flesh between his neck and shoulder.

Maybe Lidi didn't need his help after all. She hung on with her claws and teeth as her adversary tried everything to dislodge her. It wasn't pleasant, but it was effective. Blood sprayed onto the walls until, eventually, Lidi's victim dropped to the floor. When she released her grip, he twitched a few times, then became completely still.

Khan and Diablo had both won their fights. They moved into place, standing one on each side of Ged as he shifted back. A swift glance around the small storage room was enough to confirm that he had no need of their protection. All four intruders lay lifeless on the tiles. The two werecats followed Ged's lead and shifted into human form.

"Bears." Khan shook his head as he viewed the bodies. "Stubborn as hell. They never know when it's in their interests to surrender."

Lidi hadn't shifted, and with a flash of insight, Ged recognized the reason. In her homeland of Callistoya, there was no shame in making the transition from bear to human. Being naked in front of others was an accepted part of a shifter's life. But this wasn't her homeland, and she didn't know him and his friends. Keeping her head low, she moved restlessly from foot to foot, the classic sign of a bear in distress.

Slightly bemused that he was already so in tune with her emotions, Ged cast a quick look around. The storage room looked like a scene from a horror movie and they needed to move fast. These bear shifters were dead in the true sense of the word, but only silver could truly destroy their souls. The final kindness to a defeated enemy was to finish them in the manner of a true warrior. That meant decapitating them with a silver sword, the handle of which had been specially adapted so that the person who wielded it could do so without being poisoned. No one said being a shifter was easy.

Then, of course, would come the task of getting rid of the bear bodies and cleaning up. Modesty should be a long way down the list of priorities. But this was Lidi and she needed his help.

"Find something so we can cover ourselves." He jerked his head in the direction of the kitchen.

Khan blinked at him. "Are you crazy?"

"Do it." Ged wasn't in the mood for a debate.

Shrugging, Khan went through to the kitchen. When he returned, he had several white aprons over one arm and a scowl on his face. "If a picture of me wearing one of these ends up on the internet—"

"Quit griping and put it on." Diablo was already

tying one of the garments around his waist. "If Ged wants us to do it, it's done."

Ged gave him a grateful look before placing an apron close to Lidi. "Now turn your backs."

"You've got to be..." Khan caught a glimpse of Ged's expression and held up his hands in a gesture of surrender. "Okay. Okay." Obediently, he turned to face the wall opposite Lidi. "What is this?" His whisper to Diablo was just audible. "We're all shifters. Nudity is part of the deal."

"Stop being such a tiger. Just for once," Diablo growled back.

Ged could hear Lidi moving around behind them.

"I'm decent." Her voice was gruff, and when he turned, her cheeks were bright pink. The apron she was wearing was too big and she'd wrapped it tight around her, tying it so it covered her whole body, back and front. Hanging her head, she scuffed the floor with one bare foot. "Sorry."

Following on from her strength and courage, her embarrassment revealed a fragility that surprised him. It made him want to go to her, to reassure her, to hold her. *No.* He had to put those thoughts out of his head. Even if they didn't have blood and gore to clean up, bear-shifter bodies to dispose of, and a hell of a cover story to come up with, there was no room in his life for a mate. Particularly one as sweet and vulnerable as Lidi.

"Let's get moving." Determinedly, he turned away from her. "We've got work to do."

Ged had told Vasily's men that he was the King of Callistoya. Did that mean he was prepared to fight for his rights? Lidi didn't dare ask the question. Having come all this way and already faced a crushing disappointment, she wasn't prepared to go there all over again. And there were more immediate problems demanding her attention. Although she had wrapped the oversize apron as tightly around her as she could, it kept coming undone and showed an alarming tendency to flap open at the back. Clutching the two sides together, she followed Ged up the stairs.

This new modesty confused her. Until now, she had never had a problem with nakedness. Back home in Callistoya, she thought nothing of slipping out of her clothes to shift. Life would have been very difficult for werebears if everyone had tried to cover themselves before and after shifting.

Back in that storage room, she had developed a sudden awareness of her body. It had prevented her from shifting from bear to human. All she knew for sure was that it was more to do with Ged than his friends. It was about how *he* saw her. It was foolish, but she felt shy around him. And she didn't want his eyes on her body *then*. Not surrounded by carnage.

Curiously, it didn't work both ways. Since his own apron didn't come close to covering his rear, as they climbed the stairs she was treated to the delicious sight of long, muscular legs and round, firm buttocks. She was used to naked masculinity, but this was the first time she had seen a male body that appealed to her so strongly. It was rapidly becoming her favorite view.

"Khan and Diablo will deliver the mercy blows to the bodies, then Rick will clean up." Ged turned to look at her as he spoke, and, aware that she had been caught staring, Lidi felt the telltale blush stain her cheeks. She tilted her chin. If he didn't want her to look he should

have done a better job of covering up. The smile in his eyes told her he was well aware of the reason for her mortification.

When they reached Ged's room, Lidi grabbed some of the new clothes Rick had provided and headed for the shower. Although she needed to wash the signs of battle from her body, she also wanted a break from Ged's disquieting presence. Being close to him was like staring into the sun. Everything else faded in comparison with his brilliance. But she needed to step away from the glare and view her situation realistically once more.

The fight with Vasily's men hadn't changed anything. Her long and tiring journey had been a waste of time. She still had to find a way to free her father from captivity while avoiding marriage with Vasily. It seemed like an impossible task, but Lidi had never been one to shy away from a challenge. As she stepped under the jets of warm water, her mind was forming and reviewing a series of plans.

Annoyingly, her thoughts kept encountering the same barrier. Ged. No matter how much she told herself she had to walk away from him, her emotions weren't ready for that message. Deep down inside her, something fundamental had changed in the instant she saw him on the steps of the movie theater.

He's my mate.

She groaned aloud, clenching a fist against the tiled wall. Why did this have to happen now? And why did it have to be *him*? Even if he wasn't the king without a crown, he was the most unsuitable man she could have chosen. Everyone in Callistoya knew about the royal marriage pact. A Tavisha must marry the daughter of one of the five founding families. It was an ancient, un-

shakable agreement. And Lidi did not come from one of those families, so...*whoa!* Why was she even thinking about Ged and marriage in the same breath?

Straightening her spine, she let the scented gel do its work. There had been other occasions throughout Callistoyan history when this had happened. When an inconvenient attraction had occurred. It could be overcome. It was difficult, but not impossible. Nobles married for convenience, not love. Ged himself had been engaged to another woman. Clearly, since Lidi was his mate, he hadn't really been in love with Alyona.

Lidi had always been strong, able to meet any confrontation head-on. Being the bear shifter who didn't conform had always been hard. She'd grown used to the difficult task of wrestling with her unruly emotions. All it needed was focus...and in this case, some distance.

The thought instantly triggered a feeling of regret so powerful it was almost a physical pain. It was as if giant hands were pulling at her, tearing her in two. Common sense and duty were telling her to get away. These new, unfamiliar passions were prompting her to stay.

Placing her hands flat against the cubicle wall, she bowed her head as the water rinsed the last of the shampoo from her hair. She didn't have time to work out this inner conflict. While she was here in this luxury hotel, her father was at Vasily's mercy.

She snorted. *Mercy?* Vasily didn't know the meaning of the word. After stepping from the shower, she dried herself and dressed quickly in jeans, sweatshirt and boots. Thoughts of her father's plight gave her actions a new determination.

When she emerged from the bathroom, there was no sign of Ged in either the sitting room or bedroom.

Although she had intended to tell him she was leaving, she couldn't help feeling a sense of relief. This way was probably better. This way she didn't have to put her own emotional strength to the test.

Feeling a lot like a thief sneaking out into the night, she opened the door. Immediately, a security guard, who wore the same black uniform as Rick, with the Beast logo on the breast pocket, sprang to attention.

"Ged asked me to take you to Khan's room." He gestured along the corridor. "The band are all there."

Lidi weighed her options. Refuse to go and cause a scene? Go with him and waste more time? She didn't like either option. "I know my way."

"Uh…okay." He scratched his head. "But Ged said—"

"I really don't need an escort." She used her best aristocratic voice, the one that had gotten her out of so many tricky situations in the past. It was an almost-perfect impression of her mother…and no one had argued with Olga Rihanoff.

The guy actually blushed. "Then I guess…"

Lidi moved in the direction he had indicated without waiting for him to finish. The only problem now was that he was watching her and she had no idea where she was going. Luckily there was a turn in the hallway, and she followed it. Once she was out of the security guard's sight, she took a moment to lean against the wall, breathing deeply. A few feet away she could see the door marked *Réservé au personnel* that led to the staff staircase.

It was time to go.

Chapter 5

"You're leaving us?" It was Finglas who finally broke the silence.

Ged looked around the hotel room at the faces of his friends. He had known this wouldn't be easy, but the depth of the shock and hurt on their faces stunned him. It also caused an answering tug of pain deep in his own chest. For ten years, this group of people had been his family. Now he was facing the prospect of severing his ties with them. For a long time he had believed that nothing could match the misery of leaving Callistoya. Turned out he was wrong. It also turned out he wasn't that great at the whole "not doing emotions" thing.

Powering through the tightening in his throat, he forced himself to continue. "Guys, this is something I have to do."

"Why?" Sarange had tears in her eyes as she placed

a hand on his arm. "Explain it to us, Ged, so we know how to help you."

Ged glanced at the clock, judging Lidi would be finishing up in the shower and joining them soon. Khan and Diablo had followed him up to Khan's suite after they finished their grisly duty in the storage room, leaving Rick to dispose of the bodies of the intruders. Although Ged knew Lidi would be keen to get going straightaway, Sarange was right. She was one of his best friends, and he owed her, and the others, an explanation. Could he finally tell them his story? It felt like the time had come at last.

"I am the rightful king of a land called Callistoya." There. He'd said those words out loud at long last. And the rush of pride that came with them was all the confirmation he needed. Going back and fighting for his throne was the right thing to do. Getting past the obstacles was going to be a different matter. "It's a unique place. Imagine a medieval enclave high in the mountains in the center of a Siberian wasteland. A land that time forgot. Except it doesn't exist on any human map. It won't show up on a satellite image. It's only visible and accessible to shifters."

Torque frowned. "I'm struggling with the concept of a monarchy. We're shifters. That means we're immortal."

"Like you, I'm immortal and so were my ancestors," Ged said. "But we're not invincible. We can be killed by silver, fire or beheading. There are even some illnesses to which we don't have immunity, and that can be fatal. The Callistoya of my childhood was an enchanting place. In recent times, it has become a troubled land, plagued by constant battles. My father reigned for

many centuries before he was murdered. I believe my stepbrother, Vasily, was his killer. I was in the palace on the night of my father's death, but I remember nothing of what happened. I woke up two days later, here in the mortal realm. I had been badly beaten and I believe a spell had also been cast on me."

Diablo shook his head. "I can't believe we never knew about this side of your life."

"I kept it well hidden. For good reasons." The memories crowded in on him, and Ged looked at the clock again. What was keeping Lidi? "Other people were killed as well as my father, including my fiancée. She was found strangled and stabbed. In my bed."

"But you didn't do it," Hollie spoke without hesitation.

Ged smiled gratefully at her. "No, I didn't do it. But ever since then, Vasily has used her death as part of a campaign against me." He closed his eyes briefly, picturing Alyona's face the last time he had seen her. She had been laughing, making plans for their wedding, teasing him about keeping her dress secret until their big day…no. Even after all this time, it was too raw, too painful. He couldn't talk about that part of it. "I should have gone back immediately, raised an army, fought Vasily, sought justice for my father and for Alyona… but the grief and pain were too great. When I did make the attempt a few weeks later, I couldn't physically cross the border. There was some sort of magical barrier in place. Now after meeting Lidi and hearing what has been happening there, I know I have a duty to go back and put things right. I have to find a way across that barrier." He felt the tension in every part of his body. "I have to defeat Vasily."

"So this isn't forever?" The hopeful expression on Khan's face caused the constriction in Ged's chest to tighten further. These people were all his friends, but the bond between him and Khan...well, that had always been special.

"I can't say how long I will be gone. It could be for some time." He had to do this, no matter how much it hurt. "And I can't promise it won't be permanent."

"I can see how important this is to you, and I don't want to sound selfish, but what about Beast?" Torque asked.

And there it was. The all-important question. Ged had a duty to his country, but he also had a responsibility to the entity he had created. Because of him, Beast was one of the most popular rock bands on the planet. He had brought this group of incredibly talented people together. It was his vision and hard work that had taken them to the top and kept them there. Now he was telling them he was walking away. Could he do that? And if he did, what would it mean for Beast and for them as individuals?

He had an answer, but he hadn't discussed it with anyone. Not even the person it affected most. And he didn't have time for lengthy conversations...

"There is someone who has been at my right hand over the last year, someone who can take my place."

Ged looked directly at Hollie as he spoke. Her introduction into their friendship group had been unconventional. An undercover FBI agent who had been investigating a series of arson attacks, she had fallen in love with Torque, a dragon shifter. Hollie's commitment to the man she loved had been absolute, and she had taken his bite to become a dragon shifter herself.

Now they had their twin dragon babies to complete their family. While theirs was hardly a classic love story, it was definitely one that proved the theory of opposites attracting.

During her time with the band, Hollie had become Ged's unofficial assistant, to the point where he often wondered what he used to do without her. She was a fast learner, picking up every part of the job and anticipating his needs, often before he even knew them himself. He knew she enjoyed the work, but was she ready for this? And could she fit it into her new dragon-mom lifestyle?

The question was reflected back at him as Hollie returned his gaze. She was silent for long moments before she responded. "Do you think I can do it?"

"I know you can."

Her laugh was shaky. "I don't suppose I'll be able to call or email you if there's a problem?"

Ged shook his head. "Technology hasn't reached Callistoya." The clock was drawing his attention again. Lidi was taking a hell of a long time. He laughed. "Think letters written in longhand and delivered by a messenger on horseback."

Hollie looked around the assembled group. "What do you say? There are two more concerts before Christmas. Will you give me a tryout as your Ged substitute until then?"

Torque slid his arm around her waist. "We'll support you all the way. And I can take on more of the baby chores over the next few weeks."

There were nods and murmurs of agreement. Khan came forward to give Hollie a high five and Dev wrapped her in a hug. Ged exhaled long and slow. That was part one over with. The next part was even harder.

"Good. Because I have a plan that involves your help. I need you to be at the royal palace in Callistoya on Christmas Eve."

Sarange raised her brows. "Is this a royal invitation?"

"Believe me, it is not going to be that grand. Or that easy." He nodded in the direction of the children. Karina, Khan and Sarange's toddler daughter, was playing with her toys on the rug while the babies slept in cribs nearby. "And those of you with kids should probably excuse yourselves from this one. Outsiders are not welcome in my homeland. The battle will be a bloody one."

Sarange's expression conveyed her werewolf stubbornness. "Your people have never encountered *us.*" She swept a hand around the room. "Two wolves, a tiger, a snow leopard, a panther and two dragons. You wanted an army? You've got one right here in this room. We don't need to excuse ourselves. Our children are in no danger of being left without their parents...because Beast doesn't fight to lose."

Khan placed a hand on Ged's shoulder. "She's right. You've always been there for us."

Torque nodded. "It's our turn to repay you."

"Thank you." Ged managed to get the words out despite the choking sensation in his throat. He had a long journey ahead of him. He didn't want to start it by breaking down in tears. "Now I really do need to find out what's keeping Lidi."

After a group hug that tested his emotions—the ones he'd sworn he didn't have—to their limit, he left Khan's suite and made his way along the corridor toward his own room. A feeling of disquiet assailed him when he saw there was no security guard outside the door. His instructions had been simple. The guy was to escort

Lidi to Khan's room. Surely nothing could have gone wrong with such a simple plan?

He almost laughed out loud. *Rule one of shifter living: if something can go wrong, it will.*

When he entered his own room, it was empty. The feeling of unease became a squirming worm of certainty gnawing at his gut. Something *had* gone wrong with his plan.

Luckily when he called Rick, the other man answered his call immediately. "Everything is under control. There is no trace of the intruders. The police are downstairs. They're bemused, but—"

Ged cut across him. "Find the guy who was guarding my room half an hour ago."

"Dave?" Rick sounded surprised. "He's right here."

"Ask him why he left his post without permission." The impulse to smash something was becoming overwhelming. He could hear the murmur of voices as Rick relayed his message to the other guy.

"Boss?" Rick's bewilderment was even more evident. "Dave says he stayed outside your room until Lidi came out. He offered to take her to Khan's room, but she said she knew where it was. She refused to let him escort her."

Ged muttered a curse as he swiped the screen to end the call. *What the hell were you thinking of, Lidi?*

But he already knew the answer. She had gone because he had told her he couldn't help her. Now she was out there all alone, with no money, no transport and no one to turn to next time Vasily's men caught up with her.

It was like déjà vu. In another time and place, he had failed the woman he was responsible for. Alyona had died and now Lidi was facing the same fate. *Because I didn't protect her.*

Feelings of hopelessness and unworthiness crowded in on him, crushing his chest until he couldn't breathe. He was immobilized by fear, his usual decisiveness deserting him. Gradually, he forced his limbs into action.

Do something.

He was the guy who rescued shifters from danger. Since Alyona's death and his exile from Callistoya, it had been his way of giving something back. His personal mission. For Alyona and for his missing brother, Andrei. During the years of his exile, Ged had built up a worldwide network of contacts, shifter and human.

Focused now, he moved with increased purpose. If anyone could find Lidi, he could. All he had to do was get to her in time.

The prospect of retracing her steps across thousands of miles made Lidi's heart sink, but she had no choice. At least she was able to slip out of the hotel without anyone noticing her. Although the lobby was swarming with police officers, they were too busy concentrating on the ruined furnishings and the traumatized employees to pay attention to anything else. The scene was chaotic and, even though Lidi couldn't understand exactly what was being said, there was clearly some confusion around exactly what had taken place.

Once she stepped outside, she could barely move for the hordes of people. The elegant promenade had become a battleground as reporters and photographers vied for the best story and camera shot. Keeping her head down, Lidi pushed her way through, emerging close to the beach. Feeling slightly disoriented, she followed a route that led her away from the town toward the harbor. Anything to get past the crowds.

Cannes harbor was huge, with a range of vessels moored within its confining walls. Lidi guessed some of the larger, gleaming yachts must belong to the celebrities who were staying in the same hotel as Beast. With their helicopters and satellite systems, they resembled floating palaces. Nearby, the tiny, colorful fishing craft were dwarfed by them. She followed the line of the water's edge before sitting on the harbor wall, planning her next move.

After a while, one boat drew her attention away from her thoughts. Long, low and colorful with loud pop music blaring from its decks, it didn't fit in with either the billionaires' yachts or the working vessels. Intrigued, Lidi got to her feet and moved closer so she could read the painted sign on its side. Although it was rough and ready, it had been translated into several languages, including English.

Party Boat! Cruise with Us from Cannes to Genoa.

The Mediterranean climate was mild, but the middle of winter seemed a strange time to offer cruise parties. Then again, what did she know about such things? If there was a cruise happening, it interested her for one important reason. The Italian port of Genoa was a long way from home, but if she could get there, she would be heading in the right direction.

Lidi studied the boat, considering her options for how to get on board and remain hidden for the duration of the journey. As she did, a man sprang down from the deck. Landing neatly on the quayside next to her, he gestured to the vessel with a grin.

"N'est-elle pas belle?"

Although she didn't speak French, Lidi understood enough to know that he was inviting her to admire the boat.

"Beautiful," she agreed, speaking English. It wasn't necessarily the first word that occurred to her as she looked at the garish craft, but politeness prevented her from telling the truth.

"Ah, you are English? American?" He switched languages easily.

"Russian." It was the language that was closest to her mother tongue and it was easier than trying to explain where she actually came from.

Since she was trying to figure out a way to stow away on the boat, she didn't really want to get into a conversation. But it seemed the man had other ideas. It was impossible to judge his age. With skin that was tanned almost mahogany and dreadlocks tied back in a ponytail, he was dressed in jeans and a sweater that were both faded almost to the point of extinction.

"Ah. So, you say *'preevyet.'* Yes?"

"Preevyet." Lidi returned the greeting with a smile. Despite the urgency of her predicament, it was impossible not to like him. And by talking to him, she might be able to find out more about his journey. "Are you going to Genoa today?"

"Tonight. This is not usually the season, but it's a private party."

Having spoken to him, she felt bad about her plans to trick her way on board. Not bad enough to abandon the scheme, of course. Getting to Genoa would take a big chunk out of her journey. She decided on a risky strategy.

"I could use a lift to Genoa, but I don't have any money." She mimed turning out her pockets.

He studied her thoughtfully. "Can you tend bar?" When Lidi looked confused, he elaborated. "Take orders? Serve drinks?"

"Oh." She shook her head. Her life of privilege had never included anything so menial. "No."

He started to laugh. "When someone is offering you a job, the correct answer is always *yes*. And on a party cruise, the most important qualification for tending bar is good looks, so you pass the first test." He held out a hand. "I am Julien, captain of *La Fantaisie*."

"Lidi." Feeling as though she was being swept along by events beyond her control, she returned his handshake. "I don't want a permanent job. I only want to go as far as Genoa."

"Then we'd better begin your training right now." With a slight bow, Julien gestured toward the plank that led onto the boat.

Lidi paused. Looking back, she could just see the white facade of the Palais Hôtel. A sharp pang of regret hit her in the center of her chest. Had Ged noticed her absence yet? Maybe he'd be glad she'd taken the decision making away from him by leaving. She hunched a shoulder. Getting away might be the right thing to do, but it still hurt.

Aware that Julien was waiting for her to accompany him onto the boat, she took a breath. Although her heart was prompting her to stay with Ged, that wasn't an option. Pinning a smile to her face, she stepped onto the gangplank.

"Let's go."

Three hours later, Lidi was ready to tear out her hair before throwing herself overboard. How did anyone remember all these drinks? Then there were the prices and mixes, and Julien had explained that people would fire multiple orders at her and expect her to remember them.

"There will be three other people working with you."

"Are you sure?" Lidi studied the tiny bar in disbelief. She wasn't sure two people could fit behind the wooden structure, let alone four.

Julien laughed. "There will always be one person collecting glasses. And the others are used to working in a confined space. Trust me."

Did she trust him? She wasn't sure. But it wasn't important. Julien was her ticket to Genoa. If he proved to be untrustworthy, she had nothing to be afraid of. He was human and she was a shifter. She could overpower him using only half her strength, probably with a tray of drinks in one hand.

Even so, she had an uncomfortable feeling. This whole thing had been too easy. Lidi had walked out of the hotel needing to travel north, and the first person she had encountered had offered her the means to do so. What were the chances of that happening? She was going with slim to nonexistent.

The first of the guests were arriving along with her fellow bartenders, and, swept up in the chaotic atmosphere, she didn't have much time to think of anything except work. Her colleagues, a guy named Franz and two women, Eloise and Heidi, were all frighteningly efficient. Lidi felt like a baby elephant lumbering around in their wake.

Eloise, shimmying past her in the confined space, appeared bemused by a new presence behind the bar. "Julien never mentioned he was going to employ someone else."

"Maybe it's because this party was planned at the last minute. The host is English, so maybe he needed someone who spoke the language?" Franz suggested.

"You all speak English," Lidi pointed out.

"Ah, but the accent. We can't disguise that we are French, but you look and sound like a member of the British royal family." Heidi laughed. "Julien must be planning to go upmarket."

The comment re-ignited Lidi's suspicions. As *La Fantaisie* set sail and the cruise got under way, it became increasingly clear that she wasn't needed. The other bartenders worked as a tight-knit team, and although she tried to make herself useful, she often ended up getting in their way.

Although her disquiet remained, she couldn't find a focus for her suspicions. Her shifter senses were on high alert, but Julien, her colleagues and the party guests were all human. Unless Vasily had started recruiting mortals, none of his men were on board this boat. Vasily, like most of Lidi's country-folk, had never ventured beyond the borders of Callistoya or interacted with anyone other than werebears. She doubted he'd suddenly struck up a rapport with humans.

When he'd offered her the job, Julien had mentioned her looks. Lidi might not know much about the world, but she speculated briefly about whether he might have an ulterior motive. To be fair, he hadn't given any signs that he intended to try to seduce her. Quite the opposite. Now the voyage was in progress, he was interacting with his guests and had barely glanced her way.

She was being overly suspicious. Jumping at shadows where none existed. It was a new trait and one she needed to overcome. They would be in Genoa the next morning and she would need all her wits about her for the next stage of her journey.

Smiling, she turned to one of the party guests who was holding out his empty glass. As she served his drinks, her attention was caught by a woman on the small dance floor. With her silvery hair and pale coloring, she was unmistakable. It was Allie, who Lidi had met in the crowd outside the movie theater on the previous day. Then, clad in a Beast sweatshirt and jeans with her hair in waist-length plaits, she had blended with the rest of the excited fans. Now, wearing a designer dress, heels and makeup, she looked like a catwalk model.

As Lidi moved out from behind the bar and headed toward the dance floor to speak to Allie, the boat was rocked by a resounding crash. Lidi lurched and managed to stay on her feet. Behind the bar, bottles and glasses came raining down. Luckily she was several feet away and was able to escape the shards of flying glass.

There were screams and shouts as the boat tilted to one side and people dashed about in helpless panic. Pushing past them, Lidi made her way in the direction of the deck. All around her, she could hear speculation about what was going on.

"We've been rammed by another boat," a man said. "It appears to be a deliberate attack."

"Pirates?" A woman's high-pitched screech answered him. "In the Mediterranean?"

Lidi didn't need to join the discussion. She already knew what had happened. This was what the crawling feeling at the back of her neck had been about. This was what she'd been waiting for. It wasn't a pirate attack. Vasily's men had made their move.

Before she could mount the short ladder that would

take her onto the deck, a hand closed over her wrist. Looking up, she met Julien's gaze. "I can't let you go up there."

Anger flooded Lidi's whole body. Why hadn't she trusted her instincts? She had known something was wrong, had sensed all along she shouldn't trust him. As she raised her fist to strike him, she detected a presence behind her. Rough hands grabbed her around the waist. Reluctant to shift in a confined space when so many people were already afraid, Lidi remained in human form but began to struggle.

She elbowed her assailant hard in the ribs. The move was met with a muttered curse and a blow to the back of her head that brought her to her knees. Pain ricocheted through her skull and her vision blurred.

Only partly conscious, Lidi heard Julien's voice as though from a long way off. He was issuing orders. A fight was going on around her—*about* her?—and she was hauled into a pair of strong arms. Drifting in and out of consciousness, she tried to keep track of her surroundings as she was carried from the party room, along a corridor and into a cabin. When she was dumped on a bed, she tried to cry out in protest, but the only sound that left her lips was a weak croak. Although she attempted to leap up, her limbs refused to move.

As the dark spots behind her eyelids finally merged together, she heard the sound of the door closing and a key turning in the lock.

Chapter 6

Lidi became aware of two things at once. The first was the pain in her head. It felt like an ice pick was being repeatedly jabbed into the back of her skull. The second was how still and quiet the boat had become.

When she'd been placed in this cabin, there had been a party going on and the boat had just been rammed. Those things were out of place with the current silence and lack of movement. And the light…that was different too. It had been dark when she was overpowered. Now weak sunlight filtered throughout the confined space. Sensing that night had become day and that the boat was no longer moving, she turned her head toward the porthole.

It was a mistake. The pain intensified and the world swam out of focus. Covering her eyes, she uttered a groan. A movement close by drew her attention and she forced herself to focus. Pain or no pain, nausea or no nausea, there was someone in the room with her.

From her position on her side, she could only see a pair of long, denim-clad legs. Carefully, she tilted her head back until the rest of the body came into view. When she reached the face, she decided she was hallucinating and closed her eyes again.

"It really is me." The bed dipped as Ged sat next to her.

"Water?" She couldn't cope with explanations and a dry throat.

"I can do better than that." He held out a bottle of water and eased her into a half-seated position. Cradling her against the strong muscles of his chest, he held her as she gulped a mouthful of the refreshing liquid. "Now these." He opened his palm to reveal two white tablets.

Lidi regarded them warily. This had turned out to be the cruise from hell and she was no longer sure who she could trust. "I'm okay." Her voice rasped slightly and she took another drink.

Ged reached to one side of the bed for the bottle, holding it up so she could see it. "Just everyday painkillers." When she didn't reply, he frowned. "Why would I try to harm you, Lidi?"

"I don't know. I don't know anything anymore." She eased away from him slightly. "Such as why you're here. On this boat. So soon after I was attacked."

He ran a hand through his hair, the action drawing her attention to bloodstains and scratches on the back of his hand. "Look, take the damn tablets. Then we can talk."

Carefully, she moved into a sitting position. Although she felt slightly disoriented, the nausea was re-

ceding. Resting her back against the scarred panels of the cabin wall, she took the tablets from him and swallowed them with another swig of water. She might not know what was going on, but she did trust Ged. She supposed it was part of the whole mates-for-life thing. Even if they didn't want it, they were bound together.

"Where are we?"

"Genoa."

Lidi blinked so hard it hurt. "But the boat was rammed. There were attackers. I thought it was Vasily's men—" She raised a hand to touch the back of her head, wincing as she felt the lump at the base of her skull.

"It *was* Vasily's men." Ged's expression was tight with anger. "And I will never forgive myself for exposing you to danger. But I thought you'd be safe in the middle of the ocean."

Lidi's head was spinning, but this time her dizziness had nothing to do with the blow it had suffered. "Wait... you *knew* I was on this boat?"

Ged moved so he could sit next to her. Since the bed was narrow and he was big, she was pressed up tight against him. The effect was far from unpleasant, but Lidi was in no mood to relax and enjoy the sensation.

"Answer me, Ged."

He turned toward her, and the full-on impact of his face just inches from hers took her breath away. *Kissing close.* The thought almost destroyed her self-control. Then Ged was talking, and her concentration was restored.

"Julien is a friend of mine. Maybe I should say *was* a friend of mine, since he let you get hit over the head."

"Ah." That explained a lot, but by no means all, of what had happened the previous night. Although frown-

ing hurt her head, she couldn't stop herself. "But I'd only just left the hotel when I met him. And how could you have known I would go in the direction of the harbor?"

He raised his knees, clasping his hands loosely between them. For a few moments, he stared down at his entwined fingers. "I have a network of people I can turn to whenever a shifter is in trouble."

Lidi took a few moments to process that information. "So the rumors are true? You rescue shifters who are in danger?"

A corner of his mouth lifted. "They must be some powerful rumors if they've managed to penetrate as far as Callistoya."

"I told you. Vasily is scared of you. He tries to keep track of what you are doing. So do others. There are many who want you back on the throne." She studied his face. "It didn't matter which direction I went in? There would have been someone there to help me?"

He looked sheepish. "I contacted everyone I knew in the Cannes area. They were all on the lookout for you."

Lidi was quiet, unsure how to feel about that. Part of her was uncomfortable at the thought that she hadn't been free of Ged's watchful presence. Another part was glad of his protection. Her conflicting emotions only reinforced how much her life had changed since she met him. "You must know a lot of people."

"Like I said, over the years I've managed to make a lot of contacts. Julien was possibly the most colorful…" He gave it some thought. "But maybe not."

"Why do you do it?" she asked. "Rock band manager and shifter rescuer…the two halves of your life don't fit together."

He sighed. "Where do I start? But I suppose the first reason is the most obvious." When she looked puzzled, he explained. "Andrei."

"Of course. You've been searching for your brother." She knew that Andrei Tavisha had disappeared along with Ged on the night of the massacre. Unlike Ged, nothing had been heard of him since. No stories, no whispers, not a murmur. He was the young prince who had vanished without a trace. "Have you found out anything about him?"

His eyes were dark with pain as he shook his head. "Whenever I hear about a shifter in trouble, I think this might be the time I find him. Or the time I find some information that leads me to him. It's not the only thing that drives me, but it's the most important."

She took his hand. The painkillers must be starting to work because she was able to move without feeling like the action was about to lift the top off her scalp. "The rest of it...is that because you feel a sense of obligation?"

Lidi knew what duty was. She had been raised within the ancient tradition of Callistoya nobility. Even though her parents had left her to fend for herself from a young age, they had imposed rules upon her. She had been expected to conform to the lifestyle of an aristocrat. Every attempt had been made to ruthlessly crush her rebellious streak. It wasn't their fault she had constantly thwarted them.

When she reached the shifter age of maturity at eighteen, she had expressed a desire to join the king's army. Her father's outrage had been almost comical. Her mother had refused to discuss the matter.

"It is your destiny to make a good marriage." Umbert, Count of Aras had turned away as though that was the final word on the subject. "Besides, you are a woman. The life of a warrior is not for you."

"I can fight as well as any man." It wasn't true. She could fight better than most men.

"We will not speak of this again."

That had been two years ago in mortal time, and it was the last time she'd seen her mother. Her parents had been traveling to visit relatives when they were attacked by robbers, possibly from Vasily's rebel force. Her mother had been killed outright. Although her father had survived his injuries, he remained a shadow of the powerful soldier he had once been.

Caring full-time for her disabled father, Lidi had been unable to fulfill her dream of a military career. Instead she had joined the troops who guarded the castle when they took part in their military training. Honing her skills until she matched and then outstripped the professionals was one of her greatest pleasures...and most bitter regrets.

Duty was what she owed to her father, whom she loved despite his autocratic nature. Her loyalty was to his lands, his tenants, the castle in which she had been raised, the land of her birth. But if she had been given a choice, she would not have followed in the footsteps of centuries of her family. The decision had been taken from her with her father's injuries, but Lidi would never bow her head in the way expected of a Callistoya noble woman. If Vasily expected her to succumb obediently to his will, he had chosen the wrong person. The man who called himself king had picked a warrior instead of a maiden. And Lidi was prepared to teach him the difference.

She could see her question about obligation had resonated with Ged. His eyes were on her face, but she sensed his thoughts were far away. When he spoke, the sadness in his voice tore into her soul.

"I've lived in the mortal world for a long time, but Callistoya has kept its hold on me. I sometimes wondered if I could ever explain to my friends about my life back in my homeland." He laughed. "I decided I couldn't. How do you describe what it's like to step inside the pages of a history book? To them, Callistoya would be like going back in time six hundred years."

Lidi started to wrinkle her brow, then decided against it. Facial expressions still caused too much pain. "Is that a bad thing?"

"In many ways it is. Callistoya is like a medieval kingdom. It has all the charm of knights and chivalry—with a dash of shifter magic, for good measure—and when my father was alive, we mostly lived in peace. Since his marriage to Zoya, Vasily's mother, our beautiful land has become a place of fierce feuds and bloody battles. Although—" A corner of his mouth lifted. "We should probably be thankful that technology hasn't reached our magical corner of the world. At least we haven't progressed beyond silver and fire as a means of destroying each other."

"You still love it." Her voice was gentle.

He leaned his head back. "Of course I do. But after the massacre it seemed like there was no hope. I tried to go back. I wore a disguise and attempted to cross the border, but Vasily had used powerful magic to close down the frontiers. I don't know how he did it, but there was an invisible barrier and I couldn't get past it. In the end, I smuggled a message to my uncle Eduard and we met in secret in a Siberian forest." His lips thinned into a line and Lidi could tell how much the experience had damaged his pride. "Everything I once knew was gone. The king was dead, my family had been wiped out, there was no government—" He broke off, rubbing a hand over his eyes.

"How did you and your brother escape?"

He shook his head. "I don't know. I've been over it in my mind a hundred times since. There's no way Vasily would have spared us. Someone who knew of the murder plot must have rescued us before the killing started."

"Wouldn't it have been easier to have informed your father of the plot?" Lidi asked. "That way Vasily could have been stopped before he killed anyone."

"I wish I knew the answer to that. To all of it." There was no escaping the pain in his eyes and she remembered he had lost his fiancée as well as his father that night.

"Your loyalty is to the people who died as well as to your country." With every minute she spent in his company her insights into his motives gained depth. It was like she was rolling down a hill, picking up speed and unable to stop. The question was, did she want to?

Ged nodded. "Doing nothing wasn't an option. Eduard stayed in Callistoya and promised to rally our supporters. In the meantime I did what I could to find Andrei, and this—rescuing endangered shifters—felt like I was giving something back. It was for my home, my family, for the people who died." His expression clouded again and she could feel the tension in his body. "For Alyona."

Lidi could tell how much it cost him to say that name out loud. She didn't know who moved first. Did she turn toward him, or did Ged draw her into his arms? Perhaps both actions happened at once. All she knew was she was being held tight against his chest as he pressed his cheek to her hair as though he would never let her go.

They stayed that way for long, silent moments, drawing strength from each other in an embrace that had no place in a bear shifter's existence. Hugging wasn't a feature of Callistoya life, but it felt so good that Lidi wished she could find a way to introduce it. When she finally tilted her head back to look at him, Lidi saw Ged's calm had been restored. His expression was determined.

"It's time to go back." She didn't need to ask him. They both knew it was going to happen.

He smiled. "We'll go together."

For someone who had spent her whole life in Callistoya and been brought up in the noble tradition, Lidi was unlike any other bear shifter Ged had ever encountered. Once she knew Ged was prepared to travel with her to Callistoya, she wanted to set off at once. Bears were cautious by nature, and her impulsiveness was the opposite of his own personality.

"I did it once." She tossed her head, wincing slightly as the movement clearly reminded her of her injury. "I can do it again."

"But we don't need to trek across continents on foot this time," Ged patiently explained. "I've got plenty of money. And we need a plan."

"Plan?" She said it as though she had never come across the word before.

He smiled. A bear who didn't plan? Yes, Lidi was definitely unusual. "What were you picturing? You march up to Vasily and demand the release of your father while I tear the crown from his head?"

She sat on the edge of the bunk, scuffing the worn floorboards with the toe of her boot. "Pretty much."

He placed a hand on her shoulder, feeling its frailty beneath her sweater. "Where do you think that would get us, Lidi?" When she didn't answer, he gently turned her to face him. "If Vasily let you live, you would be back in your prison cell. I, on the other hand, would not survive the encounter. Vasily would make sure I met the same fate as my father."

Her smooth brow creased. "Are you telling me it's hopeless?"

"Not at all. I want to make sure we win this fight, but if we're going to do that, we have to remember who we're dealing with."

Her lip curled. "Vasily is a coward."

"He is a cunning coward and he is a killer. If we are going to outsmart him, we will have to be more devious than he is."

"It will be hard to do that if you can't even set foot in Callistoya." Wearily, Lidi rested her head against his shoulder. The movement seemed unconscious, just a natural reaction to tiredness and the aftermath of her injury. He slid an arm around her waist, pulling her closer. His reasoning was she needed comfort. The truth? He couldn't help himself. He had never had a problem with self-control. Now it was being tested to its limits. It was going to be an interesting journey. "And even if you do, you will be recognized."

"Exactly. I'm going to have to find a way to bypass the spell Vasily has put on the border. Once I've done that, I'll need a hell of a disguise." He considered the matter for a few moments. "Vasily's greatest fear will be my return at the head of an army. I'm the rightful king. He will expect me to act like it. That's why I need to behave like something completely different."

"A servant, maybe?" Lidi suggested.

"Yes. I will be your new servant."

He felt her sigh reverberate through her slender body. "I can't return to my home, remember? As soon as I do, Vasily will have me thrown back into a cell."

Ged placed his hand beneath her chin, tilting her face up so he could look into her eyes. This was going to be the hard part. "There is one way you can stay out of prison."

"No there isn't. Vasily will not grant me my freedom unless I agree to marry him." Understanding dawned and her eyes widened. "Oh." She backed away from him, shaking her head. "No. Oh, no."

"Just listen to me—"

"You want me to marry Vasily?" She got to her feet, swaying slightly.

Ged was at her side, sliding a hand around her waist to support her. "No, I want you to *say* you'll marry him."

Lidi made an attempt to move away, but she was obviously disoriented. With a sigh, she subsided against him. "Isn't it the same thing?"

Despite the seriousness of the situation, he started to laugh. "Lidi, look at me." She huffed out a breath, turning her face up to his. "Do you trust me? Enough to place your life in my hands?"

When he looked at her, everything else faded away. How had he reached this point in his life without knowing he could feel like this? That another person could be the center of the universe?

As they gazed at each other, Lidi's stubborn expression gradually faded. "You know I trust you."

"Then believe me when I say I won't let Vasily harm you. He won't come close enough to touch you. But we need a pretense, a reason to get into the royal palace."

Her lips curved into a smile. "He used your engagement to Alyona as an excuse to wipe out your family. I suppose using a fake engagement as a means of revenge would have a sort of poetic justice."

"I would never put you at risk because of Alyona." He didn't know what the future held for them, but he needed her to understand that.

"Did you love her?" As soon as she spoke, Lidi shook her head. "I'm sorry. I have no right to ask you that question."

"That's not true and we both know it. The fates might have horrible timing, but these feelings between us aren't going away." His expression became serious. "You know what Callistoya politics are like. It gets worse when you are royal. Tavisha kings and princes can only marry within the five founding houses who are deemed to be descended from the goddess Callisto herself. The House of Ivanov is one of the five and I had been engaged to Alyona since we were both children. So in answer to your question, I loved Alyona very much." He frowned, unsure whether he was explaining himself properly. "But I didn't love her in the way a mortal man would love the wife he has chosen for himself."

"But what about the feelings you and I have for each other?" Lidi blushed as she asked the question. "If Alyona hadn't died and you had married her, there is a chance you and I could still have met. We would still have been fated to be mates."

"This 'fated mate' business is so complicated. I sometimes envy member of poorer families in Callistoya. They are free to choose who they marry and can wait until they find their mates. Those of us from royal and aristocratic families are not as fortunate. But within the Callistoya royal family, love and marriage are viewed as very different things."

"Oh." He watched her face as she assimilated that information. "You mean—" He nodded and her blush deepened as she looked at her feet. "I would not have had an affair with a married man, Ged."

"We are speculating about something that will never happen. But I like to think that even though Alyona wasn't my mate, I'd have been a good husband. I would never have hurt her by being unfaithful."

Lidi looked up with a smile. "I'm glad. Can we go now?"

"What about your head?"

"It will be painful whether we stay here or we start our journey." She took his hand. "We can plan as we travel."

"Why do I feel like I am no longer in control of my life?"

Her grin was pure mischief. "Because you've met me?"

Although he laughed, his face was serious. "And you changed everything."

Chapter 7

Although Lidi understood Ged's reasoning, she was having a hard time keeping her natural impulsiveness in check. Her instinct was to keep going, to seize very opportunity for action. When he checked them into a small hotel overlooking a bustling square in the heart of Genoa's historic city center, it felt like they were marking time instead of moving forward.

"I promise this will not take long." Ged sat on the bed, watching her as she restlessly paced the room. "But there are some things I have to do before we can start this journey."

She huffed out an impatient breath. "It's easy, you know. You put one foot in front of the other and keep doing it."

"Vasily's men have found you twice."

Lidi paused in front of the full-length windows that

led to a tiny balcony. "And you have defeated them twice. We'll do it as often as we need to."

"If we're fighting Vasily's men all the way to Callistoya, my plan to return in disguise will be doomed to failure. And they'll know you are with me. Vasily is unlikely to believe you have had a change of heart and wish to marry him if his men carry *that* interesting piece of information back to the royal palace."

She sighed. "What do you suggest?"

"We can either keep fighting—over and over—and ultimately lose, or avoid them until we choose the time and place for the final confrontation. I assumed Pyotr and his group were the only ones after you, but then there was the attack on the boat." Ged frowned and rubbed his knuckles. "With Julien's help, they were easily overcome, but somehow they have impeccable sources about where you are. Someone is following you, and they are good at it. In normal circumstances, you'd notice another werebear on your tail. We're not exactly subtle."

An image of a woman with silver hair and light eyes came into Lidi's mind. "Allie."

"Pardon?" Ged regarded her in confusion.

"There was a woman called Allie…she was in the crowd outside the movie theater when Beast arrived, and we walked together to the Palais Hotel," Lidi explained. "Last night I saw her again, just before Julien's boat was rammed."

"Is she a shifter?"

Lidi shook her head. "Absolutely not."

"Does that mean she's human?" Ged asked. "I'd be surprised to learn that Vasily has ever communicated with a mortal, let alone persuaded one to work for him."

Lidi tried to recall her interactions with Allie. Her senses were finely tuned, enabling her to differentiate between shifters and other beings. Could she say with certainty that Allie was mortal? The other woman definitely wasn't a shifter. Looking back, she couldn't remember getting *any* vibes from Allie. But she'd been so focused on Ged and on meeting him that she hadn't been thinking of anything else.

"I don't know who, or what, she is," she confessed. "When we first met, I wasn't paying much attention to her. On the boat, I only caught a glimpse of her."

"She may be following you, but her presence in both places is more likely to be a coincidence." Ged seemed inclined to dismiss Allie's involvement.

Ignoring the finger of doubt that was prodding insistently at her spine, Lidi decided he was probably right. When Vasily had an army of fighters at his disposal, why would he need to send a lone woman to spy on her?

"Whether they have been using this woman or some other means, Vasily's men have been aware of your location. Instead of confronting them, I suggest we find a way to slip past them."

"We are bears. Sneaking isn't one of our strengths," Lidi said.

Ged laughed. "That's why we need a disguise."

"Good plan." She nodded approvingly. "What do you suggest? Mice? High-stepping ponies?"

He got to his feet and led her to the window. Outside, the square was a traditional Christmas market scene. Stalls were festooned with red and green garlands and white lights hung from every tree. Even from the second floor, Lidi could smell roasting chestnuts and mulled wine. She knew about the festive season. A few centuries earlier when Ged's mother had been alive, some travelers had visited the royal palace. When they told the queen of the colorful traditions, she had been so enraptured, she had introduced them into her own country.

Lidi followed the direction of Ged's pointing finger. At one end of the square, there was a stage decorated with festive greenery. "For two nights, a group of traveling actors and musicians will put on a performance as part of the Genoa Christmas market. When they leave here tomorrow night, they are taking a bus to Frankfurt. We'll be with them."

Lidi was silent for a few moments. "Do they know?"

"Not yet." Ged held up his cell phone. "Their organizer is about to get a call from my personal assistant. In exchange for a large donation, she'll ask them to allow a couple of musicians to join them for the remainder of their Genoa dates and to travel with them to Frankfurt. Two days will give me enough time to get your fake passport organized." He studied her face. "What have I said?"

"Musicians? Ged, I haven't got a musical bone in my body."

"Okay. We'll compromise and be dancers instead."

She started to laugh. "I'm a *bear*."

He grinned. "Then I guess I'd better make my calls before we start the dancing lessons."

Lidi hung her head, half laughing, half embarrassed. "I don't understand. You're a bear shifter, as well. How can you possibly have any musicality? It's like expecting an elephant to perform in the ballet."

"Years ago, there were dancing bears. But you're right—it had nothing to do with ability. It was a cruel method of enslaving our wild counterparts that has, fortunately, been outlawed in most countries." As he spoke, he tried to imagine a life without music. It was impossible. Like picturing food without flavor or a poem without sentiment. But Lidi was right; most bear shifters viewed themselves as lumbering, clumsy creatures, far removed from any artistic endeavor. "I suppose it depends how dominant our human senses are. My mother was a singer and music was her life. I guess she passed that passion on to me."

"Is that why you started a rock band?"

When they stepped back inside, Ged had moved the furniture to the sides of the room, clearing enough space so he could show Lidi some simple dance steps. From her demeanor, he had a feeling it wasn't going to be easy.

"Partly. I'd rescued the members of the band from some very difficult situations. Once I recognized their abilities, I realized bringing them together would be a form of therapy. For all of us." He smiled at the memory. "None of us could have foreseen what Beast would become." He took his cell phone out of his pocket and scrolled through to find the song he wanted. Music, slow and sensuous, filled the room. Ged held out his hands. "No more delays. Let's dance."

Although Lidi took his hands, she shook her head. "You have set yourself an impossible task. The part of me that is human may be even clumsier than my inner bear."

"That's why we're going to stick with something that requires you to be in my arms for the duration of the dance. It's very slow and romantic. All you need to do is follow my lead."

He raised her hand to his lips and pressed a kiss onto her fingertips. Sliding a hand down her back, he drew her close, holding her so the length of their bodies was connected. "I want you to copy what I do." He placed his right hand on Lidi's left shoulder and gripped her waist with his left hand. Obediently, she mirrored his stance. "We start with only a slight swaying of our bodies. Slow at first, increasing in tempo as the music builds. The important thing is to maintain eye contact throughout the dance. I need to see your feelings reflected in your eyes, just as you will know from my face what the feel of your body is doing to me."

The familiar deep pink blush stained her cheeks. Ged focused on the amber lights in her eyes, seeing shards of brighter gold in their depths, noticing the shadowy sweep of her lashes against the porcelain tint of her skin as she looked down.

"Uh-uh. Eyes on mine." Her breath shuddered as she lifted her gaze to his again. "Every dance tells a story. In this one, it would be easy to believe that the man is in charge. But that is only half-true."

He moved his hips slowly against Lidi's, feeling the tension in her frame. He slid his left foot forward, sliding his thigh between her legs, and her eyes widened.

"Relax and follow my movements." Moving his hand from her waist to the small of her back, he pressed her pelvis tighter against his own. "This dance will work better if there is no choreography, if it tells a story of a passion that is real."

Passion that is real? Just touching her set him on fire. There would be no need to pretend. Not on his part.

Gradually, he felt her respond to his prompting. Hesitantly at first, she started to shift her hips from side to side. He took her hand from his shoulder and held it to his throat, right over the pulse that beat there.

"Feel what dancing with you does to me, Lidi." He kept his voice low. "Understand the power you have over me."

She drew a shuddering breath and relaxed slightly against him, her movements changing. No longer following his instructions, she was swaying in time with the rhythm of her own desires and twin emotions coursed through him. Lidi *could* dance, but his triumph was outstripped by his own rising desire. Reaching up, he freed her hair from its ponytail and tangled a hand in its mass, using it to tug her head farther back.

"Don't close your eyes."

Ged's senses were swimming. The windows were still open and an icy breeze drifted in, bringing the sounds and scents of the market square into the room. Together with the pulsing, romantic music, they created a new, erotic memory for him. But nothing could match the warmth of Lidi's breath on his cheek, the rustle of her clothing against his and the sweet weight of her body in his arms. As the music increased in tempo, their hips undulated in perfect time.

Lidi reached up and stroked the back of Ged's neck. Her smile was shy as she ran her fingers through his hair. "I like dancing with you."

"I'm glad." His voice was husky and he could feel the hard ridge of his arousal pressing against the hollow of her stomach. His gaze dropped longingly to her mouth.

"What about the eye contact?" Lidi said.

He laughed as, maintaining the sensuous rhythm, he swung her around in a half circle. As he gripped her buttocks, she gasped. "Lift your knee and drape your leg over my hip."

Lidi followed his instruction, the action causing her to lean back. Ged moved a hand along her thigh, holding her in place and allowing her to arch her spine even further until her hair swung almost to the floor. She bit her lip, uttering a soft groan.

"Did I hurt you?" Ged helped her up, supporting her against him.

"No, it's not that."

"Ah." He understood immediately. "I think we forgot we were supposed to be dancing."

There was an edge of nervousness to her laughter. "I thought it was just me."

How could he explain it would never just be her? The line was temptingly close, and it would be so easy to cross it. He was alone with his mate. They were in a bedroom. She was in his arms...

Why the hell were the fates torturing him this way? He was doing his best to resist temptation, but his resolve had never been so severely tested. Every minute spent with Lidi was like a whisper of certainty growing stronger as it wrapped its tendrils around him. He was in deep, already beyond the point at which he could claw his way back. She was in his blood. It was an admission that scared the daylights out of him.

For a long time, his life had been mapped out. It may have been predictable, but he had known what his future held. He had been a prince of Callistoya. Wealth, land, servants, a beautiful wife...they had all been his by right. Then the massacre had tilted his world off course.

Ged had survived. Dragging himself back from the edge of despair, he had carved out a new existence.

His time as Beast's manager could not have been more different from his time as a royal bear shifter. He had learned to live among humans, to master technology, to cope with the intrusion that came with his semicelebrity status, even to stave off his feelings of loss and inadequacy by fighting to save other shifters.

But throughout that whole time, his emotions had been armor plated. Although he had formed friendships with the other members of the band, he had never allowed himself to get close to a woman. He knew why. Of course he did. Alyona's image haunted him. He would never forgive himself for what had happened to her, never get over the guilt of not being there to protect her. All he could do was make sure it never happened again. If he didn't forge those bonds, he couldn't let the other person down. It was true then, and it hadn't changed now. Not even when he looked into Lidi's huge, golden-brown eyes.

"We have to be performance ready in a few hours." Even though he spoke lightly, his words had the effect of shaking her out of her near trance. "So we'll have to ignore the simmer and pretend we're professionals. Okay?"

She tossed back her hair, tilting her chin in the manner that was becoming familiar. "Of course." Returning her hand to his shoulder, she stepped in close. "I'm ready."

Ged almost groaned aloud. *Pretend we're professionals?* What was he thinking? She only had to touch him and he melted. Lidi was looking at him with a glint in her eyes that was midway between hurt and pride. The message was clear. She was going to do as he asked and ignore the heat between them. Ged wished he could follow his own instructions. Instead, her nearness was a delicious agony.

Clenching his jaw tight and doing his best to ignore the fire in his blood, he nodded. "Right. Remember the eye contact…"

When the time came for the performance, Lidi wasn't sure there was any way she could be described as a dancer. Or prepared. The only thing she was able to do with any confidence was remain in Ged's arms and follow his lead.

She was increasingly surprised at the scale of Ged's influence. In her own world, the royal family and nobles of Callistoya were all-powerful. Here in the human realm, it seemed that money held the key to everything. Ged wanted them to have a place on the stage and on the transport to Frankfurt. He offered a donation and those things were theirs. Costumes and makeup? A few calls and the items he requested were delivered to the hotel lobby.

"I still don't see how this helps us slip past Vasily's men," Lidi said as she donned a long, white shift dress and laced a red corset over it. "We still look like *us*. By appearing on stage, we will be attracting more attention, not hiding from it."

"Remember that disguise I mentioned?" Ged reached into one of the boxes that had arrived along with their costumes. "Try this on."

He handed Lidi a long, blond wig. Inside the box were instructions and everything she needed to fix it in place. She headed for the bathroom, carrying a cap to cover her own hair, gel to protect her skin, adhesive tape and bobby pins. After a few unsuccessful attempts, she emerged sometime later with the flowing tresses in place.

"What do you think?"

Ged stared at her, taking in the medieval-style gown and golden wig. Picking up a circlet of red roses entwined with Christmas greenery, he placed it on her head. "I don't think you look much like Lidiya Rihanoff anymore. Once you add makeup, the masquerade will be complete."

"What about you?"

He held up another box. "It's my turn to be transformed."

Lidi stared at the bathroom door as he closed it behind him. Even though they would only be temporary, she didn't want him making any alterations to his appearance. Her inner bear didn't like change. She sighed. Who was she kidding? From the moment she had first seen him, Ged had been her idea of perfection. She didn't want *anything* to spoil that image.

She didn't want anything except *this*. When she was alone with him in this tiny room, locked in his arms, it felt like the rest of the world was on hold. If only it could stay that way. Why did there have to be momentous events dragging her attention away from the dark enchantment of Ged's eyes?

He was her addiction. She had known that from the moment she had first seen him the steps of the movie theater. A craving that sparked through her nerves and into her brain, taking over her mind until she could think of nothing but him. One touch of his hand and she was lost, her senses swirling with the feel, scent and heat of him. As they danced, her imagination had been alight, stealing the present from her and tempting her with glimpses of what lay ahead. Because it *would* happen. She had seen that in his eyes and felt it in his touch. No matter what his lips said to the contrary, Ged was equally addicted to her.

The thought sent a surge of mingled anticipation and desire powering through her. So much for her determination to be a fierce warrior-aristocrat who had no time for the opposite sex. She didn't know where this attraction between them was leading. The only thing she knew for sure was that she couldn't ignore it. She could condemn the fates who had chosen this time and place to throw her and Ged together, but did she really wish things were different? If she had a magic wand, would she change what had happened? She was too honest to pretend she would step off this emotional roller coaster before the ride had ended. Even so, she should probably stop daydreaming about Ged and put the finishing touches to her disguise.

Lidi rarely wore cosmetics, and when she did, she applied them sparingly. The items Ged had provided were much heavier than those she usually wore, and she guessed it must be stage makeup. By the time she heard the bathroom door opening, she was close to despair. The face that stared back at her from the mirror more closely resembled a clown than her own reflection.

She was about to launch into a complaint about her own limitations as a makeup artist, but the change in Ged's appearance reduced her to silence. An iron-straight, jet-black wig covered his own hair and was held in a ponytail at the nape of his neck. A pointed beard and neat mustache covered the lower part of his face.

"Oh." Lidi studied him with her head on one side.

"What do you think?" Ged stroked the fake beard. "I think it makes me look distinguished."

"That's not the first word that came into my head," Lidi said.

"It's not?"

She continued to stare in fascination at him. "No. You look sinister."

He started to laugh. "Seriously?"

Lidi nodded. "The change is quite alarming."

"As long as I look unlike myself, that's the most important thing."

"Oh, you do look different." She decided not to mention just how much she disliked the change. How much she wanted his own dark brown hair and clean-shaven features back. She wanted him to look like her Ged again. She took a moment to acknowledge how quickly she had come to think of him as *hers*. The only scary part of that thought was how right it felt. As if all the pieces of her life were finally in place.

He belongs to me. She had no idea what that meant long-term. Because she was looking at her *king*. The path back to his crown would be long and bloody…and not just in a physical sense. Ged had many internal battles to fight before he could face his future with pride. And was Lidi prepared to see herself differently? Her ambition to lead armies did not sit well with an image of herself at the side of a monarch. The fierce independence that was so much a part of who she was would never be subdued.

And there was that whole wife-or-mistress question. He was a man who could only marry where directed. She was a woman with a strong moral code. She felt the corners of her mouth pull down. Too many questions. The answers to which would have to wait for another time.

With a sigh, she turned to look in the mirror again. "On the subject of looking different—"

Ged came to stand behind her. "If you were aiming for startled marionette, you've done a remarkable job."

She began to laugh. "That wasn't quite the effect I wanted."

Placing his hands on her shoulders, he turned her to face him. "In the early days, I used to perform a variety of functions for the band. I've even applied some greasepaint in my time." He held up a Kleenex. "May I?"

His touch was gentle as he smoothed away the worst excesses and reapplied a fine layer of the makeup to her cheeks and eyelids. When he reached her mouth, he paused with the pad of his thumb resting lightly against the cushion of her lower lip. The touch wasn't a caress...not quite. Not yet.

There was a question in his eyes as he looked down at her, and Lidi knew Ged was signaling that, at least for now, he had stopped fighting his feelings. He was letting her know she was in control of what happened next.

Reaching up a hand, she hooked it around the back of his neck and pulled him down to her. Ged placed both hands on her waist and Lidi wrapped her arms around his neck, leaning into him, wanting to be closer, tighter. He held her like she was made of glass, and she could feel the hammering of his heart against her breast. He was nervous, and she wasn't. She had never been so sure of anything in her life.

"I won't break." She whispered the words against his mouth.

He made a sound that was midway between a laugh and a groan. "I want this…want *you*…so much. But—"

She silenced him by pressing her lips to his. The kiss started sweet and achingly slow. They stood still and straight, exploring each other. And Lidi finally understood what kissing was all about.

She was a rebel. Her mother wanted her to make a good marriage and remain chaste until her wedding night. That was how it was done. In Callistoya, anything else was unthinkable. That had been enough for Lidi to decide she needed to be impure. Unfortunately, since she had discovered she wasn't very good at relationships, none of them had progressed beyond the kissing stage. The reason was simple. She hadn't found anyone she'd actually liked kissing. Until now…

Because the feel of Ged's mouth on hers was devastating, breaking down her defenses and changing every perception she had about herself. She had already known that with him she was vulnerable, but this was like opening her heart to him. There was no part of her that wasn't his.

Her fingers caressed his neck, avoiding the wig. He tasted like toothpaste and coffee. When he eased her mouth further open, she gave a soft moan. Her fear of losing herself was forgotten. This was a new self, a different persona. Nothing mattered except Ged and the feel of his lips, the strength of his arms, the warmth of his body.

She could feel his rapid heartbeat answering her own, hear his ragged breathing, the slight trembling in his hands as they moved upward along her spine. When he broke off the kiss and raised his head, he looked stunned.

"Don't stop." She would beg if she had to.

Begging wasn't necessary. This time the kiss was fierce and hungry, both of them abandoning any attempt at restraint. Ged's mouth was demanding, his hands gripping her hips and pressing her tightly to him.

Lidi gave herself up to need and sensation, to the seductive dance of their tongues and the delicious movement of his lips against hers. When the kiss finally ended, she was breathing hard, but not as hard as Ged.

He rested his forehead against hers. "Um…we should go down to the square."

She closed her eyes, still clinging to him. "My knees don't seem to be working."

"If this is an excuse not to dance…"

She opened one eye. "I mean it, Ged. You kissed me into immobility."

"That's never happened to me before. Admittedly, I haven't kissed many people." He scooped her up into his arms. "If I carry you down the stairs, maybe your knees will start working by the time we reach street level?"

Lidi rested her head on his shoulder. "I don't know. I don't know anything anymore."

Laughter shook his large frame. "I think you'll recover."

She was glad they could make light of something so momentous. It meant she could hide her emotion behind amusement. And she liked Ged's confidence. So he thought she could be restored to normality? It was good news that one of them did. As for Lidi herself, she wasn't convinced she would ever get over the enchantment of his lips on hers, or the raw, uncontrollable emotion he had stirred in her. More importantly, she wasn't sure she wanted to.

Chapter 8

Kissing Lidi had been one of the best things that had ever happened to him. Even so, as Ged emerged from the hotel into the brightly lit square with her still in his arms, he did spare a moment to regret the awfulness of their timing.

He needed to keep his wits sharp in case Vasily's men were close by. Instead, his mind was filled with the memory of Lidi's lips on his and the feel of her body tight against him.

"You can put me down now." Even her breath on his cheek was a delightful distraction.

"Are you sure?" He smiled into her eyes as he set her down. "You're not going to fall at my feet?"

She rolled her eyes, but not before he caught a glimpse of her mischievous smile. "Really, Ged. The kiss was good, but it wasn't faint inducing."

She was about to turn away, but he caught hold of her wrist. To hell with common sense. Drawing her close, he pressed his lips to her ear. "Does that mean I need to try harder next time?"

Her tiny indrawn breath and the little shiver that ran through her were worth every second of increased danger. *Next time.* He liked those words and, from the added sparkle in her eyes, he could see Lidi did too.

Clasping her hand, he navigated the crowded square. Shoppers and tourists were out in large numbers and they passed booths selling wooden toys, scented candles, carved angels, ceramic tree ornaments and music boxes. The mingled aromas of gingerbread and spiced wine made his stomach rumble, reminding him that they hadn't eaten. He made himself a promise. Once this performance was over, he was going to find a cozy Italian restaurant and order an enormous pizza. Briefly he was going to put everything else to the back of his mind and pretend he and Lidi were a normal human couple on a normal human date.

Since "everything else" included a group of dangerous bear shifters who wanted to assassinate him and kidnap Lidi, he forced himself to remain vigilant. The stage had been erected in front of a church. Darkness had fallen, and lights twinkled amid the greenery that surrounded the canopy and bright spotlights illuminated the scene. A choir sang traditional songs, and nearby, a group of musicians were tuning their instruments.

Ged felt comfortable in this setting. It wasn't on the same scale as one of Beast's arena concerts, but the fundamental details were the same. There were artists, and an audience, and a performance would take place.

Okay, so he was usually behind the scenes making those things happen. It still felt like a safe place.

It was clear that Lidi didn't share his peace of mind. Casting a glance over her shoulder at the crowded square, she moved closer to Ged. "Couldn't we have simply paid these people to pretend we are part of their theater company? That way we could travel to Frankfurt with them without actually having to take part in the show."

"We could do that," Ged agreed, as he paused at the side of the stage.

He took a moment to scan the immediate area. As Lidi had already pointed out, stealth was not one of the strengths of their species. That was the case in the wild and for bear shifters living among humans. They were creatures who relied on their size and strength. Their natural confidence gave them an unmistakable swagger. If Vasily's men were in the vicinity, they would be hard to miss.

Ged knew exactly what he was looking for. He had been raised among werebears. Although wild bears were solitary animals, the shifters of his homeland lived a human lifestyle. A group of Callistoyan men together would exude off-the-scale levels of confidence. They would behave as they did in Callistoya, jostling among themselves for the alpha position and not caring who was watching their antics. Unless Vasily's men had adopted a new, subtle approach, he was certain they weren't nearby.

Protecting another person was new to him. He'd failed at it once without ever really having a chance to succeed. He was going to make sure he got it right this time.

"We have to blend in." He returned to Lidi's question with a sense of relief, keeping his voice low so that only she could hear. "There are at least a dozen performers in this group. We couldn't swear each individual to secrecy. If they started discussing the two strangers who were traveling with them, that information could fall into the wrong hands. This way, they might talk about the performers who have joined their group." He grinned. "They could even speculate about what terrible dancers we are. But anyone overhearing that information is unlikely to make the connection between Lidiya Rihanoff and Gerald Tavisha and the new recruits."

Her expression remained unconvinced. Or possibly nervous. He lifted her hand and lightly grazed her knuckles with his lips. "Trust me, Lidi?"

The troubled look lightened. "You know I do."

Her response ignited a new glow in the center of his chest. He had shut himself off from companionship for so long, believing himself unworthy of those basic elements that others took for granted. Friendship, loyalty and trust in their truest sense had seemed far beyond his grasp. Now this beautiful woman, with her warm, honest eyes and open smile, was offering him all of those things—and more—in one package.

For the first time, he glimpsed what lay beyond the instant attraction he had felt when he knew she was his mate. He finally understood what his friends had. It was a connection of brave hearts, strong minds and healed souls. A contentment that was almost mystical. Lidi offered him completion.

And…why now? Not just this realization, but all of it. Meeting her at a time when Callistoya needed him to step back in and be the hero his people needed almost seemed too good to be true. He needed her strength and she was there. As if they had been brought together by an unseen guide.

The thought hung in the air for a moment, like the shimmering cold of his exhaled breath. Then it was gone as a man's voice hailed him in halting English. "You are the dancers?"

They turned to face a tall man who wore the same costume as the other musicians. He looked harassed. "I am Rico. Every year I tell myself someone else can do the organizing." He shrugged. "Yet here I am again. So, the person who called me said you are called *Romanzo. Si?*"

"That's right." Ged didn't elaborate or offer their individual names. The less information Rico and his colleagues had about them, the less they could give away.

Rico didn't appear to notice the omission. Glancing over his shoulder as though something was demanding his attention, he gave them an apologetic smile. "There are other performers, but we don't really have a schedule. You have music?" Ged handed him a note, and after scanning it, Rico nodded. "We can play that. Just let me know when you are ready."

There was a crash and an exclamation from among the musicians and Rico hurried away in that direction. Reminding himself that it wasn't his responsibility, Ged resisted the temptation to take charge. Instead, he turned back to Lidi, who was looking bemused.

"I guess we don't get top billing?" She studied the stage, where a man dressed as an elf was juggling oversize candy canes. He was being watched by a small, chocolate-colored dog with a Santa hat perched on top of its long, floppy ears.

"Are you complaining?"

She linked her arm through his. "No. But if I'd been aware in advance of the standard, I might have been less worried about my own ability."

He regarded the juggler for a moment or two. "You think you're better than that?"

Lidi choked back a laugh. "Maybe equal?"

He gently patted her hand. "Just keep telling yourself that."

She gasped. "You…" Struggling to regain her composure, she shook her head at him. "Do you find something to laugh at in every situation?"

He gazed down at her, drinking in the smile that was lifting the corner of her mouth even as she tried to maintain a severe tone. "No. My friends would tell you I'm actually a very serious person."

It was true. His friends would also say he used humor as a shield. Get close to anything resembling real emotion and Ged would be guaranteed to make a joke to keep the mood light. But this zest for life? This was *new*. In spite of the danger facing them, he was enjoying himself. So this was what having fun felt like. It seemed that every minute of this adventure added a new layer of discovery, not only about Lidi, but also about himself.

"It looks like the warm-up act is almost over." Lidi pointed to the stage.

Ged had been caught up in the moment of just relaxing and savoring her company. Postponing reality wasn't an option, but for an instant, he wished it was. Wished he could suspend time and not have to think about anything except the smile in her eyes.

Reluctantly, he sighed. "Let's get on with this."

* * *

In the end, dancing on the stage didn't feel too bad. That probably had something to do with the atmosphere. It was festive and lighthearted. People paused to watch as they sipped their mugs of aromatic wine or hot chocolate, but they didn't linger. Possibly, it was also because the whole setup had an amateurish charm. Although the musicians played the music Ged had asked for, it wasn't quite perfect. As they danced, the little dog with the Santa hat sat at the edge of the stage and watched as though critically assessing their performance.

None of those things relaxed Lidi quite as much as the smile in Ged's eyes and the feel of his arms around her. She allowed herself a tiny daydream in which this was all there was. No kingdom to be saved. No father to be rescued. No evil usurper to be defeated. Just this dance. This moment. This man.

"I'm glad dogs in the human world don't get a sense of who we really are." Ged twirled her around as he spoke. "Otherwise that little guy would be spoiling our artistic endeavors by trying to attack us."

"He seems lost in admiration," Lidi agreed.

There were no dogs in Callistoya. There was a myth dating back to the time of Callisto, the hunter-goddess-turned-bear after whom their homeland was named. According to the legend, canines and bears were natural enemies. In Callistoya, there was a belief that dogs brought bad luck to werebears, signaling their intention by attacking their age-old adversaries whenever they met. Since her entry into the mortal realm, Lidi had encountered several canines, all of whom had calmly accepted her. She had even met Ged's werewolf friends, although they were shifters, and their half-human genes gave their instincts a rational edge.

Ged was right. Clearly dogs in the mortal realm couldn't recognize bear shifters. Either that, or the Callistoya fables had it all wrong.

Since the musicians mistimed the piece of music, ending several bars before Ged and Lidi had finished dancing, she didn't have time for any more thinking. Unexpectedly, she was released from Ged's arms and the small crowd clustered at the edge of the stage were clapping, whistling and stamping their feet.

"My goodness, is that for us?"

"I guess so. Unless it's for the Christmas mutt over there—" Ged indicated the dog. "We should take a bow."

Laughing, they clasped hands and moved to the edge of the stage to acknowledge the applause. With a bark of delight, the dog accompanied them.

"I think we have a new friend," Lidi said.

"Well, he can buy his own pizza." The audience was dispersing as Ged led her from the stage.

All around the square, the streets were an intricate muddle of ancient alleys. They found a small restaurant in the center of the maze. Although the place was busy, they were shown to a table overlooking the cobbled road.

"I'm so hungry I could eat everything on the menu," Lidi confessed.

"Be my guest." Ged signaled to the waiter to bring them a bottle of red wine.

She smiled. "I may be half-human, but my appetite is all-bear."

By the time they had ordered several dishes and Ged had poured them each a glass of wine, Lidi was starting to unwind. At the back of her mind there was still a feeling that this was wrong, that she should be racing back home to rescue her father. Every moment she delayed felt like a betrayal, but she had placed her trust in Ged. Although his methods might be unconventional, she believed he would make good on his promise to rescue her father from Vasily's clutches.

"Relax." Ged watched her over the top of his wineglass. "We'll do this."

"Are you a mind reader?"

"You have a very expressive face." The look in his eyes warmed her insides almost as much as the wine. "Tell me about your family."

She toyed with her wineglass. "There isn't much to tell. My parents were very traditional. All they ever wanted was for me to marry well."

"Doesn't that mean your father should be happy with Vasily's proposal? He would see his daughter on the throne of Callistoya."

Lidi, who had been taking a sip of her wine, gave a little choke. "No, absolutely not. The Rihanoff family has always been loyal to your father. And, indirectly, I believe Vasily was responsible for my mother's death and my father's disability."

"Indirectly?" He seemed content to sit back and watch her as she talked.

"My home is in the northernmost part of the kingdom. When Vasily rebelled against your father, he drew the worst elements in our society to him. Our peaceful corner of the world became plagued by lawless mobs who claimed they were fighting against the king." She frowned at the memory. "In reality I believe they were out for what they could steal. My father and the other landowners in the area waged a constant battle to protect their property. My mother was murdered by one of those gangs, and my father was left incapacitated by his injuries."

"But the attackers weren't acting on direct orders from Vasily?" Ged asked.

"I'm not sure, and I don't think we'll ever find out. As far as I know, Vasily didn't know my parents. When he decided he wanted to marry me, we had never met. The only reason he proposed to me was that he felt an alliance with one of the oldest and most respected families in Callistoya would strengthen his claim to the throne. He sent an envoy to Aras with a letter informing me of the time and date of the ceremony."

"Romantic."

She considered the comment, then shrugged. "It wasn't the lack of romance that made me refuse."

"What was it?"

"Vasily is a weak, cowardly bully who thinks he can make himself look strong by murdering his opponents. No amount of flowers and presents would have made him acceptable to me." Her lip curled at the idea. "But my future doesn't include marriage with *anyone*."

Ged had been leaning back in his chair, watching her with a lazy smile in his eyes. At those words his brows snapped together. "Why ever not?"

"When you get your throne back, you will have to work hard to stabilize your kingdom, and I will be your most loyal subject. But even before Vasily broke away from your father, the lands in the north had grown increasingly lawless."

He nodded. "It was one of my father's biggest worries."

"The problems are centuries old. Those groups who

live off the land have suffered as a result of the changing climate. Milder winters, warmer summers and melting ice caps in the mountain regions have reduced the traditional hunting grounds. Where there was harmony there is now competition." She grimaced. "You know what that's like among bears."

"Bloody?"

"And bitter." She twirled her wineglass, staring into the depths of the ruby liquid. "Before my father became ill, I pleaded with him to let me join the king's peacekeeping army."

"I take it the idea was not well received?" Ged asked.

Lidi laughed. "It was about as popular as a dog at a royal feast."

"Ouch." He winced at the comparison.

"But now my father is not able to carry out his duties as the Count of Aras. I must do much of it for him." She looked up from her glass. "That includes bringing stability to our region."

"I see. So you wish to be part of the peacekeeping force in that area?"

It occurred to her that she was looking at the man who could destroy her ambitions with a single word. She had come to think of Ged as her friend, but he was also her king. They lived in a patriarchal society where, once he was restored to his position, his word would be absolute. If he forbade her entry into the military, she would be powerless to fight him.

Even knowing that, her pride would not allow her to back down. She lifted her chin determinedly. "I want to become a general."

"And you couldn't do that while being married?"

She was still laughing too hard to answer the question when their food arrived. Had Ged seriously thought about what he was suggesting? In their male-dominated world, could he actually picture a situation in which any Callistoya bear shifter would permit his wife to have a career, let alone lead her troops into conflict?

Any further conversation was suspended as they started to eat. Lidi was so hungry her focus remained on the food, and it was some time before she looked up from her plate. She smiled across the table at Ged. "That was delicious."

A noise in the street outside attracted her attention, making her turn her head in that direction. A group of people were passing the restaurant, and one woman in particular caught her eye. Dressed in a warm, padded jacket, jeans and boots, she was tall and slim. As she drew level with the window, the light shone on the long, silvery length of her hair. For an instant, she looked directly at Lidi, maintaining eye contact for several seconds before moving away.

"Allie!" Lidi was on her feet and moving toward the door before she had time to think.

"What the—" Out of the corner of her eye, she saw Ged throw a handful of cash onto the table as he hurried after her.

Once she got outside, Lidi paused. The narrow street was crowded, and although she couldn't see Allie, she knew which direction the other woman had taken. Hitching up her long skirt, she set off at a run. Dodging in and out of the crush of bodies, she scanned the people around her for a glimpse of that distinctive, shimmering hair.

"Lidi." Ged was just behind her. "What's going on?"

"It was Allie." She turned her head to look at him

but didn't slow her pace. "The woman who was in the crowd outside the movie theater in Cannes and on Julien's boat. She just walked past the restaurant window."

"Are you sure it was her?"

"Completely. She looked right at me." They had reached the square and she paused, looking all around her. There were so many people it was almost impossible to pick out just one. "It was almost as if she wanted me to see her."

"Can you see her now?" Ged asked.

"No." Her shoulders sagged in defeat. "But it *was* her."

He scanned the busy area. "Was she alone?"

"I'm not sure. A group of people went past at the same time, but I don't know if she was with them." She shivered as the cold night air hit her. "They weren't bear shifters. I noticed that much."

"Whoever she is, and whatever she's doing here, it seems your mystery woman has disappeared. Standing around here isn't going to bring her back." Ged nodded across the square in the direction of their hotel. "Let's get out of the cold."

As they walked across the cobbles, Lidi scrutinized the faces of the individuals they passed. Allie was too distinctive to mistake. When they reached the hotel steps, a thought hit her, and she stopped.

"Distinctive." When Ged raised a questioning brow, she touched a hand to her blond wig. "I was in disguise, yet in those few seconds when we exchanged glances, I'm certain that Allie knew it was me. She found me, Ged, even though we went to all this trouble to hide who I am. How did she do that?"

"I don't know." His expression was grim. "But if you see her again, I intend to find out."

Chapter 9

As they climbed the narrow staircase to their room, Ged had half his mind on Lidi's mysterious stalker and the other half on the forthcoming conversation about sleeping arrangements.

His decision to book them into one room had been about safety. With the possibility that Vasily's men might find them, he didn't want to let Lidi out of his sight. That had been the simple, common-sense explanation. Until the moment that had changed and complicated everything.

Because, having shared one kiss with Lidi, he wanted more. Wanted more *than* kisses. And he knew Lidi shared that desire. It would be so easy to succumb, to let themselves be carried away on this tide of enchantment. But every time he let that pleasurable line of thought intrude, the tangle of complications pulled him back to reality.

Ged was an intellectual. Although his rescue operations required action, each was meticulously planned. He had been the restraining influence when the members of Beast got up to some of their wilder antics. One of Khan's jokes was that he and his friends could easily sneak off the tour bus. All they had to do was wait until their manager was reading Dostoyevsky in the original Russian. That was why Ged's purely physical reaction to Lidi confused him. He didn't recognize himself as this person who was alight with sensation, who couldn't reason away these feelings...who didn't want to. Nevertheless, it had to be done.

"You take the bed." He closed the door to their room and locked it. Turning, he remained where he was, leaning his shoulders against the wooden panels. "I'll sleep on the sofa. Oh, hell..."

So much for restraint. It lasted the two strides it took him to reach Lidi and drag her into his arms. "I told myself I wouldn't do this."

She uttered a sound midway between a laugh and a sob as she reached up to touch his cheek. "So did I."

He kissed her. "I was going to fight it."

"Me too. Kiss me again."

He groaned and pressed his lips to the curve of her neck. "Lidi, the fates really screwed up this time. I can't offer you forever. Even if I knew what that meant..."

She placed a hand each side of his face, holding him so she could look into his eyes. "I may be new to this, but let me see if I've got it right." Even beneath the makeup, he could see she was blushing. "When we are in human form we can have sex, and, like other mortals, it can just be an enjoyable act. Is that correct?" He nodded. "It's only when we shift and mate as bears that we seal our bond and make a lifelong commitment?"

"Yes, but…"

She pressed her fingers to his lips. "I've already told you I don't want forever. With you, or anyone else. So can we stop talking and get on with having right now?"

He could see the simplicity of what she was saying in the depths of her eyes. Lidi was everything he wanted. And she wanted him. Here and now. Anything else could wait. But the problem went much deeper than he had suspected. Because even though he couldn't offer her eternity—he didn't even know if he could offer her tomorrow—this was a fine time to discover that forever might be exactly what he craved.

He reached up to tangle a hand in her hair, drawing back when he encountered the stiff wig instead of her own soft curls. "I need to say one more thing. This is probably important enough to merit a return to our own identities."

Her smile flipped his heart over. "You're right. Spontaneity is good, but I prefer you without the beard."

While Lidi went into the bathroom, Ged moved to the mirror over the dressing table and studied his own disguise. The beard and wig had done their job, but he would be happy to remove them. He wasn't sure about the whole villain-in-a-melodrama look.

As he turned away, he became aware of a curious sound. It seemed to be coming from the square outside. Going to the window, he threw back the drapes and stepped onto the balcony. There on the cobbles below him was the dog who had watched their dance earlier. With his head tilted back, the little hound was uttering a low, mournful howl. There was no sign of the Santa hat.

"What's that dreadful noise?" Coming up behind him, Lidi placed a hand on Ged's shoulder.

As soon as she came into view, the dog stopped wailing. Wagging his tail, he sat up on his hind legs and waved his front paws at her.

"Oh, how sweet," Lidi said. The dog gave a single bark in response, as though agreeing with her.

Seriously? Ged stared down at the animal with a bemused expression. He had just decided to throw caution to the wind and follow his instincts. Now he was being upstaged by a *dog*? Perhaps those legends about canines bringing bad luck to bear shifters weren't so very far-fetched after all.

"Sweet or not, he can't come in here." Ged turned away and started to close the window. The dog immediately commenced his sorrowful howling again. "Is that aimed at us?"

"It looks that way." Lidi leaned over the edge of the balcony and addressed the dog directly. "It's late. Go home."

"I don't think it understands English." Ged was unable to hide his annoyance as the animal pranced cheerfully around in a circle before returning to sit beneath the balcony.

"If we leave him there, he'll disturb the other guests with his crying." She clasped her hands against her chest.

"If we bring him up here, his death throes will bother them even more." Although he tried to sound savage, Ged found himself unable to resist the plea in her eyes. His growl subsided into a sigh of capitulation. "I'll go and get him."

Lidi laughed as she looped her arms around his neck and kissed his cheek. "Thank you."

When he reached the street, the dog greeted him as if he was a long-lost friend. Jumping up and down with excitement, it tried to lick his hands. "You can stop that nonsense right now." Ged spoke harshly to it. "If I had my way, your ass would be frozen to the cobbles all night."

He scooped the animal up under one arm, tucking his jacket around it to hide it from prying eyes. Seeming to understand the need for secrecy, the dog stopped wriggling and remained quiet.

When Lidi opened the door to the hotel room, the dog began to struggle and whine quietly. As soon as Ged released him, he pranced around Lidi with obvious delight. She lifted him up, stroking his long, silky ears and reducing him to a state of instant bliss.

"I don't know much about dogs, but I think he's only young." She looked over the hound's head at Ged.

"Either that or stupid," he agreed.

"I don't know what it is—some sort of intuition, maybe—but I'm sensing that you don't like him."

"Lidi, we're Callistoya bear shifters. If you believe the legends of our homeland, that thing…" He pointed to the creature that was almost grinning with pleasure as she continued to stroke it. "Well, it's not exactly a lucky charm. Even if you don't believe the old stories, we are supposed to be lying low and not attracting attention to ourselves. Getting ourselves a pet was never part of the agenda."

"But he's so cute." The dog lolled his tongue out of the corner of his mouth and rolled his eyes. "And, if you think about it, Bruno adds to our disguise."

"Bruno? The mutt has acquired a name?" Ged asked.

"It's the Italian word for *brown*. I think it suits him, don't you?" Lidi asked. Bruno gave an enthusiastic yelp of agreement.

Even though he knew he was losing the fight, Ged bit back a laugh. "How do you work out that he adds to our disguise?"

"Because we *are* Callistoya bear shifters. No one would ever expect us to get close to a dreaded canine."

"He can stay here tonight." Ged gave the dog a stern look. "On the floor. Tomorrow we take him back to Rico and tell him to find his owner." As he headed for the bathroom to remove his disguise, he got the distinct feeling that neither Lidi nor Bruno were listening to him.

He was right. When he returned to the bedroom, he viewed the scene that met his eyes in thoughtful silence. Lidi had fallen asleep fully clothed on top of the king-size bed. Sprawled diagonally across the remaining space, with his head on the pillow next to hers, Bruno was snoring lightly. When Ged attempted to move him, the dog grunted but refused to budge. For such a small animal he had managed to make himself surprisingly heavy.

With a sigh Ged pulled the bedclothes over Lidi and moved to the sofa. As he pulled off his boots, he gazed at her face. The sweet curve of her cheek and the soft shadow of her lashes had a soothing effect on his troubled spirit. Wearily, he switched off the lamp before curling his long limbs into the small space. It was hard to believe that mere days ago, the only person he'd had any obligation to was himself. Now it seemed he was collecting new responsibilities at an alarming rate.

If he had the chance, would he go back to his solitary, unfettered existence? He uttered a short laugh. Lidi had lifted him out of an emotional fog. Wherever he was going now, at least he could see clearly. How much of the journey she would make with him in the future remained to be seen. But he wouldn't have missed this adventure for the world…even with the unexpected addition of a troublesome canine.

Ged came slowly awake to find a wet nose inches from his face. He closed his eyes in an attempt to recapture sleep and banish the image. A soft laugh drove away any trace of slumber.

When he opened his eyes again, he found that Bruno had moved closer. "If you lick me, you will regret it for the rest of your life."

The dog settled for wagging his tail and wriggling delightedly as though they had been reunited after a lengthy separation. Ged tilted his head to look at Lidi, who was seated on the end of the bed. Although she had donned her blond wig, she wore her jacket and boots.

He scrubbed a hand over his face. "Have you been out?"

"We had to take care of the toilet situation." She pointed to Bruno.

Ged sat up abruptly. "What if Vasily's men had been around?"

She indicated her hair. "I was in disguise. And I had my guard dog with me." She stroked Bruno's head and he promptly flipped over onto his back, inviting a tummy rub.

"I somehow doubt Vasily's thugs would be deterred by the presence of a cloud of fluff with butterfly ears."

"You are forgetting the legend," Lidi said. "Any self-respecting bear shifter would be scared that Bruno would bring them bad luck."

"Of course." Ged got to his feet, preparing to head for the bathroom. "Thank you for reminding me that I have forfeited my self-respect to something with all the intelligence of a cupcake."

"Just ignore him." Lidi told Bruno. "I don't think he's a morning person."

Once Ged was showered, dressed and wearing his own disguise, they headed out. Lidi explained that she had used a combination of the ribbons from her corset and one of Ged's belts to make a collar and leash for Bruno.

"I hope you don't mind?"

"Not at all," he said as the dog chewed excitedly on his five-hundred-dollar designer accessory.

Lidi laughed and tucked her arm through his. "I can tell you like him, really."

For a moment he let himself be distracted by the soft weight of her breast against his bicep and her delicious scent. Then he forced himself to focus. Lidi was enchanting, but standing in the middle of a busy square smiling into her eyes was probably not the best idea when a group of vicious killers were on their tail.

"Let's find Rico." He headed toward the stage. "He may be able to help us find out who owns the dog."

Although it was early and the market was quiet, Rico was behind the stage taking inventory, presumably in preparation for their departure that night. He shook his head when Ged questioned him about Bruno.

"I had never seen that dog before last night." Rico had the ability to look distracted even when performing the most minor of tasks. "I noticed it on the stage just before you arrived to do your dance, and it disappeared just after you finished."

"Can you ask around? See if anyone knows who it might belong to?" Ged asked.

Leaving Rico to his paperwork, they went to one of the outdoor stalls and bought coffee and pastries for themselves and sausages and water for Bruno. Taking their breakfast to a bench, they watched the square grow busier as they ate.

"We may not find his owner." Ged kept his voice gentle as he looked at Lidi's profile.

"I know that." She didn't look at him.

"We leave for Frankfurt tonight."

"I know that, as well." She had finished eating, and her fingers strayed to the dog's head.

"He can't come with us."

She didn't answer, but there was something about the set of her jaw that tugged hard at a point right in the center of his chest.

It's a damn dog.

Even in ordinary circumstances, that would be his stance. And these were far from ordinary circumstances. So why did he want to say *To hell with it* and do whatever it took so that that she could keep the dog? Why, for that matter, did he want to give her anything else she wanted? Roses in winter? Ice-skating in summer? If Lidi asked for it, he would move heaven and earth to make it happen. He decided not to inquire too closely into why, since he had a feeling the answer might lead him along a route from which there was no turning back.

He withdrew his cell phone from his pocket. "This

place is like a maze, but why don't I check out a map of the local area and find a park so we can take him for a walk?"

Lidi turned her head, catching him unawares with the radiance of her smile. Was this how it felt to be under the influence of a magic charm? Could that be what was going on here? Was there a chance that the mystery woman called Allie was a sorceress who, instead of a cat, had chosen a dog as her familiar? Had she sent Bruno to continue her work, weaving a charm that pulled Ged in deeper by the minute? He already knew the answer to that question. He was under a spell; that much was for sure. But there was no magic involved. The truth was a whole lot simpler and scarier.

The cause of his enchantment got to her feet, brushing crumbs from her jeans. "Tell me about the plan once we reach Frankfurt."

"When we get to Frankfurt we'll fly to Anchorage in Alaska. From there we'll travel to Russia, and cross the Callistoya border in Siberia." He studied the screen of his cell phone before leading the way across the square and down a winding side street. They walked on a little farther. Ged was about to take a left turn into a narrow road that would lead them to the park when Bruno started to behave oddly. Instead of continuing to prance eagerly at Lidi's side, the little dog sat down and refused to move. When Lidi tried to coax him, he flattened his ears, dug in his heels and stayed in place.

"I'll carry him." As Ged reached down to pick him up, Bruno, who was trembling all over, started to whine and look back in the direction from which they had come.

"He doesn't want to go this way." Lidi pointed to the road into which they had been about to turn.

Ged's lips tightened. "I think it's about time Bruno learned who is in charge around here."

Lidi placed a hand on his arm. "No, Ged. Look. He's terrified."

She was right. Ged's respect for Bruno's intelligence might not be high, but he couldn't ignore the evidence from his own eyes. Something around that corner was scaring the hound half-to-death.

"Take Bruno and wait on the steps of that church." He indicated a building they had just passed. The doors were open and people were going in and out. He figured that if there was any risk, Lidi would be safer among a group.

Her face paled. "What about you?"

"I'm not going to put myself in any danger. I just want to find out what the problem is."

She cast a nervous look in the direction of the street before nodding. "Be careful."

There were a number of things he could have said in the instant before she turned away. He could have told her that for the first time in a long time, he *would* be careful. Until that moment, he had been a reckless fighter, seeking danger and exulting in it. Walking around a corner into the unknown would have been exactly the sort of situation he'd have sought out. Now he would take care. Because of Lidi. Because he finally had a reason to be cautious.

Because I want to see how our story ends.

"I will."

Although Bruno willingly went with Lidi when she walked toward the church, he did cast a few looks in

Ged's direction as though questioning his decision not to accompany them. Ged watched them walk away, then turned the corner into the street that had caused the dog so much anxiety.

At first sight, he couldn't find any cause for concern. The road was short, with a few shops and cafés on either side, and he could see the park gates at the other end. As he progressed slowly along the sidewalk, he became aware of voices. A group of people, hidden from his view, were talking loudly, apparently disagreeing about something.

As he drew closer, his heart rate kicked up a notch. Genoa was on the northwest coast of Italy. It was a cosmopolitan area. It wouldn't be unusual to come across a wide variety of languages in this region, so Ged wasn't surprised to hear a tongue other than Italian. What did shake him was that the conversation he could hear was being conducted in his own language. Since it was not known to mortals, Callistoyan was not usually spoken outside his homeland.

Keeping close to the buildings, Ged moved stealthily toward the voices. When he reached an olive oil shop, he paused. After this point there was a break in the line of buildings. A quick glance around the corner showed that his next steps would take him past the courtyard of a large bar. It also confirmed the presence of a group of five male bear shifters.

Ged wanted to listen in on their conversation, but he was not yet close enough, and he needed to remain hidden. Another swift look revealed a narrow alley between this shop and the bar. Crouching low, Ged slipped into the alley and found a space between two dumpsters where he could stay close to the ground and hear what was being said.

"We are wasting our time here, Artem." The speaker sounded frustrated.

"I agree, but do you want to be the one to tell the king we have failed in our mission?"

There were a few moments of silence followed by the sound of glasses being placed on a table. "Coming to Genoa was a mistake. While we've been chasing our tails here, the Rihanoff woman and Gerald Tavisha have been able to get away."

There was a thud, as if a fist hit a flat surface, then an enraged growl. "I stand by my decision to check this city out. This is where that damn boat was headed, the one owned by Tavisha's friend. If Tavisha hadn't shown up when he did, the others would have been able to snatch the woman then."

"So what now? The mortal realm is a big place. We have no way of finding them." The words, as well as the tone, conveyed both despondency and fear.

"True, but we know the woman has an incentive to return to Callistoya." It was the voice of Artem, who Ged surmised was leader of this group. "Her father is imprisoned there. To get there, she will have to cross the border."

"The king has already ensured that Tavisha cannot make the transition from the human world into Callistoya. The spell that has been cast means his banishment is permanent." The laughter that ensued made Ged clench a fist hard against his thigh. "All we have to do is wait for the Rihanoff woman to show up at the crossing point."

"You are sure she will take the conventional route?"

There was a spluttering sound as though Artem, having been caught unawares, had choked on his drink. "Are you crazy? Even the Rihanoff spitfire would not brave the mountain crossing at this time of year."

Ged had heard enough. Easing his way carefully out of the cramped space, he made his way back to the street and headed toward the church where he had left Lidi and Bruno.

Chapter 10

Lidi sat on the church steps and hugged Bruno close, keeping her eyes fixed on the point where she had last seen Ged.

"I should have gone with him." Until Bruno licked her hand, she wasn't aware she'd spoken out loud. Ruffling his silken ears, she sighed. "What was it? What did you sense in that street that frightened you so much?"

The dog gave a whine and ducked his head under her arm as though keeping out of sight. If Lidi hadn't been so worried about Ged, she'd have laughed at his antics. It was nonsensical to suppose he could understand what she meant, even though that was how it appeared. He seemed determined to turn away from the street where Ged had gone. Lidi might even have suspected he was hiding his face. But that was nonsensical. He was a *dog*, incapable of such a complex train of thought.

Her mind refused to stray far from Ged. What would she do if anything happened to him? She didn't mean the question in any practical sense. She was more than capable of looking after herself. But in the short time since they had met, she had come to depend on his companionship as much as his support. Now, she couldn't imagine her life without him in it.

Telling herself it was foolish to think that way, that one day, sooner rather than later, she would have to cope without him, didn't work. Right here, right now, she was gripped with a paralyzing fear that she might never get the chance to tell him what he meant to her. Which in itself was a problem. Because…what *did* he mean to her?

She wasn't sure she could put her fledgling emotions into words. Physically, he sent her senses into overdrive. And, because she was new to this, she couldn't be sure that wasn't all there was to it. What if she was mistaking desire for something more?

"How would I know?" She asked Bruno, and the dog tilted his head to one side, as though attempting to understand what she was saying. "It's not like I'm experienced at this sort of thing. I hardly know any men."

Bruno gave a bark, which she took to be a sign of encouragement. She soon realized it was something else entirely. The dog had turned away from her and was wagging his tail. As she looked up, the source of his excitement became obvious. Ged was walking toward them.

All her soul-searching about her feelings became meaningless. As she tucked Bruno under her arm and ran to him, she took a moment to register the truth. This was more than physical. Meeting Ged had been like opening the page of a new book and finding there were stories within it that were so wonderful they took her breath away. She was still finding her way through the layers of these mysterious new emotions, each discovery as wonderful, and, at the same time, as life changing, as the last.

"Hey." Ged caught hold of her as she charged into him. Unable to hold her close because of the dog who was squirming and trying to lick his face, he leaned in and briefly pressed his lips to her forehead. The caress instantly grounded her and chased away the gnawing anxiety. "I told you I'd be okay."

"What happened?" She clutched his sweatshirt with her free hand. There was a strong possibility she might never let him go.

He looked over his shoulder. "Not here."

They walked downhill from the historic city center, heading toward the port. Although the colder weather meant that many of the quayside cafés were closed, a few had remained open. Finding one that was dog friendly, Ged chose a table overlooking both the harbor and the roads that approached it. Lidi could tell his selection was deliberate and waited for him to explain why.

He got straight to the point. "A group of Vasily's men were in the street that Bruno was afraid to go down."

"Oh." While he ordered coffee for them and water for the dog, she considered the implications of what he was saying. "Does that mean they know we are here?"

"No. They suspected we could be, but, from what I overheard, they've given up the search and are about to leave town."

Lidi slumped back into her chair, relief hitting every part of her body. "Surely that's a good thing?"

"It's not a bad thing." Ged's attitude was cautious. "It means they're moving on. For now."

The waiter brought their drinks and Lidi remained silent until they were alone. "It sounds like there's more to it."

Ged explained that he had listened in on a conversation between Vasily's men, during which they plotted to wait for her at the magical border that existed between the human world and Callistoya.

"They speculated that you would take the conventional route, since no one would attempt to cross the Callistoya mountains during the winter months."

Her lip curled. "They may lack the courage to do so. I do not."

Ged sighed. "How did I know you were going to say that?"

Lidi frowned. "None of this answers the question of how *you* will enter Callistoya."

He took a sip of coffee before answering. "There are several ways of getting to Russia. Going via Alaska is not the most direct route, but I have my reasons for choosing it."

She reached across the table and took his hand. "Does that mean you think there may be a way you can bypass Vasily's magic spell and cross the border?"

"I know someone who may be able to help." There was a distant look in his eyes as though he was briefly gazing into the past. "We'll know for sure when we get to Anchorage."

While they were taking, Bruno had made an alarming discovery. It involved his tail. This strange, plumy, waving thing was following him and, no matter what he did, it wouldn't stop. In a determined effort to get rid of it, he started charging around in a circle, growling and snapping wildly at his rear end.

"I have a horrible feeling that canines are considered superior to bears on the intelligence scale," Ged observed.

Lidi laughed as Bruno, exhausted by his exertions, flopped, panting, onto his side. She looked up at Ged. "He did warn us not to go down that street."

"Do you really believe that was anything other than coincidence?" His expression was skeptical.

She gave it some thought. "Yes, I do. Bruno knew there was danger awaiting us and he did everything he could to stop us."

Ged shook his head. "He was frightened, Lidi. Pure and simple. Maybe he sensed Vasily's men were bear shifters—"

"Oh, no." She pounced quickly. "If that's the case, why is he okay with us? We're bear shifters, but we don't scare him. And there's more to it." She was warming to her theme now, a mild suspicion growing into a certainty. "You heard what Rico said. Last night, Bruno turned up in the square around the same time we did. He left the stage when we finished our dance. Then he showed up outside our hotel. He was looking for *us*, Ged."

He didn't answer. Instead, he finished his coffee, keeping his eyes on Bruno. Eventually he turned his gaze back to her. "You really think the furball is some sort of protector?"

"Don't you?"

"I'm not sure what to think." He reached down and

rubbed the top of Bruno's head. "But I guess we've got ourselves a traveling companion after all."

Luckily, he gripped the sides of his chair in time to steady himself as, with a squeal of delight, Lidi leaped up and threw her arms around his neck.

That night, after Ged and Lidi had danced, they boarded the coach with Rico and the other performers and set off on the journey to the German city of Frankfurt. They both carried lightweight backpacks containing a few changes of clothing. Lidi also had the forged passport that had cost Ged a fortune to arrange in such a short space of time. Ged, having lived in the mortal realm for so long, already had documents to prove his human identity.

Bruno, who wore a new red leather collar and matching leash, had taken an initial dislike to the idea of being confined on the bus. After a few minutes of vocal objection, he had heaved a long-suffering sigh and fallen asleep on Lidi's knee.

Before long, Lidi, her head eyelids drooping, had also succumbed to slumber. Ged carefully eased her head onto his shoulder, shifting his position to ensure she was comfortable. He knew from years of experience of touring with Beast, on a considerably more luxurious bus, that he wouldn't sleep. Leaning his head against the window, he watched the lights of the freeway flash by and gave himself up to his thoughts.

This was a journey he had convinced himself he would never make. Because of shifter immortality, human and Callistoya years were different. But in mortal time, thirteen years had passed since he had left his home. He had barely reached the age of shifter maturity when his life had been destroyed by the assassins' silver blades.

He couldn't pretend that everything about the intervening years had been bad. Although his friendships with the members of Beast and the band's success had undoubtedly been the highest points, there had been other triumphs.

Khan described Ged's rescue missions as *the Red Cross for shifters*. Ged was proud of those words and of what he'd achieved. There were men and women—wolves, dragons cats…shifters of every description—who were only alive today because of the network of liberators he had established. But underlying everything there had been an ache that couldn't be assuaged.

Home. Callistoya had been the pain in his heart that wouldn't go away. He had denied it, even without knowing it.

It wasn't about wearing a crown. Ged had always known that. It was about the principles his father had stood for and the proud name of Tavisha. It was about the history of their family line and the land bequeathed to them by the descendants of Callisto herself. For a long time, he had been unable to see past the grief and shock caused by the massacre of his family and friends. Feelings of guilt had overwhelmed him. He should have been able to prevent what had happened. He should have protected Alyona. Even once he had been exiled, the feelings of inadequacy persisted with his inability to find his brother.

He knew he could have made more of an effort to return. When his only attempt had ended in failure, his emotional turmoil had raged out of control. By closing the border with a magic spell that excluded Ged, Vasily had been one step ahead of him. Unable to see a way out of his predicament, Ged had been forced to leave the resistance in his uncle's hands.

"The Tavisha name *will* rise again." Eduard had placed a hand on Ged's shoulder. "You cannot see it now, but one day your broken spirit will heal."

Thirteen years. Every day, he had waited for a sign that his uncle's prediction was coming true. That Vasily's reign was ending. That his own fear and inertia toward his exile were subsiding. It had never happened.

Ged had always assumed he was seeking a transformation that would start within himself. That, whether gradual or instant, his own attitude would be the catalyst he sought. Now he knew he had been wrong. He glanced at the slender figure beside him, and a warm feeling washed over him. His uncle had been right. It was Ged who had been mistaken. *One day* was here. Lidi was the change he had been waiting for.

She had lifted him out of the trough of his own despondency, making him search for possibilities when in the past he had only seen barriers. The difference was internal, but she was the driving force behind his new approach. Her full-on attitude made him realize he had been living a half-life, hiding from reality. Looking back, it was as if, after the horror of what had happened, he had crawled under an imaginary comfort blanket and stayed there, waiting for the world to come to him.

And it had. In the most unexpected, exciting way imaginable. As Ged stared at Lidi, Bruno opened one eye. Yawning, the dog stretched until his head rested on Ged's knee.

"Yeah. You too." Ged realized as he spoke that he was going to have to be creative with the travel arrangements. Getting a dog from Germany to America without any paperwork was going to require all his ingenuity. Taking a dog to Callistoya, a magical land where canines were viewed as a symbol of bad luck? "I don't know how you fit into this adventure, but I hope you're worth it."

Bruno wagged his tail and went back to sleep.

Lidi stirred as the dog in her lap became restless. She had fallen asleep in total darkness; now, as she opened her eyes, she could see a hint of lighter color to the sky through the bus window. Dawn hadn't arrived, but it was heralding its approach. She stretched and turned her head.

Oh, my goodness. Ged's smile. Up close. Just as she was waking up. It did things to her insides that were both delicious and unnerving.

She cleared her throat, more to give herself a few seconds of thinking time than because the action was necessary. "Where are we?"

"Just outside the German city of Freiburg. You've slept through three countries."

Her hand went to her hair and she grimaced as her fingers encountered the wig. "I have? Were they interesting?"

"No. Rest assured, the freeways of Italy, Switzerland, France—and now Germany—are identical to those of any other country."

She leaned across him to peer out of the window, conscious of the hard muscles of his chest against her shoulder. As she did, Bruno whined and shuffled as though attempting to get comfortable.

"I think he may need a comfort break," Lidi said.

"He's probably not the only one. It's been a long time since we last stopped," Ged said. "Let me talk to the driver and see what I can do."

He made his way to the front of the bus, returning a few minutes later. "He said he was planning to stop in an hour for gas. He'll reschedule and do it now."

Before long, the bus was slowing as it pulled into the brightly lit parking lot of a large rest stop. Ged looked out of the window. "We can get some breakfast."

On cue, Lidi's stomach gave an enormous rumble. "That sounds like a great plan."

Because they didn't have much time, Lidi took Bruno to the designated "pet area" while Ged went to check out the menu in the dog-friendly restaurant.

"I want the biggest cooked breakfast they do, washed down with a vat of coffee," Lidi told him.

After the dog's basic needs had been taken care of, Lidi headed toward the restrooms, tying Bruno's leash to a metal post outside while she used the facilities. When she returned and untied him, they walked toward the main rest-stop building.

Once they were inside, Lidi took a moment to look around, scanning the multilingual signs for directions to the restaurant. The interior resembled a smaller version of some of the shopping malls she had seen on her travels. She was standing in front of an array of all-night stores that offered drivers and passengers the essentials for their journey and tempted them with a few luxuries. There were also some stands, similar to market stalls, dotted around the space and, despite the early hour, the vendors were setting out their wares. Her mind was on her breakfast and Lidi barely noticed the collection of arts and crafts produced by local artists.

She was forced into abrupt awareness when Bruno unexpectedly pulled hard on his leash. Before Lidi could stop him, he had dragged her across to one of the booths and jumped up excitedly at the woman who was arranging her goods. Placing his paws on the back of her knees, he uttered a sharp bark. Startled, the woman dropped the stack of pictures she'd been holding.

"I'm so sorry." Lidi knelt on the marble tiles as she helped the woman gather the scattered images together. "I don't know what got into him."

The salesclerk laughed. "I have dogs." Her English was near perfect. "Sometimes they don't need a reason."

The prints Bruno had knocked over were an array of photographs depicting pretty German villages and fairy-tale castles. As Lidi handed them over, another picture, lying on the floor a little distance away, caught her eye. As she reached for it, she had the strangest sensation of time slowing to a crawl.

Unlike the other images, this was a painting, a haunting scene in which tall trees stood like sentinels guarding soaring mountains. While the lower slopes were dappled with greenery, the higher reaches wore a lacy shroud of snow. Above the granite peaks the sky, brooding and bruised, rolled on into infinity.

I know that sky. The thought caused Lidi's heart to beat out a new rhythm. *But it can't be what I think it is...*

She lifted the picture closer, knowing as she did that her gaze would catch the distant, mirrorlike glint of a lake, and—*there!*—high upon a distant summit, she would just make out the distinctive, colorful turrets of an ancient fortress.

Pressing a fist tight against her chest, she took a moment to regulate her breathing. How was this possible?

How was it that here, in a rest stop in the heart of Germany, she was looking at a painting of the mountain region around the royal palace of Callistoya?

It must be a coincidence.

Telling herself that meant she was able to regain a sense of calm. Yes, the painting was perfect in its detail. But the person who painted it couldn't have been to Callistoya. Unless, of course, he, or she, was a bear shifter. The chances of that were almost nonexistent. Add in the possibility of that person painting a picture and Lidi coming across it here, *today. The bus wasn't even meant to stop in this place.* She shook her head. It was more likely that the painter had chanced upon a scene in his or her imagination and that it happened to look scarily like her homeland.

Wait until I tell Ged about this.

On the subject of Ged…he would be waiting for her, and so would her breakfast. She took another look at the picture, shaking her head over the striking similarities to the scenery of the Callistoya mountain range. Who was the unknown artist who had captured it so perfectly? Tilting it to the light, she read the tiny signature in the bottom corner of the painting.

Andrei Tavisha.

Chapter 11

Ged wasn't sure what was keeping Lidi, but if she wasn't back soon there was a very real danger of him making inroads into her breakfast as well as his own. Just as he was wondering if she would miss one of those delicious sausages, he noticed her approaching him.

He was about to make a joke about his evil intentions toward her food when he realized something was very wrong. She looked like a sleepwalker. Pale-faced and wide-eyed, she stumbled into the seat opposite him and thrust an item into his hand.

"Coffee." He pointed at the cup he had already poured. "Good and strong."

Lidi tied Bruno's leash to the leg of her chair before gratefully wrapping her hands around the coffee mug. She indicated the flat package she'd given him. "Look at it."

Ged carefully removed several layers of protective tissue paper, then turned the picture over. Long, silent moments passed as he gazed at it. He felt as though his body was closing down, one shallow breath at a time. Although his heart was still beating, his eyes still seeing, he was no longer functioning. So this was what shock felt like. But it was more. Anger, bitterness, pain, relief...all of those things crowded in on him, as well.

He recognized the image in the painting immediately. There was nowhere in the human world quite like Callistoya. Something about the light was different. Or maybe those who came from the magical kingdom just believed it was. Even so, those mountains were unmistakable. As a child, he had believed the peaks were the spine of a sleeping dinosaur.

The painful tug of longing was nothing compared to the rush of emotion that hit him when he saw the signature. Thirteen years of searching for his brother. Now this. He didn't know whether to be hurt or happy. Didn't even know if he could allow himself to feel anything in case his hopes were about to be dashed into a thousand pieces.

"Where...?" The word was a croak, forced out through a throat that was almost closed.

"A booth near the entrance." Lidi had finished her coffee and started eating. No amount of shock could come between a bear shifter and food. Bruno, seated under the table, was eagerly devouring his own breakfast.

Ged looked toward the door. He had waited so long for this moment, he was almost scared to ask. "Is he...?"

"No. Andrei isn't here. I'm sorry. I should have made that clear straightaway." Lidi placed a hand on his arm.

"The woman who sold me the picture explained that she sells the work of local artists. She takes a commission and passes the rest of the proceeds on to the creator of the work."

"Does she know where he is?"

"Yes and no. She said that this particular artist is very reclusive. *Mysterious*, that was the word she used to describe him." Lidi tapped a fingertip on the picture in his hand. "He only ever paints this scene. Every few weeks, he sends a new batch of pictures to her home address and she forwards any payment to a bank in a town called Branheim." Ged reached for his cell phone, but the action was unnecessary. Lidi tightened her grip on his arm. "I already asked. It's an hour's drive from here."

He leaned back in his chair, his mind whirling as he tried to reach a decision. After all these years of trying and encountering a brick wall of silence, to come this close to finding Andrei...but he had made a commitment to Lidi. Every minute spent on the road was another minute during which her father languished in a cell. Another minute that might draw Vasily's men closer to tracing her.

Anguish tore at him as he tried to work through the arguments for and against halting their journey and going to Branheim. Apart from his uncle, his brother was all Ged had left of his old life. In human years, Andrei had been fifteen at the time of the massacre. The five-year age difference meant the brothers had been close, but their interests had been dissimilar. The idea of Andrei growing up in the mortal realm, reaching shifter maturity, without anyone to support him deepened the ache in Ged's heart.

"We have to find him." Lidi took control, overriding his indecision.

"But your father…"

"No. You don't understand." She pointed to the animal at their feet. Bruno, having finished his meal, was carefully removing any trace of grease from his whiskers by rubbing his face against Ged's jeans. "Bruno made us stop the bus. He dragged me to a booth where that painting wasn't even on display. He knocked it out of the stall owner's hand, so I was forced to pick it up."

"Are you saying he knew it was there?"

Shifter DNA was unique. Half-human, half-animal, they had the ability to adapt to either environment. While their human counterparts were raised in a world of science and technology, shifters knew magic was real. They were the living proof that the supernatural existed. Even so, Ged was still having a hard time believing the funny little dog was an enchanted being.

"Think about it, Ged." He might have been struggling with the idea, but he could tell from her solemn expression that Lidi was convinced. "We only stopped here, an hour from the town where your brother lives, because of Bruno. This was meant to happen."

He shook his head, trying to clear the jumble of thoughts that were threatening to overwhelm him. Could it be true? He was inclined to treat the dog as a joke, a living, breathing fluffy toy. Yet the evidence that Bruno was something more than an ordinary canine was stacking up so high it could no longer be ignored.

Even so, he felt the need to issue a challenge. "What if we hadn't decided to travel to Frankfurt? We could just have easily have decided to fly from Milan to Moscow."

The set of Lidi's jaw told him he wasn't going to win this argument. "Bruno would have found a way to stop us. He'd have made sure we came this way." She ducked her head to look under the table. "Wouldn't you, boy?"

Bruno gave a joyful bark and bounded up onto the seat next to Ged. Placing both paws on Ged's leg, he gazed up at him. It would be crazy to imagine there was anything in that face beyond canine affection. Yet as he looked into the shining depths of the dog's eyes, he knew there *was* more. Whether it was empathy, or a deeper understanding, it was impossible to say. All he knew for sure was he couldn't dismiss Lidi's certainty as lightly as he wanted to. But that didn't mean he wasn't going to try.

"Just remember we have a no-licking rule." He spoke lightly and Bruno gave him his best doggie grin in return.

He was conscious of Lidi watching him. Part of him wanted to explain. *This is what I do. Keep it light. Brush it off. Never delve too deep into the emotions.* But if he told her that, he'd be halfway to opening up.

Before he could speak, she was getting to her feet. "We should get our bags from the bus." She stooped to untie Bruno's leash. As she straightened, she leaned closer, her face tilted up to Ged's. "One day, you should try opening up to your feelings and forget about hiding behind the jokes." The touch of her lips against his cheek was so fleeting he might almost have imagined it. "Who knows? You might enjoy it."

"There's one thing I don't understand," Ged said.

The only rental car available on short notice had been a two-door Volkswagen. While it was functional, it was very small. Ged, who was driving, was hunched over the steering wheel as he glanced from the dashboard GPS display to the road ahead.

"Only one?" Lidi turned in her seat so she could study his profile. One positive result of this detour was that they had temporarily discarded the disguises. It was a relief to see him without the beard and mustache. "You are several steps ahead of me if you are able to make sense of the woman called Allie as well as our magical tour guide." She jerked a thumb in the direction of the back seat on which Bruno was stretched full-length as he slept off his large breakfast.

"Actually, I was thinking of something more mundane." He managed a quick glance in her direction. "You've spent all your life in Callistoya, where motor vehicles are almost unheard of. Yet once you entered the mortal world, you not only managed to hot-wire a car, you also knew how to drive it."

"Ah."

"Just *ah*? Not *ah, you've stumbled upon my dreadful secret, which is that I am a human car thief*?"

She laughed. "Nothing so exciting. My father sent one of his generals on an undercover mission to the mortal realm, and to make it look realistic, he had to learn how to drive. Much to the dismay of my parents, I was always snooping around, trying to discover any new techniques the soldiers might have. When I saw this…thing they'd acquired, I was intrigued. They humored me by showing me what they were doing."

"How did they get a car in the first place?" Ged asked.

"It was stolen from across the border. To be fair, I don't think anyone would have missed it. It was more a pile of rust than an actual car. As for my driving ability?" She smiled at the memory. "I sort of made that up as I went along. Luckily I was able to stay on quiet roads while I mastered it."

Ged groaned. "So asking you to take over to save my spine isn't an option?"

"Sorry." She looked out of the windshield at the busy freeway. "That sounds like a surefire way to get stopped by the mortal traffic police."

They drove on in silence. Lidi was aware of the tension emanating from Ged and wished she could find a way to broach the subject with him. If only he would talk to her about his feelings. In the short time she had known him, she had learned that his coping strategy was to use humor when things got too close to his emotions. To a certain extent, she understood. Although her own bear genes acted as a barrier to feelings, in Lidi's case, her human persona was stronger. That impulsive, passionate side of herself was what her mother had ruthlessly tried to suppress. Until now, she hadn't analyzed it, but she realized that part of her was responsible for her rebellious streak. She wasn't letting go of who she was. Bears were meant to be impassive. Lidi couldn't live a cold, colorless life.

Had Ged always been this way, or had his responses been affected by the awful events leading up to his exile? She had already answered the question in thinking about her own life. Ged took the typical bear-shifter indifference to a whole new level. And yet…at times like this, she could sense the raw emotion within him.

Maybe it was because they were drawn together as mates, but her intuition told her he wasn't unfeeling. On the contrary. He felt too much. That big, powerful body was a mass of quivering nerves, and he was fighting to suppress the conflict raging inside him. If only she could find a way to break down the barriers and help him.

They left the freeway and drove along narrow country lanes. Snow dusted the fields like icing on a cake, and the trees, long bare of their leaves, pointed icy fingers toward the iron gray sky. Because they didn't have an exact address, they would be turning up in the town of Branheim and starting their hunt for Andrei with no real clues as to his whereabouts.

"The internet search I did showed that Branheim is little more than a village," Ged said.

"That may be a good thing," Lidi said. "If we were heading for a big city, our task would be so much harder."

His expression was grim. "Maybe the hardest part will come once we find him."

After a few more miles, some buildings came into view, including a white-painted church and several traditional German houses. Ged parked the car near a town square and eased his long limbs out of the cramped space. Lidi followed him, lifting Bruno from the car and placing him on the frosty ground. The dog, thoroughly overexcited at being out in the open, ran around in circles, tangling himself in his lead.

"I see our psychic guide is being as intelligent and dignified as ever," Ged remarked. "Can you see anything that looks like a bank?"

Lidi frowned. "Will they give us any information about one of their clients?"

He shook his head. "Probably not, but at least we'll have a starting point."

They walked around the town square and made the discovery that there wasn't a bank. The closest thing was a post office counter inside the general store. There was a handful of businesses dotted around the square, including a bar. Ged gestured in that direction.

"Time to find out if I can make myself understood in German."

The interior of the bar was deliciously warm in contrast to the icy temperature outside. A roaring log fire and the scent of hot chocolate contributed to the comforting atmosphere, and Lidi experienced an overwhelming desire to sink into one of the cozy-looking chairs and stay there for the rest of the day. The place was quiet, and the bartender nodded in response to Ged's inquiry about whether Bruno was welcome.

Having ordered two mugs of hot chocolate, Ged did his best to strike up a conversation. Since his German was limited and Lidi's was nonexistent, it was a relief to find that the bartender spoke English.

"We are close to the French border here. Most people speak French and English as well as German."

Ged got straight to the point. "We're looking for the person who painted this." He held out Andrei's painting. "We were told he lives in Branheim."

They had already discussed the possibility that Andrei might not actually reside in Branheim. He had his money sent there, but that wasn't conclusive. They had no idea what his life had been like since he had come to the mortal realm. All they knew for sure was that he was a werebear trying to make his way in Germany. Like all shifters, he would be attempting to fit in and protect his anonymity.

The guy behind the bar studied the painting. "Good

picture. Like a setting for a film." He looked closely at the signature. "But I don't recognize the name. Sorry."

He moved away from them along the bar, and Ged carried their drinks to a nearby table.

"This is a very small town," Lidi said. "If Andrei was a regular here, I'd expect the bartender to know his name."

Ged nodded in agreement. "Perhaps he goes into the general store to collect the payments for his artwork. We'll try there next."

When they'd finished their drinks, they retraced their footsteps across the square. Tying Bruno's leash to the dog hooks provided outside the store, they stepped inside. Typical of a small-town convenience store, every inch of space had been used to display goods. Ged, always at a disadvantage in a cramped space because of his size, was forced to turn sideways and squeeze between shelves to reach the counter at the rear of the shop.

He went through the same routine, holding the painting up to the glass security screen of the counter. "We are looking for the man who painted this. His name is Andrei Tavisha."

The clerk looked over the top of her glasses. *"Nein."* Although her understanding was good, her spoken English wasn't as good as the bartender's. "I do not know this person."

"What now?" Lidi asked as they headed toward the exit.

"I guess we keep asking around—" Ged broke off as they stepped outside, his gaze fixed on the point where they had left Bruno.

Although the collar and leash were still attached to the metal hook, the dog was gone.

* * *

"The little…" Ged choked back an expletive as he registered the look of concern on Lidi's face.

She bit her lip as she unfastened the dog's collar from the post. "It's so cold and he doesn't know this place."

He placed an arm around her shoulders, drawing her close as he resigned himself to the inevitable. "We were only inside the store for a few minutes. He can't have gone far."

Even so, he was unsure where they should start looking. Fortunately, the matter was taken out of his hands. As he looked across the square toward the church, he glimpsed Bruno heading in the direction of the forest.

"There!"

Ged grabbed Lidi's hand and broke into a run. Seeing them approaching, Bruno stopped. He waited until they got almost near enough to grab him and then dashed into the trees.

Although Lidi called out his name, the little dog pranced in and out of the tall trunks. Now and then he stopped, as though he was prepared to let them catch him, but every time they got close, he darted away again.

"We don't have time for these games," Ged growled, his breath pluming in the icy air.

"I don't think he's playing," Lidi said.

"You don't?" He spared a glance in her direction as they ran deeper into the forest.

"No." She was breathing hard, a combination of exertion and cold turning her cheeks an alluring rose pink color. "I think he's leading us."

And—*damn it*—once she'd said it, it was obvious. Bruno was waiting for them to catch up with him so they didn't lose sight of him, then he was moving on again. He was *taking* them somewhere. But where? And how the hell did a stray dog they had found in Genoa know his way around a German forest? The answer was obvious, and Ged didn't bother to fight it this time. *Magic*.

Bruno really was their supernatural guide. The thought almost rocked him off balance. As the realization of what was happening hit him, the dog led them to an area where the trees thinned.

After a minute or two, they reached a clearing and a small cottage came into view. It looked like the sort of place where a witch might be holding small children captive. Or Ged could be letting the fact that he was following an enchanted dog affect his imagination. With a glance to check they were still behind him, Bruno ran right up and sat on the doorstep.

"What do you think?" Ged asked Lidi.

"I think Bruno brought us here for a reason."

"That's what I thought." His instinct was to shield Lidi with his body, but he had already learned that she didn't appreciate being kept in the background. Taking her hand, he approached the cottage.

Before he could raise his fist to knock on the scarred wooden panels, the door opened. A young woman faced them with her arms folded across her chest and a frown on her face. His shifter senses told him everything he needed to know about her. She was nervous, uncomfortable…and she too was a bear shifter.

"Das ist Privateigentum."

Glad of something to focus on other than his feelings of unease, Ged concentrated on what she was saying.

During his years of traveling with Beast, he had picked up a smattering of a few languages, including German.

Privateigentum. "Private property."

He dredged through his limited vocabulary, trying to come up with a reply. *"Es tut mir Leid."* He knew that was an apology. *"Mein Hund—"* What was the word for run? He pointed to Bruno before miming a fast walking motion with his fingers. Helplessly, he lapsed in and out of English. "He escaped through the trees. *Die Bäume.* We got lost…*verloren.*"

Her expression remained blank, and he couldn't tell if she had understood him. Hugging her arms tighter around herself, she glanced down at Bruno. Her expression changed, becoming one of distaste.

To his relief, she replied in English. "You should go."

Before she could close the door, Lidi darted forward. "Please wait." The woman paused. "We are looking for someone. A local artist. His name is Andrei Tavisha."

There was a flicker on the other woman's face. It was so slight it was almost imperceptible. If Ged's senses hadn't been on high alert, he would have missed it. But it was enough.

She knows something about my brother!

Before he could react, a man's voice called out from behind the woman. *"Sasha, wer ist da?"*

At the same time, Bruno gave an excited bark before dashing across the doorstep and into the house.

Chapter 12

Lidi made a wild grab for Bruno as he darted past her, but it was too late. He had already entered the cottage.

"I'm so sorry." She hesitated, trying to decide what to do next. This was someone's home, but she was sure Bruno was trying to get her to follow him inside. Before she was forced into a choice between trespass and canine abandonment, a noise drew her attention toward the shadowy depths behind the woman. It sounded like wheels scratching over floorboards.

The man who came into view was large. That much was obvious, even though Lidi could only see his upper body. From the waist down, he was obscured from view because he was seated in a wheelchair with a blanket covering his legs.

Lidi had time to take in that information before her gaze fixed on his face. Then everything else faded away. Because she knew she was looking at Andrei Tavisha. There could be no mistake. Not only was he a bear shifter, the likeness between him and Ged was remarkable.

"Wer sind diese Leute?" He looked at Ged and Lidi before turning to the woman, who he had called Sasha.

Although Lidi didn't understand German, she could tell what he was asking. *Who are these people?* Bear shifters were a rarity in the human world. Luckily, they had a unique ability to recognize each other. Yet Andrei and Sasha were regarding her and Ged with suspicion. It made her wonder if they'd had a bad experience with other werebears.

She cast a sidelong glance in Ged's direction, attempting to gauge his reaction. He appeared frozen to the spot, staring at Andrei as though he was too emotionally overwhelmed to deal with what was happening.

Andrei, on the other hand, did not appear to have noticed anything about Ged that struck him as unusual. Was it possible Andrei could look at his brother and *not* recognize him? She didn't see how. It must be like looking in a mirror.

"We wanted to find you." She spoke directly to Andrei, using their home language of Callistoyan.

He looked up at Sasha with a bemused expression. She shrugged, before responding to Lidi in English. "We don't understand what you are saying."

Confusion had a devastating effect on Lidi's brain cells, frying the connection between them and leaving her feeling disconnected from reality. Could she be totally wrong about who this man was? Could everything that had happened be a coincidence? The painting, his name, his likeness to Ged…she shook the thoughts aside. Even if she could dismiss the startling similarities between the two men, she couldn't ignore the fact that he was a bear shifter who painted pictures of her homeland, or that Bruno had led them to his doorstep.

She switched to English. "We wanted to ask about one of your paintings."

Ged roused himself with difficulty from his trance. Withdrawing the picture from inside his jacket, he held it out to Andrei. The other man looked at it without touching it. "*Ja*, this is one of mine." He spoke English with a heavy German accent.

"So you are Andrei Tavisha?" Ged scanned his brother's face as though he was still struggling to believe the evidence of his own eyes.

"Why should I answer your questions when I don't know why you are here?" Andrei looked over his shoulder. "And please get that animal out of my house. I have no idea where the superstition comes from, but I have always believed dogs bring bad luck."

Ged stared down at him for a moment or two. Then, uttering a harsh laugh, he scrubbed a hand over his face. "I can't do this." Lidi caught a glimpse of the despair in his eyes as he turned away.

"Give me a moment," she said to Andrei. "Believe me, it will be worth it." Catching up to Ged, she grabbed hold of his arm. For an instant, she thought he was going to pull away from her, but he stopped and swung around to face her.

"That's it?" His head was bent and she had to duck low to look at his face. "Thirteen years of searching and this is how you're going to leave it?" She saw the anguish in his face and stepped in close, sliding her arms around his waist. "You've finally found your brother."

He held on to her, as if he was drawing strength from her nearness. "He doesn't know me."

"But it *is* him?"

"There's no question about that. He was in his mid-teens last time I saw him, but I'd recognize him anywhere." Even though his voice was shaky, there was no mistaking the conviction in his words.

"Then we have to find out what happened to him," Lidi said. "And why he doesn't remember you."

He sucked in an endless breath. "Okay." His grin was slightly lopsided. "Although I'm not sure how we'll even begin to explain."

"We have the picture. That will be our starting point."

She could see a mix of confusion, impatience and annoyance on Andrei's and Sasha's faces. All the things she would expect if a couple of oddly behaved strangers turned up and launched an annoying dog into their house without warning. Was she imagining something more? Could she also see a hint of nervousness?

"This would be easier if we could come inside." She did her best to sound reassuring.

Sasha was immediately defensive. "I don't think that's a good idea."

Lidi looked directly at Andrei. "Let us have ten minutes of your time. Please?"

His gaze shifted from her face to Ged's. She saw his eyes widen slightly, possibly in acknowledgment of the resemblance between them, then he nodded. As Sasha started to protest, he held up a hand. "*Kein Problem.* Let us hear what they have to say." He smiled, the sudden lightening of his expression making him look even more like Ged. "Who knows? Maybe they are here to make my fortune as a famous painter?"

The interior of the cottage was open plan and wheel-chair friendly. Bruno gave a delighted bark, as though welcoming them into his own home. Ged shook his head. Although he was no longer questioning the dog's psychic abilities, Bruno's exuberance wasn't helping to relieve the tension.

Ged and Lidi took a seat on the sofa Andrei indi-cated. Andrei nodded at the picture that was still in Ged's hand. "Why is it so important?"

Lidi didn't say anything, and Ged could sense her holding back, allowing him to take the lead. He should probably do just that, but his mind was a jumble and his nerves were shattered. Determined to make a start, he held the painting up. "Where is this?"

Andrei hunched a shoulder. "It's not real. Just a place I see in my imagination."

Ged exchanged a fleeting look with Lidi. "It looks a lot like a region we know."

Sasha moved forward to crouch beside the wheel-chair and take Andrei's hand. "My brother already told you—"

"Brother?" The word burst from Ged before he could stop it.

"Of course," Sasha said. "Oh. You thought?" She pointed to Andrei and then back to herself. "They thought...*mein Freund.* Boyfriend."

"An easy mistake," Andrei laughed. "Tell me about the mountain range that looks like the one in my paint-ings." His face became serious again. "Then tell me why I should care."

How was Ged going to do that? No matter what he did—whether he blurted out the truth or tried to find a way of easing into the subject gradually—it was going to sound like a fairy story. Luckily, because Andrei and Sasha were bear shifters, they would already understand about magic, so that part of his explanation would be easy. As he searched for the words, Lidi leaned toward him. "Just say it."

It was what he needed to hear. Straightening his shoulders, he looked directly at Andrei. "We come from a mystical land called Callistoya. Those mountains you have painted surround the royal Callistoyan palace."

The silence that followed could not have been matched if Ged had thrown a grenade and run out of the room. After a few moments, Andrei cleared his throat. "Um, I really do think you should go."

"No." Lidi leaned forward. "Please listen. We are bear shifters, just like you."

Sasha gave a little cry and covered her mouth with her hand. Placing a hand on her shoulder, Andrei glared at Lidi. "If this is some kind of joke…"

Lidi's brow furrowed. "I don't understand. You *are* bear shifters. What's wrong with that?"

"What's wrong with that?" The words burst from Andrei in frustration. "*Mein Gott.* Where do you want me to start? You talk as though it's easy, but our whole lives are about hiding who we are, living a lie, watching everything we say and do in case someone catches a glimpse of our real selves."

"And it is worse for you." Sasha gripped his hand tighter as she spoke. Her eyes filled with tears as she looked at Ged and Lidi. "Although he can still shift, my brother cannot join me when I run in the forest."

Ged bent his head, taking a moment to appreciate

the pain of being a bear but not being able to run free. What had happened to his brother? Sasha called herself his sister; that meant a family in the mortal realm must have taken him in and cared for him. It was one of the many things he was determined to find out about.

The atmosphere had changed slightly, some of the barriers breaking down since Lidi had shared the information that they were shifters. He didn't know why Andrei and Sasha hadn't instinctively recognized that. So many things about this situation were off-key, he hardly knew where to start.

"Will you let us tell you our story?" Ged asked. "No matter how strange it seems, just listen to what we have to say. If at the end you still think we're crazy, we'll leave and not bother you again."

He could feel Lidi's gaze scanning his face. *Not bother you again?* He knew what she was thinking. This was his brother. He had spent thirteen years searching for Andrei. Could he walk away and not look back? If he made that promise, he would keep it. But he was going to rely on the powers of persuasion that had made Beast the greatest rock band in the world to make sure he didn't have to.

And he was also going to count on something else. Something he'd lost sight of along the way and only regained since he'd met Lidi. It was a little thing called *hope.* Ged was going to have faith that deep down inside Andrei retained a memory of their shared past.

And no matter how hard it is, I have to find a way to reach that...

"Okay. Although Callistoya is situated here in the mortal realm, in the place known as Siberia, it is not visible to humans. Only shifters can cross its borders, and its permanent citizens are all bear shifters." He could feel Lidi urging him on, and he focused on her sustaining presence, using her to ground him as he searched for the right words. "I am the rightful king of Callistoya…and my name is Gerald Tavisha."

Andrei's brows snapped together. "The same as my name?"

"Yes." Ged waited, giving him time to process that information.

Andrei turned to Sasha. "I wonder if our parents knew my name had royal links?"

She shook her head. "They would have told you if they had any information about your background."

Interesting. Ged flicked a glance in Lidi's direction and saw she was leaning forward, her eyes shining and her hands clasped. Clearly she had also registered the revelation that Andrei's past was mysterious.

"My father, King Ivan of Callistoya, was murdered, together with most of my family, in a coup on the night of my engagement party thirteen years ago. The rebels also killed my fiancée and wiped out my father's government. The following day, my stepbrother, Vasily Petrov, claimed the throne."

Andrei looked bemused. "I don't understand. You said you are the rightful king. Clearly you survived. Why did you let your brother take over instead of you?"

They were getting closer to the hardest part of this conversation. Ged kept his gaze on Andrei's, on the eyes that were so like his own. "Only three members of my family who were present in the royal palace on the night of the killings survived the murders. Queen Zoya, my stepmother, lived through the massacre, and for some reason, my younger brother and I were spared. I have no memory of what happened that night. All I can remember is waking up here in the mortal realm. I was beaten and a spell was cast on me, then I was transported here before the killing began."

"It's quite a story." Andrei shook his head. "I can see why you'd want to know if the similarities between my paintings and your homeland indicate whether I have any information about what happened. I'm sorry I can't help you."

"That's not why we're here." Ged leaned forward. "For the last thirteen years, I've been banished from the country I am supposed to rule. But I've also been searching for the younger brother who was exiled at the same time." He saw a glimmer of understanding begin to dawn in Andrei's eyes. "How long have you been in a wheelchair?"

Sasha gasped. "What an insensitive question. And it's none of your—"

Andrei held up a hand. "It's okay." There was a glimmer of tears in his eyes as he looked at Ged. "Thirteen years. That's how long I've been in this chair, but I don't remember what caused my injuries. I don't remember anything that happened before my parents—the amazing people who adopted both me and Sasha—found me here in the forest." He started to laugh, but the sound grew muddled and ended on a hoarse sob. "I suppose it's irrelevant to ask the name of your younger brother?"

It had been a long, hard, emotionally draining few hours, fueled by tears, reminiscences on Ged's part and, eventually, some powerful German Weinbrand. It turned out that the Tavisha brothers shared a taste for brandy. As night fell, Lidi took Bruno for a walk in the woods and Sasha accompanied her.

"Let me get this straight." Lidi turned up the collar of

her coat against a wind so icy it reminded her of home. "Even though your parents were human, they were happy to adopt a pair of bear shifters and raise them as their own children? And they found you at different times?"

"They were a remarkable couple. Our father was human, but our mother was a sorceress," Sasha explained. "Sorcery is the highest magical rank and its practitioners are immortal and all-powerful. Our mother used her ability for good, looking after the creatures of this forest. When my father found Andrei, he was close to death and she nursed him back to health. She knew, of course, that he was a bear shifter, but that didn't stop her from caring for him as if he was her son."

"Did she know what caused his injuries?" Lidi asked.

"He had been attacked. My parents always believed he had been in a fight with other bear shifters. Andrei can't remember, of course." Sasha watched in surprise as Bruno ran around a tree, almost strangling himself when he reached the limit of his leash. "I don't know much about dogs, but are they meant to do that?"

"I don't know much about them either, but craziness is pretty normal for him." Lidi laughed as she freed the overexcited canine. "What about your story? How did you join the family?"

Sasha looked embarrassed. "I grew up here in Germany. I was a few years from maturity when a trafficking ring came for me. The men who ran it kidnapped shifters and other beings to fulfill orders from their customers. If a client wanted a teenage female bear shifter, the traffickers would provide one. They killed my parents and tried to abduct me, but I escaped. I didn't know what to do, or where to go. I thought that if I returned to civilization, the men who wanted me would find me.

I lived wild in these woods for a few months, until Andrei's father found me."

"Was this after he found Andrei?" Lidi wanted to be sure she had the time line straight in her mind.

"A month or two later, *ja*. We became their adopted family at around the same time." Sasha smiled sadly. "We were both not quite children, not yet adults."

Lidi paused to extract Bruno from a tangle of twigs. "What happened to your parents?"

Lidi was an immortal herself. She knew everlasting life wasn't the same as invincibility. Nevertheless, it would take something very powerful to overcome a sorceress.

"My father became ill." Sasha's mouth turned down at the corners. "My mother once told me it was the hardest part of loving a human. She knew she would have to watch him age, and even with her magic powers there was nothing she could do about it. I suspected they might have some sort of pact because she started to ask me questions about Andrei. Would I take care of him? Would I always be there for him? One day we found them, wrapped in each other's arms. My father's illness had killed him. My mother had drunk poison."

Lidi stared up at the velvet sky with its diamanté scattering of stars. The sad story felt like a punch in her gut, triggering sharp tears at the back of her eyelids. Romantic love had never featured in her life. She hadn't witnessed it, heard about it or read of it. It wasn't something she expected to experience. So why did the love Sasha's parents had shared *hurt* her? How could she possibly understand a love so strong that they couldn't survive without each other?

She didn't want to probe her comprehension because

she feared where it might lead her. Pull too hard on that thought and it could untangle a whole complex thread that would send her running all the way back to the cottage. Throwing herself into Ged's arms while spilling her thoughts and feelings was not part of their unspoken pact.

Keep it light. That was Ged's philosophy. She would do well to remember that while also making it her own.

She retrieved Bruno from the center of a small bush. "We should head back. Ged and I still need to find somewhere to stay tonight."

"We have a spare room." Sasha looked embarrassed. "I mean… I wasn't sure…" She trailed off, clearly seeking the right words. "I didn't know if you were a couple."

"We're not." *At least, I don't think we are. Not in any permanent sense, even though the fates seem determined to tell us otherwise.* "But we don't mind sharing a room."

They were close to the cottage when she caught a flash of movement at the edge of the clearing. Bruno gave a low growl that Lidi, tuning into his mood, interpreted as a warning. She didn't need it. As soon as she saw the figure darting through the trees, her whole body had gone into high alert. Although the woman she had seen was already a speck in the distance, the moonlight glinted on her long, silver-blond hair as it streamed out behind her.

Allie! She had found them again. Here in the heart of a remote German forest…

"Have you ever seen that woman before?" She drew Sasha's attention to the fleeing figure by pointing in Allie's direction.

"What woman?" Sasha appeared bemused. "I don't know what you're talking about. I can't see anyone."

Chapter 13

It was amazing how rapidly Ged's crushing weariness vanished as soon as he was alone with Lidi. It was like someone had flipped a switch, reversing all his symptoms and sending a signal to every part of his body. It was primal, urgent and impossible to ignore.

Need her. Want her. Now.

The spare bedroom was tiny but comfortable, with a log fire and a bed that occupied most of the space. Ged had already ensured that Bruno was safely established in a box under the kitchen table. Sasha had found an old blanket, and the dog had curled up with a sigh of pleasure. Even Lidi could find no fault with the arrangement.

Now Ged closed the bedroom door behind him with a sigh of relief. "Feels like I can't remember the last time I slept."

"It's been quite a day." Her gaze scanned his face, concern in their depths. "How does it feel to have found Andrei at last?"

He sat on the end of the bed. When Lidi joined him, sitting right up close so their bodies were touching, the world felt a whole lot better. "It feels good. Of course it does." He scrubbed a hand over his face. "But the circumstances…"

She wrapped her arms around him, resting her cheek against his bicep. "You couldn't help him. You didn't know where he was."

He lifted a hand to trace the curve of her neck, tucking a silken strand of hair behind her ear. When he touched her, he melted. Like butter on toast, every part of him gave way to a warmth that radiated outward.

"Lidi, I am an alpha-male bear shifter. One of the greatest alphas of them all, the heir to the Crown of Callistoya. My prime function is to defend and protect." He gave a hollow laugh. "A fine protector I turned out to be. Everyone I love has died or been maimed, while I have been unable to save them."

She answered him by placing a hand each side of his face and gazing into his eyes. "You have to stop torturing yourself with this. It's not possible to protect someone when you have been purposely separated from them."

Without further hesitation, he pressed his lips to hers, capturing them in a deep, searing kiss. There was no awkwardness or embarrassment in the action, only perfect clarity. This was meant to be. It had been that way from the moment they met. He felt it in the awareness of his own body, heard it in Lidi's tiny murmur of appreciation.

Time stopped for them. His tongue danced with hers. As Lidi changed position, her soft curves molded to fit his body and Ged smoothed his hands over the contours of her back. Each touch left him wanting, aching, longing for more.

"Remember what I said?" Lidi whispered the words against his lips. "I won't break."

He laughed softly, taking her hand and holding it against his racing heart. "No, but I might."

She tilted her head back, looking at him from beneath smiling eyelids. "Only you can decide if it's worth the risk."

Sliding a hand beneath the fabric of her T-shirt, he followed the angle of her waist, delighting in the smoothness of her skin. Moving upward to her breasts, he massaged them gently through the lace of her bra as his lips returned to claim another kiss.

Pushing her down onto the bed, he nibbled lightly along her jawline, neck and earlobes until Lidi was sighing and writhing with pleasure.

She looped her arms around his neck, pressing a kiss below his ear and setting his flesh on fire. A wild thought intruded into the euphoria that was seeping through his nerve endings. Everything that had gone before was worth it because it had led him here. Without the pain of loss and the years of loneliness, he would never have been able to fully appreciate this perfect closeness.

He couldn't tell Lidi how he felt. Not yet. The sensation wasn't ready to be put into words. All he could do was hold her in an embrace that lingered into eternity. For the first time, he knew how it felt to be whole. A missing part of his soul had been found. Even as that thought registered, he remembered all he had lost and fear struck him.

Not Lidi. Not this. His arms tightened around her.

"Um." Her voice was husky. "I'm quite fond of breathing."

"Sorry." He relaxed his hold slightly.

She smiled contentedly and brushed her lips against his. "I like it. Just maybe not quite so tight." She lay on her side with her leg draped over his. Curling her fingers in the neck of his T-shirt, she pulled him closer.

"Lidi…" He needed to speak while he still could. "We have to talk about this."

She pressed a finger to his lips. "You can't offer me forever and I'm not asking for promises. This is fine."

He caught hold of her hand, kissing her fingertips. "That's not what I was going to say. I want to be sure you are okay with this."

Her adorable blush colored her cheeks. "You mean because I haven't…?"

"Yes, but I think you may be laboring under a misapprehension if you believe I have extensive experience."

Lidi frowned, raising herself on one elbow so she could look at his face. "Are you trying to tell me you are a virgin, as well?"

"Alyona and I became engaged as soon as we reached maturity, but we never had sex. We were good friends and we were able to talk about it without embarrassment. We agreed to wait until we were married." He cupped her cheek with his hand, running his thumb along the length of her jaw. "When I first came here to the mortal realm, I was hardly in a frame of mind to start seeking a partner." He kissed her again, feeling the delicious fingers of fire trailing over his skin. "After a few years, I realized I was missing something in my life. As you know, shifters can have sex without commitment in human form, but that was a problem for me."

"What do you mean?" Lidi curled her fingers into his hair as she spoke.

"It wasn't enough. I couldn't do the whole meaningless-sex thing that the other guys in the band enjoyed so much." He managed a shaky laugh. "I tried. Twice. So I can't tell you I'm a virgin. Not *exactly*. But *experienced*? No, I don't think I'd call myself that."

Lidi was quiet for a moment or two. Then she sat up abruptly. "We should get rid of these clothes." Her smile became mischievous. "And this time I don't need an apron to cover me. I want to be naked with you."

She tugged her T-shirt over her head and unfastened her bra. Ged helped her pull the straps down her arms, his throat tightening as his feelings spiked almost out of control. He kissed the curve between her neck and shoulder before moving his hands over the soft mounds of her breasts. Lidi showed no shyness as he touched her. Her eyes sparkled as his thumbs stroked lightly across the pink nipples that hardened at his touch.

Ged leaned forward, unable to control his desire, covering one taut peak with his mouth. Lidi shivered, and a matching tremor ran through his own body. He moved to the other breast, tasting it as his heart began to race. It had been too long, and it had never been like this. Those twin thoughts were fleeting but certain.

"You're beautiful." He swirled a fingertip around one nipple and she gasped. "Roses and pearls."

"Being poetic is all very well—" Her voice was shaky, but the smile in her eyes warmed his heart. It wasn't the smile of someone who was unsure of what she was doing. "But it's your turn to undress."

The rest of their garments tumbled to the floor and he moved to kiss her lips again. Lidi's hands traveled over his back, her thigh moved between his and she pressed closer. Ged's erection throbbed, hot and hard against the softness of her belly, but he wanted to take it slow. They would only have one first time; he wanted to prolong this moment.

"We don't need to worry about protection." He kissed her earlobe between the words. "You are a bear shifter, so you are only fertile during the mating season. And I joined the band in their regular medical check-ups. I'm clean...hardly surprising given my limited experience."

Lidi bit her lip as she looked down his body. Cautiously, she wrapped her fingers around his straining cock before bending to lightly kiss his crown. Ged's whole body jerked as though he'd been scalded. When she raised her head, her cheeks were flushed, her hair tumbling wildly about her face. "I think we should do something about that lack of experience you keep talking about, don't you?"

Their lips met again as Ged moved his hands over her body, wanting to claim every part of her. Taking his hand, Lidi moved it between her legs and he used his fingertips to gently explore her soft folds. Lightly, he ran a finger along her slit, feeling for her entrance. Lidi opened her legs wider and he slipped a finger into the warmest and most inviting embrace.

"You feel like paradise." He was mesmerized by the perfection of her body as he took the time to enjoy her. Lidi moaned as he explored her with his finger. Ged loved being the cause of that tiny sound. He wanted to hear it again. Her hand tightened around his hardness, and his hips jerked in response.

"Please, Ged." She lifted her hips from the bed. "I want..."

As she looked into his eyes, he knew he couldn't last much longer. When he positioned himself between her legs and felt her delicious heat, his anticipation went off the scale. Lidi kept her hand on his erection, guiding him to her.

He pressed forward slowly and the first touch of perfection enveloped his shaft. Lidi gasped and threw back her head.

Ged paused, staring down at her in concern. "We can stop..."

"Don't." She clutched his shoulders, urging him on. "Feels so good."

Reassured that he wasn't hurting her, he pushed further. She gave a soft cry as she took all of him while gazing into his eyes. Ged was trying desperately not to lose control. Pleasure surged through him, sending electric currents down his spine, and he stifled a groan. He never wanted this moment to end.

Tentatively, Lidi began to move her hips. The sensation of her pelvis grinding against his groin was like scalding honey. The sweetest torture. He tried to hold back the building storm just another second...

"Feels like you are inside my soul." Lidi's whole body began to tremble as she whispered the words.

It was too much. As her hips jerked upward and her frame tensed, Ged gave a groan of surrender.

"Too much heaven." He grasped her hips and began to drive into her. "Oh, Lidi. I won't last."

Lidi's muscles were already quivering around him,

massaging him into a frenzy of desire. Carried away on a wave of sensation, his own release flooded through him. With a final thrust, he cried out her name as the waves pulled him under and everything faded except a white-hot flash of ecstasy and her arms twined around him.

As he turned onto his side and looked into Lidi's eyes, he realized she was laughing. "Care to share the joke?"

"I was scared that I might not know what to do, or that we wouldn't be compatible." She traced a fingertip along his collarbone. "Now, I wonder if we'll ever be able to stop."

He cradled her face in his hands. "Why don't we get some sleep? Give me time to recover before we put that theory to the test."

When Lidi woke, the orange glow of the fire was the only light in the room. Conscious of the warm body pressed tight against her back, she turned on her side, studying Ged's features. He looked younger, some of the cares of wakefulness driven away by slumber.

Her feelings threatened to overwhelm her. *Keep it light?* She almost laughed out loud. The words had become meaningless, just like her vow to devote her life to the peacekeeping force of the northern region. All that mattered was her need to be close to him. Always.

She gave a little cry as Ged's arms clamped around her and he trailed kisses down her neck.

"I thought you were sleeping." She gasped as his hands gripped her buttocks, lifting her against him.

"I was." His grin was wickedness personified. "You woke me with your lustful thoughts." He slid a hand down over her stomach. "Do you know what I'd like to do now?"

Lidi bit her lip. "I think I can guess."

"You might be wrong. At least about the starting point." He sat up abruptly, reaching for his clothes. "I want to go for a run in the forest—" He looked back over his shoulder. "As a bear."

They dressed quickly, managing to sneak out of the house without waking Bruno. They walked until they reached the dark depths of the forest.

Ged turned to face her. "This looks as good a place as any."

He quickly undressed and Lidi began to remove her own clothes. Although she had seen Ged in his bear form once before, the danger of the situation at the Palais Hotel meant she hadn't been able to fully appreciate his beauty. Now she paused to watch him, her breath catching in her throat as he shifted.

He rose up to his full height and kept on going, his body thickening as his face elongated and dark fur sprouted from his skin. Lidi had spent her whole life among the brown bears of Callistoya. Her father was an alpha and she had seen other dominant males, but none of them came close to Ged's magnificence once he had shifted. As he rose onto his hind legs, he towered over her, his shaggy winter coat adding to the impression of size.

Lidi tilted her head back to gaze up at him, exulting in the moment. Right now, just for this instant, he was hers and she was going to enjoy him. Ignoring the impatient rumble that started deep in his huge chest, she stood on the tips of her toes. Stretching as high as she could reach, she managed to get her hands either side of his face so she could pull him down and press a kiss onto the end of his snout.

The rumble became a growl, although she sensed he wasn't displeased at the action. Laughing, she finished shrugging off her clothes. "Patience, my bear."

Lidi shifted fast, exulting in the feel of the cool forest air rippling through her fur. Moving to stand next to Ged as he dropped onto all fours, she sniffed along his neck, rubbing her face against his jaw to signal her submissiveness. In response, he rested his head briefly on her shoulder in a gesture of acknowledgment, before turning and running deeper into the trees.

The woods, although much smaller than the enchanted forests of her childhood, beckoned them. Black shadows lurked in the groves and frost-hardened snow crunched underfoot. Dawn mist lingered, writhing around their feet like the effects she had heard of at Beast's legendary concerts. Most of the time stillness hung like a canopy over the treetops. Nothing stirred in the early-morning depths. Only rarely, the piping of a songbird broke the silence.

Mahogany-brown tree trunks soared heavenward like guards lining the path. Lidi's sharp ears picked up the metallic tinkling sound of a stream, and she caught a glimpse of its tinsel-bright ribbon through the lace of leaves. Veering away from Ged, she charged toward it, splashing into the icy shallows.

This was what she craved. The earthy smell of the forest floor and the sweet scent of pine sap. The crisp snowy remnants and now the clear stream running over her fur as she drank from its crystal waters.

And her mate at her side, nudging her playfully with his nose. Then swiping her with one giant paw until she was lying on her back in the gurgling brook. Then rolling over and over with her until they were both drenched.

Clawing her way to the bank, Lidi changed back into human form. Although she was laughing, her teeth started to chatter. "Enough bear games, Ged. I'm frozen."

Shifting back, he scooped her into his arms with a purposeful look in his eyes. "I know a way to warm you up."

Twining her arms around his neck, Lidi nestled into his embrace and, as he carried her into a dark copse, allowed herself a tiny daydream about forever. An eternity with this strong, sexy man. She knew it was too much to ask, but she could fantasize. Just a little.

She shivered as he placed her on her back on a bed of leaves, but this time it was the look on Ged's face that was the cause of her tremors. Hunger and determination, all of it directed at her.

He knelt and ran his hands along the length of her thighs. Lying back, she stared at the canopy of leaves through which the first light was just peeking. It lent a secret, magical tone to the scene.

Ged's breath was warm on the inside of her knees as he moved them apart. Lidi held her breath as he slowly kissed and nipped his way higher. Her legs opened wider of their own accord and she caught the gleam in Ged's eyes as he gazed at her.

The first soft kiss on her sex had her jerking wildly in shock. Then, as his tongue traced a lazy path back and forth, she melted into the forest floor. By the time he pressed his tongue deep inside her she was clutching his hair and crying out his name as she lifted her hips in time with his movements.

Deep growls issued from his throat, vibrating against her clit with each pass of his tongue. The intimacy of him licking, sucking and driving his tongue into her roused so many intense emotions she hovered at a point between ecstasy and tears.

Helplessly, she grabbed handfuls of the leaves either side of her, wild animal sounds pouring from her as she tumbled over the edge. Arching her back, she came so fast and hard she thought there was a danger she might never breathe again. Drowning in pleasure, she gazed up at Ged as her body pulsed.

He was watching her, jaw tight, muscles tensed and his gaze on her like he had just discovered a treasure for which he'd searched all his life. He was glorious in his nakedness. With his bulging muscles and aristocratic features, he looked like a statue of a Greek god. His erection pulsed rigid between them and Lidi reached out a hand to stroke the silken flesh.

"We should maybe do something about this." Her voice was breathy. Ged's reply was a helpless groan.

Somehow he found the strength to flip her over. Gripping her hips, he positioned her on all fours and moved his body in place over hers. The combination of his strength and tenderness, the bear mating position, the scent of the outdoors...all those things combined to send Lidi's already-heightened senses into overdrive.

As Ged nipped the flesh between her neck and shoulder, she arched her back, rubbing her body suggestively against his.

"Is this how you want it?" His voice was hoarse in her ear.

"Oh, yes. Right now, please."

His breathing came fast and uneven as he angled her until she could feel him teasing her opening with the head of his cock. She was so wet and ready that one quick push and he was halfway inside her. Gasping, Lidi dropped onto her elbows, electric shockwaves of pleasure radiating through her.

Turning her head, she craned her neck until she could reach Ged's lips, tangling her tongue with his. He growled louder as he pulled her back, stretching her and driving deeper. He moved his mouth to the back of her neck, his teeth sharp on the tender flesh as he rocked his shaft in and out of her.

"More." She barely recognized her own ragged cry.

"More than this?"

She could feel his thigh muscles quivering as he battled to keep control. The pressure inside him matched her own coiled tension. The coarse hair on his chest rubbed against her back and his pelvis was iron hard pressed into her soft buttocks. She didn't want him to hold anything back.

"Let it go. I want all of you, my bear."

His roar joined her cry to shake the treetops as his hips bucked and he filled her completely. How could anything feel so good? How could pleasure be so powerful it threatened to tear her in two? How, when it felt so wonderful, could her body still be demanding more? She closed her eyes, giving herself up completely to the intensity of a connection that was more than physical, more than human. This went beyond their bodies meeting in this time and place. This was about the bond they had forged when they ran through the trees and rolled in the stream, but it was so much more. Ged was her mate and nothing would ever replace the potency of that emotion.

Ged drew out, then drove back again, picking up the pace each time. Lidi moved in time with his thrusts, her buttocks slamming against his groin. Her growls turned to whimpers as she writhed beneath him. Ged's fingers dug into her flesh as he pulled her up and slammed even harder. The next masterful thrust of his muscular hips gave her what she needed, dragging his length along her sensitive nerve endings with exquisite friction. Lidi threw her head back with a hoarse, sobbing cry.

Pleasure burst through her, hot and heavy. It spun out from her core in waves that grew stronger as Ged continued to drive in and out. As her muscles tightened around him, he was like iron, pumping in and out and in. His pelvis slapped hard against her once more before he stilled, pulsing inside her as he bit her on the shoulder, the action muffling his howl until it was a deep grunt.

Lowering her slowly, he turned her and cradled her in his arms, kissing her forehead, her nose and, finally, her lips. Lidi tightened her arms around his neck, scared of what he would see if he looked into her eyes in that moment. Afraid he would see it all, that he would know she had given him more than her body. How would he react if he knew she had been changed by him on a soul-deep level? She didn't want that pressure, for Ged or herself.

"Which reminds me—" She sat up, gazing into the trees. It was fully light now, and while the shadows were a blend of ghostly outlines and inky shapes, she couldn't see any movement in their depths.

Ged had been lazily tracing circles on her shoulder with his fingertips, but he frowned. "What is it?"

"I saw Allie again last night. Right here in the trees."
She turned her head to look at him, unease making her
chest constrict. "But Sasha didn't see her, even though
she ran right past us."

"It was dark when you and Sasha went out. If Allie was
running, perhaps it was difficult for Sasha to see her?"

Although Lidi was glad Ged accepted without question that *she* had seen Allie, she couldn't agree with his
summary of the situation. "No." She shook her head.
"Allie's pale coloring is so distinctive it's impossible
to miss her, and with the moonlight shining on that silvery hair of hers—" She broke off when Ged flinched
as though he'd been struck. "What have I said?"

He sat up, staring down at her. "Have you ever met
a member of the noble house of Ivanov?"

"No. Why?"

"They are a very distinctive-looking family." Even
though he spoke slowly with no emotion in his tone, she
could sense that he was stunned by what he had just
heard about Allie. "Unlike other Callistoya bear shifters, the Ivanovs do not resemble Siberian brown bears
when they shift. They are a unique species of white
bear. And in their human form they have pale skin,
light eyes and silver hair."

"Oh." Lidi drew her knees up under her chin, hugging her arms tight around them. "Allie? Alyona? Is it
possible?"

He frowned, following her train of thought. "You
mean could the woman you have seen be Alyona Ivanov? My fiancée, who was supposedly strangled then
stabbed the night my father and most of my family were
massacred?" Ged sucked in a shaky breath. "I have to
say *no*. How can it be her? Her body was identified by

several people including my own uncle, a man I trust with my life. And yet…"

"And yet, we are shifters. We have to believe in the impossible." Lidi's voice sounded lost, even to her own ears. "Because we *are* the impossible."

The possibility that Ged's rightful queen could be alive cut like a knife. Lidi had never believed there was an "us" in any true sense, but the idea that their closeness was a sham was brought home now with an abruptness that splintered her happiness like the icicles dropping from the trees.

She could tell from Ged's expression that he knew what she was thinking. The change in atmosphere from the warmth of their lovemaking to this sudden chill of foreboding was unmistakable and dramatic. He got to his feet, reaching down and holding out his hand to help her up. "If it was Alyona, why would she only show herself to you? Surely she would approach me? She knows me. She'd be comfortable enough to confide in me. And why wait thirteen years?"

Drawing her close, he wrapped his arms around her, pressing his lips to her forehead. Comforted by his nearness, Lidi melted into his embrace. He was right. Of course he was. Alyona was dead. Lidi didn't know who Allie was, or why she was following them, but the name and the coloring…they were just coincidences.

She lifted her head to smile into Ged's eyes. Then she looked just beyond him. And froze. "You are certain Alyona would speak to you?"

"Absolutely. We might not have been lovers, but we were friends." His tone was firm. His manner confident and reassuring. "Why do you ask?"

"Because Allie is standing right behind you."

Chapter 14

Ged's heart was still racing out of control as he pulled on his clothes. Although he hadn't seen anyone else in the forest, he knew Lidi was convinced she had seen someone standing behind him a few minutes earlier. And she had left him in no doubt that the person she had seen was the woman who had been his fiancée.

Lidi had never met Alyona. Yet the description she had given had been perfect, right down to the other woman's height and build. Even if that hadn't been the case, Ged knew Lidi was telling the truth. He trusted her absolutely. In the short time he had known her, he had come to believe in her more deeply than anyone he had ever known. More than Khan and the other members of the band, more than his uncle, more even than the brother he had just rediscovered. He didn't question that faith. It just was.

That didn't make it any easier to fathom what was going on. Had Alyona survived? If so, how? Why was she following them? And why did it seem that Lidi was the only person who could see her?

There were other issues, ones that would have to wait. Ones he didn't want to probe. Not now. Not ever. Because if Alyona was alive, everything was different. His future, never certain, had just undergone a radical change. Once, in what felt like another life, he had accepted the inevitability of his arranged marriage. Now he looked at Lidi as she tugged her sweater over her head, and he wondered if there was any such thing as inevitability.

"We don't know what the future holds." Her face was forlorn as she took his hand.

"No." They retraced their steps toward the cottage. Was there a chance a king of Callistoya could decide his own fate? It was a radical idea and there was only one way to find out.

Since he wasn't officially the monarch, right at this moment he was more concerned about Lidi. She looked lost, as though seeing Allie again had pierced her soul. Ged wanted to take that look away and make sure it never came back. He wanted to make sure all he ever saw on her face were smiles of joy. If he had his way, Lidi's life would be one of sunshine and roses. Gallant thoughts for a bear.

He took her hand, twining his fingers with hers, and she turned her head to look at him. Although her smile was a watered-down version of her usual expression, it still caused his heart to swoop with delight. And while the things going on around them either made no sense or were life-threatening, the thrill he got when he gazed into her eyes had somehow become the most important thing in his life.

As they stepped through the door, Bruno hurled himself on them with hysterical barks, as though he had been under the impression they had abandoned him. It was some time before the noise died down and they were able to sit down to enjoy the breakfast Sasha had prepared.

"As soon as we've eaten, we have to leave for Frankfurt," Ged explained to Andrei. "We've delayed long enough."

"I wish I could come with you. But—" Andrei indicated his wheelchair.

Ged caught Lidi's eye. He knew they were both thinking the same thing. The journey across the mountain border into Callistoya would be arduous for them. For Andrei, it would be almost impossible. But he had found his brother. Even though Andrei had no memory of their homeland, he was a prince of Callistoya. He deserved his place at Ged's side when the resistance overthrew the man who had murdered their father.

"I cannot enter Callistoya until I break the charm Vasily has cast. It is one that bars me from entering my own country. That's why we are flying from Frankfurt to Alaska. There is someone there who may be able to break the spell." He didn't want to build up Andrei's hopes unnecessarily, but he also wanted his brother with him for the final fight. "She is a powerful healer and there is a chance she may be able to restore your ability to walk."

Sasha shook her head. "Our mother was a sorceress. If anyone could help Andrei, she would have done it."

"My friend is very unusual." Ged held Andrei's gaze. "I'm not going to make you any promises. The decision must be yours."

"I don't want to slow you down," Andrei said. "But I do want to see my homeland."

Lidi cut through his indecision. "Come to Alaska. If Ged's friend can't help, you can always come back here. If she can…"

"If she can?" Andrei's eyes sparkled as he clasped Ged's hand. "Then I will be right with you, my brother."

"I have to pack." Sasha jumped up from her seat. "I've never been in a fight in my life, but you don't think I'm going to miss this adventure, do you?"

Ged laughed. So much for being a loner. "Welcome to the resistance. We need all the help we can get."

Ged had always liked Alaska. He loved the crisp, clear air, the wide, open spaces and the stunning scenery. They all reminded him of home. Although, after a journey of over twenty-four hours, he was almost too tired to notice.

Once they left Branheim, Ged's organizational skills had kicked into overdrive. Using a combination of his network of connections, persuasiveness, authority and vast amounts of money, he had a private plane waiting for them on the tarmac when they reached Frankfurt.

Since Andrei and Sasha both had passports confirming their status as German mortals, the biggest problem was Bruno. After trying out various schemes, the simplest solution had been for Andrei to hide the little dog under the blanket that covered his legs.

"Can he be trusted to remain still and quiet while the customs checks are carried out, both here in Germany and once we land in America?" Andrei asked.

"In my experience, Bruno can only be trusted to do the exact opposite of what I want him to," Ged said, ignoring Lidi's look of reproach.

On this occasion, Bruno curled up in Andrei's lap and slept through the official checks. No one in Germany suspected a dog was departing on the plane, the pilot remained unaware of his presence and they were able to leave the airport at Anchorage without anyone having noticed he was there.

"You are a very clever boy," Lidi told him once they were safely in the rental car that was specially adapted to meet Andrei's needs. She spoke as though Bruno had used some canine magic to sneak past the officials who had conducted the checks. When Bruno barked delightedly and wagged his tail, Ged began to wonder if she might be right.

"And we are all criminals." Ged maneuvered the vehicle into the traffic as he spoke. "Although I think smuggling livestock into the United States may turn out to be the least of our problems."

As they left the town, the roads became quieter and he followed a route toward the mountains. Pine-covered hillsides flashed by as he took the twisting bends and narrow passes that stirred memories of his early days in the mortal realm.

"How do you know this sorceress?" Lidi's words, together with her eyes on his profile, told him she had picked up on his tension.

Ged examined his reluctance to speak of it. It was part of a time in his life that was filled with pain and humiliation, when he had been fighting to cope with what had had happened to him. His lips quirked into a half smile. Who was he kidding? Thirteen years later, he was still struggling to come to terms with it.

But this was Lidi. He could tell her anything. At least he thought he could. Now was a good time to put that belief to the test.

"I told you I woke up in a ravine here in the mortal realm two days after the massacre?" The road was quiet and he risked a glance in her direction. Lidi nodded. "Pauwau was the person who found me."

"Found you?"

"Like Andrei, I'd been badly beaten." He grimaced at the memory. "Unlike him, I could still walk. Just. Pauwau took me to her home and nursed me back to health. If it wasn't for her, I probably wouldn't have survived."

"I don't understand any of this." He heard the hint of tears in Lidi's voice. Tears for him. The thought caused a corresponding tightening in his own throat. When had anyone in his life cared enough to cry because he'd been hurt? He was a bear. The answer was *never.* "Why did someone take the trouble to rescue the two of you from the massacre, only to have you beaten before they dumped you here in the human world?"

"If we knew that, we might have a clue about who it was," Ged said. He didn't want to sound dismissive. Feelings, piled on top of exhaustion...he just couldn't do it. Lidi placed her hand on his knee and he took the gesture to be a signal that she understood.

He was driving along the track that led to Pauwau's cabin now. As they approached the ridge on which the tiny log structure stood, he heard Lidi draw in an appreciative breath. Even though the light was fading, the views were spectacular. In the far distance, the hazy outline of far peaks could just be seen in the golden sunset. Closer to the cabin, a swooping valley led the eyes down to a silver lake. Its silver waters were a mirror for the whole scene. The cabin was the ideal vantage point from which to enjoy the tundra in its late-evening perfection.

By the time Ged had helped Andrei from the vehicle

and into his wheelchair, Pauwau had come out onto the porch and was watching them. When Ged first met her, she had been dressed in traditional Inuit clothing, a hood lined with fur pulled up over her long black hair. Now she wore jeans and a hand-knitted sweater. Her two Siberian huskies, Jet and Sable, sat like statues on either side of her.

Ged could never see her without being reminded of two things. The first was that he owed her his life. The second was that he was in the presence of the strongest magic he had ever known. Pauwau's name meant *witch*, but her powers went far beyond any earthly understanding. Hers was a sacred, age-old link to the very fabric of the universe.

As she gazed his way, a smile as wide as the Alaskan mountain range split her broad face in two, and, holding out her hands in greeting, she descended the porch steps.

"You have stayed away too long, my friend."

Ged took her hands in his, feeling, as always, the slight electric charge of her touch. He bent to kiss her cheek. "I know."

"I forgive you." Her smile encompassed the others. "Especially as you have brought new friends to my home."

Ged introduced Lidi, Andrei and Sasha. He looked around for Bruno and discovered him cowering behind Lidi. "I think he may be intimidated by your dogs."

Pauwau squatted and placed her hand on Bruno's head. When she looked up at Ged, he was surprised to see tears in her eyes. "This little guy reminds me of a dog I had many years ago. She died giving birth to her first litter."

"What happened to the puppies?" Lidi asked.

"Sadly, none of them survived." Pauwau gave Bruno a pat before straightening. "I feel this is a very special animal, one with an enchantment that goes beyond what any of us understand."

For once, Ged couldn't find anything sarcastic to say.
Instead, he picked Bruno up and stroked his ears. "You
could be right." His voice was unexpectedly gruff and,
sensing a momentary weakness, Bruno took the opportunity to give him a quick lick on the chin.

Ged's shout of surprise broke the ice, and, laughing,
the whole group went into the cabin. The visitors sat
around Pauwau's kitchen table while she brewed a pot of
strong herbal tea and took a large pie from her freezer.

"I know you are bears." Although the aroma coming from her cooker as she heated the food was delicious, her voice was apologetic. "But I don't eat meat."

"Did you know we were coming?" Lidi regarded the
feast that was being laid out in front of them with an
expression of wonderment.

"I may have had a suspicion." Pauwau's eyes crinkled
into a smile. She flapped a hand. "Eat. Then we can talk
about how we are going to get you home."

Home. Ged was finally starting to feel like they
might really be able to make it happen.

After they had eaten, Pauwau listened carefully to
everything they told her. Lidi thought she had never
seen anyone so still. It was as if the other woman had
the ability to blend into her surroundings. Perhaps that
was the essence of her magic. Whether she was dealing
with the mountain birds, the trees surrounding her cabin
or a group of bear shifters on a dangerous mission, she
would afford them all the same courtesy.

"Can you help us?" Lidi finally broke the lengthy
silence that followed the end of their story.

Pauwau turned ageless dark eyes in her direction.
"*I* cannot do anything." She softened the impact of her

words with a gentle smile. "But I will seek guidance from the spirits."

She began to make preparations, murmuring softly to herself as she lit aromatic candles and placed them on a low table on the porch.

When she was ready, Pauwau invited Ged, Lidi and Sasha to join her on cushions placed around the table. Andrei remained in his wheelchair. Pauwau commenced a ritual of deep breathing and incantations. Lidi could feel the temperature dropping even further. A breeze came from nowhere, stirring the trees and sending the leaves flurrying across the ground.

Pauwau's dogs lay at the top of the porch steps as though guarding the house. Bruno, having inspected them and decided they were of no threat, sniffed the air suspiciously before settling between the larger canines. He had clearly decided to give them the honor of being his guardians.

Lidi wondered if it was a trick of the light, but Pauwau appeared to grow in stature. And then—could she be imagining the change in the air blowing around them?—she could see vague shapes moving in and out of the fluttering light cast by the candles.

Pauwau drew in a deep breath. "They are here."

Silence resumed, during which Pauwau sat with her eyes closed. Occasionally she tilted her head, as though listening to a voice the others couldn't hear. Now and then, she nodded. Once, she smiled and clasped her hands beneath her chin. Finally, she turned to Ged with shining eyes.

"The spirits have spoken to me of your problems."

Ged reached for Lidi's hand, his grip just the right side of painful. Although his face was partly turned away from her, she could see tension quilting the muscles of his jaw. "Do they see àny solutions?"

Although Pauwau's face was serene, Lidi caught glimpses of other expressions flitting across her features. It was a like a pond rippling in sunlight. Now and then, it was possible to see what lay beneath the surface.

"Your stepbrother fears you." Pauwau's voice was soft, her gaze fixed on the candles. "The enchantment he used against you is a simple barrier spell, easily cast and just as easily broken. If you open your mind." She lifted her eyes to Ged's face. "The hardest part will be overcoming your own fears—I think you have always known that."

"I guess that's why I stayed away. The fear that I won't ever cross that border, that I won't be able to defeat Vasily, that I won't be strong enough to avenge my father…" He sucked in a breath. "Do you know if Vasily was responsible for the murders?"

Pauwau bent her head. "You don't need the spirits to confirm what your heart already tells you."

Ged clenched a fist on his thigh. "He did it." He kept his gaze on the distant mountains for long, silent moments.

"What about our rescuer?" Andrei asked at last. "Who got Ged and me out of the palace on the night of the massacre and brought us to the mortal realm? And what was the motive for doing that if he, or she, then had us beaten until we were close to death?"

"She. It was a woman."

Pauwau's answer startled Lidi, and she automatically glanced over her shoulder. *She? Allie?* Was she seeking a connection where none existed? Ever since she had discovered that Allie matched the description of Ged's murdered fiancée, Alyona had occupied a place at the back of her mind.

"The person who got you out of the palace that night was conflicted, but she wanted to help you. It was never her intention to cause you harm." Pauwau turned her head as though listening to an invisible speaker. "Her identity is unclear to me."

"No harm?" Andrei indicated his legs. "Are you sure?"

"I only know what the spirits tell me," Pauwau said. "I'm sorry."

Ged leaned across and placed a hand on his brother's arm. "The most important question is whether anything can be done to help Andrei."

Lidi could feel the people around her holding their breath as they waited for the answer. Her own heart was thumping out an irregular beat. What if Pauwau gave them a flat-out negative?

"I can try...but I can't make you any promises."

Lidi was caught off guard when Sasha collapsed into her arms, her whole body shuddering with sobs. Comforting the other woman gave her an opportunity to hide her own emotions. So much for her upbringing as a hard-hearted noblewoman trained to hide her feelings. Right now, as she patted Sasha's shoulder with one hand and clung to Ged with the other, she felt incapable of rational thought.

Looking up, she was surprised to find Pauwau's gaze fixed on her face. "Look inside your own heart." Although the healer's lips didn't move, Lidi heard her voice clearly. "It will give the answers you seek."

Chapter 15

Before she started the healing ceremony, Ged took Pauwau to one side. "I'd rather not do this at all than build up Andrei's hopes only to find nothing can be done to help him."

She turned her serene gaze to him. "There is nothing physically wrong with your brother."

His brows snapped together. "What do you mean?"

"Often, what I get from the spirits are impression, rather than complete images. Like the story of your rescue from the palace on the night of the murders. I can sense the emotion of the person who saved you. I even know it was a woman, but I can't *see* her. I can't tell you who it was."

"I understand that," Ged said. "The spirits guide you. They don't give you a perfect picture."

Pauwau nodded. "Except, when it comes to your

stepbrother, I have a very strong sense of who he is and what drives him."

"Vasily?" Ged frowned. "He is an evil cur, driven by greed."

Pauwau drew him down to sit next to her on a large rock. Ged spared a moment to think about the weather. As a bear shifter, the cold didn't affect him, but this tiny woman appeared not to notice the biting wind. No matter what her surroundings, she was at one with nature.

"I don't like the word *evil.*" She nodded in the direction of the house. The golden glow of the lamps strung along the edge of the porch roof illuminated the ground beyond the house. Bruno, his initial timidity long gone, was trying to tempt Jet and Sable into a chasing game. The other dogs were regarding him with bemused dignity as he charged around them, ears flapping and tongue lolling. Ged was convinced he saw the huskies exchange a canine eye-roll or two. "An animal is not born bad. If a dog becomes vicious, it is because life has taught it to behave that way. We are animals too. People are shaped by their early experiences."

"But Vasily was born into a life of wealth and privilege. His mother, Zoya, doted on him. She gave him everything he wanted," Ged said. "We were young when our parents married, but I remember thinking even then that he was a spoiled brat."

"And you? What were you like?"

Ged was surprised at the question. "I'm not sure. Although my father was fit and healthy, I was being raised as the future king. I spent a lot of time with my father, but that wasn't a hardship." He felt the familiar tightening of his throat. "I loved him." His glance went back toward the house. "And Andrei, of course. The three of us were a tight group. Beyond that, I was mad about sports and wildly competitive. I had to be the best at everything." He laughed. "Still do, if I'm being honest."

Pauwau placed a hand over his. "You have just described the person Vasily wanted to be."

Ged jerked slightly. "You're saying this was all about jealousy? Of *me*?"

"Think about it. Vasily had always been given everything he asked for. Suddenly, he was presented with a stepbrother who was stronger, quicker, better looking and more popular than he would ever be. A stepbrother who had a loving father and a younger sibling who worshiped him. For the first time in his life, Vasily's mother couldn't make it all better for him."

Ged gave a soft whistle. "I knew he never liked me, but I hadn't thought about it from that perspective."

"Hatred breeds evil. Vasily couldn't take away who you were, but he could take what you had…and what you would become." Pauwau's voice was gentle.

"You mean my family?" Ged asked.

"And more. Your royal status, your country…those things were your identity. But he was not content to stop there. Vasily vowed to take even more from you." Pauwau removed her hand and placed it on his shoulder. "He wanted to take your mate."

Ged's shoulders slumped as he felt despair hit him all over again. "I know. Alyona was attacked because of me."

Pauwau shook her head. "No." She raised a hand, directing his gaze to the porch where Lidi was chatting quietly with Andrei and Sasha. "Alyona was to be your wife. Vasily has sworn to take your *mate*. Your one true love."

Ged stilled, shock and truth hitting him like twin punches to his gut. His brain tried to shut down. *Too much. Can't take it.* At the same time, his heart gave a sigh of relief and acceptance. *At last. Just admit it and get on with loving her.* Unfortunately, reality had a way of intruding. Usually the old barriers got in the way. A lost kingdom, an ancient agreement between five noble families, a fragile heart too afraid of the past to let go… this time there were questions. So many of them he hardly knew where to start.

"How could Vasily possibly know Lidi was my mate? I didn't know it myself. We hadn't even met when he decided he wanted to marry her."

Pauwau shrugged. "I am relaying the information given to me by the spirits."

"That's the problem with spirits. They have a tendency to be even more enigmatic than bears," Ged said. "I remember how Zoya, Vasily's mother, always consulted her personal spirit guide before she took any action."

"She sounds like a sensible woman. The spirits steer us wisely."

"It used to drive my father demented. He said she couldn't decide what to wear without conferring with her oracle." Ged smiled at the memory. "Take me back a step to why all of this is connected to Andrei's injuries."

"That's where things become less clear to me. Vasily is the key to everything—of that I'm sure. And I'm also convinced that the person who arranged to have you and Andrei removed from the palace meant you no harm." Pauwau gave a frustrated sigh. "But, in trying to ensure your safety, something went wrong. Perhaps the spell she cast on you failed. Or the people she entrusted to bring you here didn't carry out her orders the way she wanted. Possibly it was a combination of both. Whatever happened, you were left with physical injuries and emotional scars."

"I always believed that was the intention," Ged said. "Certainly in my case. Mess me up so badly I would never go back." And it had worked. Until now, his fear of returning to Callistoya had been a greater impediment than the spell that prevented him from crossing the border.

"That's not what I feel." Pauwau turned her face up to the night sky. "Modern technology would have us believe that we live in an ever-changing world, but we know the truth. You are a shifter. Like me, you understand the earth and its magic. Andrei believes his injuries were caused when he was attacked. They weren't. When he was removed from the palace and brought to the mortal world, some fundamental change took place within him. His confidence was destroyed." She cast a sidelong glance in Ged's direction. "The same way yours was."

Ged smiled. "For the last thirteen years, I have managed one of the most successful rock bands in the world while also running an underground rescue network for endangered shifters. Do you really think I lack confidence?"

"Yes." Her answer shook him with its blunt truth. "We both know the image you present to the world is not the reality of who you are."

He frowned. *Not going there.* "You are saying that Andrei's condition is caused because he had convinced himself he can't walk?"

"That's it, my friend. Deflect attention from yourself." Pauwau's smile deepened and she continued before he could protest. "Yes. Your brother's psyche has been badly damaged and his physical symptoms mask a deep emotional distress."

Ged rubbed a hand over his face. "He is a shifter, so his adopted parents would have had limited access to medical care."

"It's possible conventional doctors—human or shifter—would not have reached this conclusion. They could have spent his whole life searching for an underlying medical cause."

"But you can cure him?" Ged asked.

"I can show him how to cure himself," Pauwau said. "Then it will be up to him."

Ged looked across at the porch again, seeing the figure of his brother in the wheelchair. "Surely he will take that chance?"

"I hope so." Pauwau took his hand as she got to her feet. "But what about you? Even though it didn't take away your ability to walk, the harm done to you was just as real and devastating. Will you take this chance to heal your heart?"

Lidi watched Ged as he approached them with Pauwau at his side. He walked like a man in a trance, but his face wore the stunned expression of someone who had just been given life-changing news.

She wanted to run to him and wrap her arms around his waist. Most of all, she wanted to drive that lost look from his eyes. Did he know she felt that way about him? That her heart had become so entwined with his that even the tiniest pain he felt was like an arrow piercing her flesh?

Cut him and I bleed. Burn him and I scar. Hurt him and I will fight you to the death.

He couldn't know that was how she felt. Not unless she told him. She smiled sadly, knowing she would never be able to do that. The standards of their world were simple. *Bear before human. Follow the orders of the council. Don't allow emotion to cloud your judgment.* Although Lidi understood the Callistoya code, she had never been able to follow it. Ged, as ruler of the bear-shifter state, had to lead by example. Once he regained his crown, he would have to live and breathe those rules.

That meant he would not be able to ask Lidi to be his wife, even if he wanted to. He would be constrained by the decree that stated that he must marry within one of the five founding families.

The thought was like acid in her veins, driving out the sweetness of her longing for him. The irony of her mother's words came back to her now. "Cursed with feelings." That was how she had described her daughter.

Would I change who I am? Given a choice, would I be more like my mother so I didn't have to feel this knife thrust every time I look at him and know that one day I will watch him walk away?

The answer to her question lay in the smile Ged gave her as he drew closer. Because when he looked at her that way, the warmth in his eyes touched her soul. She would never trade her own ability to feel and replace it with the bear-shifter coldness she was supposed to cultivate. All she had to do was convince Ged she was still playing by the "keep it light" rules.

"Okay?" His eyes scanned her face, making her wonder how well her plan was working.

"Fine." She pinned on a bright smile and knew by the way his brow drew together that she was overdoing it. Seeking a distraction, she pointed to a large dog bed in one corner of the porch. "Does that look like a familiar scene?"

Bruno was sprawled in the middle of the dog bed, while Jet and Sable lay on the wooden boards nearby. Ged laughed. "If I ever get my crown back, I'll expect a challenge from that dog in the near future."

"I think the canine will win." Although Andrei smiled, he appeared nervous. "Are we going to do this?"

Ged nodded. "Let's get on with it."

Pauwau came to kneel beside Andrei's wheelchair. Placing her hands on his knees, she gazed into his eyes. "I can take away the toxin that another has placed inside your body. That has poisoned your soul—it has not damaged your limbs. Once the contamination has been removed, you are the only one who can heal your legs. To do that, you must believe in your ability to walk again."

Andrei raised his eyes to Ged's face. "Do you think I can do this?"

"You are a Tavisha." Lidi could see the pride of generations of Callistoya royalty in Ged's expression. "You can do anything."

Andrei nodded. "Then let's get on with it."

Pauwau closed her eyes and began to hum softly under her breath. Almost immediately, Andrei started to tremble all over. After a while, the tremors became more violent until he was shaking like a young tree in a thunderstorm.

All around her, Lidi could feel the air shimmering, not only with tiny shards of ice, but also with a different energy. Pressure, powerful, elemental and positive, was increasing all around them.

As she turned her head to look at Ged, she could see that Andrei wasn't the only one who was feeling the full impact of Pauwau's treatment. Although the effects were less pronounced in his case, Ged was pale and shivering as though he had been struck by a sudden fever.

As Lidi was about to go to him, Pauwau rocked back on her heels. Tilting her head to the skies, she gave a single hoarse cry. The force that had been building reached its peak before swirling around them like an invisible river breaking its banks. Then it was gone. Andrei slumped forward in his chair and Ged shook his head as though waking from a deep sleep.

As Pauwau got to her feet and moved away from the wheelchair, Sasha took her place. Kneeling beside Andrei, she took his hands, rubbing them as he took a few deep, shuddering breaths.

Pauwau staggered slightly and Lidi caught hold of her, steadying her. The other woman smiled her thanks. "It uses a lot of energy."

"Is that it?" Lidi asked. "Is it over?"

"I have done my part. The poisonous spell that was cast thirteen years ago has been removed." She looked at Ged as she spoke. "From both of you."

"I feel…" He looked stunned. "Lighter."

Pauwau laughed. "That is an illusion. Your physical weight is unchanged. Don't ask me to carry you, my friend."

Lidi could see him struggling to achieve a smile. "What happens now?"

Pauwau patted his hand. "That, as I told you, is up to you and your brother."

* * *

It was almost midnight and the wind had dropped when Ged and Lidi went for a walk. Andrei, exhausted by the healing ceremony, had fallen asleep in his wheelchair without talking about what had happened. So far he had made no attempt to use his legs. Sasha, reluctant to leave him even when he was sleeping, was helping Pauwau prepare supper.

Bruno, having sleepily opened one eye as they left the house, was now bounding ahead of them, examining every pebble and blade of grass and attempting to eat the occasional unseen object.

Ever since Pauwau had performed her ritual, a strange peace had settled over Ged. After spending so long battling his feelings of guilt and inadequacy, it was as if he had finally reached an awareness of who he was. He had been trying so hard to achieve perfection when all he needed was to accept that he was the best person to follow in his father's footsteps. He knew it now, and that was good enough for him.

He paused, looking down at Lidi's face in the moonlight. Her smile gave him a hint of new hope. Maybe he was one person's idea of perfection? Or at least the mate Lidi wanted? If that was true, it was more than he had ever dreamed of. And for the first time, instead of seeing obstacles, he started to think of possibilities.

"You look like the cat who has got the cream." She moved closer, resting her cheek against his chest.

"Uh-uh. Let's not talk about cats." He pointed to Bruno. "We already have one pet. Besides, we don't want to make Khan, the ultimate alpha feline, jealous."

"You make it sound like we'll see Khan again soon," Lidi said.

"That's the plan." He ran his hand down the length of her hair, enjoying its silken feel.

She sighed. "Do we have a plan? Beyond the pretense that I will marry Vasily?"

"We have several plans, all of which will become clear at the royal Christmas-Eve ball."

Although the Callistoyans did not follow the Christian traditions of the festive season, they enjoyed the color and vibrancy of its customs. Trees, decorations, parties and the giving of presents had become part of the winter way of life in his homeland. The Christmas-Eve ball, held in the royal palace, was attended by all the noble families of Callistoya.

"Before we go back and start partying, we'd better follow Pauwau's instructions," Ged said.

Between them, they carried the items the healer had given them. Ged held a fireproof dish, an old-fashioned brass compass and a candle. Lidi had tucked four pieces of paper, a piece of charcoal and a box of matches into the pocket of her padded coat.

Pauwau had been very precise. They were to write the names of the northern, southern, eastern and westernmost places in Callistoya on each of the pieces of paper. Lidi took out the piece of charcoal and started writing. Once she was finished, Ged took out the compass.

"North." He turned to face that direction. Lidi placed the piece of paper with the word *Aras*, her own home county, written on it into the bowl. Solemnly, Ged struck a match and set light to the piece of paper. They watched it catch fire and blacken. When it had turned to ash, they repeated the process with the other three compass directions.

Once all four pieces of paper had been burned, Lidi sighed. "Pauwau said that means the spirits who control the earth's magnetic fields will now open the borders. Vasily's spell is destroyed and Callistoya is no longer closed to you. She also said that Bruno, who is an enchanted being, can come with us, as well."

Ged closed his eyes briefly, relishing the chill air in his face and her warm presence. It was finally happening. The dream that been out of reach for so long was becoming a reality. Step by step, he was moving toward his homeland. Tomorrow they would fly to Moscow and then to Siberia. That was the last leg of the human journey. After that, they would use their shifter abilities to get them across the mountain range and into Callistoya. The revolution had begun.

Would it rest with him and Lidi, or would Andrei and Sasha be able to join them? That question still remained unanswered. And once they arrived in Callistoya, Lidi had the hardest job of all. Her acting abilities would be tested to their limits as she pretended to capitulate to Vasily's demands. Ged, meanwhile, would make contact with his uncle and the other members of the resistance.

There was still a long way to go, but he smiled as he drew Lidi into his arms. "We're going home."

"And we won't be not alone." Her gaze fixed on something over his shoulder and Ged turned slowly to see what she was looking at.

His heart gave a thud of joy as, holding Sasha's hand on one side and Pauwau's on the other, Andrei walked toward them.

Chapter 16

The wild beauty of the Siberian landscape reminded Lidi of the northern territory of Callistoya. Breathing in the pure mountain air and drinking from the crystal clear water of the lakes and rivers made her heart soar. They were getting close. She could feel her homeland in her blood.

After hiring a Jeep, they had left civilization behind and were now in a land of snow, ice and forests. Ged had been concerned about his brother's ability to cope with the demanding conditions.

"I won't slow you down," Andrei promised.

"You know that's not what worries me," Ged said. "You've only just started walking again after thirteen years in a wheelchair. I don't want to do anything that will cause a setback to your health."

So far, Ged's fears had been unfounded. Andrei

seemed to become more energized with each passing mile. The only thing that saddened Ged was that Pauwau's spell hadn't restored his brother's memory.

"I don't remember Callistoya, but I can feel something new." Andrei breathed deeply. "As though I have a deeper recollection imprinted in my cells and, as we get closer, it's revitalizing me."

Lidi smiled. "I've only been away from home once, but I know there's nowhere like it."

"What about me?" Sasha asked. "I don't belong there."

"You are one of us," Lidi said. "The Callistoya borders are magical. Closed to humans, but open to shifters. You will be welcome in our homeland."

"Except for being part of the plot to kill the king," Sasha reminded her.

"Ah, yes. But the plan is to kill the Usurper, the man who calls himself king." Lidi felt her features harden at the thought that she would soon be face-to-face with Vasily. She had never met him, but he had dominated her life recently. "He will not do so for much longer."

Ged remained silent, his eyes fixed on the view ahead of them. Lidi knew why. The mountains they could see belonged in the human world. But there was another set of peaks, just out of sight. They were the Aras Range, the border between Siberia and Callistoya. Visible only to shifters and other enchanted beings, they were the gateway to the magical land that would take them back in time.

There were no roads here and, as the climb became too steep for the vehicle, Ged called a halt. "This will be easier if we shift, but we face the problem of arriving in Callistoya with no clothing."

"We can go straight to Aras House," Lidi said. "My childhood home is situated just over the border in the northernmost mountains. The servants are loyal to my family. We can spend the night there in safety while we arrange the journey south."

"I have to carry my disguise." Ged held up the cloth bag he had bought in Genoa. Inside were his wig and false beard. It had a cord that he could slip over his neck so even when he was in bear form he would be able to keep it with him. "Once we reach the palace, I'll have to wear this at all times. Vasily hasn't seen me for thirteen years, so I'm hoping that the disguise, coupled with the fact that he won't expect me to have the audacity to enter his stronghold, will buy me enough time to get everything in place."

Lidi wasn't so sure. Her fear was that Vasily would be hyperalert and on the lookout for Ged's return. "You will also need to stay out of his way," she said, firmly.

"He is the king—for now—and I will be disguised as your servant. I don't imagine we'll have much interaction." She wasn't reassured that he would avoid trouble, particularly when he went for a swift change of subject and nodded at Bruno, who had turned his face into the wind. His eyes were half-closed against the chill, his ears were blowing back and his expression was almost thoughtful. "Are you sure about the dog? Pauwau reassured us that he is indeed an enchanted animal, so he will have no problems entering Callistoya, but taking a canine into the land where dogs are hated is not going to be a popular move."

Although Lidi knew he was right, she had grown to love the funny little animal who had been such an important part of their adventure. She felt strongly that

Bruno had more to give them, but even if he wasn't a mystical protector, even if he was just a dog, he was *her* dog.

"I will care for him." She tilted her chin upward, looking Ged firmly in the eye.

To her surprise, he nodded. "We all will."

Even Andrei, who had been unimpressed by Bruno at their first meeting, placed a hand on the dog's head. "He's one of the team."

"Will he be able to keep up with us as we cross the mountains?" Sasha asked.

Ged laughed as he pulled his sweatshirt over his head. "We're bears. He's a dog. He'll probably enjoy trying to chase or herd us."

Although Bruno inspected them thoroughly once they'd shifted, he appeared to find nothing strange about the fact that they had been humans one minute and were bears the next. Moving in a group, they set off toward the mountains. They climbed high peaks, ran through gentle valleys and into steep ravines, skirted glaciers and lakes, and plodded along plateaus. As a human, Lidi would have struggled with the pace. As a bear, she was enjoying herself.

Even so, the approach was physically draining. Ged kept close to Andrei, but his brother coped well with the terrain. After a few grueling hours, Lidi recalled the conversation Ged had overheard between Vasily's men. They had said she wouldn't take this route into Callistoya. Perhaps they had been wise.

Finally, up ahead, she saw the ridge topped with white-veiled polar birch trees that marked the Callistoya border. This was where the atmosphere changed and became charged with an extra, supernatural dimension. She could feel it, a magnetism in the air that was unique to Callistoya. Very few humans would come to this remote part of the world. Those who did would remain oblivious to its enchantment, perhaps experiencing only a shiver down the spine as they passed. Only a true shifter or those with enchanted genes would feel the pull of the magical realm and be able to see the land that existed beyond those earthly peaks.

As they drew closer, Bruno began to whine and trail behind her. Lidi nudged him with her nose, but the little dog sat down, refusing to go any farther.

She looked up at the ridge, catching a glimpse of what was causing Bruno's distress. The movement was so slight it was barely perceptible. Lidi drew level with Ged, bumping his shoulder to get his attention. He followed her gaze. There it was again. A figure walking among the trees. Someone, or something, was patrolling that section of the ridge. Yet again, Bruno was warning her of danger. Could it be that Vasily's men had changed their minds? Was her arrival expected?

At the base of a rocky outcrop, well out of sight of the ridge, Ged gave the signal to shift back. Lidi recalled her former modesty about nakedness and was pleased to find it was gone. She had a feeling there were going to be several shifts between human and bear on this journey. Worrying about other people's eyes on her body wouldn't help the resistance cause.

"We need to check that out." Ged nodded toward the ridge above their heads. "It may be nothing, or it could be that Vasily has posted guards along this section of the border. We have more chance of stealth in human form."

"From a wheelchair to a naked rock climb in the

space of a few hours." Andrei shook his head. "Who knew finding myself a brother would prove so interesting?"

They ascended the opposite side of the ridge to where they had seen the figure, passing Bruno between them until they reached the top. In spite of the icy breeze blowing powdery snow in her face, it was an easy climb. Lidi enjoyed the harshness of the rocks beneath her bare feet and hands and delighted in the freezing temperatures on her flesh. The mystery person ahead was yet another obstacle, but they were within touching distance of Callistoya at last.

Lidi carried Bruno as, stealthily, they moved toward the woodland. The forest grew denser as they approached from behind the point where they had seen the movement, but weak sunlight penetrated, showing them a path through the trees. She stayed close to Ged, drawn to his side even in this situation. Her need for him was primal and uncontrollable. She could try to contain it, tell herself she was a warrior and this was a dangerous mission…it was no good. She may as well tell her heart not to beat.

The border wasn't physical, but it was real and it was right here in this forest. Almost like a film shot in soft focus, it made the trees ahead of them look slightly faded compared to the ones close by.

"Are you ready for this?" Lidi whispered to Ged. She knew how hard it had been for him to face this challenge. Even now, could they really be sure the spell was broken? Would he walk toward that haze only to be driven back once more?

His jaw was so tense she wondered if he would be capable of answering. Then he smiled down at her. "With you at my side, I'm ready for anything."

Lidi had only crossed that invisible barrier once, but she clearly remembered the sensation. It was like the creepy chill that would sometimes shimmy down her spine for no reason and have her looking over her shoulder even though she knew no one was there. Gone as soon as it started. A collective indrawn breath, a shared shiver, and they were across. They were inside the magical land of Callistoya.

"We did it." She gripped Ged's forearm, unable to celebrate any further because of the mystery person up ahead.

He dropped a kiss onto her temple and Bruno wagged his tail as though sharing the caress.

Andrei looked at Sasha with a shrug. "If I'm meant to feel something, I don't know what it is."

"Bewildered." She managed a slight smile. "That's what I feel. Oh, and cold."

"Let's keep moving," Ged said. After a few hundred yards, he dropped into a crouch and the others copied the action. From their position, shielded behind a clump of trees, they watched as a man in military-style garments walked along the edge of the ridge and back again.

"What is he wearing?" Ged kept his voice low. "That is not the uniform of the Callistoya army."

"No." Lidi smiled as joy built in her chest and warmed her whole body. "It's the clothing worn by my family's household guard. I know that man. His name is Bogdan. He is known as Bogdan the Brave, and he was one of my father's closest friends."

She was about to rush forward to greet the man she had known since she was a baby, but Ged placed a hand on her shoulder. "Wait. We don't know what's been happening while you've been away. Let's make sure he's alone."

They remained hidden while Bogdan patrolled the line of trees several more times. When they were certain there was no one else around, Ged nodded and they moved out from their cover. The contrast between the mortal world, where four naked people would be shocking, and Callistoya, where it was normality, caused Lidi to bite back a smile. Yes, she was home at last.

Hearing a noise behind him, Bogdan swung around. His eyes widened as he recognized Lidi and he smiled before bowing his head. "My lady!"

"Bogdan." She stepped forward to take his hand.

As she did, Bogdan caught sight of Bruno. His face paled and he took a step back. "My lady, is that wise? To touch such a creature…one known to carry bad luck in its very pores…"

"Bruno is my friend." Lidi spoke firmly. "I don't expect others in Callistoya to share my liking for him, but I will not have him maligned or harmed."

Bogdan cast a wary look in Bruno's direction. "No, my lady."

"Why are you here?" Lidi asked. Although her home was close to this mountainous border, it was still several miles away, and it was unusual for one of the Aras guards to patrol here.

Bogdan cleared his throat and looked at her companions. Since he seemed to be uncomfortable talking in front of other people, Lidi looked over her shoulder at Ged. The people of Aras had always been loyal to King Ivan, and she didn't believe their allegiance would have changed in the short time she'd been away. Even so, she and Ged had agreed to keep Ged's identity secret.

Following her train of thought, he gave a small shake of his head. She understood what the gesture meant. *Keep my identity secret.*

"You can talk in front of my friends, Bogdan. They are loyal to the true king."

It was only now she was able to observe Bogdan up close that she noticed how much he had altered. Time was measured differently in Callistoya. Once a bear shifter reached maturity, their immortality kicked in and the aging process slowed. It became almost impossible to judge a person's age, but their bodies were marked by experience. Gray hair and lined faces were a sign of wisdom and expertise, but they were acquired over many centuries.

To Lidi, Bogdan had always looked old. Now he appeared old *and* ill. And exhausted. The lines on his face could have been carved with a knife, and his dark eyes were bloodshot, as though he hadn't slept since the last time she saw him.

"Aras House has been under attack. Vasily the Usurper has declared your father to be a traitor and has claimed his lands." Bogdan shook his head. "He sent soldiers to take the house by force. We fought them off, but they will be back. The next attack could come from any direction, so we have posted lookouts on each of the mountains surrounding the house."

"How long ago was this?" Ged asked.

Bogdan turned to face him. His hesitation was momentary, and Lidi could see the instant in which he deferred to Ged's obvious authority. "Two days. The commander of the Usurper's troop declared his intention of returning once he had reinforced his numbers."

"Can you get a message to Eduard Tavisha?"

Bogdan's eyes widened. "I don't know where the leader of the resistance is hiding."

"No, but I do," Ged said. "Lead us to Aras House. We can talk more once we get there."

Lidi took Ged's hand, her touch branding him like white-hot iron. No matter where they were or who they were with, she would always affect him this way. May as well get used to it. Whether she knew it or not, she had claimed him for life. Could he do the same with her? She had made an emphatic declaration to the contrary. It was up to him to put that to the test.

"Aras House." Lidi sighed as she said the words. "My romantic heart always aches when I hear that name. It's an incredibly dull name for what must surely be the most beautiful castle in this or any other world. It was typical of my traditional bear-shifter parents that they never gave the aesthetics of our surroundings a thought."

"Oh, it's like something out of a fairytale," Sasha exclaimed as soaring white turrets came into view.

Perched dramatically on a perilous cliff, the castle overlooked the rolling hills around it and could only be reached by a narrow drawbridge.

"Vasily must have been mad to send his soldiers to attack this place," Ged said, assessing his surroundings.

Bogdan gave a harsh laugh. "Have you never heard of our so-called king, my friend? He is not known for his military acumen."

Lidi smiled in response to Ged's wry expression. "Vasily Petrov? I've come across that name once or twice."

The drawbridge was closed so that the castle entrance resembled a mouth twisted into a rocky snarl. As they stepped closer a trumpeter sounded a few bars across the valley, the signal that friends were approaching. Slowly, the drawbridge was lowered.

"Have you heard any news of my father?" Lidi asked Bogdan.

"Only that he is still alive," Bogdan replied. "I sent a spy south disguised as a traveler. He was able to ascertain that the Count of Aras is still held in the dungeons beneath the royal palace."

Lidi's shoulders slumped and Ged knew it was with relief as well as sadness. She had been afraid that her escape might have prompted Vasily to take revenge against her invalid father.

"We will free him," he told her.

"I know. It's just…" She brushed away a tear and managed a weak smile. "That prison is like hell and he doesn't know we are coming for him." She turned to Bogdan. "Can we avoid the central courtyard? I've no wish to be greeted like a celebrity. Not until I've had a chance to bathe, sleep and dress."

He nodded. "I understand."

Once they had crossed the drawbridge, he led them to the right and up a narrow staircase. When they reached a gallery, they were able to look down on the open courtyard below. It resembled a small, bustling village. Some of the inhabitants were in human form and were clothed. Several, like the new arrivals, were naked, clearly having just shifted. A few bears wandered freely among them.

"Where do they all live?" Sasha asked. She appeared stunned at the way she had stepped from her own world and into the pages of a history book.

"Most of these people are servants, or castle guards. A few will be travelers, come to sell their wares," Lidi explained. "The members of my family reside in the central tower of the castle and the rest of the inhabitants live in other accommodation within the fortified walls." She smiled. "It can feel overcrowded sometimes, but I've never known a different way of life." She turned to Bogdan. "We will need rooms in the family quarters and my friends will require clothing."

"Consider it done, my lady."

Although Ged could appreciate Sasha's feelings, he felt at ease with the difference between the mortal realm and Callistoya. He had often speculated about how it would feel if he came back. The contrast was so sharp, he had wondered if it would jar on his nerves. The old-fashioned courtesy. The rules and regulations that had been in place for centuries, their original purpose lost in the mists of time. The lack of technology. No more pressing a button to get what he wanted.

But he slipped back into the rhythm of Callistoya as easily as breathing. He had barely even noticed the border when they crossed. A slight tingle. An awareness of the difference, and then nothing. No pain, no barrier spell pushing him away, no sense that this was not the right time. He was home.

For good? He considered the question. Yes, of course. He would stay, but to make it happen, there were two things he needed. His crown and the woman at his side. Not necessarily in that order.

Bogdan showed them to their separate rooms. Ged looked around the wood-paneled chamber with its four-poster bed and log fire with a smile as he remembered his modern New York apartment. Some things would take a little getting used to.

After a moment or two, there was a knock on his door, and before he could answer, Lidi slipped inside. She was wrapped in a bedsheet and she walked straight into his arms.

Ged removed the bag from around his neck as he held her close. "I know why I'm naked, but you have access to your own clothes."

"I didn't want to waste time dressing. I couldn't wait another minute to be with you."

As he lifted her so her face was level with his and their lips could meet, Ged knew nothing mattered except this. Fine dining, luxury hotels, the celebrity lifestyle? Those things were in his past. In his arms, he held his future. But there was a long way to go before he could begin to claim her.

Chapter 17

Lidi sighed with pleasure as Ged carried her to the bed and placed her on it. This was what she had dreamed of during the long hours of traveling. Just the two of them, alone together. They might have worlds to conquer and villains to vanquish, but when his arms were around her, she was at peace.

"This question may be a mood killer," Ged murmured. "But what have you done with Bruno?"

"My room is next door. As soon as we got inside, he dived onto the bed and fell asleep." She turned her face into his neck to hide a smile. Her big, strong bear tried hard to pretend he didn't care about the dog. "I've locked the door and we'll hear him if he barks."

"If he barks?" He growled the words against her lips. "If that little cur interrupts us, I'll tie those ridiculous ears of his in a bow around his snout."

She rose up on her knees and moved closer, stopping just inches away. Taking one of his hands, she placed it on her breast and leaned in, kissing him slowly and passionately. When she broke the kiss, he was smiling, his eyes alight with desire.

"I think we can find better things to do than talk about a dog, don't you?" she asked.

She pulled him down onto the bed. With a firm hand flat on his shoulder, she pushed him onto his back and crawled up his body until her thighs straddled his naked waist. Ged tucked his hands behind his head, his smile widening.

"You have my full attention."

Lidi leaned close to whisper in his ear. "That journey was torture. Not being able to touch you when I wanted to drove me crazy. But I'm going to make up for it now. I'm going to start by caressing you…" As she spoke she slid off the sheet she had wrapped around her body, enjoying the flare of pleasure in his eyes. "Then, I'm going to taste you." She changed position slightly, letting him feel the heat of her arousal rubbing against his erection.

"What happens next?" His eyes were locked on hers, his voice hoarse.

"Then, I'm going to let you take over. I hope you'll have come up with a few ideas of your own by that time." She smiled as her gaze wandered down his body. "Perhaps you already have."

He groaned. "Lidi, are you trying to torture me?"

"That's the idea."

She moved to his side. Starting at his feet, and with a featherlight motion, she began to lightly massage first one leg, then the other. When she reached his straining erection, her fingertips danced teasingly close, making his throbbing flesh jump and twitch. Ged's hips jerked upward, but Lidi moved on to his chest, shoulders and arms, ignoring his gritted teeth and moan of frustration.

When she reached his mouth, she paused to kiss him again. Ged seized the chance to twist his head and ease his lips over one hardened nipple. Lidi whimpered, her whole body starting to shake as she almost forgot her resolve to take this slowly. His hands moved down to her waist and he locked her in place as he licked, sucked and nipped. Pulling away, she shook her head, laughing as he muttered a curse.

Gliding the whole length of her body against his, she moved all the way back down.

"I know what you're doing. You're trying to kill me." Although she couldn't see him, she could tell Ged's teeth were tightly clenched.

Laughing softly, she pushed his legs apart so she could kneel between them. Caressing his right leg, she licked and lightly nibbled her way up his left leg until she reached his groin. Moving along his hip bones with long, rough swipes of her tongue, she finally reached the area that was straining for her attention.

Leaning in, she ran her tongue in one long, slow motion up his erection and ended by swirling lightly around the rim. Although this was outside her experience, from the way Ged gasped and arched his back, she guessed he was enjoying it. She decided to go with her instincts.

I'm *enjoying it*. Her whole body was on fire at the taste and feel of him. Her only goal had been to give him pleasure. How had she not anticipated that pleasing him would inflame her own desires to the point of torment?

Opening her lips, she slid her mouth over him, covering his head and sucking gently. Out of the corner of her eye, she could see Ged's hand scrabbling to grip the sheets, and his breath came out in one long, slow hiss. Pushing down further, she used her tongue to trace a pattern on the sensitive underside of his cock, sliding up and down and applying more suction. Ged lifted his hips in time with her movements.

"Oh, Lidi. Don't want…not yet…"

As his body started tensing and trembling, Ged's hands gripped her shoulders, hauling her up to face him. He was breathing hard as he plunged a hand into her hair, kissing her like his life depended on it.

Rising up onto her knees, Lidi straddled his hips once more. Taking hold of his rock-hard length, she lined him up with her entrance and slowly lowered herself down until he was buried all the way inside her. Gripping her lower lip with her teeth, she remained still, adjusting to the incredible feeling of him filling and stretching her. Then, leaning forward, curtaining them with her hair, she began to move.

Ged gripped her ass, holding her cheeks wide apart, opening her fully against him as the feelings intensified. Heat consumed them both, searing them. Lidi's soft moans mingled with his deep groans.

With tantalizing slowness, she lifted up until he was almost all the way out, then slammed down. Ged's pelvis jerked upward at the same time, grinding into her. Gripping her hips, he flipped her over and onto her back.

"No more going slow."

He lifted her legs over his arms and thrust into her with hard fast strokes. Passion and pleasure mounted, and a light sheen of sweat slicked their skin. Lidi gasped and her head fell back. Ged drove into her one last time, and the world flew apart. She cried out as everything faded except his body inside hers and the slick sounds and musky scents.

Ged dug his fingers hard into her hips, holding on to her as she shuddered. She was dimly aware of him stiffening and jerking through his own orgasm. Then he relaxed, dropping his head onto her shoulder. She could feel his heart pounding as he nuzzled his face into her neck.

They lay wrapped in each other's arms for a long time. Just resting. Maybe dozing. When Lidi hitched in a breath, Ged tilted her face up to his.

"Are you crying?" His face was concerned as he raised himself on one elbow.

She sniffed. "I don't cry."

"Right. I almost forgot about you being a tough, no-nonsense warrior." He smiled into her eyes as he tracked a finger down her cheek. When he held it up, it was wet with her tears. "Do you want to talk about this?"

Did she? It would be so easy to give in to her feelings. To let it all pour out. But where would that leave them? They would be setting out on the last, and most dangerous, stage of their journey under an embarrassing cloud.

They had both known the rules when they entered into this. *Keep it light.* It was simple enough. It wasn't Ged's fault she had stepped outside those boundaries. Maybe they both had. But they had enough to deal with. She wasn't going to add emotion into the mix.

Plus, she genuinely didn't know *why* she was crying. She meant it when she said she didn't do tears. There was just something so wonderful about being in his arms. Aware that Ged was still waiting for answer, she squirmed slightly.

"I'm tired. And being home again is all a bit over-whelming."

His gaze probed her face. "Care to tell me the real reason?"

Her lips parted. For a moment, her response hung in the balance. Then a muffled volley of barks reached them from the adjoining room.

"Good timing that the dog wants to be let out?" Ged asked as Lidi wrapped the sheet around herself again. "Or bad?"

She paused with her hand on the door handle. "I suppose that depends on whose perspective you're in."

Ged had spent some time pondering the difficulties of persuading Bogdan to send a message to Eduard Tavisha at the secret headquarters of the resistance. He discussed the matter with Lidi, Andrei and Sasha when they met in his room before they went downstairs for the evening meal.

"The only way to get Bogdan on our side will be to tell him who I am," he said. "If I don't, we can't expect him to follow my orders, or believe me when I tell him I know where my uncle is."

"Bogdan can be trusted," Lidi assured him. "I am sure of it."

"Then that's decided."

When they descended the grand staircase, there was a flurry of excitement as Lidi was recognized by several servants who had known her all her life. There were hugs and exclamations, although these were subdued by the presence of Bruno. The curious glances cast in the direction of her companions made Ged glad he had donned his disguise.

"Is there any news of your father, my lady?" It was the question on everyone's lips.

"I hope to hear something of him very soon."

The exchange told Ged a lot about both Lidi and her father. The servants loved the Count of Aras and his daughter. It was obvious in the way they spoke about their master and the delight they displayed on seeing Lidi again. And the trouble Lidi took to talk to them and reassure them confirmed everything he already knew about her. These people were paid to serve her. Yet the relationship she had with them was one of mutual love and trust. Even now, when she was desperately worried about her father and preparing for the fight of her life, she was putting the needs of others first.

His heart clenched with love. He allowed himself to recognize and accept the emotion. To *welcome* it. He had once believed this would never happen to him. Now, he was bowled over by its force. Just a few more steps...

"Usually, we would eat in the great hall," Lidi explained. "But I think the fewer people who see you, the better. I have asked for dinner to be served in a smaller dining room. It will just be the four of us and Bogdan. That way, we can talk without fear of being overheard."

The room they entered was opulent but comfortable, with dark paneling on the walls and crimson drapes shutting out the darkness. A roaring log fire crackled in a huge fireplace, and, after regarding it with suspicion, Bruno curled up in front of it.

When Bogdan entered the room just after them, he paused on the threshold, regarding Ged in surprise. Remembering that he hadn't been wearing his dark wig, beard and mustache when they first met, Ged tried to come up with a suitable excuse.

Bogdan closed the door behind him before coming into the room. "The disguise is probably a good idea, Your Majesty."

Lidi gave an exclamation of surprise and Ged shook his head. "You knew?"

Bogdan went down on one knee, placing his hand on his heart. "It is impossible to mistake a Tavisha. You are very like your father." He raised his head and looked at Andrei. "As are you, Prince Andrei."

Ged placed a hand on his shoulder. "Rise, Bogdan. You are the first person to have sworn allegiance to me."

"I'll not be the last, sire."

Ged felt his heart swell with pride. "So I've no need of the arguments I'd prepared to persuade you to send for my uncle?"

"I have a party of men ready to leave," Bogdan said. "They await my orders. Just tell me where to find your uncle and I will send them on their way."

They took their seats at the table. "My uncle is staying with the Earl of Vitchenko," Ged said.

Bogdan sat up straighter in his chair. "But Vitchenko is a friend of Vasily the Usurper."

Ged smiled. "That is what Vasily believes."

Bogdan pursed his lips. "This changes everything. With a man as powerful as Vitchenko on our side, we can't lose. We could march against Vasily tonight."

"Not so fast." Ged paused as a group of servants entered. They staggered under the weight of platters laden with slabs of raw meat and freshly caught fish. One of them carried a small bowl of salad. That was another advantage of being home. Everyone knew exactly what he wanted to eat. When the door closed behind them, Ged continued. "We need to know our strength and also what we're up against. My uncle will able to tell us the true size of the resistance forces, but the only way to assess Vasily's power will be to get inside the royal palace."

Bogdan shook his head. "He is a coward. Ever since he stole the throne, he has feared an assassination attempt. We'll never get anyone close enough."

"I'm going to do it," Lidi said. Briefly, she outlined the plan to trick Vasily into believing she would accept his offer of marriage.

Bogdan had been about to take a slug of wine, but he slammed down his goblet and half rose from his seat. "No, my lady. I cannot—"

Bruno, who had given all the appearance of being in a deep slumber, jumped up. With his hackles rising, he ran to Lidi's side, baring his teeth at Bogdan. She patted his head reassuringly. "It's okay, he's on our side." The dog sat down, but continued to glare at Bogdan as though warning him not to try anything.

"I will be with her," Ged explained. "Hence the disguise." He smiled. "And I have a few unexpected Christmas presents for Vasily."

He could see Bogdan was torn between his dislike of the idea and his obedience to his king. They ate in silence for a few minutes before the older man raised another concern. "What of Prince Andrei and Miss Sasha? Vasily will never admit them into the palace, as well."

It was a valid point. Ged regarded Andrei across the table. "Could you stand to wait here until we send for you? There will be a very important mission attached to your stay here at Aras House."

Since their arrival in Callistoya, Andrei, who had coped well with the journey, had been looking tired. Now he looked up from his plate with an inquiring expression. "What would it be?"

"We can't take Bruno with us. Someone has to remain here and keep him out of trouble."

Andrei laughed. "My God. So we get the hardest job of all?" He turned to Sasha. "What do you say?"

She took his hand. "This is a beautiful place where you can convalesce, and we can catch our breath while we adjust to our new lives." She smiled at Lidi. "And I'm getting used to the dog. We'll look after him and join you when the time is right. We don't want to miss all the fun."

As she finished speaking, Bruno placed his paws on her knee and, eying her plate, gave the plaintive whine of a dog who has not been fed for weeks. Sasha patted his head and gave him a large piece of meat, which he took back to the fireside.

Ged smiled at Lidi. "That's the pet sitting taken care of. When my uncle arrives, we'll draw up a battle plan."

Chapter 18

As Lidi crossed the central courtyard with Bruno, the contrasting receptions they received amused her. While she was greeted with cries of delight, the dog's presence provoked universal horror. Although she explained that the creature at her side—who was prancing delightedly while chewing on his leash at the prospect of a walk—was harmless, it was clear no one believed her.

When she reached a quieter area of the castle grounds, she paused, pushing back the hood of her cloak and breathing in the pure, clean air. Ged was expecting his uncle to arrive within the hour. As soon as they had consulted with Eduard Tavisha, she and Ged would travel south to the royal palace. The last stage of the journey to freedom would begin.

What comes after freedom? After my father is re-

leased from his cell and I no longer have this threat hanging over me...what then?

She looked back at the castle that was her home. Then...*this*. A return to her old life. The life she loved. Would that be such a hardship? Tears blurred her vision briefly. Yes. Because her life would no longer contain Ged. And he was her whole world.

Just as the thoughts threatened to overwhelm her, a woman approached. Lidi averted her face, wanting to escape recognition. She didn't want another conversation, not now, when her mood was so low, but Bruno's soft growl drew her attention.

She looked back in time to see the woman as she drew level. Although the hood of her cloak was pulled up, strands of her hair were clearly visible. They were silver blond.

"Allie?"

The other woman turned, pressing a finger to her lips. Beckoning with her other hand, she led Lidi in the direction of the ornate rose garden. Set right against the farthest of the castle walls, this was one of the quietest areas of the grounds.

Allie pushed back the hood of her cloak and Lidi noticed she wore the same beautiful, expensive scarf that had been wound around her neck in Cannes. As Allie took a seat on a stone bench, Lidi didn't know whether to be angry or scared. She went for a combination of both. "What the hell is going on? Why have you been following me?" And, more important than anything else: "Who are you?"

That question became doubly important because now she was close to Allie once more, she was reminded of what she'd told Ged when he'd asked her if Allie was shifter or human. Last time she'd met this woman, Lidi had been on a single-minded mission to find Ged. The minute he'd come into the scope of her consciousness, nothing else had mattered. That was why she had paid very little attention to Allie, only noticing her as a means of gleaning information about Beast.

Although Callistoya was an insular nation, enchanted beings sometimes passed through its borders, and during her life, Lidi had encountered several different species of shifter as well as the occasional sorcerer, dragon and nymph. But her finely tuned senses weren't working around Allie. The other woman was a complete blank, giving off no clues to her persona.

"Look inside your own heart. It will give the answers you seek." They were the unspoken words Lidi had heard the night Pauwau had performed her healing ceremony. Hearing them again, this time from Allie's lips, sent an icy chill down Lidi's spine. At her feet, Bruno gave an answering shiver and slunk into the folds of her long skirt.

Look inside your heart. What was it telling her? Taking a steadying breath, she stated the unthinkable. "My heart tells me you are Alyona Ivanov."

To her amazement, slow tears rolled down the other woman's face. "Thank you. You have no idea how sweet it is to hear my name spoken out loud after all this time."

Lidi tried to shake off the feeling that she had stepped into someone else's dream. Or possibly her own nightmare. "I don't understand. How did you survive on the night of the massacre? Your body was identified by Eduard Tavisha himself."

Slowly, Alyona removed her scarf. "I didn't survive."

Lidi raised a shaking hand to her lips as she gazed at

Alyona. A deep crimson mark ran all the way around the other woman's neck. Above and below it, the skin was red and swollen in angry contrast to the whiteness of her surrounding flesh. Where the bodice of her dress revealed her collarbone and chest, Lidi could see a deep, gaping stab wound, bloodless now after thirteen long years.

"You're a…" Lidi shook her head, still struggling to take in what she was seeing.

Alyona's smile was the saddest thing she'd ever seen. "I think the word you're looking for is *ghost*."

"That's why I don't feel anything from you. When Ged asked me if you were shifter or human, I didn't know *what* you were."

Tears spilled down Alyona's cheeks again. "How is Gerald? Truly?"

Lidi took a few seconds to weigh the situation. Was she really doing this? Having a conversation with the ghost of Ged's murdered fiancée? Deciding that if she was going to do it, she may as well do it properly, she took a seat next to Alyona on the bench.

"How does this work? Don't you know how he is?"

Alyona shook her head. "Although Gerald is the reason I am here, you are the only person I can interact with."

There was a world of information in that sentence, but Lidi decided to unpack it slowly. "Ged is—" Where to begin? "I think *conflicted* is the best word, but it's only the start. For many years, it was like he died in the massacre along with the rest of you. A part of him did. He hates himself because he wasn't able to stop the killings." She turned her head to look at Alyona. "And he blames himself for not being there to protect you."

"I will always love him, but not in the way you do," Alyona said. "Gerald was my best friend, my confidant, the person who made me laugh and lifted me up when I was down. But he was never my lover. He is *your* mate. And that is why I am here."

"I don't understand any of this," Lidi said. "And please don't tell me to look inside my heart to find the answers, because I can tell you now…they aren't there."

Alyona smiled. "I was going to say *it's simple*, but that sounds patronizing. Perhaps it's easier to understand if, like me, you have been part of the spirit world for the last thirteen years. Thirteen years ago, the foul massacre in the royal palace tore apart the very fabric of this land. The spirits who watch over Callistoya could not allow it to go unavenged. But while Gerald remained absent, it was hard to find a way to restore the true regime."

"Couldn't those spirits have found a way to remove the spell Vasily had used to prevent Ged from crossing the border?" Lidi asked.

"We both know that the spell was not the reason Gerald stayed away," Alyona said. "The barrier was in his heart, not on the border. Sadly, we—for I had become one of those determined to redress the wrong that Vasily caused—were forced to wait until the time was right."

"How did you know when that was?" Lidi was conscious of Bruno moving out from her skirts and lying on the grass, his relaxed attitude confirming her own conviction that Alyona meant her no harm.

"It happened when Vasily turned his eyes in your direction. From that moment on, although you didn't know it, I was always close by."

Lidi managed a smile. "If that was the case, couldn't

you have stopped Vasily from throwing me and my father into prison? Or at least helped me when I escaped?"

Alyona returned the smile. "My physical presence is an illusion. I am here to guide, but I cannot intervene."

Lidi couldn't help wondering if there might come a point when Alyona would tell her she had run out of questions. Her best option was probably to keep going while she could. "If you are his guide, why can't Ged see you?"

"I'm not here as Gerald's spirit escort." As Alyona spoke, Bruno jumped up onto the bench and positioned himself between the two women. "I'm here for you, Lidi."

Lidi took a break from the conversation to stroke Bruno. As a supernatural being herself, she was no stranger to the concept of unseen forces at work behind the scenes, but this was a little too personal. The idea that the spirits had their watchful eyes upon her was both comforting and unnerving. While it gave her hope that the good guys would win, it made her uncomfortable about her privacy.

"I am not always with you." Alyona's words addressed at least one of Lidi's unspoken concerns. "But once you passed into the mortal realm, it was decided that I should materialize and appear to you from time to time."

"But why?" Lidi asked. Although she had no wish to offend a spirit, she couldn't see what Alyona had actually *done*.

"I was to be there if you needed my assistance. Most times, you've been doing just fine on your own." Alyona's smooth brow wrinkled. "In fact, I can only think of one occasion where I nudged you in the right direction."

Lidi stared at her with a blank expression for a moment before she remembered what the other woman was talking about. "You told me which floor the band would be staying on in the Palais Hotel." Suddenly the whole situation struck her as funny. "You dared me to get into the hotel. By telling me I couldn't, you knew I would. I have a guardian angel who is my—" still unsure how to describe Ged in relation to herself, she hesitated "—a matchmaking guardian angel who is Ged's ex-fiancée and whose job is to make sure I stay with him."

Alyona appeared bewildered by her amusement. "That's it exactly. You are the key, Lidi. You are the person who will save our king and, with him, our country."

Lidi shook her head, the amusement fading. "No pressure, then. And that's the reason you've hung around for thirteen years? To make sure Ged and I find each other?"

Alyona's hand went to her neck. "Not the only reason. Revenge is a powerful motivator."

Lidi swallowed hard at the thought of what Alyona must have endured that night. "Did Vasily do that to you?"

"Yes." Alyona closed her eyes briefly. "I relive that night constantly. By the time the engagement feast was over, both Gerald and Andrei had begun to feel unwell. I wondered if it was something they'd eaten, but the other guests were all fine. Soon, they were so ill that they were forced to retire to bed. After about an hour, the party ended and everyone else went upstairs. Something woke me in the early hours of the morning. I'm not sure what it was. A sound that was out of place, maybe. I tried to get back to sleep, but then I heard a scream and the sound of running footsteps."

"Were you in your own room?" Lidi remembered that Alyona had been in Ged's bed when she was murdered.

"Yes. I was scared, so I put on my dressing gown and went along the corridor to Gerald's room. When I got there, the room was empty and his bed hadn't been slept in. I'd only just closed the door behind me when Vasily burst in." She swallowed hard, and Lidi could see the effort it took for her to force herself onward. "He wore some sort of protective glove that came all the way up his arm, and when I looked at his hand, I could see the reason why. He was holding a silver dagger. The glove was to protect him from the effects of the silver. The knife was dripping with blood."

Lidi wasn't sure if she would be able to touch Alyona. When she placed her hand over the other woman's, she was pleased to find she could feel it. Perhaps it wasn't quite flesh and blood, but it was there. Alyona looked down at their entwined fingers for a long, heartbreaking moment before continuing her story.

When she spoke again, her voice was stronger. "Vasily screamed at me, wanting to know where Gerald was. He wouldn't believe me when I told him I didn't know. He showed me the blood on the knife and told me he had just killed the king. Now it was to be Gerald's turn. I tried to run, but he caught hold of me. He took the cord belt from my dressing gown and twisted it around my neck, trying to get me to tell him where Gerald was hiding." Her voice hitched on a sob. "Because I didn't know, I couldn't tell him. I was losing consciousness when I heard another voice. It was a woman and she was crying. She pleaded with Vasily to stop." Alyona turned tear-filled eyes to Lidi's face. "That was when I felt the burn of the silver dagger and...nothing."

"A woman? Ged's friend Pauwau told us that the person who saved him and Andrei that night was a woman," Lidi said.

"Queen Zoya, Vasily's mother, was the person who rescued them. She was the one who tried to stop Vasily from killing me. Zoya had heard rumors of the assassination plot and was placed in a terrible position. If she took the story to her husband, the king, he would have Vasily executed for treason. But she knew she couldn't sit by and do nothing. She consulted the spirits and devised a spell to incapacitate Gerald and Andrei on the night of the feast. Then, she ordered her servants to carry them to different locations in the mortal realm."

Lidi frowned. Although the picture was clearer, she was still confused. "If Zoya wanted to save Ged and Andrei, why did she have them beaten? Ged was seriously injured, and Andrei was left in a wheelchair as a result of his injuries."

"When her servants returned, they told her that, even though they were under the influence of a powerful spell, the Tavisha brothers had fought them and had needed to be physically restrained. Zoya was angry and had the men responsible punished, but it was too late by then to do anything. And she had other things on her mind. Zoya herself was suffering the aftereffects of Vasily's anger."

"Did he know what she'd done?" Lidi asked.

"He didn't know she was the person who had rescued Gerald and Andrei. Even though Zoya is his mother, that would have meant certain death," Alyona said. "But he was furious because she tried to save me."

"But her husband died that night. How could she have let that happen?"

Lidi didn't get an answer to her question. To her surprise, Alyona disappeared as she was speaking. The reason soon became obvious when Bruno gave an excited bark and leaped from the bench.

"Talking to yourself?"

Lidi turned her head to see Ged walking toward her.

"Or talking to Bruno? I'm not sure which is more troubling." His gaze scanned her face. "Hey…are you okay?"

Since the information Alyona had given her would take more than a few minutes to share, she smiled. "Just gathering my thoughts."

He held out his hands, helping her to her feet. "I came to tell you that my uncle has arrived. And also that Bogdan has been dealing with a possible rebellion from the staff over the theft of meat from the kitchen."

Lidi linked her arm through his and they strolled back toward the courtyard with Bruno trotting beside them. "That sounds strange."

"Doesn't it? Some people were inclined to blame the devil-dog you brought with you from the mortal realm."

Lidi huffed out an impatient breath. "If they would just take a little time to understand him—"

"That's what Bogdan told them." Ged held the door open so she could step through in front of him. He lowered his voice as she passed so that only she could hear. "Bruno hid the remains of his robbery under your bed. I've already removed them."

She had only just stopped laughing when they reached the drawing room where Eduard Tavisha awaited them.

Ged could never see his uncle without being reminded of his father. And memories of his father brought a combination of joy and pain. Ivan Tavisha had been a king in every sense of the word. Big and powerful, he had reigned over Callistoya with an understanding of his subjects and their needs that was deeply intuitive. Taking into account the fact that he was a bear, it was also remarkable.

He knew now that his homesickness and anger at Vasily's behavior had prevented him from grieving properly for his father. Maybe avenging his death would be one way to begin that process. It would certainly make Ged feel as though he was doing something to redress the balance.

As he gripped his uncle's hand, he thought he could see some of the same thoughts reflected in Eduard Tavisha's eyes.

Eduard smiled as he indicated Ged's disguise. "It's a little unsettling, but I'd have known you anywhere."

Ged frowned. "I hope Vasily isn't as perceptive."

His uncle shook his head. "Vasily is too interested in himself and too busy trying to deal with the threats to his reign. He doesn't notice anything beyond the end of his own nose. I wouldn't underestimate his cunning or his instinct for self-preservation, but together, we will reclaim what is yours. This land needs a Tavisha on the throne once more." He looked around. "Can what Bogdan tells me really be true? Is Andrei with you?"

"He is, but his experiences have taken their toll. My brother has no memory of his life in Callistoya."

As Ged finished speaking, Andrei entered the room with Bogdan. With no time to waste, they launched into a discussion about the size of the resistance forces and the plan to overthrow Vasily. It soon became clear that his uncle had devoted the last thirteen years of his life to building the resistance into a formidable army.

"I believe that we, with the addition of Vitchenko's forces and the support of Bogdan here on behalf of the Count of Aras, we can defeat Vasily's army," Eduard said.

Ged's heart swelled with pride at the news he was hearing. When he was forced to leave Callistoya, he had never dreamed of leading an army. He had been relatively young, and his experience of military action had been limited to combat training with the royal army. But, back then, his father had been alive. If he had thought about it, he supposed that one day he would ride out at his father's side on his missions to quell the rebels. "One day" had seemed a long way off.

Now he was preparing to lead the resistance, and he found the prospect exhilarating. Curiously, his time in the mortal realm had been good preparation for this moment. Managing a rock band might not appear on the surface to have many similarities to leading a revolution, but the skills he had honed were the same. He was used to being in charge. And managing Beast meant he knew how to cope with the unexpected.

In addition, he had spent his time deliberately facing peril by rescuing other shifters from danger. For thirteen years, he had thrown himself from one wild adventure to another, never pausing to consider his own safety. Looking back, he supposed it was the best possible training for what he was about to face.

"I want you to approach the palace from the south," he told Eduard.

"The south?" His uncle shook his head. "That would be a mistake. You haven't been to your old home recently, but the south plain has become an encampment for Vasily's men. We should take him by surprise and storm the palace from the east."

"No." Ged's expression was determined. "As far as possible, I want the palace left untouched."

Eduard laughed. "A wise move. A battle inside the building would leave it in ruins. Do you have any other requests?"

"Yes." He handed Eduard a slip of paper. "You will need to get someone into the mortal realm to contact this man. His name is Khan and he will be waiting close to the border. Once he and his companions arrive in Callistoya, have them escorted directly to the royal palace."

Eduard blinked, but nodded. "As you wish."

Ged turned to Lidi. "I think that's it. We should start our journey."

"I have just one question." She turned to Eduard. "Where is Queen Zoya?"

He looked confused. "I'm not sure. Vasily has effectively closed the royal palace off from the rest of the country. After King Ivan was killed, the queen went into mourning. Although she has not been seen in public for many years, she is believed to reside in the royal palace. Why do you ask?"

"I was just curious." Lidi spoke casually, but Ged knew her well enough by now to be sure she had a very specific reason for asking.

They left soon after. Sasha reassured Lidi that she would take care of Bruno, who, with his uncanny sixth sense, seemed to understand that he couldn't accompany the mistress he had chosen for himself. Instead, tucked under Sasha's arm, he watched as Ged and Lidi mounted their horses.

They had discussed the method of travel. Although

the journey would have been quicker if they had shifted and crossed the Callistoya landscape as bears, Lidi's reasoning had prevailed. This time her arguments about nakedness had nothing to do with modesty and everything to do with first appearances.

"It is my intention to arrive at the royal palace and request a meeting with Vasily. Once I present myself to him, he will assume that I am willing to marry him after all. I will feel more comfortable if I am not naked when we have that conversation."

Ged's feelings had threatened to overwhelm him at the image of Vasily's eyes on Lidi's naked body. As the time drew closer when they would play out their charade, it was bad enough to contemplate him anywhere near her.

Not for long. That was how he managed to deal with it. *We will get inside the palace, spoil his festive ball and then destroy him.*

Horses were not naturally comfortable around bears, but over the centuries, the Callistoya nobles had bred sturdy packhorses to carry them and pull their carriages. This breed was large and functional rather than beautiful, but they displayed no nervousness around bear shifters and could be relied upon to carry Ged, Lidi and their belongings without any problems.

Ged leaned forward in the saddle to grasp Andrei's hand. "Any regrets about this mad adventure so far?"

"Only one." Andrei smiled in response to Ged's raised brows. "I'd have liked to be there to see you kick Vasily's ass."

Ged raised a hand as he departed. "Don't worry. I will make Vasily pay for what he did to you…to all of us."

Chapter 19

Situated high in the Callistoyan mountain range, the royal palace was a breathtaking sight. It was said that the very first Tavisha king, upon being granted his kingdom by Callisto herself, had decided to create something unique and romantic amid the snowcapped peaks.

Although Lidi had seen the colorful building, it had been when she was brought here as a prisoner. On that occasion, she had been in no mood to admire the royal residence. This time, it drew a gasp from her as they approached. "It's like…" She paused, lost for words.

"My mother, who was musical, once described it to me as an opera made from bricks and mortar," Ged said.

Lidi, who *wasn't* musical, couldn't understand the comparison. She gazed at the towers, facades and architectural flourishes that appeared to have been thrown together from a bunch of different castles. One portion resembled medieval European parapets, while the section next to it was modeled on an Islamic tower dome. And so it went on. Each part of the facade was also presented in a different color; a long purple wing was flanked by a red clock tower and a yellow minaret, the bright colors eye-catching against the stark landscape. It was opulent, indulgent, foolish…and incredible.

"It's beautiful."

"I'm glad you like it." Ged seemed relieved, and as they moved closer to the palace, Lidi took a moment to wonder why that was. She knew he cared about her. After everything they'd been through and all they'd shared, it was obvious his feelings for her were strong. But she would never be part of *this* life. So why should it matter what she thought of his home?

She shrugged the thought aside. There were more important considerations right now, such as the impending meeting with Vasily. She still hadn't told Ged about her encounter with Alyona. Not because she didn't want to. On the contrary, she really wanted to share what she'd learned, but the details of what had happened on the night of the massacre had been devastating to hear. If it could distress Lidi, who hadn't known Alyona, how would it affect Ged? He needed a clear head for the coming encounter. If his judgment was clouded by a red mist of rage, he might jeopardize the whole mission. Worse, he could endanger himself.

The approach to the castle was winding and treacherous, and for the last few hundred yards, they dismounted and led their horses. In addition to his wig, beard and mustache, Ged wore a cloak with the hood pulled up to shadow his face. He paused when they drew close to the palace and pointed at the view below them.

"The south plain. That is the army encampment my uncle spoke of." His voice was tight with repugnance. "Vasily's determination to keep his soldiers close has destroyed the landscape. It reminds me of shantytowns I have seen in the mortal realm."

Although Lidi didn't know what he was referring to, she could understand his distaste. The far side of the plain was a mass of rusting roofs slung across mud and rocks. Buildings were stacked precariously on top of each other with piles of trash in between. This was the view from the palace. King Vasily's focus was on his own protection rather than aesthetics.

When they arrived at the huge, gilt-decorated gates that marked the entrance to the palace, their way was barred by two guards wearing ornate uniforms and carrying huge curved swords.

"State your business," one of the soldiers demanded.

"I am Lady Lidiya Rihanoff, daughter of the Count of Aras. I request an audience with King Vasily." Even though she was playing a part, Lidi found it difficult to use the royal title when referring to Vasily.

The guard looked her up and down. Turning away, he engaged in a muttered conversation with his companion.

It was several minutes before he turned back to them with a curt command. "Wait here."

The guard who had challenged them entered the palace through a small door at the side of the larger gates, leaving them alone with his comrade. Lidi wrapped her cloak around her. The wind was whipping straight off the highest peaks of the Callistoya range and seemed to be biting right through to her bones. She didn't dare speak to Ged, who was now supposed to be her body-

guard. Once or twice she caught his eye and saw a reassuring twinkle that warmed her more than the heavy
material of her cloak.

It was a full twenty minutes before the guard returned. Without speaking, he signaled to his companion and, together, they opened the huge gates until there
was just enough space for the horses to pass through.
The sound of the hinges creaking closed behind them
made Lidi want to move closer to Ged. Determinedly,
she straightened her spine.

"It has been a long journey. Kindly arrange to have
my horses stabled."

"Your groom can see to your horses while I escort
you to the king." The guard led them across a courtyard that was similar to the one at Aras House, although
this was larger and quieter. The few people who were
around scurried about their business with their heads
bent and avoided eye contact.

Being separated from Ged was not part of the plan
and Lidi shook her head. Realizing they hadn't agreed
on an alias for him in his role as her bodyguard, she
thought fast. "Robert is my bodyguard, not my groom.
He can't be trusted with my horses."

Ged made a slight choking sound, but collected himself before the guard noticed. As he walked ahead of
them, calling for a stable-hand to come and take the
horses, Ged leaned closer. "Robert?"

"It was the name of one of my cuddly toys when I
was a child."

Although his lips twitched slightly, he didn't say
anything more. The guard led them toward the central

palace building. Once they passed through its doors, it was eerily silent.

They came to a halt in a grand, highly ornamented reception room. The furnishings were rich and ornate, with oil lamps glowing in every alcove. Light bounced off the gold filigree ceiling and reflected the colors of high stained glass windows. The effect enhanced the sensation of peace and tranquility.

"You are to wait here until the king's secretary sends for you," the guard said. He indicated a group of chairs organized around a table upon which there were a number of books.

"How long will that be?" Lidi asked.

He gave her a pitying look and left. Although she risked a quick glance in Ged's direction, she didn't dare speak to him. They had no idea if anyone was watching them or listening in on their conversations. With a sigh that was a combination of impatience, annoyance and nervousness, she took a seat on a high-backed chair and began to flick through a book without reading it.

After anticipating a lengthy wait, she was startled when an ornate tapestry was thrust aside and the door that had been concealed behind it opened. Getting to her feet, she faced the man who entered the room. He was shorter and darker than most Callistoya bear shifters, his features handsome without being remarkable. As she registered that information about his appearance, she was also distracted by the way Ged was acting. She could almost feel the waves of tension coming from him. She had been told to expect Vasily's secretary. Whoever this man was, there was clearly history between them.

"Oh." Realization hit her at the same time as the stranger stepped toward her.

Bowing low, he took her hand. "We meet at last." With a smile, he brushed her knuckles with his lips. "I am King Vasily, but your presence here indicates that you are prepared to call me *husband*."

Ged paced the small chamber that had been assigned to him in the servants' quarters. It wasn't easy since the room was the size of a shoebox. How had he ever believed he could do this? It was bad enough having to see Vasily again without giving in to the temptation to tear into him with his teeth and claws. Watching his stepbrother leer at Lidi and drool over her hand? He paused, his chest expanding as though he had shifted into bear form and run for miles across the Callistoya plain.

He needed action, but his secret identity was a problem. Thirteen years was a long time, but he had no idea how many members of his father's staff still remained in the palace. Reminding himself he hadn't come here to remain trapped inside this room, he stepped cautiously out into a narrow corridor. There was no one around. Following the passage for a few yards, he came to a door that led him outside.

It seemed strange that, although he had grown up in the palace, he had never stepped foot into this area. As a royal prince, there had never been any reason for him to stray into the part of the establishment that was reserved for servants. Now he was in the open air, he took a step back, taking a different look at the place that was once his home.

To the uninitiated, it would be easy to assume there was no logic to the glorious muddle of buildings. Ged, who knew the palace well, was aware that there was order amid the disarray. Although a number of decorative edifices fanned out around it, the central palace was a rounded, four-story structure. A glorious, pale yellow color, it towered above the surrounding buildings.

The first two floors were taken up with public rooms. There was a grand ballroom—where the Christmas-Eve ball would take place on the following night—a dining room, several reception rooms and sitting rooms. The third and fourth floors were taken up with the private rooms of the royal family. That was where Lidi would be now. When Vasily had shown up and fawned over her, he had offered to escort her to one of the family bedchambers. Ged had just had time to signal that he would catch up with her later before Vasily had waved him away without looking at him. A steward had directed him to his own room.

The servants' quarters were in the basement. Ged had always known, of course, that the building had a lower floor. It just hadn't registered with him that, because of their position beneath the main building, the servants' quarters would exit onto a separate courtyard. This was one floor below and to the rear of the main palace entrance.

From where he was standing now, he had a new view of the palace. He had never seen it from quite this angle, but what interested him most was that within the thick stone walls surrounding this lower courtyard there was a plain, wooden door. Ged could see that it led directly onto the mountain pass up which he and Lidi had recently led their horses.

With his mind working overtime, he approached the door. The following night, during the Christmas-Eve ball, he planned to confront Vasily. He wanted to force his stepbrother into a fight to the death. At the same time, the resistance forces would spring a surprise attack on Vasily's army encampment. The only problem Ged had foreseen was how to get Khan and his other friends into the palace. Now it looked like he might have found a way.

As he had expected, the door was locked. He was considering how easy it would be to break the lock when he heard footsteps approaching. Turning, he found himself staring into the familiar face of his father's best friend. Ivan Tavisha and Mikhail Orlov had grown up together. When Ivan became king upon the death of his father in an unfortunate hunting accident, he had appointed Mikhail to the post of his steward. There was no one Ged's father had trusted more.

"I thought—" Ged bit back the exclamation, annoyed at how close he had come to giving himself away. *I thought you were killed in the massacre.* That was what he had almost blurted out.

Although Mikhail's gaze probed his face, he gave no sign of recognition. "You thought what? Do you have someone waiting on the other side of that door? An accomplice perhaps? What's the plan? Let him in, steal what you can and get out through this door?"

It was a surreal situation. Ged had known this man all his life, but they confronted each other now as strangers. Questions crowded in on Ged. How, when everyone close to the king had been killed, had Mikhail escaped? And had this man, who would once have died for his father, now transferred his loyalty to Vasily?

"I am not a criminal. I was merely exploring the grounds while awaiting orders from my mistress."

Mikhail's eyes narrowed. "Your mistress? You are here with the daughter of the Count of Aras, the lady who is to be our queen?"

Ged inclined his head. He certainly hoped that would be the case, although not in the circumstances Mikhail expected. "I should go to my mistress…"

He made an attempt to pass Mikhail and was halted by the other man's hand on his arm. "Have we met?"

"This is the first time I have been to the palace." Ged tried to avoid looking directly at the other man. As he started to turn away, he remembered that Mikhail, who was in charge of all household arrangements, would be the very person to help him find Lidi. "Do you know which floor my mistress's room is on?"

"She has been allocated the blue suite," Mikhail said.

Ged walked away, conscious the whole time of Mikhail watching him. How the hell had his father's best friend escaped death on the night of the massacre? And why was he still working in the palace?

When a knock came on the door, Lidi flew up from the elegant sofa and darted toward it. Halfway there, she stopped. What if it wasn't Ged? What if Vasily had decided to pay her an unannounced visit? She shuddered with a combination of disgust and loathing.

Since the moment he had stepped through that tapestry-covered door, Vasily had been charm itself. But there had been an underlying threat in his manner. He had made it clear that their marriage would take place as soon as possible and that nothing less than total obedience on her part would be tolerated.

He had questioned her about her escape and subsequent decision to return. Lidi had explained that she had come back because she was afraid, both for herself and for her father. The men who had followed her into the mortal realm had made it clear that there was no place for her to hide. Although Vasily had regarded her with a probing stare, he appeared to accept her answer.

For the first time in her life, Lidi was truly afraid. She had looked into Vasily's eyes and seen…nothing. No compassion. No warmth. None of the humanity that was 50 percent of the shifter makeup. Something had gone very wrong in Vasily's life, depriving him of the basics of his mortal side.

"My lady?" Relief flooded through her as she recognized Ged's voice. "I came to see if you have any orders for me."

Her hands were shaking as she fumbled the door open, and as soon as Ged was inside, she turned the key in the lock before hurling herself into his arms.

"My God, Lidi." His strong arms closed around her. "You're shaking all over. What's happened?" His expression hardened. "Has he tried anything?"

She shook her head. "It's just *him*. I've never met anyone so—" She shuddered, pressing nearer to his reassuring warmth. "Just hold me, Ged. Even though you shouldn't be here. Even though this is dangerous. Just hold me."

He obliged, and after a few minutes her trembling subsided. Taking his hand, she led him to the sofa and drew him down to sit next to her. He studied her face, his expression concerned. "Tell me what has frightened you."

"It's hard to explain. Vasily hasn't said or done anything specific. I suppose it's being close to him and knowing what he's capable of…and what he's already done. And it's there, when you look at him. I've never seen evil in a person's eyes before. I don't ever want to see it again."

"What about your father?" Ged asked. "Vasily had

him placed in a cell because of your refusal to marry him. Now you are here, surely he should release your father?"

Lidi shook her head. Tears stung the back of her eyelids, and even though she attempted to blink them away, they defeated her and spilled over. "Vasily said he will not release him until after the wedding." A sob escaped her. "He even refused to let me see him."

Ged drew her close, holding her to him until the tears were over. As his hand ran gently up and down her spine, she could feel the anger stiffening his frame. "We may be able to find some information about how he is doing."

Lidi raised her head. "How can we do that? You are in disguise and I don't want to arouse Vasily's suspicions. Not any more than I need to."

"Let me think about it," Ged said. "Why did you want to know about Queen Zoya?" The abrupt change of subject left her feeling slightly disoriented.

She altered her position so she was able to fully face him. "It's quite a story."

He leaned back, watching her face. "I'm not going anywhere."

Although he didn't speak as she told him the details of her encounter with Alyona in the rose garden, she could see the pain in his eyes. When she finished, he remained silent for a few minutes before shaking his head. "So it was Zoya who rescued Andrei and me? It makes a curious kind of sense. I once overheard her telling my father that she blamed herself for the way Vasily turned out. She said that if she hadn't spoiled him as a child, he might have grown up to be a better man."

"I hope your father reassured her that Vasily was responsible for his own actions," Lidi said.

"To be honest, by that time I was surprised to hear

them talking at all." In answer to her raised brows, he elaborated further. "My father's second marriage was not a happy one. In fact…" He paused, his expression distant, as though he was looking back in time and trying to capture a memory. "I wonder?"

"Ged." Lidi placed a hand on his shoulder, giving him a slight shake. "Now is not the time to be mysterious."

He laughed. "You're right. I met someone today. A man who was very close to my father."

"Oh, good heavens. Did he recognize you?" Alarm spiked through her again, this time at the possibility that Ged might be snatched away from her.

"He appeared not to. His name is Mikhail Orlov and he was my father's steward. He was also very close to my stepmother."

"Oh." Lidi took a moment to assess what he was saying. Could a thirteen-year-old affair between the queen and her husband's best friend matter today? From the look on Ged's face, he clearly thought it might. "With everything else that is going on, tell me why this is important."

"Perhaps it isn't. There is one thing that is becoming increasingly clear." He smiled as he ran his thumb along her jawline. "Well, two things."

His hands had moved up to her shoulders and were sliding inside the fabric of her dress, warming her flesh and sending a ripple of pleasure to chase away the anxiety. She leaned closer, pressing a kiss onto his lips. "I approve of the first, but what is the second?"

"We need to speak to Zoya. Before we do, would you care to explain the reasoning behind your decision to name me after a cuddly toy?"

Chapter 20

"Zoya Petrov lives as a recluse." Vasily's tone was dismissive. "Her opinion about our marriage is unimportant."

Zoya Petrov? Not *my mother* or *the Queen Mother?* Although she was confused, Lidi decided against asking for clarification about the way he referred to his mother.

"Nevertheless, I should like to meet her." Lidi was astonished at the way her usual defiance deserted her in this man's company. Briefly, she imagined what it would be like if she actually went through with the wedding and married him. She would be giving up who she was and committing herself to a life of fear. It wasn't going to happen, so that feeling of alarm that tightened her chest every time she looked his way was unnecessary. Wasn't it?

"She is the only person who can truly tell me what

it is like to be queen," she explained in response to his frown. "And it is a courtesy to her, as your mother."

His laugh was harsh and mirthless. "I owe her no courtesy."

They were eating dinner in a small chamber on the third floor. Although they were alone, servants came in and out to serve various courses, providing Lidi with occasional interruptions from Vasily's company. It was like dancing with the devil and taking an occasional break to catch her breath.

"Tomorrow night at the Christmas-Eve ball, I will introduce you to the Callistoya nobles. The following day, we will be married," he said. "Other people's opinions are unimportant."

"A whirlwind courtship. How romantic." Lidi hid a wry smile. "What happened to the tradition that the king must marry a daughter of one of the five founding houses?"

"That ruling applies to the *Tavisha* kings. They are the ones who swore to be bound by honor and tradition. I am bound only by my own desires. You and I will be the founders of a new dynasty." He raised his glass. "The Petrov monarchy."

Realizing he was referring to their children, Lidi took a sip of wine to hide her face from him. Since her presence at Vasily's side was a pretense, there was no reason for any discussion of a future family to provoke a storm of emotions in her. But the sharp tug of loss and sadness had nothing to do with the man she was with. For a brief instant, she had a mental picture of a family of her own. Of a tall laughing father swinging a child up into his arms and of herself watching the scene with pride. And that man, of course, was Ged. It was an "if only" image, gone as soon as it appeared.

When the meal was finished, Lidi risked his displeasure by reminding Vasily again about his mother. "I would like to see her tonight, please."

He pouted, the expression transforming his features and making him look like a sulky schoolboy. "Very well. You will excuse me if I do not join you." Gesturing to a servant, he gave an order. "Escort Lady Rihanoff to Zoya Petrov's apartments."

When Vasily had gone, Lidi felt relief ooze from every pore. Being in a permanent state of tension was exhausting. Rising from her seat, she followed the servant from the room. Making their way along a corridor lined with gilt-framed portraits, they descended a wide staircase to the central hall.

"You will need a cloak, my lady." The young female servant bobbed a curtsy as she indicated a rack of fur-lined garments.

"Does the queen live in another building?" Lidi fastened one of the cloaks around her shoulders and followed the woman outside.

Nervously, the servant glanced over her shoulder. "Please, my lady. You must not refer to her as *the queen*. And, yes. Her quarters are in the east cottage."

Darkness was falling and flaming torches lined the walls as they crossed the courtyard. Passing between alternating pools of golden light and dark shadows, Lidi was aware of a figure following in their wake. She bit back a smile. Ged was an alpha-male bear shifter. Stealth was not one of his strongest attributes. Luckily, her companion did not appear to notice him.

The east cottage turned out to be a small, plain building as far away from the main palace as it was possible to get while remaining within the encircling walls. Lidi's guide knocked on the outer door and pushed it open without waiting for an answer.

"Visitor for you," she called out, her manner unceremonious to the point of insolence. When Lidi stepped cautiously inside, the woman walked away, closing the door and shutting her in.

Lidi hesitated on the threshold, aware of her uninvited status. She was in a small, dark room, in which two chairs faced a fireplace. The only light came from a meager fire and a woman sat in one of the chairs, her face turned toward the flames, apparently unaware that she was no longer alone.

As Lidi moved closer, the woman moved her head. Although her eyes roamed back and forth around the room as though searching the shadowy corners, it was clear she couldn't see. "Is someone there?"

"I'm sorry." Lidi reached out a hand, grasping the other woman's fingers to reassure her. Why had the servant thrust her into this room with a blind woman? "I had asked to be taken to see Queen Zoya."

The woman's lips curved into a smile. "Queen Zoya? It's a long time since anyone called me by that name."

"Oh." Lidi sank to her knees next to Zoya's chair. "I didn't mean to disturb you."

Zoya returned the clasp of her hand. "Who are you? And why are you here?"

"My name is Lidiya Rihanoff. My father is the Count of Aras." Lidi bit her lip. How did she proceed from here? *Your son is trying to blackmail me into marriage?* Too blunt. *No matter what your son tells you, don't rush out and order an outfit for the wedding?* She got the feeling the warning wouldn't be necessary. Zoya was not going to be a guest of honor at any event organized by Vasily.

"Ah." Zoya patted her hand. "Your poor father. Mikhail does what he can for him."

Lidi felt as though the world had just tilted very slightly off its natural axis. "I don't understand."

"It's a very long story." A man stepped from the shadows into the circle of firelight as he spoke. "If we are to tell it properly, perhaps your 'bodyguard' should join us?"

Lidi tilted her chin at the stranger. "This has nothing to do with my bodyguard…"

"It's okay, Lidi," Ged closed the door behind him and strode into the room, instantly dominating it with his size and presence. He looked at the other man in silence for a moment or two. "Thirteen years is a long time, Mikhail."

Mikhail nodded. "I wasn't sure it was you at first."

"What gave me away?" Ged asked.

Mikhail smiled. "When I told you your mistress was in the blue suite, you didn't ask where that was."

While the two men were talking, Zoya was listening with a frown. "What's going on?" she whispered to Lidi. "Who is this man?"

Overhearing her, Ged came forward and dropped on one knee beside her chair. Taking her hand, he pressed a kiss onto her fingers. "It's Gerald, Zoya. I believe I must thank you for saving my life." With tears streaming down her face, she reached out a shaking hand to touch his face and he smiled. "You have to ignore the beard and mustache. This is my disguise."

Slowly, she examined his features. "Is it really you?"

"It really is. And Andrei is also alive and well. You saved us both."

"But what is this all about?" Zoya held out her hand in Mikhail's general direction.

"I think your visitors have some questions for you." He came to stand at her side, looking down at Ged and Lidi, who were both kneeling beside the fire. "Is that right?"

Lidi decided there was no time for diplomacy. "Your son is holding my father prisoner in an attempt to force me into marriage. Although we plan to rescue him when we remove Vasily from the throne, there are a lot of things about the night of the massacre that don't make sense. This may be our only chance to find out the truth."

Mikhail placed a hand on Zoya's shoulder. "We always feared this day would come."

She nodded. "But we knew if it did that it would be because Ivan's sons were alive. That can never be considered a bad thing."

"Why did you save me and my brother but not my father?" Ged asked.

Zoya remained silent for so long Lidi thought she wasn't going to answer. When she did, her voice was quiet and filled with pain. "I knew of the murder plot, but I wasn't sure of the details. I had arranged to have you and your brother removed from the palace that night, but after I had made sure you were safe, everything happened so fast. When the killing started, I was faced with a hateful choice. Save my husband...or save the man I loved."

Ged closed his eyes. "You chose Mikhail."

"I'm sorry." Her shoulders slumped. "I was the only

person who knew what was happening. When I heard my son's men running through the corridors, I had seconds to decide which direction I should go in. If I went to the left, I could reach Ivan's room and warn him. If I went the other way, I could get to Mikhail and tell him to hide from the killers." She rocked back and forth in her chair. "Even though I knew what the consequences would be for our country, I went to the right."

"When Zoya told me what was happening, I refused to hide," Mikhail said. "I tried to get to your father's room by using the back stairs. But it was too late. He was already dead."

"And you went to Alyona's room," Lidi said to Zoya.

"How did you know that?" Zoya asked.

Lidi exchanged a glance with Ged. "It's what I would have done."

"It was horrible. Knowing your son is a murderer is bad enough. Watching him kill an innocent young woman, unable to stop him—" She broke off, clearly struggling with her emotions.

"When Vasily knew what Zoya had witnessed, he told her it would be the last thing she ever saw," Mikhail said.

"No!" Lidi gasped. "You can't mean Vasily was responsible for his mother's blindness."

"Vasily grew up watching me consult the spirits and devise spells. But, although he also wished to harness the powers of the spirit world, Vasily's motives were…" Zoya shook her head. "After everything he's done, I still find it hard to say it about my own son."

"I'll say it for you." Mikhail's expression was hard as flint. "The word you're looking for is *evil*. How else would you describe a man who killed his stepfather, in addition to a group of other people, and then cast a spell on his mother, leaving her blind?"

"So that's why you stayed here," Ged said to Mikhail. "It wasn't out of loyalty to Vasily. It was because of Zoya."

"Yes. Initially, I was also a target of Vasily's anger. But, although he's a foul villain, he isn't stupid. He quickly realized he would need someone to guide him through his royal duties. The thing Vasily enjoys most—next to murder, of course—is blackmail," Mikhail said. "His method of keeping me in line is simple. I do as he says, or he will hurt Zoya."

Ged clenched his fists. "Oh, I am going to enjoy tearing him apart."

"Not yet," Lidi warned. "You have to remain in disguise until the time is right." She looked up at Mikhail. "How is my father?"

"Those dungeons are hard on anyone, and your father is neither young nor healthy." His expression was grim. "But it is my job to oversee the conditions for the prisoners, and I have done what I can to make him comfortable." He smiled. "May I congratulate you on your own escape? I have never seen Vasily so angry. He tore the palace apart in his search for you."

"The only place he didn't look was here," Zoya said. "My son has not been near me since I witnessed him killing Alyona on the night of the massacre. After he cast the spell that left me blind, he banished me to this cottage and refused to have anything more to do with me."

When they left Zoya, Lidi was in a stormy mood, and convincing her not to attempt to rescue her father from the dungeons there and then used up all Ged's powers of persuasion.

"It's too dangerous." He saw the glint in her eye and continued quickly. "I'm not trying to relegate you to a subservient role, but you are undercover here. Tomorrow night, when the ball is over, I promise you can look Vasily in the eye and tell him how you really feel about him."

"Look at him?" They were hidden in a dark curve of the palace wall, but he could see Lidi's face in the moonlight. Her expression left him in no doubt about her feelings. "I will do a lot more than that."

An image of a ball-gown-clad Lidi in full-on combat mode flashed into his mind and he bit back a smile. "Vasily won't stand a chance." He dropped a quick kiss onto her forehead. "Seriously. Go back to your room. Lie low. We don't have much longer to wait."

"I'm just not good at being passive." The words came out through gritted teeth.

"I figured that out a long time ago. Around about the time you were slamming one of Pyotr's thugs around that hotel storeroom."

"It's certainly been interesting." He could hear the smile in her voice now.

"Hey, it's not over yet." He wanted to say more, but skulking in a darkened corner risking discovery by one of Vasily's guards was not exactly the ideal place for a declaration. One more day. An elegant ball followed by a bloody battle. After that, he would say *to hell with it* and pour out everything that was in his heart. "Get some sleep, Lidi. Tomorrow will be a long day."

He watched her as she hurried away, her dark cloak blending with the shadows. Although he had persuaded her to exercise restraint, his own mood was equally restless. There was no way he was going back to that tiny room with its rock-hard bed.

Because he knew the palace so well, it was easy for him to reach the room he sought without being challenged. Tucked away beneath the clock tower, the first thing that greeted him was the scent of disuse. Stepping back outside, he took a torch from the corridor and fixed it into one of the wall brackets inside the room. Its lights showed him a landscape of dust covers.

For a moment, he let the memories flood back. This had been his mother's music room, and although Ged had been very young when she died, he could still recall the hours he had spent in here listening to her playing and singing.

Flipping back the ancient sheets, he uncovered the instrument he was seeking. The guitar was slightly smaller than anything he'd played recently, and he had to adjust to its size, but, to his surprise, the strings had survived in their leather case. After retuning it and quietly strumming a few familiar tunes, he began to play the notes that had been haunting him recently.

Pour out everything that was in his heart? Maybe he couldn't do it in words. Not yet. Instead, he would put his feelings into music. During the time he had spent with Beast, Ged had rarely played an instrument. Because his friends were all so talented musically, he had been content to be the organizational brain behind the band. Now his fingers felt clumsy and the instrument had suffered through lack of use, but he knew which notes he wanted to play.

Everything he yearned to say to Lidi was right there at his fingertips. Fueled by emotion, he teased the strings into a haunting melody. It was as if the echo of the music reached inside him, finding the very point where his soul connected with Lidi's, caressing and soothing him. His throat tightened, and, even though he played quietly, he poured himself into the chords.

He was unaware of how long he remained lost in his own world. It was only the click of the door that finally drew him out. When he looked up, Lidi was framed in a circle of golden candlelight. Although she was smiling, tears glinted in the depths of her eyes.

Ged placed the guitar aside. "How did you know I was here?"

"I couldn't sleep, and from my bedroom window I saw a light in this room below the clock tower. For some reason, I was drawn to it. When I got close, I heard the music and I just knew it must be you." She put the candleholder on a window ledge and went to him. "It was beautiful. What was it?"

"It was your song, Lidi."

He gathered her into his arms and kissed her, tasting his future on her lips. She was everything he wanted and more. Hope, happiness, and forever. They were right here in his arms. And the thing he had thought he would never have…

"I love you." Her voice was husky as she smiled up at him.

When he lowered his mouth to hers again, it was the sweetest kiss, the most perfect moment, he had ever known.

"I love you too, Lidi."

Lidi tiptoed back toward her bedroom, wrapped in a bubble of pleasure.

Ged loves me!

There was still a long way to go before she could say they had reached their happy ending, but hearing those words spoken aloud by her mate had changed everything. Chaos might be raging all around them, but the world felt right. Their bond had given her so much joy. Now she also had hope. Anything that didn't end in perfect happiness just wouldn't be fair.

Shielding the flame of her candle against drafts, she slid noiselessly along the corridor that led to her room. When she left earlier, she had locked the door behind her and now, she reached into the pocket of her cloak for the key. Grimacing slightly as it grated in the lock, she turned it. Once she was inside, she secured the door once again.

"Very wise." The drawling voice startled her so much she almost dropped the candle. "We don't want to be interrupted, do we?"

It was as if a pause button had been pressed on that moment. Shock caused the strangest sensation of the moment splintering and her senses becoming heightened. She was frozen, unable to move, her eyes fixed on the wooden boards of the door.

Even though Vasily didn't move from the bed, she imagined she felt his breath on the back of her neck and ducked her head to avoid his touch. Nothing in her life had ever frightened her, so why was she letting this man strike terror into her heart?

Turning slowly, she faced the bed, where he lounged casually against the pillows. Straightening her shoulders, she called up every ounce of her courage. "I didn't realize I had forfeited my privacy when I agreed to marry you."

He laughed, the sound a masterclass in menace. Pinpricks of fear traveled up her spine, making the hairs on the back of her neck stand on end.

"You forfeited *everything* the day you refused me. Escaping from your cell was a minor distraction, nothing more. All you did was exchange those prison walls for these prison walls." He waved a hand, indicating the luxurious room. "The day I chose you to be my wife, you owed me your next breath. You don't seriously still believe I chose you because I wanted a Petrov-Rihanoff union, do you?"

"Why else would you want to marry me? Today was the first time we've met." *Look into your heart...*

"Because you are his." Vasily's smile confirmed everything she already knew. "When the spirits confirmed it, I knew I had found a way to destroy him at last."

Doing her best to hide the shaking of her hands, Lidi placed her candleholder on the dressing table. "I'd like to get some sleep. It's late..."

"So it is. Too late to be wandering the corridors of a palace you don't know." Vasily's eyes narrowed as he studied her face. "Care to explain?"

"I couldn't sleep—"

"Don't lie!" He sprang up from the bed, his voice booming in her ears as he grabbed her upper arms.

Anger spiked, driving away her fear, and she welcomed it. "Take your hands off me." Pushing with both palms hard against his chest, she shoved him away. "I don't owe you answers. I'm here because you have my father in a prison cell, not through choice."

"No. *He* is your choice, isn't he? You couldn't even stay away from him long enough to keep up the pretense." His lips twisted into a parody of a smile. "That's how it always was. Gerald was everyone's first choice."

"Don't hurt him…" The words were out before she could stop them.

He laughed, his face up close to hers. "I won't need to, Lidiya. You are going to do it for me."

She shook her head. "Never."

Reaching past her, he raised his hand, knocking three times on the door. As Lidi tried to squirm away from him, she heard a key turn in the lock, and two men entered. Fighting in earnest now, she kicked out at Vasily and attempted to run from the room.

"Tie her to the bed." His voice was calm, all trace of anger gone now. "And bring me what I need for the amnesia hex."

"No, please." Lidi struggled as the two men carried her easily between them. "Vasily, you don't need to cast a spell on me. I'll do whatever you ask—"

Her pleas were cut short when Vasily tied a scarf around her mouth. At the same time, his servants were securing her hands and feet to the bedposts. Panic was like a weight settling on her chest, making the air too thick to breathe. She forced herself to concentrate. An amnesia hex. That meant he was going to make her forget. Forget what? Ged? Never. As long as she had breath in her body and blood in her veins, she would remember the man she loved.

Vasily was lighting candles. Black and foul-smelling, they gave off a thick, choking smoke. Leaning over her, he held out a piece of twine and slowly tied a knot in its length.

"With the first knot, your fate is sealed." His eyes glittered like polished coal as he started to chant. "The memories begin to fade."

Lidi twisted her head from side to side. *No. Ged.* She

must keep him in her mind. She could see his face, hear his voice. She remembered dancing with him in Genoa, laughing when she got the steps wrong. There was no spell strong enough to make her forget him.

"With the second knot the darkness descends on your mind." Vasily held the twine closer to her face as he made another twist.

Dancing. She was dancing and laughing. And there was something—*someone*—she must never forget. It was important, but so difficult because of the blackness that was creeping into her mind pushing out everything else.

"The third knot is the one that binds." Vasily's smile was both tender and triumphant. "Sews the discord and makes you mine." He took the twine and tied it around her ankle. "While you wear this, your memory will belong to me. Only me, Lidiya, my bride to be."

Lidi frowned. Had she been trying to recall something? Surely if it had been important, she would be able to remember it? Her head hurt, and every time she tried to think, dark shadows filled her mind.

Gently, Vasily removed the scarf from her mouth and untied her hands and feet. "All done. You should sleep now."

She nodded. He was right. After all, the day after tomorrow was their wedding day.

Chapter 21

Ged only caught glimpses of Lidi the following day. Although he was slightly disappointed not to be able to talk to her, in her role as the king's fiancée, she was busy with preparations for the Christmas-Eve ball. At the same time, he was planning Vasily's downfall. It was hardly surprising their paths didn't cross too closely. When he did see her, she appeared to be playing her part well and, although he was frustrated that he couldn't snatch a private moment with her, he had several distractions of his own.

Partway through the afternoon, he tracked down Mikhail and presented him with two requests. "Can you open the gate in the wall of the servant's courtyard?"

Mikhail nodded. "Consider it done."

"And…uh, maybe get me something to wear for the Christmas-Eve ball?"

Mikhail started to laugh. "That one is not so easy. Even in Callistoya, you're not exactly the smallest guy around." He regarded Ged thoughtfully. "Would you consider wearing something that used to belong to your father?"

"It might feel a bit weird, but if that's all you've got…"

A few hours later, he was standing in front of a full-length mirror in Mikhail's room, studying his reflection. While it didn't feel strange to be wearing one of his father's well-cut, formal suits, it did strike an emotional chord. The garments fitted perfectly and his own resemblance to his father was stronger than ever. It was like looking back in time.

"If he could be here now—" Mikhail's voice had a rough edge to it.

"If he was, none of this would be necessary," Ged said. They spared a few moments of silence to remember the man they had both loved before Ged switched back to a businesslike tone. "Have my friends arrived?"

"Yes. I let them in through the door in the servants' courtyard. They are in Zoya's house. Even if Vasily was suspicious, that is the last place he would look." Mikhail gave him a sidelong glance. "You have acquired some unusual allies during your absence."

Ged laughed. "That's a diplomatic way of putting it. I suppose a tiger, two dragons, two wolves, a panther and a snow leopard do appear out of place here in Callistoya."

They went their separate ways, Mikhail heading down to the ballroom to oversee final preparations for the party while Ged made his way to the east cottage. The light was fading, but there were still a number of people around. Would anyone notice Lady Rihanoff's bodyguard as he sneaked into Queen Zoya's home? It seemed unlikely. Everyone appeared engrossed in their duties, all of which were directed toward the forthcoming celebration.

With a final glance around, he ducked his head and stepped into the small cottage. The scene that greeted him was amusing and heartwarming at the same time. Mikhail had clearly brought his organizational skills to bear and arranged some extra chairs around the edges of the room. The members of Beast, together with Hollie and Sarange, were seated on them. There was barely a spare inch of space.

"We're taking it in turns to breathe." Khan's drawling tones greeted him. "There's not enough room for us all to do it at once."

"Take no notice." Sarange rose gracefully to her feet and hugged Ged. "He's been such a tiger since he found out he can't get a cell-phone signal here." She regarded him with her head to one side. "No. I'm never going to get used to that new look."

Ged touched his fake beard. "I'm so accustomed to it, I've almost forgotten about it."

A flurry of greetings followed, and Ged's heart expanded as they slipped back into the familiar routine of jokes and fake insults.

After a few minutes, he turned to Zoya, who was listening with a slight smile on her lips. "Is this okay? We're not disturbing you with all these people and this noise?"

"I like it." Her voice was firm. "And I want to help."

"You know what will happen tonight?" Ged spoke quietly.

"Mikhail has told me. I know my son must die." There was a slight quiver in her voice. "I have accepted that is the only thing that will bring an end to his evil."

Ged stooped to kiss her cheek. "You are a very brave woman, Zoya."

She shook her head. "I made him what he is. If just once during his childhood I had said 'no,' perhaps we wouldn't be facing this problem today. I am the person who taught Vasily the power of magic. And I am the woman who chose her lover over her husband... your father."

"Many people are spoiled by their parents as children. And here in Callistoya, magic spells are not uncommon. Yet in both cases, those people rarely become murderers and dictators."

Her smile was sad. "Let me take my share of blame, Gerald. I have earned it."

"What's the plan?" Torque's voice broke in on their quiet conversation. "You want things to get fiery?"

"At midnight," Ged said. "Wait here until then. When the clock strikes twelve, come into the ballroom. That's when the action will start."

Hollie clasped her hands beneath her chin. "It's like Cinderella with fangs, fur and scales."

"Where is Lidi?" Diablo asked.

"Right now, she's playing her part as the submissive bride to be. I saw her earlier and she was doing a great job in the role, barely even noticing me. Although Vasily *was* nearby the whole time."

Khan grinned. "I can't imagine Lidi is very good at acting."

Ged laughed. "Luckily, she doesn't have to do it for

much longer. For now, she is Vasily's fiancée. In a few hours, she can drop the pretense and be one of us again."

Ged waited until the ballroom was filled with guests before he slipped quietly inside and joined the crowd. The sight of the beautifully decorated room brought back memories of similar parties when his father had been alive. He took a moment to ride the wave of pain that ricocheted through him.

So many of the faces were familiar to him. There were nobles from every corner of the kingdom, friends and acquaintances of his father, gathered together in one place. Glad of his disguise, Ged took up a position in one corner of the room. Until midnight arrived, there was only one person he was interested in.

Evergreen garlands had been hung around the room, entwined with holly berries and heavy boughs of fragrant pine. At one end of the room, a giant tree reached the ceiling, its branches twinkling with tiny white lights. At the opposite end, the royal thrones were decked with sprigs of mistletoe.

Vasily lounged comfortably in the king's throne and anger rose in Ged's gullet at the sight of him in the chair his father had once occupied. *The Usurper.* The nickname had stuck, but Vasily hadn't simply seized a crown that wasn't his. He was a killer with the blood of dozens of innocent people on his hands.

And you will pay that blood back. Every drop.

Ged's gaze moved on, his heart giving a leap of pure joy as his eyes feasted on Lidi. She was sitting very still and upright on the queen's throne. The dress she wore had a scooped neckline and a bodice of intricate beaded lace. Its muted, taupe shade emphasized her dramatic coloring, and her hair was loosely arranged in long curls that hung over one shoulder. Her beauty took his breath away.

As Ged watched, Vasily turned to Lidi. He took her hand and spoke a few words to her. She inclined her head, a soft smile touching her lips. There was something about the action that chilled Ged, but he couldn't understand why. She reminded him of a doll. it was as if she was lovely to look at and completely empty, with all her usual vivacity gone. He shook the thought aside. *She is playing a part, for goodness sake!* Perhaps she was overdoing it a little, but that was Lidi. She never did anything by halves.

When midnight struck, she would drop the pretense and run to his side. Her desire to sharpen her claws on Vasily's face would finally be fulfilled. Even as he reassured himself with the thought, he was left with a sense of unease.

The catering was in stark contrast to the celebrity parties he was used to attending in the mortal realm. No elegant canapés and dainty dishes here. The menu consisted of fish, meat, and salad, plenty of it and piled high. Ged watched as Vasily led Lidi through to the banqueting hall. His stepbrother always had a knack of looking smug. As Vasily smiled into Lidi's eyes, his self-importance was unbearable. For the first time in his life, Ged had no appetite.

The minutes dragged slowly by. All around him, the other guests appeared to be enjoying themselves. He overheard a conversation between two high-ranking nobles speculating on the absence of the Earl of Vitchenko and managed to hide his satisfaction. Ged knew exactly where Vitchenko was. With Eduard Tavisha, the earl would be assembling his troops on the plain to the south of the palace. The resistance forces were in position, just waiting to attack Vasily's army.

When Vasily led an elderly duchess onto the dance floor, Ged seized his opportunity. Unable to resist the chance to be near her, he moved to where Lidi was standing. Reasoning that no one would be surprised to see her bodyguard talking to her, he leaned in close.

"Not long to wait now." His lips almost brushed the shell of her ear and he took a moment to breathe in her delicious scent.

She turned her head to look at him, a blank look in the golden depths of her eyes. "Pardon?"

He had the strangest feeling that he had stepped into an alternate world without noticing. *Taking the act a little too far, Lidi.* "It's almost midnight. When the clock strikes, so do we."

She gave him a tight, formal smile. He knew that expression. He'd used it himself time after time when he wanted to dismiss unwanted strangers, people who thought he needed their advice on how to manage the band.

"Lidi, what is it?" He spoke softly, unable to keep the urgency out of his tone.

"My name is Lidiya and I think you've mistaken me for someone else. Now, if you'll excuse me, I see the king wants me."

Ged watched her walk away, confusion and hurt competing to be the sharpest knife tearing into his gut. Because…what the hell was going on? As Lidi reached Vasily's side, his stepbrother looked directly at Ged for the first time. The blaze of triumph in his eyes almost knocked Ged off his feet.

He knows who I am.

As Vasily placed a hand under Lidi's arm and guided her toward the royal thrones, Ged felt the fragments of his heart fall to the floor. Somehow, Vasily had taken away the Lidi Ged knew and ruined the love they shared.

He bowed his head, his mind weighed down with the enormity of what had happened. He needed time to process this, to deal with the storm of grief and rage that was powering through him, threatening to destroy him. Inside his head, there was a laughing monster shrieking a single message.

He has won.

An awful hollowness washed over him, replacing the joy he had felt only hours earlier when Lidi had said she loved him. On feet that felt like lead, he turned away. Unthinking, unseeing, he needed to get out of the crowded room, to be alone with the pain that was threatening to crush him. How was he supposed to fight for his kingdom when the only thing that had made his life worth living had been torn from him?

As he reached the door, his footsteps halted at the sound of Vasily's voice. "My friends, I would like you to raise your glasses in a toast to Lady Lidiya Rihanoff, who has agreed to become my wife."

At the same instant, the clock began to strike, and Beast burst into the room.

Even though his heart felt like a lead weight inside his chest, Ged knew he wouldn't get another chance at this. Whatever had happened to Lidi, surely they could deal with it once Vasily was vanquished? Right now, the plan to take down his stepbrother had to proceed.

For all the lives that had been lost. For his father, for Alyona, for Callistoya…

Tearing off his wig, beard and mustache, he strode forward until he was standing beside Vasily's throne. Around him, he could hear the gasps and knew his likeness to his father was the cause. Slowly, he turned to face the assembled guests.

"Merry Christmas, ladies and gentlemen. In case you haven't already recognized me, I am indeed Gerald Tavisha, your rightful king. Thirteen years ago, many of you will recall a similar occasion to this. It was one that ended in tragedy. My own engagement party to Lady Alyona Ivanov was the scene of the most hateful massacres in Callistoyan history."

"Guards…" Vasily half rose from his seat, but Ged placed a hand on his shoulder, forcing him back down. He noticed that Lidi appeared confused, as though she had never heard this story before.

You took away her memory!

"This man, whom the great King Ivan raised as his own son, organized that massacre. He wielded the knife that killed your king…my beloved father." There were shouts of anger and dismay. Many had suspected the truth, but hearing it in this elegant setting confirmed their fears. For Ged, it was cathartic to finally say the words out loud to the people who mattered. "His were the hands that choked the life from Alyona Ivanov as he tried to get her to reveal my whereabouts before he stabbed her."

He could see Vasily was shaken by that information. The only person who knew what had transpired between them before her death was Alyona herself. Deeply superstitious, Vasily would fear the spirits as much as he dreaded physical violence.

Vasily got to his feet. "This theater is all very well. But do you believe the word of a fugitive? If this is all true, ask him why he stayed away for thirteen years."

"You know the answer to that," Ged snarled. "You cast a spell that prevented me from returning. Enough talking." He turned back to the crowd. "This murdering piece of garbage is about to die. So are the thugs who have protected him for the last thirteen years. If you leave this room now, you won't be hurt. If you stay, you must decide where your loyalties lie. Tavisha or Petrov. Choose wisely."

As soon as he finished speaking, the room erupted into action. Some people ran for the door. Others began to shift and range themselves alongside Ged or Vasily. Just when he thought the ache in his heart couldn't get any worse, he saw Lidi rise from her seat and move to his stepbrother's side.

So this is where we stand, my love and I. On opposite sides of the enemy lines.

He knew his Lidi too well. Once she declared her allegiance, she would fight to the death.

Unless I can stop her.

The thought lasted half a second, then Lidi shifted and launched herself at him. Ged managed to shift just before she slammed full force into him with her claws slashing and teeth snapping. He had seen Lidi fight. Although he was bigger and stronger, he knew better than to underestimate her. How the hell was he going to get them both out of this alive?

On the periphery of his vision, he was aware of the confusion caused by the appearance of big cats, werewolves and dragons in the middle of the bear-shifter fight. Disorder would help the situation. And Beast were a formidable fighting force. Never underestimate the power of two dragons in a ballroom. Confident that he could leave his friends for the time being, Ged turned his attention back to Lidi just as she dealt him a blow to his kidneys that almost toppled him over backward.

As he struggled to remain upright, she came at him again. Crashing into him with brutal force, she bared her teeth, aiming for his throat. Ged managed to dodge out of her way and she growled in fury. As he straightened, she struck him across the face with her claws and he felt warm blood gush from his nose.

He had to stop this. Although he couldn't fight back, at this rate, the woman he loved was going to kill him. She was totally focused on her target—him—and he could feel anger and determination coming off her in waves.

When she lunged at him again, he wrapped his front paws around her, drawing her into a classic bear hug. As she struggled wildly, he backed her up against the wall. Usually, when he was in bear form, he retained an element of his human senses while his animal instincts took over. This time, his mortal self remained in complete control. With a pang of regret, he tipped Lidi back, reining in his bear strength so that her head hit the brickwork with just the right amount of force.

Knock her out. Don't crush her skull.

As he lowered her carefully to the floor, Ged changed back into human form. Through the chaos around him, he caught sight of Mikhail and signaled to him to shift. When the steward reached his side, Ged had to shout to be heard.

"It's Lidi." He indicated the unconscious bear at his feet. "Vasily has her under some sort of spell. When she regains consciousness, she will fight you. Take her to Zoya's house and tie her up." It hurt his heart almost more than he could stand to say those words. "Then stay with her until I get back."

"What will you do now?" Mikhail asked.

"Me? I'm going to kill Vasily."

Once he was sure Lidi had been safely removed from the fight, Ged scanned the room for his stepbrother. All around him, the air was filled with the sights and sounds of shifters fighting. Teeth, claws and scales glinted, fur flew, and blood arced. Screams, growls and grunts punctuated the tearing, slashing and occasional bursts of fire.

It was impossible to tell which side was winning, although Ged was hopeful that the presence of two dragons would swing the outcome in his favor. No matter which direction he looked, he couldn't see Vasily. It wasn't an entirely unexpected outcome. There was a reason why Vasily surrounded himself with thugs who did his bullying for him. The Usurper was a coward.

As he continued to scan the room, he caught a glimpse of a figure sidling toward the door. In bear form, as in human, Vasily was slightly smaller and darker than most Callistoyan bears. For that reason, as well as the fact that he wasn't fighting, he was unmistakable.

Ged shifted back into bear form and took off at a sprint toward his stepbrother, dodging fighting and fallen shifters as he ran. When Vasily saw him coming, he stopped dead in his tracks and rose on all fours, pressing his back tight against the wall. Ged didn't slow his pace. Instead, he headed straight for him, teeth bared as he aimed for his stepbrother's throat.

He had a second to exult in the fear in Vasily's eyes before he crashed into him with a roar like thunder. Vasily was thrown off balance and they rolled around on the floor, with Ged's teeth snapping while Vasily held him off with his paws.

Ged moved to one side, sinking his teeth into Vasily's shoulder. His stepbrother's yelp was loud enough to be heard above the fire and fury raging around them. Fighting back in desperation now, he rolled over, pinning Ged down. The move was bold, but the triumph was short-lived. A growl rippled deep in Ged's chest, and using his superior strength, he yanked the lighter bear off him. Throwing Vasily to one side, he sprang to his feet and drew himself up to his full height.

Without giving Vasily time to catch his breath, Ged slammed him into the wall, clamping his jaws onto the other bear's front leg, close to the shoulder. Shaking his head from side to side, he tore off a chunk of flesh with his teeth. Blood sprayed in an arc, coating them both, and Vasily howled in agony.

Using his uninjured front paw, Vasily swiped Ged's face. His claws didn't sink in, but Ged's nose had already been injured by Lidi and he grunted. The pain was enough to send a fresh charge of adrenaline powering through his veins, and he charged Vasily, sending him flying through the air and crashing to the floor.

Vasily landed on his back, the worst possible position for a bear in a fight, and Ged didn't give him time to get up. He threw himself on top of his stepbrother, pinning him down and ripping into his chest with his claws.

Vasily's squeals reminded him of an angry pig, and Ged toyed with the idea of making him suffer. Torturing him was appealing. For those who had died in the massacre. For the damage done to Callistoya. For himself and Andrei. And now, for Lidi…the thought of her tied up in Zoya's cottage saddened and enraged him all over again.

Finish this.

So he did. With one final deep gouge with his talons into Vasily's chest, he tore deep through bone and muscle right into his stepbrother's black heart. Blood gushed from the wound, pooling on the floor around them. With a final shudder, Vasily stiffened, then stilled.

Killing never felt good, but Ged had wondered what his emotions would be if this moment ever came. Would he experience triumph? A release of the pent-up hurt and anger that had held him in their grip for so long? Would there be a sense of relief that it was finally all over? Instead he was gripped by a crushing emptiness. Vasily was gone, but he had left a legacy of pain and destruction. Reversing that was now Ged's responsibility.

Getting to his feet, Ged looked around. At first glance it appeared his supporters had staged a complete victory with very few casualties. While it was a positive outcome, there was no opportunity to celebrate. He needed to join the resistance troops on the southern plain.

Chapter 22

In his bear form, Ged could outrun the fastest human on earth and then keep going. But why waste time and energy when he had the perfect method of transport right here in the palace grounds?

As he shifted back into human form and exited the building, Torque was already waiting for him. Ged's dragon friend was a magnificent creature, with wings that spanned the courtyard. When he lifted them, they billowed and created an updraft that rivaled the wildest Callistoyan winter gale. His claws were like giant scimitars, scraping over the cobbles as he moved. Sleek, iridescent scales covered his muscular body, pulsing in time with his dragon breath, and wisps of smoke curled from his nostrils.

With his neck stretched out and wings held high, Torque crouched low, waiting for Ged. Catching hold of a wing, Ged levered himself onto the dragon's back and settled into position between Torque's powerful neck and the front of his wings.

Once Ged was securely in position, Torque spread his wings and tensed his muscles. His mighty feet pounded across the ground as he broke into a run before launching into flight. Beneath them, the palace dropped away, and in minutes they were soaring over the mountain peaks before swooping low over valleys and plains.

Another dragon joined them. Hollie, who was smaller and sleeker than Torque, had scales the color of aquamarine and eyes that glinted like emeralds. When she soared high, her camouflage caused her scales to match the silver of the moonlit clouds. Dropping lower, she blended into the dark surface of the mountain lakes.

When they reached the south plain, the full moon gave Ged a clear view of the battle taking place below him. From his vantage point, he could see that his uncle's troops had taken Vasily's army by surprise. Wave upon wave of resistance bear shifters surged into the makeshift living quarters on the plain in an organized attack, scattering their startled opponents, most of them still in human form, before them.

Vasily's commanders took control, organizing their forces and staging a counterattack. Two relentless groups of werebears plowed into each other in a bloody head-on battle. As Torque swept low, Ged could see his uncle and the Earl of Vitchenko. They had positioned themselves on opposite sides of the battlefield and were coordinating the action.

The resistance forces were unyielding. Having waited this long for their opportunity, they were clearly determined to see it through. Each time Vasily's men appeared to gain the upper hand, Eduard or Vitchenko triggered a fresh assault. They even had a team at work dragging the injured free of the danger zone.

As Torque tilted his wings in preparation for landing, Ged caught a glimpse of Khan, Diablo, Dev, Finglas and Sarange joining the fray. Three big cats and two werewolves would add a new dimension to the resistance team. The addition of two dragons would increase their fire power even further.

As soon as Torque's giant claws hit the ground, Ged was clambering from his back. He shifted as he ran, his sensitive ears ringing with the sounds of battle. Screeching, growling, yelping and grunting. The crash of giant bodies slamming together and the clashing of razor sharp teeth and lethal claws. And now the roar of dragon fire was added to the mix. The coppery scent of blood was so strong he could taste it.

The ground shook as opposing forces streamed past him. Ged's aim was to reach Eduard, but his progress was slowed by the skirmishes going on around him. Driven onward by sheer determination, he barged, slashed and bit his way past any of Vasily's men who blocked his way.

Torque and Hollie cleared a path ahead of him. Wings flapped. Roars echoed off the mountain side. Boulders vibrated, and cinders rained down on the grass around him. Incinerated bear-shifter bodies lined his route.

Eduard grunted a greeting as Ged approached. From this viewpoint, the whole battlefield was lit by the full moon. Vasily's men were losing badly. The bodies of their dead and dying lay trampled in the mud as the battle continued around them. Even so, they continued to fight bravely. They were bears. Brave, loyal and intelligent. It wasn't their fault they had chosen to follow a villain.

With his empathy aroused, Ged signaled to Eduard and the two men shifted into human form.

"Speak to their leaders. Tell them Vasily is dead and they are fighting for a lost cause," Ged said. "If they surrender now, we will give them amnesty."

Eduard placed a hand on his shoulder. "Your father would be proud of you."

Ged managed a grim smile. "There are enough bodies to dispose of, including Vasily's. Once we call a truce here, there is a huge task to be undertaken. We cannot leave our fellow bear shifters in an undead state. Their bodies may have been destroyed, but only silver or decapitation can kill their souls. Our final responsibility is to lay them to rest."

"Yes, Your Majesty."

Your Majesty. Ged was naked, bloodstained and sweaty, and his nose felt like it had swelled to twice its normal size. He had never felt less majestic, but his physical state wasn't the only reason why he felt so distant from his royal status.

His duty was here on this battlefield, but his heart was in Zoya's cottage. After thirteen years of waiting, he had finally regained his crown. Was it wrong to wish he could put his royal duties on hold for a few more hours while he focused on the important business of restoring Lidi's memory?

Several hours passed before Ged was finally able to leave the battlefield. Weary and dirty, he headed for the palace. When he got there, the first person he saw was Khan. He eyed his tiger friend thoughtfully. "Give me your clothes."

Khan snorted with laughter. "It may have escaped your attention, but sometimes size *does* matter."

"Shut up and undress. I have to go to Lidi."

Khan must have heard the desperation in his voice, because he removed his T-shirt and sweatpants without further comment. Ged struggled into them. Both items were stretched impossibly tightly over his muscles, and the pants only reached to midcalf, but at least he was covered up. He gripped Khan's hand briefly before leaving the building.

As he headed for Zoya's cottage, his anxiety levels were off the scale. What would he find when he arrived? Would Lidi still want to kill him? Was it possible her memory had returned? What the hell had Vasily done to her to bring about such a change?

When he entered the cottage, the silence hit him. A quick glance around showed him Lidi was in human form. She wasn't tied up or restrained in any way. Instead, she was wrapped in a blanket and sitting quietly on the opposite side of the fire to Zoya.

"Lidi—" He started toward her, relief flooding through him.

Mikhail stepped forward, placing a hand on his arm. "Take care. She is calm now, but she had to be restrained for a few hours after she regained consciousness. She still doesn't remember anything except that she is supposed to be marrying Vasily."

"She'll remember me," Ged said. The words were more for himself than for anyone else. "She has to."

He knelt at Lidi's side. As he reached for her hand, she jerked it away. Her eyes raked his face, but all he saw in their depths was suspicion. "You are the one who knocked me out."

"Lidi, it's me. It's Ged."

"My name is Lidiya." She stared around the cottage in confusion. "Where is Vasily? Today is our wedding day."

Ged made another attempt to take her hand. "Lidi, you don't love Vasily. You love me."

She shrank back in her chair. "I don't know you."

Ged turned his head toward Zoya. "Is she under a spell?"

"I think so." Her voice was sad. "But it is not one I know, and I suspect it can only be undone by the person who cast it."

"But Vasily is dead. How does that work? Are you telling me she will never remember me?" He ran a hand through his hair. "I'm sorry. I shouldn't speak roughly to you. I know it's not your fault."

"I wish I could help." Zoya's shoulders slumped in defeat and Ged's hopes plummeted at the same time.

He made another attempt to get through to Lidi. "Please try to remember. I love you…"

She covered her face with her hands. "Leave me alone."

Wearily, he got to his feet. He had regained his kingdom. Would anyone believe him if he said he would give it away in exchange for Lidi?

"I will never stop trying to find a way to get you back."

It felt like an empty promise, but he meant it. As he moved to the door, it opened and a familiar bark attracted his attention. Bruno bounded into the room slightly ahead of Andrei and Sasha.

"When I saw the palace, some of my memories started to return." Andrei's happiness was in direct contrast to Ged's despair. "What have we missed?"

Although Ged clutched his brother's hand in greeting, he pressed a finger to his lips and indicated Lidi, who was now staring into the fire. "I'll tell you all about it later."

The tone of his voice must have been enough to deter Andrei and Sasha from asking questions. But it was not enough to stop Bruno, who, after a quick greeting to Ged, bounded over to Lidi and jumped onto her knee. As he attempted to lick her face, she recoiled in horror.

"Get it away from me."

Ged lifted Bruno down and placed him on the floor, but the dog refused to be discouraged. Burrowing under the blanket that enveloped Lidi, he began to tug at something on her leg. No matter how much she pulled her foot away, he kept returning, determinedly biting at the item that was tied around her ankle.

"I'm sorry." Ged knelt on the floor and tried to grab the squirming dog. "He really wants to get rid of this piece of twine."

"Twine?" Zoya asked, her voice becoming intent. "Lidi, why do you have a piece of twine tied around your ankle?"

"My name is Lidiya and I don't know. Will someone get this creature off me?" Lidi drew her legs up onto the chair and tucked them under her.

"Gerald, get rid of that twine." Zoya spoke urgently. "It could be the source of the spell."

Without hesitation, Ged grabbed Lidi's ankle. It was chafed and red. It looked like she had been wearing the twine when she shifted and it had cut into her flesh.

Was it possible Zoya was right and Vasily had tied the knotted length around her ankle before the Christmas-Eve ball? If that was the case, maybe the thread *was* the source of the magic. He was almost afraid to hope.

Ignoring Lidi's protests, Ged snapped the twine and threw it into the fire. Resisting the urge to grab her and kiss her until she remembered him, he watched Lidi's face. There was no change in the blank, lost look she wore. Sinking back into her seat, she resumed her contemplation of the fire.

"I guess the twine wasn't the source after all," he said to Zoya. He scooped up Bruno. "Nice try, mutt."

The dog licked his hand as though offering him a sympathetic gesture and they headed toward the door.

"Wait." Although Lidi's voice was soft and hesitant, there was something in her tone that caused a tiny flare to ignite deep within Ged. He turned to face her, his heart pounding. Bright tears shone in her eyes and a tiny smile trembled on her lips. "What happened to the 'no licking rule'?"

"Your father is fine, but a little weak," Ged said as he carried Lidi past the line of nobles who were trying to attract his attention. "A doctor has seen him, and he's been given a sedative. Although he's sleeping now, I've sent a message to the nurse who's with him to say you'll visit him later."

Her emotions were still raw and she couldn't decide whether to laugh or cry. After everything they'd been through, she could hardly believe it was true. Vasily was dead. Her father was safe. The horrible darkness that had invaded her mind was gone. She was in Ged's arms.

There was just one problem…she buried her face in

his neck in an attempt to block out the curious stares. "I think all these people want to speak to you."

"They will have to get used to the idea that one person will always come first with me." The emotion in his voice tipped her over into tears. "I don't care what their title is or why they want to see me. They will all have to wait in line before you, Lidi."

As he reached the grand staircase, the Baron Dmitriev barred his way. "Your Majesty, while the five founding families are gathered here, we should talk about your wedding." His expression registered a rigid determination to ignore the fact that there was a young woman wrapped only in a blanket in the king's arms.

"A good idea, Dmitriev," Ged said. "Mikhail?" The steward came forward and bowed low. "Start the preparations. Lady Rihanoff and I will be married this evening."

"Very good, sire." Mikhail bowed low before walking away.

Dmitriev began to bluster. "This is unacceptable. Your Majesty knows the agreement that was made between the five founding families—"

"Rip it up," Ged said.

"Pardon?" Dmitriev looked like he might cry.

"You heard me. Rip up that agreement or find yourself a new king. The only reason for me not to marry Lady Rihanoff will be if she says *no*." He smiled down at Lidi. "Please don't say *no*."

"Is this a proposal?" She smiled through her tears.

"I suppose it is." He laughed. "I had planned something more romantic…and a lot less public."

Carefully, he set her on her feet. Then he went down on one knee and took her hand in his. The people around them were a blur as, through her tears, Lidi focused on his face.

"Lidi, from the moment we met, I was yours. I'd heard about other people finding true love with their mate, but I never knew what it meant until it happened to me. Every time I look at you, I feel the union of our hearts beating as one. I want to seal our eternal bond with a marriage blessing." He raised her hand to his lips. "Will you be my wife?"

Her first attempt at a response came out as a strangled sob. Taking a deep breath, she tried again. "No one could ever understand what was wrong with my heart. It didn't work the way it was supposed to. I didn't know how to be a bear. I couldn't be enigmatic. That's because until I met you, my heart was a rose in bud. Then you came along, Ged, and it was like the sun shining. My petals unfurled and I could release all the love I had inside."

He smiled up at her. "Very poetic, my beautiful bear. Is it a yes?"

She tugged at his shoulder. "It's a yes. Now kiss me."

He did. Passionately. There might have been some cheering from the people around them, but she couldn't be sure. After a few minutes, Ged raised his head. "Aw, hell. Andrei, are you there?"

"Yes."

"Find Mikhail. Tell him we need roses at the wedding. Dozens of the damn things." He swept Lidi back up into his arms. "And now, ladies and gentlemen, if you'll excuse us, my fiancée and I need to be alone."

Lidi wasn't sure how she managed to run up the wide staircase so fast with her in his arms. Reaching his room, he slammed the door closed and set her on her feet, the smile in his eyes taking her breath away.

"Don't we have a wedding to prepare for?" she teased.

"We have hours before we have to get ready." He reached out a hand to draw her close and liquid heat burned through her veins. Her knees weakened with desire and she leaned into him. Ged grimaced as he plucked at the front of the ridiculously tight T-shirt he wore. "Although I could use a shower."

"Me too." She touched his nose gently with one fingertip. "What happened here?"

He smiled, catching hold of her hand and pressing a kiss onto the inside of her wrist. "A bad-tempered bear took a swipe at me."

She shook her head. "We need to talk about my future role. Maybe you need me as *your* bodyguard."

"A queen who is a soldier? It's an interesting idea."

Ged shed his clothes on the way to the bathroom and Lidi discarded her borrowed blanket. Stepping under warm jets of water was both soothing and revitalizing, and Lidi felt some of the horrors of the day recede as Ged soaped her body and washed her hair. By the time they were both clean, her arousal levels were off the scale.

Ged's nostrils flared as he stroked his thumb along her jawline, tracing the droplets of water. "Ah, Lidi. When I thought I'd lost you—"

She pressed her fingers to his lips. "The only thing that could drive you from my mind was powerful magic, but it's been vanquished. Never again."

Holding her captive with his heated gaze, he drew her fingers into his mouth, flicking his tongue over them and sucking. When he released them, it was to capture her lips with his own as he pushed her up against the tiled wall, holding her in place with the hot, muscled strength of his body. His tongue sought the softer recesses of her mouth, demanding a response.

"Need you now." The words came out on a whimper as she clung to him. "Hard and fast."

"Works for me." Ged growled triumphantly and slid a hard, wet thigh between her legs.

He blazed a trail of kisses down her throat, his stubble rasping a harsh caress over her skin. Awareness and need spiked higher as he pressed closer, caging her with his arms and rocking his hips tight against hers.

Needing him became an ache. The realization that their connection had almost been severed made her crave him more than ever. She had to touch him all over, to press closer, to feel his skin on hers.

Running a hand over his rock-hard abs, she moved lower. Quivering with excitement and anticipation, she stroked a hand down his straining length. The action broke through his control and he seized her. With his hands gripping her buttocks, he lifted her off her feet.

"You are mine, Lidi."

She wrapped her legs around his waist. "All yours. Always."

The breath left her lungs in a rush as he bent his knees, fitted his cock to her entrance, and drove into her with a single thrust. Arching her back, she clung to his biceps, adjusting to the delicious sensory overload. His hard chest muscles crushing her breasts, his hips between her thighs, his erection buried hilt deep inside her…everything about that instant was pleasure-pain perfect.

When he moved, it was to give her what she'd asked for. Hard and fast. Taking her and owning her. He was her mate and she loved him. As he poured his body into hers, it was a confirmation of that shining truth. Incredible friction, generated at the point where their bodies joined, taking her feelings higher. Clinging to him, she rode the rising tide of her release.

Ged's pace was relentless, his muscles tightening and releasing as his hips tilted up and forward, driving him into her. His head dropped to her shoulder, his ragged breathing matching her own. The water pouring over them mingled with the sweat from their bodies, making their flesh slippery as they rocked together.

Lidi's climax hit full force, stiffening her whole body and tightening her muscles around him. She cried out, the waves of pleasure intensifying when Ged growled and increased the speed of his thrusts. Wildly seeking his own release, he slammed into her, his hips jerking. Shaken by the depth of her feelings, Lidi held on tight, her body clamped around his as he stiffened and pulsed.

When their breathing returned to something resembling normality, Ged lowered Lidi to her feet. "Sleep."

"You have the best ideas."

Wrapping her in a huge, fluffy towel, he paused to tuck another one around his waist before carrying her through to the bedroom. Placing her on the bed, he curled his body around hers. Within minutes, she heard the change in his breathing that signaled he was asleep. A slight smile touched her lips.

I am in the arms of a king. She turned her head to look at him. *And he is the man I love.*

With a little wriggle of pleasure, she closed her eyes and felt weariness overwhelm her. She wasn't sure how long she slept, but she woke some time later, roused by the sound of frantic scratching and whining at the door. Squirming out from within Ged's encircling arms, she slid from the bed. Finding his discarded T-shirt on the floor, she pulled it on and went to answer the summons.

Bruno immediately hurled himself on her in an attempt to communicate his fear of permanent abandonment. After she had petted him for a few minutes, the dog calmed down and commenced an inspection of the room.

"No." Lidi shook her head when he showed an interest in jumping on the bed. "I don't think that will be a popular move right now."

The dog wagged his tail and headed for the window seat instead. Jumping onto the cushioned chair, he placed his front paw on the ledge and pressed his nose against the window frame. Lidi joined him, curling up on the seat. Instead of looking out the window, she faced into the room, preferring to watch Ged as he slept.

"Your mommy and daddy are getting married in a few hours." She ruffled Bruno's ears as she spoke. "And we want you to behave during the ceremony."

The dog whined, his whole body becoming rigid. Since Lidi didn't imagine her words had provoked his intense reaction, she shifted position so she could follow the direction of his gaze.

Immediately below the room, there was a small patch of lawn. Standing in the middle of the grass, a lone figure was looking up at the her.

"Alyona." Lidi reached up to open the window. Before the catch was released, Alyona had raised her hand in a parting gesture. Lidi pressed her own palm against the glass in response. For a few moments, they remained frozen in that mutual position of respect and farewell. Then Alyona gradually faded away.

"Peace," Lidi whispered. Something told her that for Alyona, it would finally be true.

A few minutes later, there was a knock on the door. Deciding a little more decorum might be required of the future queen, she retrieved her jeans and underwear and pulled them on.

When she opened the door, Sarange, Hollie and Sasha greeted her with excited smiles. "We've come to get you ready for your wedding."

"I need to see my father first," Lidi said.

"Of course. You can go visit him first, then we'll get to work." Sarange's grin was filled with girly promise.

Hearing her voice, Ged groaned and pulled a pillow over his head. "Make the noisy werewolf lady go away."

Sarange regarded him with a critical eye. "I'll send Khan up to him. If he's going to be *I do* ready in two hours, we're going to need a bit of tiger magic."

"Two hours?" The words acted like a bucket of water thrown over Ged, and he sat up. "What are we waiting for? I need Khan, Torque, Andrei…hell, I need everyone. And a glass of brandy. The good stuff." He smiled at Lidi. "Kiss me before you go."

She leaned over the bed, hooking a hand behind his neck as she pressed her lips to his. "See you on the other side of the marriage vows, King Gerald."

"Can't wait, Queen Lidiya."

Eduard Tavisha, Bogdan the Brave and Mikhail Orlov stood together at one side of the ballroom. The Count of Aras was with them. Although he was in a wheelchair, it was a temporary measure and he was already complaining that it was unnecessary. All four men were drinking the king's favorite brandy as they watched the other guests.

"I think this will be a different kind of monarchy," Bogdan observed.

"What makes you say that?" Eduard asked. "Apart from the fact that the queen has a dog for a pet and the king's best friends are a tiger and a dragon?"

Bogdan laughed. "There are a few clues about diversity that may have escaped your attention."

They fell silent again. On the dance floor, Finglas, the werewolf member of Beast, whirled past with Lady Galina Ivanov, younger sister of the tragic Alyona. Nearby, Sasha swayed in the arms of Diablo, the darkly handsome werepanther.

Karina, the hybrid tiger-wolf daughter of Khan and Sarange, who had joined her parents in time to be a flower girl, sat on the floor in a corner of the room, She had removed the circlet of roses from her head and was feeding them one at a time to Bruno. The dog carefully accepted each one from her fingers, then dropped it at her feet. Every time he did it, Karina clapped her hands and squealed with laughter.

At a quiet table, Zoya, the Queen Mother, was talking to Hollie. They each held one of Hollie's twin dragon-shifter baby boys. On another table, Prince Andrei was sharing a jug of Callistoya's finest ale with Khan, Torque and Dev.

"A bear, a tiger, a dragon and a snow leopard. There must be a joke in there somewhere," Mikhail said.

As for the new king and queen…they remained alone on a secluded part of the dance floor, lost in the music and each other.

"It's very strange," the count said. "But until now, I didn't even know my daughter *could* dance."

When the music ended, the king's friends and his brother encircled the royal couple. Some good-humored chanting, including encouragement to kiss, ensued. Then the king and queen were hoisted onto their friends' shoulders and paraded around the room.

"I remember the pomp and ceremony of previous royal weddings. Yes, this is a little different." Eduard took a sip of brandy. "It looks like there will be changes around here. Is that a bad thing?"

"Hell, no." Bogdan raised his glass in salute to the laughing group on the dance floor. "I'd say it's going to be very, very good."

* * * * *

We hope you enjoyed this story from

Unleash your otherworldly desires.

Discover more stories from
Harlequin® series and continue
to venture where the normal and
paranormal collide.

SPECIAL EXCERPT FROM

⬩HARLEQUIN®
™

ROMANTIC suspense

Tessa Wilkes has trained to become a Special Forces operator for her entire adult life...that is until she's unceremoniously tossed out of the training pipeline. But the gorgeous spec ops trainer Beau Lambert offers her the chance of a lifetime: to become part of a highly classified, all-female Special Forces team called the Medusas.

Read on for a sneak preview of the first book in New York Times *bestselling author Cindy Dees's brand-new Mission Medusa miniseries,* Special Forces: The Recruit.

Hands gripped Tess's shoulders. Lifted her slowly to her feet. Her unwilling gaze traveled up Beau's body, taking in the washboard abs, the bulging pecs and broad shoulders. A finger touched her chin, tilting her face up, forcing her to look him in the eyes.

"We good?" Beau murmured.

Jeez. How to answer that? They would be great if he would just kiss her and forget about the whole "don't fall for me" thing. She ended up mumbling, "Um, yeah. Sure. Fine."

"I don't know much about women, but I do know one thing. When a woman says nothing's wrong, something's always wrong. And when she says she's fine like you just did, she's emphatically not fine. Talk to me. What's going on?"

HRSEXP0419

She winced. If only he wasn't so direct all the time. She knew better than to try to lie to a special operator— they all had training that included knowing how to lie and how to spot a lie. She opted for partial truth. "I want you, Beau. Right now."

"Post-mission adrenaline got you jacked up again?"

Actually, she'd been shockingly calm out there earlier. Which she was secretly pretty darned proud of. Tonight was the first time she'd ever shot a real bullet at a real human being. At the time, she'd been so focused on protecting Beau that it hadn't dawned on her what she'd done.

But now that he mentioned it, adrenaline was, indeed, screaming through her. And it was demanding an outlet in no uncertain terms.

"I feel as if I could run a marathon right about now," she confessed. She risked a glance up at him. "Or have epic sex with you. Your choice."

Don't miss
Special Forces: The Recruit *by Cindy Dees,*
available May 2019 wherever
Harlequin® Romantic Suspense books
and ebooks are sold.

www.Harlequin.com

Love Harlequin romance?

DISCOVER.

Be the first to find out about promotions,
news and exclusive content!

Facebook.com/HarlequinBooks

Twitter.com/HarlequinBooks

Instagram.com/HarlequinBooks

Pinterest.com/HarlequinBooks

ReaderService.com

EXPLORE.

Sign up for the Harlequin e-newsletter and
download a free book from any series at
TryHarlequin.com.

CONNECT.

Join our Harlequin community to share
your thoughts and connect with other
romance readers!
Facebook.com/groups/HarlequinConnection

HARLEQUIN

**ROMANCE WHEN
YOU NEED IT**

HSOCIAL2018